THE SHELL GAME

REVIEWS

"Steve Alten proves his versatility in his latest thriller The Shell Game, a tour-de-force thriller tackling oil, politics, and the state of the world. Controversial, shocking, meticulously researched, and sure to raise many eyebrows in Washington, Alten has produced both a dazzling political thriller and a cautionary tale for our times. Anyone interested in the labyrinthine world of politics, international gamesmanship, and the control of oil in society needs to read this book."

—JAMES ROLLINS, *New York Times* bestseller of *The Judas Strain*

"Whether you embrace it or refute it, The Shell Game cannot, and should not, be easily dismissed. This is Steve Alten's boldest, bravest book to date. He's fearless, in fact, and his skills as a storyteller have not dulled. The Shell Game leaves you shattered, angry, and demanding change."

—ANDREW TALLACKSON, Michigan City (Ind.) *News-Dispatch* entertainment editor

"Action packed, intense and politically probing, The Shell Game is an intriguing blend of fiction and non-fiction that will most certainly disturb the practitioners of the game, because it will make readers stop and think about American foreign policy in the oil-rich Middle East."

—RICHARD FOLSOM, *Washington Daily News*

"For those who have struggled against the machine, the book holds some precious nuggets of truth, hope, and insight. For those seeking to stop the next 9/11 and World War IV, the book is a great opening for a dialogue on the painful truths and realities that most journalists and politicians do not dare to speak about. For those who dismiss the news and focus on their personal realities, and feel insulated from the struggles of the majority of people, this book will challenge their perception of reality, and perhaps inspire them to stop being a spectator and recognize their own power and responsibility to shape the future. I highly recommend it as a first choice on what to read and hope that readers follow up on the source books and give the author a hand in preventing the next 9/11."

—CAROL LIANE BROUILLET, 9/11 activist

"What if the oil reserves we thought were so plentiful were on the verge of running dry? What if a secret group of government officials formed a plan to allow terrorists to detonate a w.m.d. on American soil, giving us a reason to launch a full-scale invasion of the Middle East (under the guise of retaliation) to secure the last remaining oil fields and end the threat of radical Islam once and for all? What if the salvation of America and possibly much of the civilized world lay in the hands of one man, whose life has suddenly been turned upside down with this devastating knowledge? All this sounds like a great conspiracy thriller, something that was dreamed up by people who see secrets and shadows where none exist, where paranoia reigns and no one can be trusted, least of all the government. In fact, Steve Alten's The Shell Game is a superb thriller that does indeed ring of all these elements, but the thing that sets this book apart from similar works is that this story is actually very believable, which is what makes it so frightening."

—CRAIG HARVEY, *Movement Magazine*

THE
SHELL
GAME

SECOND EDITION

by *New York Times* Best-Selling Author
STEVE ALTEN

THE
SHELL
GAME

SECOND EDITION

SWEETWATER BOOKS
Springville, Utah

The views expressed within this work are the sole responsibility of the author and do not necessarily reflect the position of Cedar Fort, Inc., or any other entity.

Cedar Fort books and its imprints carry no political agenda, nor are we aligned with any political party or candidate. Although the author has referred to real people and events, *The Shell Game* is a work of fiction.

ISBN 13: 978-1-59955-359-7

Published by Sweetwater Books, an imprint of
Cedar Fort, Inc., 2373 W. 700 S., Springville, UT, 84663
Distributed by Cedar Fort, Inc., www.cedarfort.com

LIBRARY OF CONGRESS CATALOGING-IN-PUBLICATION DATA

Alten, Steve.
The shell game / by Steve Alten.
  p. cm.
ISBN 978-1-59955-359-7 (acid-free paper)
1. War on terrorism, 2001—Fiction. 2. Terrorism—Prevention—Fiction.
3. Intelligence officers—Fiction. 4. Conspiracy—Fiction.
5. International relations—Fiction. 6. Nuclear warfare—Fiction. I. Title.

PS3551.L764S54 2007
813'.54—dc22
2007026515

Cover art by Erik Hollander
www.HollanderDesignLab.com

Cover design © 2009 by Lyle Mortimer

Printed in Canada

10 9 8 7 6 5 4 3 2 1

Printed on acid-free paper

"THE LIE WAS DEAD,
AND DAMNED, AND
TRUTH STOOD UP INSTEAD."

—ROBERT BROWNING

THIS NOVEL IS DEDICATED TO

Michael C. Ruppert,
friend, fellow author, and former
LAPD investigator who risked
his life to report the truth

and to

Sibel Edmonds, Cynthia McKinney, Bill Douglas,
Richard Gage, Dr. Steven E. Jones, David Ray Griffin,
Richard Heinberg, Matt Simmons, Matt Savinar,
Carolyn Becker, Jonathan Mark, Sander Hicks, Jack Blood,
Kyle Hence, Dr. Kevin Barrett, Kevin Ryan,
John Heartson, Don Harkins, Don DeBar,
Scott Halfmann, Cheri Roberts,
William Rodriguez, Jason King, Tom Tvedten,
Sander Hicks, Justin Martel, Les Jamieson,
Michael Jackman, Peggy Brewster, Barrie Zwicker,
Erik Lawyer, Gabriel Day, Carol Brouillet, Mia Hamel,
Donald C. Meserlian, Paul Craig Roberts, Jon Gold,
Chris Gruener, Cheryl Curtiss, Jodie Baltazar, Jarek Kupsc,

Joseph Culp, Ken Jenkins, Ellen Mariani,
Gerhard Bedding, Jim Smart, Jack Shimek, Paul Krik,
Damon Bean, David Slesinger, Allan Giles,
Janice Matthews, Michael Berger, Dylan Avery,
Korey Rowe, Jason Burmas, Robert Bowman,
Mike Palecek, Donald Stahl, Ray McGovern,
Dwain Deets, Bill Veale, Don Plummer, Judy Shelton,
Paul Zarembka, Penny Little, Peter Thottam,
Ralph Schoenman, John Schuster, Frank Morales,
J.F. Ranger, Alan Miller, James Hufferd,
Janette MacKinlay, Donna Marsh O'Connor,
Bob Mcilvaine, Jean Canavan, Edith Beaujon,
Janette MacKinlay, Ted Walter, Justin Martell,
Michael Jackman, Barbara Honegger,
Michael Hasty, Ron Schalow, Daniel Sunjata,
Michael Springmann, Barrie Zwicker, John Feal,

*and every person who, against all odds
and extreme prejudice, fearlessly soldiers on for
a higher cause . . . a real 9/11 investigation.*

ACKNOWLEDGMENTS

It is with great pride and appreciation that I acknowledge those who contributed to the completion of The Shell Game.

First and foremost, many thanks to my friend and producer Belle Avery at Apelles Entertainment (www.ApellesEntertainment.com) my literary manager, Danny Baror of Baror International, and my terrific publicists, Trish Stevens at Ascot Media and Monica Foster at Reliant Public Relations.

Very special thanks to the great people at Sweetwater Books who believed in this project and developed a new imprint to support it. My gratitude to Lyle Mortimer, Lee Nelson, Bryce Mortimer, Heather Holm, and Liz Carlston for their commitment and friendship. Many thanks as well to Tim Schulte, Barbara Becker, and Jerry Williams.

Although this is a novel, there is much truth in the details. My gratitude to those contributors who generously offered private accounts from their own lives that added to the authenticity and richness of the story. With gratitude I acknowledge the invaluable contributions of Richard Lawrence, Charles Jones, Nathalie Tarabadi (Enyotic Designs Ltd.), Dino Garner, Ian Primosch, Mike Worley (www.PolicePractices.com), Greg Croft seismic services (www.gregcroft.com), and Kevin Lasagna. While my research involved over forty published books and two file cabinets worth of research papers, I wish to acknowledge two outstanding resources: Michael C. Ruppert's amazing *Crossing the Rubicon: The Decline of the American Empire at the End of the Age of Oil* and his latest, *An American Energy Policy*.

Very special thanks to those individuals who preferred their names not be made public, but whose information and guidance was invaluable—my heartfelt gratitude.

Thanks also go to my assistant, Leisa Coffman, for her talent and expertise in updating the www.SteveAlten.com website as well as all her work in the Adopt-An-Author program, and to Erik Hollander, for his tremendous cover design and graphic artistry.

Last but not least, to my wife and partner, Kim, for all her love and support; to my parents who have always been there to keep me going; and to my readers: Thank you for your on-going support, correspondence and contributions. Your comments are always a welcome treat, your input means so much, and you remain this author's greatest asset.

—STEVE ALTEN, ED.D.
E-Mail: Meg82159@aol.com

To personally contact the author or learn
more about his novels, click on

WWW.STEVEALTEN.COM

A PERSONAL MESSAGE FROM THE AUTHOR

QUESTION: How does a tall, bearded radical Muslim living in a cave in Afghanistan divert the most powerful air force in the history of mankind from the most guarded air space on the planet on the very day of the worst terrorist attack—an attack that will lead to the invasion of Iraq, a country that has nothing to do with the events of 9/11?

ANSWER: He doesn't.

Okay, Neo, you can take the red pill and see the world for what it is, or take the blue pill and return this book to the shelf (or toss it in the trash if you already purchased it).

The events of September 11, 2001, remain a very emotional story. To quote 911 Truth.org, perhaps the best website to acquire accurate information,

> "Understanding the full truth of 9/11 seems to require two separate awakenings. The first, awakening to the fraudulence of the 'official 9/11 story,' is a pretty simple brain function and only requires a little study, logic or curiosity. The second step, however, consciously confronting the implications of that knowledge—and what it says about our media, politics and economic system today—is by far the harder awakening and requires an enormous exercise of nerve and heart. (As the Chinese say, 'You cannot wake up a man who is pretending to sleep.') In other words, this part of the journey depends more on character than on maps and evidence."

The Shell Game debuted in hardback on January 22, 2008. This paperback release is *not* the same book. In the hardback (researched and written from 2004–07), the story involved a Republican Administration in office when the next terrorist attack strikes America, giving a Neoconservative U.S. president the "right" to unleash a retaliatory strike upon Iran. A year after the book was released, I saw the presidential candidate I had supported enter office, and former Vice President Dick Cheney begin making a series of speeches that predicted another terrorist attack. Six months later, President Barack Obama stood before an Egyptian audience and stated that there were no conspiracies on 9/11.

Wow. So much for the audacity of hope.

During the Vietnam Era, when tens of thousands of young men and women were protesting a war they refused to accept on the basis of "protecting our democracy from Communism," the FBI figured out a clever way to diffuse and disorient an entire peace movement. If you take a gallon of white paint (truth) and add 5 percent red paint (lies) you get Communist Pink. We patriotic Americans *hate* Commie Pink. The FBI called this operation COINTELPRO (Counter INTelligence PROgram) and their dirty little tricks were quite effective.

QUESTION: How does a tall, bearded radical Muslim living in a cave in Afghanistan divert the most powerful air force in the history of mankind from the most guarded air space on the planet on the very day of the worst terrorist attack—an attack that will lead to the invasion of Iraq, a country that has nothing to do with the events of 9/11?

ANSWER: What are you? One of those 9/11 conspiracy wackos who thinks laser weapons collapsed the WTC, or the Pentagon was hit by a missile . . . or that the Jews did it?

Yes, by now we know the Bush Administration lied about torture, lied about firing attorney generals, lied about weapons of mass destruction—but God help you if you ever question the actual event that pulled the trigger on two U.S. invasions.

I am not a conspiracy theorist, nor am I a lefty liberal. In researching *The Shell Game*, I managed to interview experts and foreign operatives who knew 9/11 was going to happen a full month before the attacks. (One former agent from Egypt attempted to warn the FBI, his U.S. Senator, and two newspapers about Al-Qaeda and was soundly dismissed.) For three years I worked on this book, and the facts threaded through the fiction made me physically ill. Three months after the original manuscript was finished, I was diagnosed with Parkinson's Disease. I was only 47, with no family history of the disease.

That was only the beginning . . .

Two months before *The Shell Game* hit bookstores, I began receiving threats. Photos of my home were placed on the Internet, along with my wife's name and our unlisted phone number. I started getting phone calls at 4 AM and threatening e-mails that divulged private information, the message being, "We know who you are."

All this for a fictional thriller by a guy who usually writes about giant sharks and doomsday prophesies.

Through 2008, there seemed to be an unofficial media blackout on anything to do with 9/11 Truth or Ron Paul. Networks refused to discuss it, or ridiculed the subject. As an author, I was actually disinvited to several events, and my publicist ran into a brick wall of refusals for appearances.

Ironically, *The Shell Game* is not about 9/11; it is about why 9/11 was allowed to happen (or made to happen, depending upon which 9/11 Truther you dare ask). And that reason is *oil*. The simple, terrifying fact is that the world is running out of oil, which means we are running out of the one irreplaceable resource required to feed six billion people on this planet. And all the lies, cover-ups, and corporate bailouts are not going to change that reality.

So, why am I rewriting a book that has given me nothing but pain and stress?

Because I want you to wake up before the lights go out. I want you to be prepared when the gas stations run dry and the grocery shelves go bare . . . or God help us, before a nuclear suitcase bomb goes off in a major U.S. city. I have hugged family members of those whose lives were stolen on 9/11, and they deserve better. I have many loyal fans in the military, and they deserve to come home safely. And yes, because there is the threat of another false flag event. (Ask the smirking ex-VP what would happen in the next U.S. elections if this happened on Barack Obama's watch.)

Call it the audacity of truth in fiction.

So, let's try this little exercise one last time:

QUESTION: How does a tall, bearded radical Muslim living in a cave in Afghanistan divert the most powerful air force in the history of mankind from the most guarded air space on the planet on the very day of the worst terrorist attack—an attack that will lead to the invasion of Iraq, a country that has nothing to do with the events of 9/11?

ANSWER: He doesn't. Vice President Dick Cheney does, by conducting a series of war game exercises (originally scheduled in late October) on the morning of September 11th, which purposely diverted all of our jet fighters away from the Northeastern Air Defense Sector (NEADS) where the four hijackings took place, sending them over Alaska, Greenland, Iceland, and Canada. One of these exercises, *Vigilant Guardian*, was a hijack drill designed to mirror the actual events taking place, inserting twenty-two false radar blips on the FAA's radar screens so that flight controllers had no idea which blips were the hijacked aircraft and which were the war game blips. As for the jet fighters stationed at Andrews Air Force Base, a mere twelve miles from Washington, D.C.—they were diverted hundreds of miles away so the Pentagon could be hit—a full eighty minutes *after* the World Trade Center was struck by commercial jetliners.

How was Dick Cheney able to do all this from his White

House command bunker?

Turns out "Vice" was quietly placed in charge of all war game exercises in May of 2001 by special presidential directive. These facts, which were purposely kept out of the 9/11 hearings by Bush appointee Philip Zelikow (along with a trove of other damning evidence) will never see a courtroom, despite the tireless efforts of a group of 9/11 Truth petitioners in New York.

Getting mad yet?

So . . . will it be the red pill or the blue pill? Better decide now. Your life may depend upon it.

—Steve Alten, Ed.D.

THE MIDDLE EAST

"If the United States continues to be bogged down in a protracted bloody involvement in Iraq, and I emphasize what I am about to say, the final destination on this downhill track is likely to be a head-on conflict with Iran and with much of the world of Islam at large. A plausible scenario for a military collision with Iran involves Iraqi failure to meet the benchmarks, followed by accusations of Iranian responsibility for the failure, then by some provocation in Iraq, or a terrorist act in the United States, blamed on Iran, culminating in a quote-unquote defensive military action against Iran that plunges a lonely America into a spreading and deepening quagmire, eventually ranging across Iraq, Iran, Afghanistan, and Pakistan."

—ZBIGNIEW BREZINSKI, former National Security
Adviser to President Jimmy Carter, currently
President Obama's foreign policy adviser

"When you read behind it, it's almost as if he (former VP Cheney) is wishing that this country would be attacked again, in order to make his point."

—LEON PANETTA, CIA director
to the *New Yorker*, June 2009

"Then the seven angels with the seven trumpets prepared to blow their mighty blasts . . ."

—REVELATION 8:6

PROLOGUE

WASHINGTON, D.C.
JUNE 14, 2009

THE HOTEL SUITE IS RICHLY DECORATED IN cream-colored fabrics and matching carpet. The turquoise drapes are drawn, blocking out the view of downtown Washington and any prying eyes. Aluminum steam table pans situated on warming trays cover a small side table, the aroma of scrambled eggs, bacon, and hash browns filling the room.

Ignoring the hunger pangs growling in his stomach, Colonel Graeme "the Bull" Turnbull, U.S. Army, directs his harsh blue-eyed gaze at the two civilians seated directly across the conference table. Ryan Gessaman, a rugged man in his forties, wearing a dark suit and matching bow tie, had been a senior assistant to Richard Perle, former chairman of the Defense Policy Board. Perle, known around Washington power circles as the "Prince of Darkness," is himself a close friend and adviser to former Secretary of Defense Donald Rumsfeld and a major investor in a number of defense companies. Perle is also cofounder of the Project for the New American Century (PNAC), a Neoconservative political think tank established in 1997 that promotes American dominance in world affairs.

Turnbull does not recognize Gessaman's companion, an as-yet unidentified woman with thick, shoulder-length, blond, curly hair and penetrating hazel eyes, her navy business suit partially concealing an athletic physique.

"Colonel, are you sure we can't interest you in some breakfast?"

"No, thank you, sir."

"Well, if you change your mind . . ." Gessaman opens a sealed file. "I understand you're currently stationed at Camp Anaconda. How long have you been in Iraq?"

"Since the beginning. I started in Afghanistan with the 187th Airborne Regimental Combat Team, the 'Rakkasans.' We were the first boots on the ground. Same for Iraq. *Ne Desit Virtus*—"

"Let valor not fail," the woman translates. "When did Military Intelligence recruit you?"

"The day Psy Ops found out I spoke fluent Arabic."

"So you were with M.I. two years, then Counterintelligence. Looks like you were quite busy . . . over one hundred interrogations." The woman's eyes narrow. "Tell me, Colonel, what's the most interesting thing you ever learned from these 'sessions'?"

Turnbull frowns. "You don't want to know."

"Try me."

"Back in 2005, I reported that Bin Laden had escaped to the Hadhramaut of Yemen, that he was being protected by Sayyid tribesmen. The info went up the food chain, but nothing ever happened. Seems the Sayyids of the Hadhramaut are allied with members of the Saudi Royal Family . . . to go after him would have insulted our Saudi friends. Better to just pretend the number one bad guy's hiding in a cave in Afghanistan than confront the real enemy, huh?"

The woman nods. "I share your frustration, Colonel. Off the record, CIA ran an assessment of the blowback of a Bin Laden capture. Sometimes bad guys are better left alive than dead."

"Is that why we're funding Sunni insurgents with ties to Al-Qaeda?" Turnbull watches their expressions drop. "Yeah, I know about that, most of the other grunts in M.I. do too. You don't have to be a brain surgeon to figure out where these guys are getting their money and weapons."

"It's a complicated situation, Colonel," Ryan Gessaman replies.

"Not when you're getting shot at."

"Shiite radicals must be contained."

"Look, friend, let's get something straight: I ain't in politics and the old 'the enemy of my enemy is my friend' policy doesn't fly with me, unless your definition of history is any period of time less than five years old. We supported Bin Laden to keep the Soviets in check. We supported Saddam to keep the Iranians in check. Now we're supporting Al-Qaeda to keep Iraq from turning into a Shiite nation? Ever wonder why we're not exactly being embraced these days?"

The woman stares straight ahead, saying nothing, her silence saying everything.

"Let's refocus on Iraq," Gessaman says. "The President has decided to go with a troop surge in Afghanistan. Your thoughts?"

An icy glare crosses Turnbull's eyes. "You don't want to know my thoughts."

"Off the record."

"Off the record . . ." Turnbull smirks. "The last commander-in-chief started a forest fire; the new one seems a lot smarter about tossing matches. Still, the problems remain the same. Where's the President getting these additional troops? The Boy Scouts? I'm working with soldiers that have been recycled so many times they're starting to demand air miles. My enlisted men are so fried that a third of them no longer have any business carrying a weapon, let alone participating in combat operations where their presence jeopardizes the welfare of an entire platoon. And the Reserves and National Guardsmen? Nice surprise, not telling them deployment doesn't officially begin until their boots hit sand, meaning the six months their unit spent at the MOB stations didn't count."

Gessaman interrupts, "Morale aside, Colonel, we're asking for your assessment of—"

"Morale aside? Disillusionment and morale don't mix real well on the battlefield. Our guys want to complete the mission, they're no longer sure what the mission is. Last month my soldiers killed a guy setting a roadside bomb. Turns out he was a sergeant in the Iraqi Army, the guys we're supposed to be training as our replacements! Who the hell are we fighting for? In the last ninety days, three of my Pfcs committed suicide. These were brave, outstanding soldiers—when they arrived three tours of duty ago. Two were on antidepressants, the third had already attempted suicide ten weeks earlier. His mental health officer and I had personally signed a recommendation that the soldier not be returned to active duty. My CO's response was that we had troop shortages, request denied."

"Duly noted, Colonel," said the blond. "We appreciate the severity of the situation, which is why you are here. Now, if you could refocus your comments on the activities of the enemy."

"I'm sorry, ma'am, I didn't get your name."

"No, you didn't. The insurgents, Colonel."

"Insurgents are a small piece of a larger puzzle. Two years ago we were in the middle of a Sunni-Shi'ite civil war, and now we're seeing growing signs of a Shi'ite movement designed to unleash a nationwide bloodbath aimed at American troops. The militias' objective is to lure us out of the green zone and then pin us down in hostile neighborhoods using Iranian-made rocket-propelled grenade launchers. As a result, we've now ceased all military sweeps. Meanwhile, the local Sunni population is slowly being killed off or sent packing. By invading Iraq, we essentially radicalized the entire Muslim community and turned a secular society into a Shiite nation."

"In your estimation, Colonel, what group is doing most of the damage?"

Turnbull looks hard at Gessaman. *They're playing head games, leading me somewhere . . .*

"Which group is the worst? The Shi'ite Death Squads . . . the Mahdi Army . . . the Badr Organization . . . take your pick. Essentially the groups trained by the Iranians. They come and go as they please, controlling neighborhoods, sometimes entire cities, and the Iraqi militia and police give them free rein. The civilians are too scared to venture out of their homes, and areas that used to be mixed have now segregated into either Sunni or Shi'ite simply out of necessity. Add to that the perpetual shortages of water and electricity, plus an exodus of ten thousand Iraqis a day, and you've got an almost intolerable situation. But you already know that, don't you Mr. Gessaman?"

Gessaman says nothing.

"Let's talk about you, Colonel." The blond leafs through her own folder. "Both parents trace their roots to the Scottish Highlands. Your family came to America just after World War II. Grandfather was a war hero—"

"Yes, ma'am. He fought Rommel in North Africa."

"According to your bio, you come from a long line of fighting men."

"The Turnbull clan has fought in every war since Longshanks invaded Scotland." The Colonel smiles. "We were a wild sort, the only bunch of rowdies ever to have a bounty placed on the entire clan's head."

"Tell me about John Turnbull." The blond flashes an encouraging smile.

"John Turnbull . . . now there was a crazy muther. According to Scot lore, John was reputed to have killed more English during William Wallace's raids than any other kinsman who wore the kilt. Used to bring a two-hundred pound Mastiff into battle. One time, John beheaded four English Knights while his dog chewed on their arms. True story. Some time after that, this little English dweeb by the name of Kerr beheaded the dog and John simply lost it. Forgot all his training and got his arm chopped off, then he lost his head. Literally. War is hell, huh?"

The blond again makes it a point to reference her notes. "According to Scot history, for the next two hundred years the Turnbulls waged war on the Kerr's land."

"That we did. See, we Highlanders . . . we never forget a debt."

"Killed a lot of people in the process, I imagine."

"Nothing I'm proud of, mind you. But you do what you have to."

"Women and children too?"

The Colonel's guard goes up. *She's a spook. CIA most likely. Careful, Bull, this one's a wolf in sheep's clothing . . .*

Ryan Gessaman jumps in before he can reply. "Colonel, you're right about Iraq. It's become a real quagmire. Was it a mistake to go in? We'll let history decide. But the problem that refuses to allow democracy to take root in Iraq is the same one that threatens America—Islamic radicals. And everything's coming from Iran."

"Ever hear the term 'Islamic Waqf'?" asks the blond. "It refers to an old Islamic precept that states Muslims have the right to claim any territory their people conquered by force. Any conquest, including the ones that date back over a thousand years."

"That's a radical interpretation," the Colonel counters. "Waqf is the act of giving an estate to the leaders of Islam to manage to help the poor."

"Radicals are who we're dealing with, Colonel. America stumbled in Iraq, and radical Islam used the momentum to spread its tentacles throughout the Muslim world. Sure, Obama's presence may have affected Lebanon's election results, but Ahmadinejhad is alive and kicking in Iran, fanning the flames of a dangerous ideology that thinks nothing of slaughtering Muslim and non-Muslim civilians alike to achieve their objectives. These radicals have infiltrated at least fifty-five different countries, and they won't be satisfied until they've retaken or recaptured every speck of land, from Madrid to the Middle East and then some. Their influence is spreading quickly throughout the Arab world, the more radical the violence, the more power they wield."

Gessaman nods. "This is Nazi Germany all over again, only they're killing for Allah, which is a far more powerful cause than the Fuhrer. Radical Islam is winning the war of minds through an extensive propaganda program. Children in Palestine, Jordan, Iran, and Saudi Arabia are being taught at an early age to despise the West. Text books and music videos depict Jews and Christians as blood-sucking animals, the West as Satan worshipers. We have video-taped footage of first graders chanting for Jihad and the opportunity to blow themselves up in Allah's name. And as bad as things may seem now, it's going to get a whole lot worse. Within the next three years we could be looking at Armageddon-like attacks that could lead to the end of open societies as we know it."

"Three years, Colonel," the blond repeats. "Within three years Iran will be producing enriched uranium. Think about how a nuclear Iran would change the Middle East. The Saudis would demand nukes, and then Egypt, Jordan, Syria . . . nuclear detente. But that's not even the worst of it. How do we stop Iran from supplying nuclear weapons to terrorist groups? Is there any doubt these Islamic radicals would use them? Remember how helpless you felt on September 11th? Imagine waking up one day and learning a suitcase nuke just wiped out Manhattan, or Chicago, or Philadelphia, or Miami—"

"Or all of them at once!" Gessaman says. "Hijacking planes and flying them into skyscrapers requires long-range planning and specific talents, and we still failed to stop it from happening. Smuggling in a dozen fifteen-kiloton suitcase nukes would be a cakewalk. A dozen Hiroshimas, Colonel. Think Homeland Security could stop it? What about immigration? We can't keep a thousand Mexicans a day from sneaking over the border, and eight years after 9/11 our ports still remain virtually unprotected. And you know how Washington is when it comes to terrorist threats; the politicians always wait until something bad happens before they react. You think the Dems are going to keep us safe?"

Turnbull closes his eyes, trying to imagine smoldering American cities, tens of millions vaporized, millions more dead and dying, the economy destroyed, panic in the streets.

"It's an absolute nightmare," the woman says, "and Iran is the linchpin. Rumsfeld screwed up Iraq, no argument, but the Neocons were right about one thing: Threats must be addressed before they arrive, sponsors of terror held accountable. We simply cannot afford to allow the nuclear genie out of the bottle in the Persian Gulf."

Colonel Turnbull's heart races. "Why am I here?"

"You're here because you know the enemy, because you've seen what they can do. You're here because you have access to resources we may need." Ryan Gessaman closes his folder. "For a moment, Colonel, I want you to imagine you're the Secretary of Defense. Better yet, President Obama. Your top advisors have just told you in no uncertain terms that, within the next three years, Iran will have enriched uranium to build and supply nuclear suitcase bombs to radical extremists. How do you prevent the terrorists from using those weapons to decimate our nation and Western Society?"

"A preemptive invasion, I suppose."

"Obama would never go for it," Gessaman replies, "and it still wouldn't work, at least not with conventional forces. You said it yourself—Iraq's a disaster, our troops are burned out, the military is dangerously short on manpower, and the American people need out of the Persian Gulf. Even if you went ahead, you'd need upward of half a million troops to invade Iran, maybe more to maintain control, which none of us truly believe can happen. Where do you get the troops?"

"You could institute a draft," the blond suggests, playing devil's advocate.

Gessaman shakes his head. "The American public would never go for it."

"Okay," the Colonel says, "so we don't invade, we simply take out their nuclear facilities, just like the Israelis did with that Iraqi reactor back in '81."

"A good suggestion," Gessaman states, "only there's potentially dozens of facilities, most of them unknown, many underground, plus there's the terrorist training camps, the military bases . . . no, if we do this it's got to be all or nothing. And remember what you said earlier—by invading Iraq we essentially radicalized the entire Muslim community. The days of preemptively attacking another country are over . . . unless there's just cause."

"You mean if they hit us first?"

"Exactly." The blond's eyes bear down on Turnbull. "The world had no problem with us invading Afghanistan after 9/11. Two years ago, I sat in a top-secret meeting between President Bush and his most-senior national security advisors about rewriting the rules of the Cold War. The old rules of deterrence don't apply when it comes to suitcase nukes. Before his presidency ended, Bush announced that should a nuclear suitcase bomb ever be detonated on American or Allied soil, the United States would hold the country that supplied the material 'fully responsible' for the aftermath. I think Obama would adhere to that."

Colonel Turnbull wipes a bead of sweat from his brow. "What does 'fully responsible' mean exactly?"

"The term was purposely left vague, allowing for a nuclear . . . or other type of retaliatory attack. Should such an attack be directly linked to the Iranians through nuclear forensics, the outcome would change the geopolitical landscape forever."

"You sound like Cheney . . . like you want them to hit us."

Gessaman attempts to dismiss the charge with a smile. "The former VP is simply concerned about showing our enemies any chinks in the armor. Let's not forget, it was the Bush Administration's preemptive doctrine that kept this nation safe. Not a single attack on their watch."

"Wasn't 9/11 on their watch?"

The blond loses her patience. "Iran's a very real nuclear threat, Colonel. You think Obama's 'citizen of the world' speeches are going to alter the aim of radical Islam?"

A rush of anxiety causes the Colonel to flush. "Who are you people?"

The blond leans forward, lowering her voice. "We're like you, Colonel, loyal Americans who love this country too much to see it turned into a socialist nation . . . or a parking lot. Look at the EU, they know the importance of strength. Their last elections returned hardliners to power. Spain, Bulgaria, Hungary, Latvia, Greece, Ireland—"

"Just get to the point."

"Iran's about to become a nuclear threat. The only way we stop them is to control the variables. In doing so, we can cripple radical Islam once and for all."

"How?"

"By minimizing the damage. By allowing one targeted city to be nuked."

Colonel Turnbull sits back in his chair, suddenly feeling queasy. "You're insane."

"Twenty bombs or one bomb, Colonel. Pick your poison. The difference between letting it happen and making it happen could be 50 million dead Americans and permanent martial law. Yes, a nuclear attack on an American city is a horrific price to pay, but it would limit the damage and turn the tables on our enemies, giving us the excuse to eradicate the radical element of Islam once and for all. It would change the world."

"Let me get this straight. You want to allow an entire American city to be nuked in order to turn Iran into a parking lot?"

"No, absolutely not. We hit only the desired Iranian targets. Nuclear facilities, military bases, terrorist training sites—a preemptive strike to prevent a dozen nuclear attacks on American cities."

"But to wipe out a million Americans?" The Colonel mops

sweat from his brow.

"Your grandfather fought in World War II," the blond reminds him. "Imagine what would have happened if Roosevelt had waited another six months before entering the war? All of Britain would have been lost, the Manhattan Project would have been delayed. Hitler's heavy water experiments were nearly complete. Germany would have won the war."

"But allowing a nuclear attack . . . on American soil?"

"New flash, Colonel: Roosevelt *knew* the Japanese were readying an attack on Pearl Harbor, and guess what—he allowed it to happen!"

"I heard that, I just never wanted to believe it."

"Believe it," Gessaman states. "U.S. intelligence had broken the enemy's codes months earlier. We'd been monitoring their communications long before December 7, 1941. World War I was Roosevelt's Iraq. He knew Congress and the American people would never agree to engage in another battle in Europe, not unless something drastic were to happen . . . an event so terrible, so heinous that it would incite an emotional public response and elicit a massive call to arms. When he learned the Japanese were coming, FDR ordered the carriers out to sea and allowed the devastation in Pearl Harbor to take place. The President sacrificed thousands of innocent American men and women so that our country would be forced to go to war—a war the White House secretly provoked in order to give us a fighting chance to defeat an evil that was threatening the entire world."

The Colonel's eyes grow harsh. "And Bush? Did he allow the events of 9/11 to happen in the same way?"

Ryan Gessaman smirks. "Honestly, Colonel, I didn't think someone of your stature would be a conspiracy theorist."

The blond leans forward, the conversation so overwhelming that even the taut breasts beneath the woman's white blouse cannot divert Turnbull's attention. "Colonel, this is merely think-tank conversation. The Pentagon engages in this kind of rhetoric eight days a week. But let's face facts: Islamic radicals want to get their hands on a nuke, and with Iran entering the game, the odds are suddenly even that the threat is very real. I think you'd agree we've been relatively lucky since 9/11, but our ports remain unprotected, our border patrols fail almost every test we throw at them. Sure, we could sit back and pray our intelligence network will stop the next wave of attacks, only it doesn't take a team of terrorists to blow up a city, it only takes one suicide bomber with one atomic suitcase bomb. But if we control the variables, we can destroy the threat."

"What variables do you control?" Turnbull asks. "The Republicans lost the presidency and both Houses. Obama can do no wrong, the GOP is perceived as the party of 'no,' and Neocons like Cheney and Rumsfeld will be lucky just to stay out of jail."

Gessaman smiles. "You're misreading the landscape, Colonel. We're dealing with some major players—"

"Enough." The blond waves the conversation off. "Anyway, this is just talk. Before any action can even be considered there must be a plan, and no one knows this area of the world better than you."

Colonel Turnbull clears his throat. "Nothing personal, Ma'am, but I have a family that's barely seen me these past few years. I've done my time in hell, so if it's all the same to you, I think you'd better find another man for the job."

The blond sits back, her face turning red. "You think you've been in hell? You have no idea what hell is, Colonel. I have a great-uncle who passed away a few years ago. When he was ten, the Nazis rounded him up with his parents and sisters, his aunts and uncles and cousins and the rest of the Jews in his village, and shoved them into cattle cars. The lucky ones suffocated on the ride to Auschwitz. When they arrived at the death camp, the women were separated from the men and taken directly to the gas chambers. That was before the Nazis figured out they could run the ovens day and night by using the fat from burning human flesh as a fuel.

"I may seem like a cold-hearted witch to you, Colonel, and maybe I am. But when I go home at night, I hug a husband who loves me and kiss two young children whom I adore, and if I have to be a bitch to make sure they don't get incinerated by some wacko in a turban who's been brainwashed into believing he's going to paradise for killing infidels . . . then so be it."

She pauses, looking out the window at downtown Washington. "Last week I was watching CNN . . . Glenn Beck was interviewing Benjamin Netanyahu. The Israeli prime minister was asked what the Jews learned from the Holocaust. You know what he said? He said, 'When someone tells you they intend to annihilate you, you should believe them.'"

She forces a smile, regaining her composure. "I know you're a family man, Colonel, that's why you're here. For a moment I want you to imagine you and your family living in the Highlands centuries ago, at a time when Longshanks was readying his invasion of Scotland. If you knew you could save your country and countrymen by sacrificing a few clans while forever removing the English threat, would you have done it?"

Colonel Turnbull grinds his teeth, the damaged nerves in his right quadriceps causing the leg to shake. "Okay, lady, you've got your man."

"It is well documented that the officials topping the chain of command for response to a domestic attack—George W. Bush, Donald Rumsfeld, Richard Myers, Montague Winfield—all found reason to do something else during the actual attacks, other than assuming their duties as decision-makers. Who was actually in charge? Dick Cheney, Richard Clarke, Norman Mineta and the 9/11 Commission directly conflict in their accounts of top-level response to the unfolding events, such that several (or all) of them must be lying."

—911Truth.org

"If you want to get people to fight, you have to get them to believe there is a threat, that they're in danger. This is an integral part of Islamic propaganda."

—Itmar Marcus, Palestinian Media Watch

"We know he's been absolutely devoted to trying to acquire nuclear weapons, and we believe he has, in fact, reconstituted nuclear weapons."

—Vice President Dick Cheney,
on Saddam Hussein, March 16, 2003

WINTER
2011

"The first angel blew his trumpet, and hail and fire mixed with blood were thrown down upon the earth, and one-third of the earth was set on fire. One-third of the trees were burned, and all the grass was burned."

REVELATION 8:7

"Yeah, I was in the Old Executive Office Building for those meetings, at one time or another all of us were. BP, Chevron, Conoco-Phillips, Shell, Exxon-Mobil, U.S. Oil and Gas . . . but only the top managers. The C.E.'s were purposely kept away. That was the red flag, the 'plausible deniable' factor. All of us knew what was at stake. We'd seen the reports coming out of the Caspian Basin, all of which added a sense of urgency to Cheney's plan. Rumsfeld showed us SAT images of the oil fields, while Wolfowitz did most of the selling, some nonsense about how our workers would be safe, how they'd be embraced, all the while pushing us for timetables on how long it would take us to get the oil flowing again, as if we had a crystal ball. The Brown and Root guys had detailed maps of Iraq's energy infrastructure. You could tell they'd been in it with the CIA lady from the beginning. It was one big circle jerk, and I just kept nodding, wondering what the hell we were doing here. I mean, the Bushies had just taken office, and the scenario they outlined, no one actually believed it would happen. Five months later the planes struck the Twin Towers and everyone knew. The Senate Hearings that followed . . . what a joke. I mean, no one was even placed under oath."

—ANONYMOUS OIL EXECUTIVE
on Vice President Dick Cheney's Secret
Energy Task Force Meetings

"The very word 'secrecy' is repugnant in a free and open society; and we are as a people inherently and historically opposed to secret societies, to secret oaths, and to secret proceedings."

—PRESIDENT JOHN F. KENNEDY

CHAPTER 1

Iran Claims Capability to Build a Dozen Nuclear Missiles

Associated Press: December 11, 2011

TEHRAN—Iranian President Mahmoud Ahmadinejad announced today that his country has succeeded in enriching enough weapons grade uranium to build a dozen atomic bombs. "For more than a decade we have been pressured by the West and the Zionist regime to curtail our efforts to remain a liberated power. Thanks to our great successes in bringing nuclear power to our people, we have taken the next step down the path of independence. Iran's enrichment program now yields enough uranium to arm a dozen nuclear missiles—sufficient enough to annihilate the enemies that threaten our borders. The West will no longer bully the great nation of Islam. The Zionist movement will be eliminated in one storm, the Western powers that hold Iraq in another."

The Obama Administration responded to the Iranian announcement by stating that Ahmadinejad's rule has succeeded only in taking his people down a "dangerous path of self-destruction."

Ahmadinejad's recent rise in popularity among his own people, fueled by the continued violence in Iraq, allowed him to change the Iranian constitution, extending his presidency.

Dirksen Senate Office Building
Room SD-366
December 12, 2011
9:06 am EST

Hearing before the Committee on
Energy and Natural Resources
United States Senate
110th Congress

"The hearing will please come to order." Committee Chairman David Keller grandstands a sweeping glance around the packed chamber, the senator from California reminding himself not to look directly into the C-Span cameras.

"I'd like to thank everyone in attendance, particularly the senators who have chosen to join us here today for the first in a series of meetings that I hope will lead to real change in the role energy plays in our global economy, the environment, and the security of our nation. In light of the recent events in Iran, I can think of nothing as important.

"The questions we're going to be focusing on today concern the present and future energy needs of both the United States and the world as a whole, specifically dealing with oil and natural gas. If our witnesses would share their perspectives on these specific challenges, the Committee and I would be most grateful. Senator Poschner, I believe you had some opening remarks?"

"Thank you, Mr. Chairman, and a special thank you to our esteemed panelists who have made themselves available for this morning's session." The Republican senator from Virginia pauses for the applause, nodding to the lone woman and four men seated at the witness table below the main dais. Adjusting his wire-rimmed glasses, he reads from a prepared statement.

"Ladies and gentlemen, we live in unprecedented times. The world's population is growing by a quarter of a million people every day. Whether we're able to feed and clothe, educate, sustain, and maintain our population will depend upon our ability to meet global energy demands. Little has changed over the last twenty years. Fossil fuels still supply 85 percent of our energy needs, with oil leading the way. Each day the United States uses approximately 22 million barrels of crude, representing a fourth of the world's 94 million barrel-per-day consumption. These staggering quantities are expected to increase at an annual rate of upward of 2 percent, reaching 107 million barrels of oil per day by 2020 as the economies of China, India, and other Asian countries continue their unprecedented acceleration as industrialized nations . . ."

Ashley Brown Futrell III, affectionately known to family and friends simply as "Ace," stretches his left leg beneath the witness table. At six-four and 225 pounds, the forty-four-year-old petroleum geologist and onetime football star at the University of Georgia finds it hard to remain seated for very long in one position. His left knee crackles like gravel beneath a twice surgically repaired patellar tendon, and his joints ache from chronic arthritis. On good days he can recall every pass completion thrown during a meteoric college career. On bad days, only the pain.

Ace tilts his head hard to the right and then back to the left until the vertebrae in his neck "snap" into place. He then methodically pops each knuckle a finger at a time while stealing another quick glance at his watch.

Ten after nine. Six more hours till I leave for Dulles airport. Figure an hour flight to JFK, and then another hour to get my luggage and catch a cab into the city. Eight hours . . . eight long hours until Kelli's back in my arms. No more long trips, Futrell, no matter what she says. This is it.

Ace palms his Blackberry, flipping through the stored images in his photo gallery. Kelli and their two children smile back at him, tugging at his heartstrings. He has thought about his wife every day during his travels abroad, the hardest times coming at the end of each eighteen-hour day when he lay in bed alone in some foreign hotel room, staring at the ceiling fan, wondering if she was all right. Twenty-three days, wracked with guilt over leaving her. At least a dozen times he had contemplated taking the next flight home, but his wife had insisted he stick it out. Tonight he and Kelli will finally share the same bed—a suite in Central Park—before driving home to Long Island tomorrow to see their kids.

He checks his watch again.

Ace had met Kelli Doyle during their junior year at Georgia—he the walk-on third string quarterback suddenly thrust into the limelight, she the knock-out blond with the country-girl smile and the disposition of a backroom brawler. She had been an All-American on the women's lacrosse and field hockey teams, a tough-as-nails competitor who enjoyed physically humiliating her opponents. Their relationship had lasted nearly until graduation when Ace had gone through his "gray period." Kelli, always focused on the brass ring, had moved on without him. Six years later the flame was rekindled when they ran into one another at a fund-raiser in Orlando. Within two months they had married.

Fourteen years of marriage, most of it good. A house, cars, two wonderful kids, two well-paying jobs at a time when the economy was still in turmoil—the American dream . . . all threatened by that damn lump in her left breast. Surgery, chemo, followed by a six-month reprieve before it had spread. The second round of chemo had knocked the fight out of her . . . but was it enough? He had wanted to cancel his trip, but she had insisted, promising him good news when he returned.

Three long weeks . . . never again. PetroConsultants can fire me if they want. Plenty of other jobs in the field. He turns to face the other four members of the panel. To his immediate right is Ellen Wulf, an associate director with the Energy Information Administration, to her right, Michael Bach-Marklund, a Senior Fellow for the Center for Strategic and International Studies.

Next to him is Rodney Lemeni, an economist representing Chevron/Texaco, and then Christopher Santoro, a consultant from the Cambridge Energy Research Association. CERA is a sister organization to Ace's employer, PetroConsultants, both falling under the ever-expanding IHS Energy Group umbrella. *Wonder if any of them have to travel twenty-two weeks out of the year?*

Senator Poschner drones on. "Listen to these stats. China is adding the equivalent energy demand of an entire mid-sized country every two years. Last year they added another 44,000 megawatts—more than our largest power company, and they still experienced blackouts throughout 60 percent of their country. In addition, India has—"

Ace shifts again in his chair, waiting for the senator to chew up his allotted time. He has worked as a petroleum engineer for PetroConsultants for fifteen years and has heard it all before—the statistics, the warnings, the recommendations, and the endless debates. He has never doubted the sincerity of the senators present. Not now, and not six years earlier when he last testified before the newly-installed Democratic-led Congress. But convincing a committee to act is far different than passing sweeping legislation, and the Obama Administration had lost precious seats in the 2010 midterms.

Maybe I should just quit. Not like I haven't given it some thought. I'm sure I could find a position with any of the major oil companies . . . unless, of course, I burn the bridge right now, pull back the curtain, tell Congress what I really know . . . yeah, like that'll make a difference. Most of these bozos receive campaign donations from the six sisters of sludge, the ones who don't won't survive next year's election. Your call, Ace. Feed your family, or go down in one last blaze of glory . . .

"Thank you, Senator. That brings us to our first witness of the day. Ace Futrell is a senior administrator at PetroConsultants of Geneva, now part of the IHS Energy Group. Mr. Futrell's team has been collecting data as part of his organization's upcoming report on world oil reserves—"

What about a major university? I could probably get a decent teaching job. Of course, we'd have to downsize. Lose the car, forget about that Disney cruise. Maybe I could pick up a few night shifts as a fry cook at McDonalds. Could be fun. They just bumped the minimum wage to $8.25. That should be enough to cover our cable bill. So what if we can't afford health insurance, or college tuition, or summer camp . . .

"Mr. Futrell, I know you've been traveling abroad these last few weeks. The Committee greatly appreciates you diverting your trip home to be with us this morning. Mr. Futrell?"

. . . or gasoline, or food—

"Hey, Ace, you're on." Ellen Wulf nudges his shoulder, snapping him back into reality.

"Mr. Futrell, I asked if you're ready to testify."

"Testify? Yes, sorry. Oh, and it's pronounced Fu-troll. As in petrol." Ace adjusts his microphone and then reads from his notes. "Mr. Chairman, Senators, it's an honor for me to be back with you this morning. I've been asked to address the topic of global oil production, specifically how much oil is left in world reserves. Having just returned from an extensive field trip to the Middle East, I have with me preliminary results from our latest data, however, before I share that information with the Committee, I feel it's important that we understand a few basic rules of the game. The first is a fundamental law of energy, the Law of Diminishing Returns. When the first wildcat rig is drilled, we know very little about what an oil field will yield, but by the time the last well is up, we pretty much know everything. The pattern is consistent and clear —every oil reserve peaks and drops in what M. King Hubbert, the father of petroleum geology, discovered to be a bell-shaped curve. The first oil pumped from a well is the cream, the easiest to access. Eventually the basin will peak, and thereafter production will slow. The less the flow, the more difficult and costly it is to pump. And yes, while technology continues to increase the long-term potential of each reserve, even technology has its limitations.

You're boring them, Futrell. They're not here to resolve the oil crisis, only to spin it.

"Peak oil is a term that refers to the top of Hubbert's Curve, the point at which the fruit is still easily picked among the tree's lower branches. EUR Oil refers to the Estimated Ultimately Recoverable quantity of oil remaining underground, the key word here being 'recoverable.' Bottom line, Senators: It takes energy to get energy. In this case, oil to recover oil. If it takes two barrels of oil to recover ten barrels, you pump. But if the field is in decline and you're only able to recover two barrels or less for those two barrels expended, you can't continue pumping, not with a negative energy return on energy invested. Remember that, Senators. It means we'll run out of oil long before the last drop is ever drawn out of the ground.

"Hubbert correctly predicted crude oil production in the United States would peak between 1966 and 1972. The actual peak occurred in 1970, though it would take another full year before that fact became apparent. Since then we've gone from being the world's largest oil producer to its biggest importer, a role now being challenged by China. While we still have active reserves in the Gulf of Mexico, for the most part America's domestic supply is all but finished.

"What about the rest of the world? Hubbert predicted world peak oil would occur between the years 2000 and 2005. Have we peaked? No question about it. From 2003 to today, not a single new catchment has been discovered that exceeds 500 million barrels. Okay, so how much is left? That's a bit more difficult to predict, given that these national companies exporting oil tend to operate in secrecy and deceit. Kuwait, for example, recently lied about its reported reserves in order to protect their OPEC production quotas, a practice all-too common among producing nations. Oil companies are just as bad. Because they have to pay taxes on reserves, they tend to report new findings in old fields, a practice that maintains stock prices but does little for world energy needs. Six years ago, executives at Shell had to resign after they misrepresented oil reserves to stockholders by four billion barrels of oil—an 'accounting error' worth an estimated $136 billion."

Ace reshuffles his notes. "Here's a few facts that play into the equation. Our species uses one billion barrels of oil every ten days, the United States responsible for 25 percent of that demand. While the Obama Administration has enacted policies that conserve energy and raised gas mileage standards while cutting harmful greenhouse gases, the new standards won't even take effect until 2016. Meanwhile, America's demand for oil, as well as natural gas and coal, is expected to increase by another 40 percent over the next twenty years, and we're not the only one. As Senator Poschner already mentioned, the energy demands coming out of Asia, specifically China and India, are enormous. Prior to 1990, China's energy needs grew only half as quickly as its gross domestic product, but over the last five years there's been a groundbreaking surge in China's economy that has caused their energy consumption to quadruple. We've contributed to that variable, our auto imports playing a key role in the mobilization of China's work force. Of particular concern is China's recent shift from coal to oil and natural gas, a change necessitated by the effects of carbon dioxide emissions that have reduced air quality in their major cities. As a result, China's oil demand has risen from 14 million barrels per day in 2004 to its present levels of 19 million barrels, nearly equaling that of the United States. When one considers that China's population of 1.4 billion people is four times as large as ours, it staggers the imagination to think how high their demand could eventually go. And like the United States, China receives most of its oil imports from Saudi Arabia, followed by Iran, Venezuela, and the Sudan."

Chairman Keller interrupts, "It's no secret we're in direct competition with the Chinese, Mr. Futrell. What this Committee would like to know is how much oil is left, specifically in Saudi

Arabia, which appears to be the only oil-producing nation that can sustain global increases in demand."

Ace nods. "Saudi Arabia is the key, there's no doubt. They possess five fields classified as super-giants, several of which have been pumping for close to 60 years. Ghawar is the mega-giant, composed of several super-giants. The field is 174 miles long and 16 to 20 miles wide, and it's been online since 1951. To the Saudis credit, they set the standard on maintaining their wells, with recovery rates at 75 percent—far and away the highest in the industry."

The Chairman interrupts again. "Yesterday, the Committee heard a presentation by Mr. Nansen Saleri, the Reservoir manager at Saudi Aramco. According to Mr. Saleri, the Saudis have tapped and untapped fields that could meet world demand beyond 2054. By the look on your face, you don't seem convinced."

"No, sir, I'm not, and I'm not alone. Despite their public gestures, the Royal Family has clamped down on foreign inspections of both oil wells and tankers. As a result, our data reflect basin quantities that are antiquated at best. As to these untapped fields . . . we've been listening to that song and dance for years. These days, if the House of Saud told me the desert forecast was hot and sunny, I'd probably bring a raincoat."

The remark sends smiles across the faces of those in attendance.

Nicely done, dopey. The fast-food industry can use a man like you . . .

Republican senator Bob Prichard, a staunch oil industry supporter from Texas, is not amused. "For the record, Mr. Futrell, the House of Saud has been a friend and ally to this nation for more than sixty years. Besides being our main supplier of cheap oil, they've also proven themselves to be a stabilizing influence among the other OPEC nations, as well as one of the few countries in the Middle East that supports our ongoing war against terrorism."

They also fund the teaching of radical Islam, hatred of the west, and nineteen of their nationals hijacked our planes. Ah, but what's a few thousand dead civilians among friends . . .

"I ask you now, sir, and for the record, are you in possession of any hard evidence that refutes the information presently being supplied by Saudi Aramco?"

"Hard evidence? No, Senator, however—"

"Thank you, Mr. Futrell."

Ace grinds his teeth, refusing to back down. "Senator, you invited me here to testify, not to debate politics. PetroConsultants accepts the fact that third-world nations routinely exaggerate oil reserves. In the last year alone Venezuela, Dubai, Iran, and Iraq have all been caught in lies. I'm not sure we're any different. After all, how many tens of billions of dollars' worth of aid to New Orleans was secretly diverted to rebuild oil rigs damaged by Hurricane Katrina?"

Oops, did that just slip out? Ace returns the Senator's glare.

Conversations break out as Senator Prichard's face turns a deeper shade of red. "Mr. Chairman, I demand you strike those comments from the public record. They have no bearing on this hearing."

"Senator, my only point was—"

Chairman Keller interjects. "I think we've got the point, Mr. Futrell. If you'd conclude your testimony with your latest figures?"

Ace takes a deep breath, his blood pressure refusing to settle. "One final comment, if I may, Mr. Chairman, for the record. While the Committee might eventually enact measures to replace some of the 40 percent of oil expended on power generation with natural gas, coal, nuclear, or some other form of alternative energy, there presently exists no short- or long-term solution to remedy our transportation and farming needs. Let me be crystal clear here: Without the oil used in fertilizers and pesticides, corn yields would drop from 130 bushels per acre to thirty. The same would apply for our other crops, including the grain needed to feed livestock. It's gasoline that powers industrial tractors, allowing a mere 2 percent of our population to feed 300 million people, and it's gasoline that brings those perishable goods to market. When the oil stops flowing, the masses will go hungry—and that, Senator, is fact. The only way you remedy that nightmare is to invest now in renewable energy resources and enact major policy changes that radically replace our nation's infrastructure, something that will take upward of ten years, mandating long-range planning and investment. In the opinion of many experts, it's long overdue."

Chairman Keller waits for the spectator's applause to die down. "Your recommendations are duly noted. Now the estimates?"

Ace removes a sealed manila envelope from his briefcase. "Mr. Chairman, Senators, based on all available supply indicators, including the recent exhaustion of the North Sea fields, the collapse of the Burgan field in Kuwait, and a 35-percent decrease in output of the super-giant, Cantrell, in Mexico, it is PetroConsultant's belief that world oil levels peaked in the summer of 2005, fueled, in part, by unexpected losses incurred at Iraqi well heads and insurgent attacks on pipelines in the wake of the second Gulf War. Based on current and projected demand, the ongoing war in the Middle East, the continued pattern of hurricanes affecting the Gulf of Mexico with increased ferocity, and the potential for more terrorists attacks that threaten key pipelines, we anticipate the world depleting all recoverable oil reserves by the year 2017."

A hush falls over the chamber, followed by dozens of side conversations.

"Six years, Mr. Futrell?"

Ace nods. "Or perhaps, Mr. Chairman, even sooner."

"Secretary Rumsfeld also stated that he was giving a lecture to members of Congress, in the Pentagon, on the morning of 9/11 and warned them to expect the unexpected with future terrorist attacks. Shortly after that he was handed a note stating that the North Tower was struck. Shortly after that he was told the second tower was hit. He then claims he continues with this lecture until the Pentagon was struck at 9:38. This makes absolutely no sense. If the Secretary of Defense was lecturing to Congressmen about surprise terrorist attacks when he is told two planes have hit both World Trade Towers, it is beyond belief that he continues this presentation without reacting to this 'unexpected' terrorist attack. The fact that not one member of the (9/11) Commission chose to scrutinize this statement speaks volumes."

—MICHAEL KANE, *Elephants in the Barracks:*
The Complete Failure of the 9/11 Commission.

"The most important thing for us is to find Osama bin Laden. It's our number one priority, and we will not rest until we find him."

—PRESIDENT GEORGE W. BUSH,
September 13, 2001

"I don't know where he is. I have no idea, and I really don't care. It's not that important. It's not our priority."

—PRESIDENT GEORGE W. BUSH,
March 13, 2002

CHAPTER 2

Aurora, Illinois
December 12, 2011
8:06 am CST

"Mary Chris, I'm late! Where's the Sweet'n Low?" Aurora Police Area Commander Doug Dvorak searches through kitchen cabinets and drawers, leaving chaos in his wake.

"I forgot to buy some," his wife calls out from the bedroom. "Use the sugar."

"Can't! Just started that new diet."

"Then use honey."

"It's still sugar."

"Then drink it black!" She enters the kitchen, a curling iron dangling from her chestnut hair. "Since when do you diet anyway? You're like a genetic freak as it is."

"I'm in training for the spring marathon."

"Good. You can run over to Walmart after work and pick us up a new alarm clock."

"I told you, I can fix it." He fills his Chicago Bears coffee mug, making a face as he chokes down the bitter elixir.

"Then fix it tonight. I can't afford to be late again." She wipes coffee from his goatee and gives him a kiss. "Be careful out there."

"Always."

✦ ✦ ✦

Situated forty-two miles west of Chicago, the city of Aurora is a community of 165,000 suburbanites, spread out over four counties, six school districts, and seven townships. The Fox River splits the historic downtown area into east and west districts, and is home to a renovated movie theater, as well as several churches and bridges that date back to the late 1800s.

Commander Dvorak oversees Area One, which encompasses the west side of Aurora and its downtown area. He also commands the city's bicycle patrol program and its special response team.

He is ten minutes from the police station when he receives the call from dispatch.

✦ ✦ ✦

Ray Henry has been the owner and general manager of Aurora Truck Rental since returning from two tours of duty in Iraq. Dvorak finds the former sergeant in his office, pacing behind his desk, a cell phone pressed to his ear.

Henry waves him in. Signals "one minute," as he jots down numbers on a notepad already filled with hieroglyphics. "Fine, fine. But you tell Jerry I want that truck back here in an hour with new front brake pads or I'm taking my business over to Kendall." Henry hangs up. "Sorry, Doug. Appreciate you coming by. How's Mary Chris and Simon?"

"Good. So what's up?"

"Probably nothing, then again, my 'soldier-sense' is tingling. Had two customers come in late last night to purchase one of our trucks. Middle Eastern types, supposedly college students, living at the same address. First red flag was their driver's licenses, both from South Carolina. These days, Bin Laden could probably get a license from that security sieve. Anyway, they got real antsy when I told them I had to make copies for my records. Second red flag was paying me in cash—$17,500 in cash, to be exact."

"What kind of truck?"

"Seventeen footer, one of the temperature-controlled units used for hauling perishables."

"They say what they needed it for?"

"Produce, but I could tell they were lying. Here's a copy of their licenses." Henry hands him the photocopies.

Dvorak reads the names. "Jamal al-Yussuf, age twenty-seven. Omar Kamel Radi, twenty-nine. Okay, I'll check it out." He stands to leave. "Tell your girls I'll see them Saturday at soccer practice."

"Sure thing. But I didn't tell you the last red flag. Schmucks were wearing Cub jerseys. Who wears a Cub jersey in December, especially the way the Bears are playing? Am I right or am I right?"

✦ ✦ ✦

The apartment complex is a two-story brick face, located six miles from the College of DuPage. Commander Dvorak verifies the refrigerated truck is nowhere in sight and then locates the landlord, Dawn Darconte, a local woman in her mid-thirties.

"They rented the apartment back in October. Told me they were students."

"Ever give you any trouble?"

"No. They pretty much kept to themselves. And they paid for the year in advance."

"Isn't that a bit unusual for students?"

"Bit unusual for anyone."

"Ever see them carrying textbooks?"

"I work full-time in a video store. They could be moving a library in and out of here and I'd probably miss it."

She leads him upstairs to apartment 2-D. He knocks several times. Waits.

No answer.

"When do you recall last seeing these guys?"

"Maybe a week ago. The tall one, Omar, he jogs in the mornings. I have a key. Want me to let you in?"

"Without a search warrant, I'd need consent of the occupant or evidence of abandonment. What about their car? Is it still out front?"

She peers over the rail. "Nope, it's gone."

Dvorak fishes inside his pocket for a business card. "Call me if they show up."

✦ ✦ ✦

Commander Dvorak was back in his office by eleven-fifteen. By noon he'd established that neither Jamal al-Yussuf nor Omar Kamel Radi were officially enrolled at the Community College in DuPage. By two-fifteen that afternoon he learned that both suspects had closed their checking accounts at a local Citicorp branch, having withdrawn more than $65,000. A check on the deposit histories of both men traced back four months, all monies originating from a bank in the Cayman Islands."

By six-thirty that evening, Commander Doug Dvorak had his signed search warrant.

"When NEADS (Northeastern Air Defense Sector) was informed of the first real-world hijacking, members of its staff initially assumed this was part of the (war game) exercise. For example, Master Sergeant Maureen Dooley, the leader of the ID section, told the other members of her team: 'We have a hijack going on. Get your checklists. The exercise is on.' Major Kevin Nasypany, the mission crew commander, actually said out loud, 'The hijack's not supposed to be for another hour.' Like the numerous hijacking scenarios described in the 'NORAD Exercises' document, there was no mention of this simulated hijacking scheduled for the morning of September 11th in the *9/11 Commission Report*."

—History Commons Group
June 14, 2009

"The U.S. air defense system failed to follow standard procedures for responding to diverted passenger flights. The various responsible agencies—NORAD, FAA, Pentagon, USAF, as well as the 9/11 Commission—gave radically different explanations for the failure (in some cases upheld for years), such that several officials must have lied; but none were held accountable. Was there an air defense stand down?"

—911Truth.org

"After all this I saw another angel come down from heaven with great authority, and the earth grew bright with his splendor. He gave a mighty shout, 'Babylon is fallen—that great city is fallen! She has become the hideout of demons and evil spirits, a nest for filthy buzzards, and a den for dreadful beasts. For all nations have drunk the wine of her passionate immorality. The rulers of the world have committed adultery with her, and merchants throughout the world have grown rich as a result of her luxurious living.'"

—Revelation 18: 1–3

CHAPTER 3

DIRKSEN SENATE OFFICE BUILDING
ROOM SD-366
DECEMBER 12, 2011
10:27 AM EST

HEARING FOR THE COMMITTEE
ON ENERGY AND NATURAL RESOURCES
United States Senate
110th Congress

"THE HEARING WILL COME TO ORDER!" Chairman Keller strikes his gavel until the room quiets. "Six years, Mr. Futrell? This committee's been assured by multiple sources on more than one occasion that world reserves should continue to meet demand until at least 2029. The Energy Information Agency's own Annual Energy Outlook Report stated that—"

"With all due respect, Mr. Chairman, EIA estimates are based on nontechnical considerations. While the DOE's data on current and past supplies tend to be fairly accurate, future projections were concocted so they'd equate to anticipated domestic supply growth. They were political projections, Senator, nothing more. It's like asking an economist; all you'll get are unsubstantiated sunny expectations."

More cross-conversations fill the chamber. Ellen Wulf turns to face him. "Hey, Ace, I'm sitting right here."

"It's nothing personal, Ellen. Your department simply

functions as saccharine—it artificially sweetens."

Keller pounds the gavel until the sound echoes above the din. "Mr. Futrell, I have a question. It seems every year we're hearing and reading about some huge new reserve discovered, like the one a few years back off the coast of Brazil."

"It's all nonsense, Senator, perpetrated by the industry to sucker potential investors. The Brazil field you mentioned . . . that was the Carioca field discovered back in 2008 in the deepwater Santos Basin. One test well was drilled. Someone claimed he heard an estimate of 33 billion barrels, and the next thing you know, it's all over the news as fact, causing the stocks belonging to BG Group, Repsol, and Petrobras to skyrocket like a pyramid scheme selling fluff. No one noticed when Brazil began denying the claim, or that there's still no oil being produced from the basin. Pumping oil from a deepwater offshore reserve requires very expensive platforms, each one costing in the neighborhood of $150 million. Speculation won't fill up your gasoline tank, Senator, nor will it get these big oil companies to invest unless they are absolutely certain they'll receive a positive return."

"Thank you for clarifying that, Mr. Futrell. The Chair recognizes Senator Ashton."

The representative from Alabama appears quite animated for a man stricken to a wheelchair. "Mr. Chairman, I want to readdress Mr. Futrell's previous statement. Yes, it is an undeniable fact that the world will eventually run out of oil, but to suggest that we'll actually run out of oil within six years is simply irresponsible. Last year I personally attended an energy conference hosted by the Center for Strategic and International Studies right here in Washington. I listened to testimony from numerous experts, including directors at Saudi Aramco, who presented us with in-depth maps of their oil fields. The Saudis' projections, backed by the U.S. Geological Survey, go far to refute Mr. Futrell's 'personal opinions.' Conservative estimates indicate reserves of 600 billion barrels, not counting a significant part of the Rub' Al-Khali Basin, which has yet to be drilled. As such, I formally request that Mr. Futrell's estimates be stricken from the public record."

"Seconded."

Ace sits back, a numbness creeping over his being as Republicans and Democrats argue whether to remove his statement from the event's recorded history.

Chairman Keller retakes control of the proceedings. "We shall table a vote on any motions until after the Committee hears testimony from the other panelists. Mr. Santoro, I'd like to hear your opinion on Saudi reserves."

"Thank you, Mr. Chairman." Christopher Santoro repositions his microphone, allowing him to stare down the table at Ace. "CERA has conducted our own study of the Saudi oil fields in question. We agree with Senator Ashton that these reserves hold more than 600 billion barrels, plus an additional 200 billion barrels in undiscovered resources, and perhaps another 100 billion in fields that have peaked but still hold reserves that can be pumped using new technologies. That's 900 billion barrels of oil, enough to meet global needs well beyond 2035. We also believe that, as technology evolves, oil companies will continue to drill deeper and more accurately, and I think even Mr. Futrell has agreed, no one does it better than the Saudis. By producing slow and steadily, Saudi Aramco has expanded the life cycle of each of their big reservoirs, with depletion rates averaging a mere 1 to 2 percent a year. Sure, we'd love for the Sauds to open the valves and double production, but sending a glut of cheap oil into the market can also destabilize the industry. The Saudis realize this and use their vast reserves to stabilize prices. Still, as history has shown, whenever there's a crisis, be it a hurricane in the Gulf or a harsh winter in Japan, the flow of oil is always increased to compensate for demand. Based on CERA's studies, and taking into consideration new extraction technologies and alternative energy sources coming on line, we feel confident global reserves will last us beyond 2043, perhaps as long as 2050."

Several Committee members applaud the statement.

Rodney Lemeni, an economist from Chevron/Texaco, half raises his hand, adding, "I would agree with Mr. Santoro, provided the oil companies continue to receive the strong backing and support of the United States government."

Yeah, because the oil companies need a few billion dollars more of our tax money each quarter in order to keep the lights on . . .

Ace raises his hand. "Mr. Chairman, so there is no confusion, our analysis of the data took into account all factors, including improved extraction technologies. Granted, we did not add the untapped fields located in the Saudi's Empty Quarter, the reason being—we've yet to see any geological or seismic evidence that shows us what's really down there."

"Yes, but given the vast fields and their proximity to the Ghawar, wouldn't you assume more of the same?"

"Sir, if I've learned one thing in my fifteen years in this business, it's this: If it doesn't smell right, something stinks."

"Senator Thornton, you wish to reply?"

Robert Thornton, the Republican senator from Alaska, leans into his microphone as he addresses the Committee. "I want to thank all of our distinguished guests for attending this morning's session. After listening to Mr. Futrell's comments, I hope our friends on the Democrat side of the aisle are now convinced that drilling in the Arctic National Wildlife Refuge is no longer an option, but a critical necessity in meeting our nation's present and future energy needs. As former governor Palin has rightly said, 'Drill, baby, drill.'"

The reference to Sarah Palin draws mixed responses from the audience.

"Response? Yes . . . Mr. Futrell."

Ace grabs the microphone, his psyche now fully engaged in battle. "With all due respect to Senator Thornton, while some 'experts' have tossed around quantities of 16 billion barrels of oil being found in ANWR, the U.S. Geological Survey's numbers are far more accurate, dealing with EUR Oil, not volume.

There's less than a year's supply of recoverable oil in the Arctic, and what little is there is spread around in small pockets in areas that have no roads, no pipelines, no infrastructure whatsoever. It would take at least ten years to bring that supply to market and it would barely make a dent. The Arctic supply is nothing more than a Band-aid, and a small, expensive, and, in my estimation, a politically motivated one." *Now who's your daddy, Senator? Me or the Moose Queen?*

"How dare you, sir!" Senator Thornton barks. "This is a bipartisan hearing! We're committed to seeking solutions, not votes, and I will not be chastised by a . . . "

A what? Future fry cook? Droplets of sweat drip from Ace's armpits, though he refuses to break eye contact with Thornton, who is backing Sarah Palin's presidential run in the upcoming Republican primaries.

Chairman Keller allows him to ramble another minute. "Senator Henk?"

Mrs. Danelle Henk, the Democratic Senator from Louisiana, offers a motherly smile to the panel. "Thank you, Mr. Chairman. I'd like our panelists to comment about nonconventional energy resources, specifically heavy oil and tar sands. It's my understanding these resources can yield significant supplies of oil."

Ellen Wulf is first to reply. "Senator, EIA projects the equivalent of 200 billion recoverable barrels of oil in Canada's Alberta tar sands. While processing tar sands isn't cheap, we believe the potential yield warrants the expense. There has also been talk about expanding a new field in Venezuela."

"Okay, Mr. Futrell, but keep it short."

Ace feels his face flush. "It's not my intent to be a nay-sayer, Mr. Chairman, but I feel it's important the Committee have all the facts. Despite U.S. pressure, Canada has been hesitant to increase tar sand operations because of the nature of the job. Tar doesn't flow out of the ground the way oil does. The technology involves hot-water flotation to remove thin layers of oil from the sand, while adding a petroleum distillate to upgrade the tar to a synthetic crude. It's essentially an open pit mining operation, but it produces lake-size amounts of polluted refuse water. It's also costly in terms of energy, requiring upward of 20 percent of Canada's entire natural gas production, which they've been understandably hesitant to sacrifice. In regard to Venezuela, while the Orinoco oil belt contains one of the largest known accumulations of bitumen in the world, the synthetic crude project has a low yield of only 5 to 10 percent based on current technologies. Once again, it comes down to economics."

"What about synthetic fuel, Mr. Futrell?" This from Senator Bill Rawlins, a veteran of the first Gulf War. "The Senate has been debating the virtue of subsidizing Syn-fuel as long as I can remember."

It's a setup question, and a good one. "Senator, Syn-fuel is nothing more than a giant tax dodge created by a handful of greedy companies who found a way to take advantage of a tax incentive enacted by Congress back in the 1980s. Synthetic fuel is made using bromide and coal, but the companies running the fifty or so Syn-fuel plants across the United States—and I use the term 'plant' loosely—are simply spraying coal with diesel fuel or pine tar resin so they can collect enormous tax credits from a loophole the Senate refuses to close. The subsidy's buried in Section 559 of the Tax Relief Bill, and the Syn-fuel lobby, which uses the Orwellian name 'Council for Energy Independence,' spends about $2 million every year to keep it in place."

Senator Rawlins smiles in satisfaction. "Thank you, Mr. Futrell. Perhaps our friends on the other side of the aisle will take note of your comments."

Senator Keller registers the weight of the chamber. "This is an issue we need to address at a later date. However, since we are discussing fossil fuel alternatives, I'd like to hear from the panel on solar wind, and other potential resources. Mr. Bach-Marklund."

"Thank you, Mr. Chairman, and thank you Senator Ashton for joining us at last year's conference. The Center for Strategic and International Studies has submitted its report on current forecasts in regard to alternative energy solutions to fossil fuels. Natural gas is the leading alternative fuel, currently supplying about a quarter of our energy needs and slightly less around the world. Natural gas can be burned cleanly in internal combustion engines, the challenge is in developing a storage capacity that renders it feasible to use in automobiles. Compressed natural gas lacks the range of a tank of gasoline, while liquified natural gas requires extremely low temperatures for storage. At the same time, natural gas, like oil, is a finite resource. While EIA estimates supplies lasting until 2050, industry analysts agree we'll most likely run dry before 2025. That's because newer fields tend to be harder to find and are far smaller, depleting faster. Unlike oil, gas doesn't taper off. It just shuts down when depleted. Natural gas can be imported by cooling it into a liquid form at minus 260 degrees Fahrenheit; however LNG requires special tankers and ports, of which there are currently only three in the United States.

"Wind may be our most promising renewable source to fuel electricity, and the technology continues to advance, with the latest turbines capable of producing up to three megawatts. At present, wind supplies less than 2 percent of America's energy needs, though countries like Denmark have reached levels as high as 10 percent. To contribute significantly, the industry requires additional funding to resolve certain technological challenges, and much of our transmission lines will have to be revamped in order to bring wind power to the masses. As Mr. Futrell indicated, the commitment entails significantly altering our nation's infrastructure.

"Solar power currently supplies less than 1 percent of domestic needs. Like wind, solar is clean, renewable, and the technology continues to improve, with new thin-film panels and PV dye coatings, showing real promise in reducing costs. The

Swiss are close to completing their new Titania Dye Sensitized Cell, which could yield the most inexpensive photovoltaic panels yet.

"Hydro-electric power currently accounts for 3 percent of global energy needs—9 percent here in the States—but expansion is quite limited as the rivers that can handle dams have already been exploited. Micro-hydro projects utilizing smaller rivers and streams show promise to assist less-populated communities.

"Geothermal power remains stagnant. Nuclear power has also stagnated, due to costs, radioactive wastes, and the potential for these facilities to be targeted by terrorists. Nuclear currently supplies 20 percent of our electricity, but less than 4 percent of our total energy needs.

"Of all the alternative energy sources available today, there are only two that can replace or supplement oil as a transportation fuel. The first is hydrogen fuel cells. While hybrids continue to sell well, shifting to a total hydrogen community requires a trillion-dollar upheaval in our infrastructure. Hydrogen is also very combustible, and big business is not apt to outlay substantial investments in the technology unless they see a full commitment by the federal government.

"More promising is ethanol, or E85, a mixture composed of 85 percent ethanol and 15 percent gasoline. In Brazil, E85 has already replaced pure gasoline at service stations. Most Americans don't know it, but all new American cars possess flex-fuel engines, meaning the consumer can switch back and forth between E85 and gas without service required. Whether ethanol is generated by cornstarch or sugar, it's a clean fuel, good for farmers, and good for the environment. But switching to an ethanol-nation again requires a serious commitment by the federal government to make changes within our infrastructure, in this case, the farming sector."

"Thank you, Mr. Bach-Marklund. And I agree, this Committee must look into ethanol and some of the other alternatives you mentioned. Mr. Futrell, I cringe every time you raise your hand."

The audience laughs.

"Believe me, Senator, I wish I had better news to add. But this Committee and this Administration need to take its head out of the sand, and if I have to be the one to deliver the sobering news, then so be it. In regard to E85, it's not practical. Ethanol is fuel converted from food, and food requires lots of energy to grow. U.S. wheat reserves are already dangerously low. Several hundred million people in China are in danger of starving. Keep in mind, a lot of these food sources also feed our livestock.

"Natural gas is vital for electricity, but it can't be used to power vehicles, unless you want to drive to the local supermarket strapped to a bomb."

"Okay, uh . . . thank you. Before we break for lunch, we have time for one last speaker. The Chair recognizes the Senator from Pennsylvania."

Senator Edward R. Mulligan waits until the chamber quiets.

Ace doodles over his notes, his thoughts slipping back to his travel plans. Following the usual script, the energy hearings have degenerated from fact-finding exercises to posturing and speeches. Congress will again banter back and forth politically for months but delay the "major impact" decisions until after the 2012 Presidential election. The public will continue to complain about high energy and fuel costs and the issue will certainly be debated in the fall, while behind the scenes the corporations with major contracts at stake will use their eight-figure donations to seed those candidates who share their "mutual interests." In the end, Congress will most likely pass an energy bill loaded with pet projects and "tax incentives" designed to encourage Big Oil to explore. Perhaps there will be a new port or infrastructure development or two "awarded" to the usual suspects. But in the end, there will be no impact-generating long-term solutions, no major infrastructure commitments . . . nothing to stave off the "big rollover."

Senator Mulligan clears his throat. "Mr. Chairman. I'm not going to read any prepared speeches today, but I do have a few comments. You know, my father was always a straight-shooter, and if he was in this room, I think he'd say all this digging and drilling and data collecting is a yesterday-forever policy that's finally run its course. The American people are fed up. Hell, I'm fed up with energy policies that rely on third-world countries, half of which would rather see us dead than alive.

"Electric cars and hydrogen fuel cells are a pipe dream. According to the University of California, it takes over 1,100 gallons of gaseous hydrogen to equal the energy in one gallon of gas. There are 700 million internal-combustion powered vehicles on the planet . . . anyone here really think fuel cells are the answer? "

Ace stops doodling, his attention now fully focused on the speaker.

"Mr. Chairman, fellow committee members, we have a serious set of problems staring us in the face—a failing world economy, pushed to the brink by the sudden end of the fossil fuel era. There are 200 million Chinese starving, and drought is ravaging many areas of the planet. If there are any of you still around from the Bush Administration who thinks the war in Iraq had to do with 9/11 and weapons of mass destruction, I have some prime swamp land in Scranton I'd be willing to sell you. No, my friends, Mr. Futrell is right. We either address this problem as a unified nation and world, or we'll end up annihilating one another to secure the last drop of oil, the last acre of food, and the last reservoir of water. How do we do that? We conserve. President Carter preached conservation back in 1973 when OPEC decided to grab us by the short and curlies and shut off the spigot, thinking they could dictate foreign policy to America, and it made a real difference. Well, isn't that what's happening now? My Republican friends might rightly state that we could go back to the Ford Administration when Vice President Rockefeller pushed a plan to develop alternative energy sources. Of course,

Dick Cheney helped derail those plans thirty-five years ago, and he and his cronies have profited quite well from those policies ever since. But this is our watch now, and we're all responsible. There are six billion of us on this planet, and we no longer have the energy capacity to handle our needs. We need to end the wars in Afghanistan and Iraq, if for no other reason than we can't afford it from both an economic and an energy standpoint. Most of all, we need to accept the fact that we can no longer sustain new growth. That means, my fellow Democrats, that the American empire must shrink . . . along with the rest of the world. We either accept that fact, or we'll end up sinking this lifeboat we call Earth and drowning together. It is our responsibility as elected officials to map out a radical course of action that conserves our resources, while we bring online solar and wind farms and other means we can afford, in order to save as much oil as we can for food and transportation.

"Rest assured, there are those among us who aren't interested in cutting back and sacrificing. They'd rather go to war. We must unite against these psychopaths of power, or deal with their solution: Nuclear warfare, biological attacks, genocide . . . or the elimination of the lower class through systematic starvation. One thing is for sure, when the lights go off and there's no food at the grocery store, every person in this chamber will be to blame."

Ace Futrell can't help but grin in admiration. Finally a politician, perhaps a presidential candidate with the guts to take on the big boys.

Too bad he doesn't stand a chance.

"Life is what happens while you are busy making other plans."

—JOHN LENNON

"Washington Air Traffic Control Center knew about the first plane before it hit the World Trade Center. Yet the third plane was able to fly 'loop-de-loops' over Washington, D.C., one hour and forty-five minutes after Washington center first knew about the hijackings. After circling in this restricted airspace, controlled and protected by the Secret Service, which had an open phone line to the FAA, how was it possible that this plane was then able to crash into the Pentagon? Why was the Pentagon not evacuated? Why was our Air Force so late in response? What, if anything, did our nation do in a defensive military posture that morning?"

—9/11 WIDOW KRISTEN BREITWEISTER
from a testimony given before the Joint
Senate House Intelligence Committee.
September 18, 2001

"Then the second angel blew his trumpet, and a great mountain of fire was thrown into the sea. And one-third of the water in the sea became blood. And one-third of all living things in the sea died. And one-third of all the ships in the sea were destroyed."

—REVELATION 8:8

CHAPTER 4

Aurora, Illinois
December 12, 2011
8:03 pm CST

"Unit One in position."

"Unit Two in position."

"Acknowledged. We're entering now." Commander Dvorak nods to his patrolmen. The lead officer keys open apartment 2-D, the second and third men in line coming in low, guns and flashlights drawn.

A quick search of the two bedroom apartment confirms the occupants have moved out. Dvorak enters, followed by another officer carrying a forensics kit. He looks around.

The L-shaped living and dining room area is small. A thirty-three-inch plasma screen television is mounted on an otherwise bare wall facing a second-hand sofa. The dining room light fixture hangs above empty floor. Brown curtains conceal a balcony overlooking the parking lot. The kitchen is overflowing with trash from fast-food joints.

"Commander, we found something."

Dvorak heads back toward the bedrooms and enters the master suite. One of his officers is holding up the queen-size mattress, exposing the box-spring . . . and a laptop computer.

THE DINING ROOM IS ALIVE, its heated air recirculating an aroma of lobster bisque and filet mignon, its clothed tables spilling over with patrons bundled in sweaters, feeding among a sea of overcoats and parcels, fine paintings and chandeliers. Frosted windows glitter with holiday lights, everything multiplied in a frenzy of etched glass and mirrors.

Ace weaves past patrons and waiters as he makes his way through a twisting hall of mirrors into the Chestnut Room, the paneled dining area one of three looking out onto a central garden.

Kelli Doyle is seated alone at a table for two, staring at her reflection in a large hourglass clock. The remains of her blond hair, once thick, shoulder-length curls, have been reduced to dried strands tucked beneath a matching wig, set in a tight ponytail. Her weakened body slumps against the padded chair, seeking equilibrium against the pain. The scorching residue of her last treatment of chemo still swims in her tissues, burning out the cancer and everything else the clear elixir has come in contact with.

She glances at the faint brown discoloration along the inside of her forearms—burn marks from her fourth and final cycle. Chemotherapy is an all or nothing endurance race against death as your body is eaten away from the inside out while your mind shuffles in and out of a dementia interrupted only by spasmodic episodes of vomiting. Only her self-imposed mission has kept her going, the morality of her choices giving her a newfound strength. *What doesn't kill you . . .*

"Hey, stranger." Ace beams at his wife but gets no response. "Kel?"

The frail blond looks up, her thin face creasing into a smile. "Hey, you." She stands, half-falling into her husband's arms.

"You were gone so long—"

"But now I'm home for good. So? What did Dr. Eastburn say?"

Her eyes glisten. "Blood count's normal. I'm in remission."

Ace hugs her again, easing back as he feels her ribs caving beneath his grip. Kelli's two-year battle has taken an emotional toll on his psyche, each day lived with uncertainty, every joy hollow. Remission—a death sentence commuted.

"Ace, honey, you okay?"

He pulls away, Kelli's thick wool sweater leaving fuzz against his five-o'clock shadow. "Am I okay? You just gave me the best damn Christmas gift a guy could ask for."

"Sit down, there's more." She reaches into her purse, pulls out an envelope, and places it on the table. "Merry Christmas."

Wiping a stray tear, he removes his overcoat and pulls his chair close to hers. "What's this?"

"Open it."

Ace peels back the flap and stares at the tickets. "A cruise?"

"To the Bahamas. Just the two of us. My mother said she'd watch the kids."

"Are you strong enough to travel?"

"I'll deal. I really need to get away."

"We both do."

She studies his expression. "What happened in D.C.?"

"Nothing. Same old, same old." He scans the menu.

She pulls it away. "You're not getting away that easy. What did you say?"

"Nothing."

"Liar. You told them everything, didn't you? I knew you would. Good for you!"

"It means nothing. Half my comments were stricken from the public record, the other half refuted by the Senators on the oil lobbyists' payrolls."

"Maybe I can help deliver your message." She squeezes her

husband's hand. "Ace, I wrote a book."

"A book? What kind of book?"

"A tell-all memoir."

His heartbeat jumps. "CIA stuff or White House days?"

"Both. Focusing mainly on a period I spent working with the Strategic Support Branch."

"You never told me much about that."

"The SSB's a clandestine espionage arm of the Pentagon created by Rumsfeld and Cheney after 9/11. We were essentially an independent wing of Special Ops with no Congressional oversight. Cheney used us as his own private assassination ring."

"You killed people?"

"Not me personally, but my hands have blood on them. The whole thing was a Neoconservative initiative, pushed by Dick Cheney, who believed Iran-Contra failed only because the CIA and Pentagon were involved and secrecy couldn't be maintained."

"These guys don't give a damn about the Constitution or the law, do they?"

"Let's just say they have a very specific vision about how the Middle East should be realigned, and Iraq was only the beginning. The SSB allowed the Neocons to operate in secrecy, outside the jurisdiction of the CIA. Just after Cheney left office, I was tasked with organizing . . . well, let's just call it a Middle Eastern contingency plan. I can't give you any details, at least not yet. Just suffice it to say it was bad stuff."

"How bad?"

She looks him straight in the eyes. "As bad as it gets."

Ace feels his skin crawl. "And you want to go public with the information?"

"My soul is tarnished, Ace. I didn't realize it until I started studying Kabbalah. The cancer . . . its cause and effect. The memoir is a way to warn people, a way to expose the plot before it happens so that it never happens."

"What plot?"

"I can't say."

"You can't say, but you're going to publish this information?"

"Yes . . . I mean no, not publish . . . release, over the Internet. But I can't do it yet. I'm still gathering details. I've been out of the loop a bit over these last eight months."

"Then how do you even know it's still happening?"

"The same reason you know we're running out of oil. You're in the trenches . . . you hear things. In order to do what I want to do, I'm going to need your help."

"My help? Against the SSB, the Neocons? The entire fossil fuel industry?" Ace massages the growing ache in his sinuses. "Kelli, I'm not Superman, I'm just mild-mannered Clark Kent, a regular guy trying to provide for his family."

"Every Clark Kent has a Superman in them."

"More Kabbalah?"

"Don't make fun. It's my lifeline to salvation. And don't change the subject. I know you, Ace. You're as sick of these do-nothing politicians as I am. How many times have you testified before Congress? How many times have you warned them? The system's broke. It'll take all of us down with it . . . unless we act."

"And exactly how do you propose we do that? The Feds own the banks, the banks are in bed with Big Oil, the Neocons are in bed with the defense contractors, who in turn are in bed with the media—and the rest of the world is lining up to sleep with King Sultan. Remove Sultan and there's five hundred other royals waiting in line, daggers poised, to take his place, backed by about a trillion dollars in Saudi assets, a quarter of the remaining oil left on this planet, and, oh yeah, did I mention the White House? Or will you be rewriting sixty years of U.S. policy in your memoir as well?"

"I admit it's a challenge."

"No, going to the moon was a challenge. This is more like a massacre."

"Sort of like your first game, huh? Georgia—Tennessee?"

"Save the speech."

"What a game. First Gary Archer breaks his leg, then his backup goes down, forcing the coach to turn to third-string quarterback, Clark Kent."

"Okay, enough—"

"Down 17–3 late in the game, the Vol's defense blitzing you on every play. Ace, I swear, you had so many guys chasing you it looked like a jail break. The game was over, and everyone in Sanford Stadium knew it . . . except my man. Every time they sacked you, you just kept getting up, clapping and yelling, rallying the troops."

"Seriously, if you're looking to get laid tonight, I'm a sure thing."

"Then it turned. Another third and long, the pocket collapsing on you, when out of nowhere, 'boom,' you took off running . . . fifty-two yards—first down! They never saw it coming, the scrawny little white boy from West Virginia."

"I wasn't scrawny."

"Another run, another first down, and now you've got Tennessee's defense thinking. The coverage on your receivers eased up, Mark got loose in the end zone, and you nailed him with a 30–yard laser—touchdown! Everyone's going nuts, but you're the calm in the storm, like you saw it all before it happened. Crowd's back in the game, our defense holds, and you've got the ball again. With twenty seconds left, you tied the game. You brought us back from the dead."

"We lost in overtime."

"My point is one man's effort against impossible odds not only changed the game, but changed our season. The team suddenly believed again, and you guys made it all the way to the Orange Bowl. Not too shabby for a walk-on. You had no fear. I really loved that about you."

"Loved?"

"Love. I meant love."

"We both know what you meant." He glances down at his sleeves and the set of three thin white scars that run along the inside of either wrist. Two inches long. Twenty-three years old—his scarlet letter.

"Guess every Superman has his kryptonite, huh, Lois?"

"Ace . . . I didn't mean—"

"Yeah, you did. You say everything that crosses that conniving little brain of yours and you mean everything you say."

They pull away from one another as the waiter interrupts, "Good evening, sir. Something to drink?"

"Arsenic. Leave the bottle."

Kelli shoots him a look.

"Coke."

"Madam?"

"Another water, please."

The waiter leaves.

"Ace—"

"It was a long time ago, Kelli, a lifetime ago. Things change. I'm not the same person, this isn't a football game, and there's no 'S' on my chest. Start mouthing off to the wrong people and there'll be bullets flying . . . and those will just be coming from the American side of the equation."

"I have something in mind."

"And I told you I'm not interested." He kneads his eyelids. "Look, I'm tired. We both are. Right now, all I want is for us to be together."

"It doesn't work like that. I have access to information that could change a lot of people's lives. We have a responsibility—"

"My first responsibility is to my family."

"All the more reason to—"

"Damn it, Kelli, I said no!"

Heads turn. Ace looks away.

Kelli stares at her husband. *Maybe I was wrong. Some scars run so deep they never fade.* She reaches out for his hand. "Hey? I'm sorry."

"You don't know when to stop."

"I said I was sorry. You gonna be grumpy all night?"

"This is dangerous stuff. Because of my little tirade in D.C., I'll be flying way above the radar. And technically, you're still part of Cheney's machine."

"Exactly. I know where the mines are laid and the bodies buried."

"We're not discussing it anymore, end of story."

Her eyes grow harsh. "No, Ashley Futrell, let me tell you how the story really ends. Things are going to happen. Bad things. Nine-eleven kind of things, only on a different scale. The world's become a tinderbox, and there are people on either side of the equation tossing matches."

"And some of those people you and your cousin helped get into office."

"Guilty as charged, and now I want to do something about it. Something radical. The clock's ticking, Ace, the question is—are you ready to get back in the game?"

✦ ✦ ✦

An hour later they're outside, breathing in the cold winter air. The appetizer of conversation had turned their meal into a chore, and barely a word had been spoken during the main course.

Ace raises his arm to hail a taxi.

"No, let's walk. Please?"

They head north, Central Park on their right, the night alive with Manhattan traffic and festival lights.

"Ace, I'm sorry I ruined our evening. It's just . . . I've been thinking about things."

"I can see that. Too bad you never gave these things a thought while you were working for Dick and Rummy."

"Stop." She blocks his way. "No more cheap shots, okay? Let's just be together tonight. We'll sort the rest out in the morning."

Ace sees the urgency in her eyes. "Okay. No more fighting."

She points across the street to the northwest corner of 72nd and the Dakota Building. "That's where John Lennon was shot. Let's walk in the park. I want to see the Strawberry Fields Memorial."

Before he can object, she's leading him east through Central Park. They follow a narrow path that opens to a clearing, its garden laid barren by the cold. A mosaic composed of inlaid stones from all over the world lies before them, a tribute to the late musician and peace activist. The word *Imagine* is visible in the moonlight.

Two women are leaving flowers, setting them among others that have accumulated since the last anniversary of Lennon's death only a week earlier. The women nod to Ace and Kelli and then head back up the path.

Ace stares at the memorial. "I can still remember the day he died."

Kelli squeezes his hand for warmth. "He had the right idea. What do you think Lennon would do if he were alive today? Do you think he'd sit tight? Move to Montana?"

"Probably throw a concert, make people aware. Organize a political rally or something."

"You think it'd make a difference?"

"I don't know. Maybe against Nixon, but not with these guys. Their roots run too deep."

She moves closer. "Ace, the only way we keep society from running off the cliff is with a radical change in course. Think about that."

Before he can respond, she leans in and kisses him passionately, surprising him.

After a long moment she pulls away and hugs him, tears in her eyes. "I love you Ace. I know you've been suffering inside, and I know what happened years ago changed you, but the strength that made you special . . . it's still inside you, waiting to come out. I know that sounds corny, but isn't it time you found your way home?"

He starts to reply when shadows move, catching his eye.

The man is tall, at least six-foot-four. Long and lean. Tan complexion. Dressed in a dark raincoat, hands buried deep in his pockets. Dark eyes and heavy brows are just visible beneath the wool *N.Y. Giants* ski cap. Clean shaven. European.

Ace's scalp tingles as he approaches. A heavy whiff of aftershave arrives first, followed by words that glide over a trace of Russian accent. "Never was a Beatles fan, you know. The Rolling Stones, they were more to my liking."

A false smile.

A blinding spark of light, accompanied by a double *whooft* in the crisp December air, and sound is silenced.

Kelli's frail hand slips from Ace's grip. He catches her as she goes down, his mind racing to catch up with the fleeting moment, everything moving surreally, his pulse a timbering drumbeat in his ears, his lover's pained expression frozen in time. His eyes instinctively search for the stranger—gone—even as a steady stream of blood slides between his fingers, warming the hand now pinned against his dying wife's back. He presses his face against her cheekbone as blood rises up her larynx, choking her last words.

A final heartbeat . . . and she's gone.

Ace gags on his emotions, unable to comprehend what has just happened—what is still happening. Reality explodes. He shatters the night with a guttural yell, unable to tear himself from his wife's broken body. He screams rebuttals at the fleeing killer, cursing, raging, his soul lost, his existence plunging into a maelstrom of insanity, an abyss so deep he will never find his way home.

For Ashley "Ace" Futrell, the tsunami has struck. The world as he knew it is gone—never to be the same again.

"Our society is run by insane people for insane objectives. I think we're being run by maniacs for maniacal ends, and I think I'm liable to be put away as insane for expressing that. That's what's insane about it."

—JOHN LENNON

"A blueprint (Rebuilding America's Defenses) written in September 2000 by the Neoconservative think tank: Project for the New American Century, was drawn up by Dick Cheney, Donald Rumsfeld, Paul Wolfowitz, Jeb Bush, and Lewis Libby. The plan shows Bush's cabinet intended to take military control of the Gulf region whether or not Saddam Hussein was in power."

—MICHAEL MEACHER, MP,
UK Environmental Minister (1997–2003)
Excerpted from "The War on Terrorism Is Bogus,"
The Guardian,
September 6, 2003

"How was it possible the Pentagon was hit 1 hour and 20 minutes after the attacks began? Why was there no response from Andrews Air Force Base, just 10 miles away and home to Air National Guard units charged with defending the skies above the nation's capital? How did Hani Hanjour, a man who failed as a Cessna pilot on his first flight in a Boeing, execute a difficult aerobatic maneuver to strike the Pentagon? Why did the attack strike the just-renovated side, which was largely empty and opposite from the high command?"

—911TRUTH.ORG

CHAPTER 5

Located in downtown Chicago in the U.S. Customs Building, the Chicago Division of the FBI is composed of thirty-six squads assigned to investigate counterintelligence and terrorism, as well as organized crime, drug violations, violent crime, and white-collar crime. Included in their state-of-the-art facility is the Regional Computer Forensic Laboratory (RCFL), which is used to examine and analyze computers and related systems in terrorism, child pornography, and other forms of Internet crime.

Computer Forensic Science is the discipline of acquiring, preserving, retrieving, and presenting criminal data that has been processed electronically. With personal computers averaging thirty to sixty gigabytes of storage capacity (thirty gigabytes of printed data would create a stack of paper sixty stories high), new methods of training must be combined with technology to aid an examiner in determining which files are critical, especially in accordance with time limitations and judicial constraints.

Of the seven forensic examiners currently assigned to the Chicago RCFL, Steven Klemz is the newest recruit. Klemnz has suffered through six weeks of classroom training and more than two months of dealing with nothing but chat logs and cyber-porn. Then, three days ago, his director, Adrian Neary, handed him the laptop confiscated from the Iraqi suspects' apartment. Suddenly the young recruit's life had meaning. He was being given a chance. He was in the game: counterterrorism.

Time was of the essence—Director Neary wanted to return the laptop to the suspects' apartment, which was being watched by the local police department. Agent Klemz' first action was to copy the laptop's files into a SAN. Short for Storage Area Network, the program was essentially a single repository used by examiners to download large amounts of data.

With the data now copied, Klemz began sorting through files and segregating e-mails, using a Netcase program to translate Arabic into English. He refused to leave the facility, eating his meals at his station, taking hour catnaps when waves of exhaustion would hit. Still he continued on, building a profile of the subjects through the websites they visited and their e-mail correspondence.

Both suspects were born in Iraq. Jamal al-Yussuf was a Shi'ite, his home—Baghdad. He was an artist and had been taking courses in graphic design. He was also a photographer, his website portfolio dark and descriptive: amputees lying in dust-caked streets, cloaked policemen armed with machine guns, explosions raining upon civilian neighborhoods, the strafing ripping out chunks of stucco. Through blogs and intercepted e-mails, Agent Klemz learned that Jamal had lost his father and grandmother in the opening air raids of the 2003 invasion. An eleven-year-old brother, Kudair, had been wounded with shrapnel from a car bomb, and Jamal had carried the boy two miles to the hospital, describing in horrifying detail, how the boy's liver kept slipping out of his open abdominal wound between his fingers. The younger brother had died in the waiting room.

Omar Kamel Radi was a Sunni, tall, just over six-feet-five inches. He had been a soccer goalie in Haditha, a farming town on the Euphrates River, and hoped to play for the national team. After the U.S. invasion, Omar's neighborhood became a battleground between American troops and Iranian insurgents. A roadside blast reportedly destroyed his family's home, with two children listed among the dead. The military offered no details of the account.

Two civilians. Two men with motive . . . their own personal torment unleashed by the American invasion.

Agent Klemz lost his enthusiasm for the project. He stopped reading the e-mails, allowing the program to sort the correspondence using key words. Tonight he'd go home, eat a hot meal, sleep in his own bed. *I should give mom a call . . .*

The blinking red alert catches his attention—an encoded video file has been detected. Agent Klemz pages his director, his eyes glued to the screen as the lab's computer resolves the encrypted codes and opens the file.

Clean-shaven and scarred from head to knees, Chicago FBI director Adrian Paul Neary had spent his first seventeen years with the FBI as a field agent working in conjunction with the DEA. He had been forced to accept a desk job after three suspects wielding barbed wire had jumped him. The FBI director's body still bears the evidence from the attack, including a jagged two-and-a-half-inch scar in his chin that runs clear past his lip.

Neary joins Agent Klemz at his station, the two men staring at the video-taped footage.

The opening scene, taken by a hand-held camera, is of a classroom of Arab grade schoolers, ages five to seven . . . singing a song. Neary listens carefully. Translates: "Arabs are beloved and Jews are dogs."

"This is what they teach their kids?"

"They indoctrinate them into hatred early."

The scene changes to a graduation ceremony. Suicide bombers, their faces cloaked in black masks, their vests holding plastic explosives. Chanting in Arabic: "Death to America, death to Israel."

Neary shakes his head. "The psychosis of hate."

The next scene is far more disturbing. A small Palestinian girl is holding a Glock 9mm pistol, emotionally spent as she chants to small public gathering, "I want to die Shaleed! I want to die Shaleed! I want to die Shaleed!"

Agent Klemnz shakes his head. "She's no older than my seven-year-old niece. What are they teaching these kids?"

"How to die for Allah."

One of the suspects, Jamal al-Yussuf, appears next, dressed in combat fatigues. He is alone in a room, the walls bare, a cot visible in one corner. Facing away from the camera, he kneels in prayer. Bows. Turns to face the camera, an object held in his hand.

It is a child's skull.

Agent Klemnz shudders.

Al-Yussuf rattles something off in Arabic at the camera.

Neary translates. "We knock on heaven's gate with the skulls of Jews . . . with the skulls of Americans."

"Lovely."

Neary pats his rookie on the shoulder. "Put out an APB. I want these two found."

"All political parties in America are abysmal failures when it comes to energy and economics both. They cannot tell people bad news and they suppress those who try to. In fact, I believe that we are long overdue for a Jeffersonian approach; we should throw all archaic political constructs, buzz words, orthodoxies, and ideologies out the window and start with a fresh sheet of blank paper. We have entered a new human paradigm. It was and is of little benefit to keep refining Industrial Age government and philosophy in a new era."

—MICHAEL C. RUPPERT,
An American Energy Policy

"Multiple allied foreign agencies informed the U.S. government of a coming attack in detail, including the manner and likely targets of the attack, the name of the operation (the "Big Wedding"), and the names of certain men later identified as being among the perpetrators. Various individuals came into possession of specific advance knowledge, and some of them tried to warn the U.S. prior to September 11th. Certain prominent persons received warnings not to fly on the week or on the day of September 11th."

—911TRUTH.ORG

"The great enemy of the truth is very often not the lie, deliberate, contrived and dishonest, but the myth, persistent, persuasive and unrealistic."

—PRESIDENT JOHN F. KENNEDY

Book Excerpt:
To the Brink of Hell:
An Apology to the Survivors
by Kelli Doyle
White House National Security Staff Advisor
(2002-2008)

Frankly, I hope this scares the hell out of you.

I remember the moment it first hit me, the realization that something was terribly wrong. One moment you're fine, your mind consumed by the trivial, the next . . .

Those first moments are the toughest, when mortality hits you like a ton of bricks. Cancer? Can you operate? What about chemo? Well then, doc, what can you do?"

At some point, through tears and the tightness in your chest, you expel the words you never imagined having to ask: "How long?"

The doctor's answer is hard to hear, maybe harder than the death sentence itself, because even if he's wrong, even if he's off by a week or a month or even a year, it doesn't really matter — you know your clock is ticking. Of course it's always been ticking; it's been ticking backward ever since birth. We're born in an instant and die in an instant, our life, those precious moments in between, and like it or not, no one gets out alive.

When it comes to mortality, being human is both a blessing and curse. Aware of life's limits, we're forced to process something we can never fully comprehend. The first stage of coping with death is denial, a stage you'll be entering into momentarily. This will progress to blame and then anger. You'll punch the walls, kick the dog, and curse God, asking, "Why me?" Eventually you'll negotiate and try to make peace with your maker, because you'll need him now more than ever. And if you're a fighter, you'll fight for every last glorious moment.

That's what I want you to do. I want you to fight. I want you to act! Because the clock is ticking backward and the bells are tolling, only they're tolling for you! They're tolling for your children and your parents and friends, and every loved one and acquaintance . . . every human being you know or knew or might never know. There are six billion of us who share this planet, and soon — very soon — every one of us, save an elite few, are going to perish.

That's right, a massive die-off. To most of you it will appear gradually, as gradual as climbing into a giant pot of cold water and turning on the burner. At first you won't know anything is happening, and then slowly . . . slowly and painfully, like an IV drip of chemo burning into your veins, the realization will kick in that there's no escaping this death sentence, that the chaos that surrounds you won't be going away, that the food left in your refrigerator and on your shelves won't last very long, and that you and your family are going to starve to death.

Or freeze.

Or be incinerated by a weapon whose impact you'll never hear. Or succumb to a virus you'll never feel. You will be as helpless as the victims of the tsunami that struck Indonesia the day after Christmas 2004, or the lost souls of Hurricane Katrina, abandoned without food or water in flooded New Orleans . . . only this time there will be no rescuers, and CNN won't be covering the event, because there won't be any electricity to power their cameras . . . or your TV. Shooting the messenger won't help. Call me a liar, refute my warnings, curse my existence — it won't change a thing. The brakes are shot and civilization is being diverted . . . instructed to gaze in the rearview mirror as we drive ourselves off a cliff . . . only you're too busy micro-managing your life to see what's happening.

Open your eyes! Read the signposts! It's already begun — the opening moves played out as if upon a great political chessboard:

The 1973 oil crisis — the first taste of things to come.

The Reagan-Bush years—moves within moves, corruption behind smiles.

Iran and Iraq: A fostered war designed to temporarily control the center of the board.

Saddam's invasion of Kuwait: The manipulation of a pawn.

The rise of Islamic fascism: A cancer spreading throughout the Muslim world.

Secret 2001 energy meetings: Our path of self-destruction, mortared in greed.

The manipulation behind 9/11, the sacrifice of a noble knight.

The invasion of Afghanistan: A feint in the conquest of Iraq — our fateful plunge into the abyss.

The election of Hamas, the deceit of Hezbollah: The tentacles of Iran.

Attempted coups. Rigged elections. Laws "to protect the public" penned straight out of a George Orwell novel . . .

The collapse of the global economy, part I.

The board's still in play, but the outcome was decided long ago, and soon the final piece shall fall, but not the way the self-appointed autocrats would ever have predicted. When the house of cards collapses, everybody loses, from the rainmakers to the reign-enders, and the meek shall indeed inherit the Earth, at least what's left of it. As for me, I'll be long dead by then, and yet the cancer that riddles my body's been a blessing in disguise, for it has given me a newfound strength . . . an insight to set in motion my own little series of events that might stave off some of the impending doom, and perhaps buy back my own auctioned-off soul in the process.

For me it's too late. For my children, my loved ones . . . for you, I toll these final warning bells: The end of civilization as we know it is on the horizon, a tsunami of death on its way . . .

And you're asleep on the beach!

"Therefore, I have asked Vice President Cheney to oversee the development of a coordinated national effort so that we may do the very best possible job of protecting our people from catastrophic harm."

—PRESIDENT GEORGE W. BUSH,
altering a long-standing protocol by placing the VP in charge of all federal programs and agencies dealing with terrorism.
May 8, 2001
(4 months prior to the events of September 11th)

"U.S. military and other authorities planned or actually rehearsed defensive response to all elements of the 9/11 scenario during the year prior to the attack—including multiple hijackings, suicide crash bombings, and a strike on the Pentagon. The multiple military war games planned long in advance and held on the morning of September 11th included scenarios of a domestic air crisis, a plane crashing into a government building, and a large-scale emergency in New York. If this was only an incredible series of coincidences, why did the official investigations avoid the issue? There is evidence that the war games created confusion as to whether the unfolding events were 'real world or exercise.' Did war games serve as the cover for air defense sabotage, and/or the execution of an 'inside job'?

—911TRUTH.ORG

"Then the third angel blew his trumpet, and a great flaming star fell out of the sky, burning like a torch. It fell upon one-third of the rivers and on the springs of water. The name of the star was Bitterness. It made one-third of the water bitter, and many people died because the water was so bitter."

—REVELATION 8:10–11

CHAPTER 6

THE POLISHED WALNUT CASKET RESTS STARKLY upon its steel-wheeled chariot, its presence an emotional black hole that tugs at Ace's being. His insides tremble against the finality of its weight—he cannot bear to be in its presence much longer, nor contemplate standing by the graveside in the coming hour as his wife is lowered into her final resting place. Too weak to move, he remains seated in his designated place of honor, his left arm draped protectively around his eight-year-old son, Sam, his right hand wedged in between the hands of his thirteen-year-old daughter, Leigh. Kelli's parents, Sharon and Bruce, are seated behind him, along with Kelli's grandfather, Fitch. Ace registers the strength of their presence, yet inside he remains an island of combusting rage.

From his seat he watches Kelli's first cousin, Jennifer Wienner, take charge of the precession. For years the two had been known around Washington's inner circles as Butch and Sundance, pet names anointed by the GOP's top political strategist, Karl Rove, who himself had been nicknamed Turd Blossom by the second Bush he had maneuvered into office. Kelli, of course, was "Butch," a former CIA analyst promoted in 2002 as an advisor to the National Security Council, overseeing the Gulf Region. Jen was "Sundance," a campaign strategist who trained under Rove to oversee election "hot spots," seats vital to maintain control of the Houses by the GOP. Following the mid-term elections of 2006, Jennifer had left politics, accepting a high-paid lobbyist's position for a major pharmaceutical company specializing in flu virus vaccines. Like her cousin, Jennifer knew where the mines were laid and the bodies buried . . . along with the treasure.

Ace watches Jennifer as she shepherds each guest, accepting their condolences.

Divorced and in her early forties, Jennifer is roughly the same age as her deceased cousin and cut from the same cloth. She greets each guest as if closing a deal.

"Jen, I'm with Monsanto. The Board sends its condolences and specifically wanted me to ask you if the police have caught the bastard yet. If there's anything we can do—"

"Jennifer, how are you holding up? Katherine sends her love. She couldn't make it with the trial and all, but said she'll call you next week about financing a congressional run in her new state. Things in Florida just weren't working out . . . and after all her hard work."

"Ms. Wienner, I am so sorry for your loss. Do you remember me? Laura Whisenant. We worked together on Saxby Chambliss's campaign back in '02. Ol' Max Cleland never knew what hit him."

Black suits, nameless faces. Crocodile tears and Cheshire cat smiles . . . everyone networking.

Ace registers everything. Tucks it all away, adding it to the rage that fuels his fire.

"You're the husband, right?

He looks up, gauging the Monsanto lobbyist that has somehow managed to slip past Jennifer to invade his private island of grief.

"One of our board members, Owen Hollifield, asked me to send his personal condolences. Mr. Hollifield worked with Mr.

Rumsfeld when he was CEO at J.D. Searle back in 1977. He became friends with your wife years later when—"

"Maggot."

The man breaks into a nervous half-smile. "I'm sorry, what did you say?"

"Your ears not working? I called you a maggot. That is what you are, isn't it?" Ace's eyes bore through the false smile, causing beads of sweat to break across the man's forehead.

Sensing a disturbance in her universe, Jennifer moves to the approaching storm.

"Sir, if there's something I said—"

"Did you know that your pal, Rumsfeld, was hired by J.D. Searle just so he would use his political clout in Washington to coerce the FDA to approve Aspartame, despite the fact that every legitimate study showed it caused brain tumors in rats and all sorts of other health related problems? The FDA's scientists rightly shut it down and filed a grand jury investigation against J.D. Searle for filing false test results. But that didn't stop Rummy—"

Jennifer steps in between them. "Ace, let me handle this—"

"Instead, he waits until Reagan is sworn in. The new Prez selects one of his cronies to head the FDA board. And guess what happens next?"

"Ace, stop."

"America gets a new toxin in its food supply, the rich guys get a whole lot richer, and my wife, who drank a lot of diet soda, gets cancer!"

The lobbyist pushes past Jennifer, only to be trapped in the procession line as he searches for the nearest exit.

"Run, Forest, run!" His blood still broiling, Ace stands, waving to the funeral director. "Mr. Goldstein, this viewing is officially off-limits to anyone associated with Capitol Hill, Monsanto, or any other scumbag corporation."

"Ace, enough!"

"Back off, Jen!" He turns to face the gathering crowd

buzzing at the rear of the chapel. "If I can have the attention of the dirtbags exchanging business cards in the back. Yes, that would be all of you."

The room quiets.

"Thank you for your condolences. Now if you leeches would kindly crawl back inside your limousines or beneath your rocks, Kelli's family and friends would like to say our good-byes in peace."

Stunned expressions. No one moves.

Jennifer shoots Ace a venomous look and then quickly herds the group outside.

Ace returns to his seat, receiving a nod of thanks from Bruce Doyle as he draws his children in close.

❖ ❖ ❖

A cold rain falls from a sky more brown than gray. Mourners huddle beneath a canopy of black umbrellas, half-listening as a rabbi leads them in prayer and Kelli's casket is lowered into the ground.

Grief is an emptiness only time can fill; in its waxing moments it can swallow you whole, in its waning respite it will rise to ambush you with a long-forgotten memory when you least expect it. The death of a parent causes reflection, the death of child can shatter faith—

The death of a spouse forces change.

Ace trembles as the casket bearing his wife's remains disappears from view.

What do you do when your existence is shattered in an instant, when the pain is so intense that you can't stand to be inside your own skin, when every waking moment is consumed by endless emptiness? How do you go on when you are so sickened by life that you wish you'd simply disappear . . . the urge to drink your thoughts into numbness stayed only by your newfound responsibilities as a single parent, your children's pain far more important than your own, their innocence an emotional anchor that forces you to live out each hellish moment?

For days Ace Futrell has wept only in private. Around detectives and doctors, among family and friends, he has remained a rock. But as he whispers his last good-byes to his soul mate and sweeps his children up in his arms, he knows he will weep no more. As he climbs back into the limousine, another emotion will slowly seep into his being—one so cold it will suffocate his heart.

How do you quench a fire that burns inside you like a furnace, fueling an anger so hot that it consumes all thoughts, all logic, all tears?

There is only one way . . .

Revenge.

Today Ace Futrell's fury will cement his life's new mission—to find his wife's killer, to assassinate the assassin—

To punish those responsible for destroying his family.

"What we want is not a united Arabia, but a disunited Arabia split into principalities under our suzerainty."

—LORD CREWE, BRITISH STATESMAN,
1858–1945

"Oil is too important to be left to the Arabs."

—HENRY KISSINGER

"The truth is that the United States wants to eradicate our religious and Islamic identity."

—NAGI AL-SHIHABI,
Egyptian Newspaper Editor,
2004

CHAPTER 7

THE BOEING 747 JUMBO JET LANDS with a double thud, the spoilers—small hinged plates situated along the top portion of the wings—flipping up into the air stream to kill the plane's lift and keep the massive aircraft on the ground. Bypassing the airport's main terminal, the pilot taxies the vehicle to a private hangar—a temporary embassy for the visiting V.I.P and his traveling entourage.

King Sultan bin Abdel Aziz—ruler of Saudi Arabia, head of the Al Saud family, absolute monarch of the world's largest oil-producing nation, and guardian of Islam's two holiest shrines—relaxes inside the jumbo jet's private sauna with two of the dozen "stewardesses" who have accompanied him on the trip from Riyadh. As the 747 slows to a halt, the King exits the heated chamber and showers, his naked followers washing him down and then patting him dry.

Feeling refreshed, the King slips on a silk robe and enters his master suite, a chamber complete with oversized bed, fifty-two-inch flat-screen satellite television, and a crystal chandelier. Touching a keypad on his internal communications system, Sultan speaks Arabic to his son, Prince Bandar bin Sultan, ambassador to the United States. "Is he here?"

"Yes. He is in the hangar, waiting for an audience."

"Tell him I'm concluding an important meeting. Awaken me in two hours."

◆ ◆ ◆

Scott Swan finishes checking his e-mail on his Blackberry and glances at the time: 4:47. The CEO of Tech-Well Industries, a defense contractor recently purchased by the Carlyle Group, has been waiting in the airport hangar office for nearly three hours, and his patience has worn thin.

Lousy Saudi bastards . . . no appreciation for the working man.

◆ ◆ ◆

The Carlyle Group is a private equity investment firm whose financial assets, estimated between $30 billion and $50 billion, are topped only by its members' ability to directly and indirectly affect world policy. Founded in 1987 by David Rubenstein, a domestic policy advisor to President Carter, along with his partners William E. Conway, Daniel A. D'Aniello, and Stephen L. Norris, the Carlyle Group's list of partners, advisors, and associates reads like a global Who's Who of the rich and well-connected. Their power players include former Presidents George H. W. Bush and his son George, former Secretaries of State, James Baker III and Colin Powell, the former prime minister of Britain, John Major, as well as Park Tae Joon, the former prime minister of South Korea, former Secretary of Defense Donald Rumsfeld, and Frank Carlucci (also a former Deputy Director of the CIA), as well as a growing list of ambassadors, heads of state, and regulatory agencies from around the world.

While political access helped launch the company, it was money from the House of Saud that propelled the Carlyle Group to its present heights.

Carlyle's first transaction with the royal family took place in 1991 when Prince Al-Waleed bin Talal, the largest individual shareholder of Citicorp, purchased nearly $600 million of Carlyle stock. That investment opened the floodgates to the Saudis, who were shepherded by former President Bush, James Baker, and John Major, three world leaders who had supported Saudi Arabia during their terms in office. From that point on, the Carlyle Group soon found itself selling everything from AWACS to weapon systems, the profits from which enabled them to purchase defense contractors LTV, Harsco, and BDM International, which they later sold to TRW, Boeing, and Lockheed Martin. In the wake of the first Gulf War, Carlyle's defense contractors won major contracts to support the Royal Saudi Air Force while The Vinnell Corporation, on the verge of bankruptcy, landed a big contract to modernize the Saudi National Guard (following a Carlucci trip to Saudi Arabia).

In recruiting key players from former White House administrations as well as outgoing subordinates from the Pentagon and CIA, the Carlyle Group has become more than just a successful investment firm, it has become a political arbitrage—a trading entity that relies on insider information and "the persuasion of access" to forecast political stability among foreign activities.

For "normal" trading to be legal, it must be based on publicly available information. However, when it comes to former presidents and secretaries of state, this black and white area often turns gray. The Carlyle Group uses this gray area as a hedge against the unknown, such as investing in foreign government bonds, or accepting contracts in war-sensitive sectors dealing with oil and arms. With direct access to the White House, Carlyle's advisors not only gain insider information, they have the ability to sway foreign and domestic policy. By "riding the board," Carlyle has minimized the risks in purchasing struggling companies, turning them around and selling them for huge profits.

✦ ✦ ✦

Scott Swan tucks away his Blackberry and picks up a

two-month-old issue of *TIME* Magazine, the front cover depicting the world's continuing struggle to control the Avian Bird Flu, which again threatens to become a global pandemic. He skims through the article, a grin creasing his face as he reads about the pharmaceutical companies now working on a vaccine.

Stock's up another dollar, should split by next April . . .

He tosses the *TIME* magazine aside as Prince Bandar bin Sultan enters the office. "Mr. Swan, my father will see you now. I am truly sorry for the delay."

The executive forces a smile. "Business is business." Swan kisses the Prince on his silk-robed shoulder. He grabs his briefcase and follows him out of the office and up the portable steps leading onto the 747 jet.

King Sultan bin Abdel Aziz, now dressed in his own traditional white *thobe* and matching *ghotra* headpiece, greets his guest in the study. "Mr. Swan, *Masaa al-Khair.*"

"*Masaa an-noor.*"

"And how is your chairman?"

"He sends his best."

"But the chairman has chosen not to greet his biggest investor in person?"

"Due to the nature of this meeting, he felt it best I come alone. Officially this is simply a social call between the two of us. It has nothing to do with Tech-Well or Carlyle."

"Understood." The King signals to his son and visitor to take a seat. "Still, I am very uncomfortable with certain elements of this transaction. I need reassurances if we are to proceed."

"Remember, it was you who came to us."

"The timing concerns me."

"Would you prefer to wait until your country is invaded by Iran, or seized by an Islamic revolution?"

"I would feel more comfortable if President Obama was not in the Oval Office."

"There is an election coming up."

"You wish to make jokes?"

Swan looks the King in his piggish eyes. "Obama will not be a factor."

The King raises an eyebrow. "Is there something I should know?"

"Events change elections, Your Highness. The world is at a crossroads and your kingdom needs stability. These are tenuous times, and it will get worse unless we act now. Difficult decisions have been forced upon us—terrible decisions, still we do what we must. Historians not yet born will celebrate our courage."

"The House of Saud cannot be implicated—"

"There will be no loose ends."

"And if something does go wrong?"

"It won't."

"Now you speak for Allah?"

Scott flushes. "I am a liaison, nothing more. However, I've heard there are contingencies . . . backups in case of unforeseen events. That is all I am at liberty to say."

"Mr. Swan, I too have contingencies . . . the United States economy is my contingency. If anything does go wrong—a blogger selling conspiracy theories, a former CIA agent writing a tell-all book," the king's eyes blaze, "then the House of Saud shall reevaluate America's standing in the Middle East . . . and OPEC shall no longer sell oil in U.S. dollars."

King Sultan's cherub face creases in a frigid smile.

Swan clears his throat, finding his voice. "Enjoy your visit with the President."

BALTIMORE, MARYLAND

Jamal al-Yussuf lies in the strange bed in the strange room, staring at the ceiling, the uneasiness he feels reminding him of his childhood back in Iraq. For as long as he could remember his father had instructed him to sleep under his bed, that it was the best place to be in case the house came crumbling down or the American jets broke the sound barrier. Under the bed, Jamal would be protected from flying glass. Under the bed he would be safe.

The year was 1991, and Jamal was seven years old. As he lay underneath his bed, night after night, he tried to think of what he had done wrong to deserve this. When the American planes came low and the sirens would go off, he would stick his fingers in his ears and sing his favorite songs as loud as he could, just as his mother had instructed. He had asked her once when he should stop singing. She had replied, "When I come and get you, Jamal."

Winters were the worst, because it got dark out faster and turned very cold. Saddam had cut off electricity to give the enemy less to shoot at, and Jamal was not even allowed to turn on a flashlight to read. Night after night the family would huddle together, listening to the BBC on the radio, waiting to hear updates about the war. At some point water became rationed, and when the pipes had burst from the bombings, Jamal's mother had to boil it to make it potable—without any electricity.

Then there were the shopping trips. The entire family would pile into one car and lie down in the backseat while Jamal's father drove through decimated streets to find supplies. On one occasion, Jamal had peeked out the window at the carnage, the bodies wrapped in bloodied white sheets along the roadside, people crying and screaming over them. As the boy lay back in the seat he started to sing, wishing he was back in his safe place.

Twenty years later, Jamal registers that same familiar fear gnawing in his gut. Grabbing his pillow and blanket, he rolls onto the floor and curls up beneath the iron-framed bed, humming his favorite song until he falls asleep.

"The people can always be brought to the bidding of the leaders. That is easy. All you have to do is tell them they are being attacked, and denounce the peacemakers for lack of patriotism and exposing the country to danger. It works the same in any country."

—HERMAN GORING,
at the Nuremberg Trials

"It could happen tomorrow, it could happen next week, it could happen next year, but they will keep trying. And we have to be prepared."

—VICE PRESIDENT DICK CHENEY

"On August 13, 2002, the CIA completed a classified, six-page intelligence analysis (dubbed "Perfect Storm") that described the worst scenarios that could arise after a U.S.-led removal of Saddam Hussein. According to then-CIA director George Tenet, it was relegated to the back of a thick briefing book handed out to President Bush's national security team for a meeting on September 7, 2002, where the Iraq war was Topic A."

—WALTER PINCUS,
The Washington Post, June 2007

CHAPTER 8

The beach hamlet of Montauk represents a seventeen-square-mile tract of land bordered on the south by the Atlantic Ocean, to the north by Long Island Sound. The Doyle-Futrell home is a contemporary two-story, with cedar shake shingles, located in the Hither Hills section, within walking distance of the beach. Inside, maple walls and bamboo floors maintain a beach decor, while the two stone fireplaces create a ski-resort effect—a practical aesthetic put to good use during Montauk's harsh winter months.

The mourners have gathered in the great room, warming themselves by the main fireplace, eating and comforting one another with memories of the deceased. Every so often Ace's name is referenced in hushed tones:

"He travels so much. Who's going to stay with the kids? The housekeeper?"

"What about that live-in nurse of Kelli's?"

"No, she was part of a service. He'll have to get one of those full-time sitters."

"They should move. A beach town is no place to raise kids."

❖ ❖ ❖

The study is on the second floor. Bookshelves line three of the walls, with an L-shaped desk situated between two ocean-facing windows. Winter gusts howl in defiance outside the storm glass. A Dutch Zaanse wall clock continues its soothing cadence from its perch above a worn sofa bed. The inscription on the timepiece reads *Nu Elck Syn Sin*. Written in Old Dutch, the saying had been translated by the gift giver as, "To Each His Own."

Ace remains sequestered in his office, alone with his thoughts. Leaning back in his leather chair, his eyes linger on a family Christmas photo taken years earlier that sits on one corner of his desk. *Everyone smiling. Everyone healthy. Did I appreciate those times like I should have? If I could only turn back the clock—*

A double knock and Jennifer opens the door. "Can I come in?"

He motions to the sofa. She closes the door behind her and takes a seat. "You hiding out?"

"The kids' friends are over. I needed a reprieve."

"Understandable. Can I bring you some food?"

"Maybe later."

"I'm sorry about earlier. I'm here for you, if you need me. You know, with the kids."

"Thanks."

"What are you going to do? I mean, I know you and Kelli talked about it. I'm sure you made plans."

"We talked about it."

"And?"

"Things have changed." His eyes lock on hers, delivering the message.

"Ace, you're angry, and you have a right to be, but just let the police handle this."

"The police aren't handling anything. The FBI's in charge. Case closed."

"What's that supposed to mean?"

"Do I need to spell it out for you?" Ace gets up from his desk chair. Locks the door. "She was sanctioned, Jennifer. A few of her old pals in Washington, no doubt. Maybe some of the buzzards circling at the funeral."

"Is that why you went off? Ace, that's ridiculous. Why would they target Kelli?"

"You tell me?"

"This is crazy talk."

"Then I guess I'm crazy."

"No, but you're under a lot of stress. How about if I move in for a few weeks. I could help with the kids, let you get back to work—"

"I was fired."

"What?"

"They called this morning. Left the message on my machine. Apparently I ruffled the wrong feathers in D.C. Nice of them to wait until the day of the funeral, knowing I wouldn't be home."

"What will you do? Do you need money?"

"We're okay. Your cousin earned a good living. Paid for it in the end."

"That's enough! There is no conspiracy—"

A knock. The locked door handle jiggles. "Ace, you in there?"

Ace unlocks the door for Bruce Doyle. His father-in-law looks pale. "Son, I think you'd better come downstairs."

✦ ✦ ✦

The four vans are parked on his front lawn. The occupants, all wearing black jackets with the letters "FBI" in yellow glow-lettering, are already unloading equipment. The team leader waits impatiently at the front door.

"Mr. Futrell, my name is Special Agent Geordie McGillivray with the FBI. I have orders to search your premises."

"Orders from who?"

"The Department of Homeland Security."

"Homeland Security? Why? What's this all about?"

"I'm not at liberty to say."

"Then tell me what you're searching for."

"I'm not at liberty to say."

"Then you'd better show me a damn search warrant!"

"Homeland Security is not required to have a search warrant when dealing with acts intended to intimidate or coerce a civilian population."

Jen shakes her head. "Damn Patriot Act."

"You think my family is out to coerce a civilian population?"

"I'm sorry, sir, I'm not at liberty to say."

Ace feels his blood pressure boiling over. "You keep using the word 'liberty.' I wonder if you really know the definition."

Jennifer pushes her way into the conversation. "Is this in any way related to my cousin's death?"

"I'm sorry, ma'am, I can't answer any of your questions at this time. Now if you'd step back and allow us to search the premises." He nods to two armed FBI agents who barge their way in, each man carrying a heavy suitcase.

"Today was my wife's funeral. I have a houseful of guests."

"My condolences. However, please be aware that all guests currently on the premises will be subjected to a search. Cooperate and we'll try to make this as least invasive as possible."

"Cooperate? You invade my home, refuse to tell me why you're here or what you're searching for, and you want me to cooperate? Ever hear of the Constitution, pal? It wasn't written to be used as a doormat!"

Agent McGillivray touches the walkie-talkie mounted over his right shoulder. "Security, we have a situation. North entrance."

Before he can react, another agent barnstorms the door, taser in hand. He points the black stun gun at Ace and fires.

Zap!

The blue bolt of electricity instantaneously penetrates Ace's clothing and skin, jolting his central nervous system like a bucket of ice water. Purple lights flash across his vision, his body turning to electrified jelly as it hits the floor.

Special Agent McGillivray looks over the gathering circle of guests. "Anyone else have an objection? Good. Then in an orderly fashion I'd like you to line up against that far wall, arm's length apart. There's nothing to fear. This is a security matter that most likely doesn't concern you."

Sensation returns. Ace pulls himself up into a sitting position on the floor, his fingertips still singed with hot electrical impulses. Through watering eyes he sees his daughter racing down the staircase.

"Dad! Why are they doing this? Dad, are you okay?"

Ace nods, his voice box still unable to form words.

"Miss, I need you up against the wall with the others."

"Dad, they're taking everything! My laptop . . . all my CDs and DVDs! Why are they doing this?"

"Everything will be inspected and returned. Now line up with the others." The FBI agent grabs the thirteen-year-old girl by her arm.

"Get your paws off me!" Leigh twists free, retreating up the stairs.

The security man wheels, aiming his stun gun at the fleeing teenager.

No! A wave of adrenaline drives Ace off the floor. Wobbly hands grab for the weapon, twisting the barrel at its moment of discharge—the blue bolt striking Agent McGillivray, who drops to the floor in spasms.

An elbow clubs Ace in his face. The former quarterback shakes it off, slamming the FBI agent against the hallway mirror, their images shattering on contact.

And then everything goes black as Ace Futrell sinks into a midnight sea of velvet.

"Normal FAA procedures for responding to even minor deviations from air traffic control protocols were followed routinely and without complication sixty-seven times between September 2000 and June 2001 before a new convoluted order was released by the Pentagon on June 1, 2001. That order inserted the Secretary of Defense into a decision-making and action protocol, normally the domain of senior military commanders. Why? It took only minutes for [scrambled] fighters to get there after golfer Payne Stewart's plane had missed only one turn and failed to respond to radio transmissions for just a few minutes [October 25, 1999]. Why the enormous difference in responses between 1999 and 2001 when an obviously greater emergency existed and was widely recognized? Part of the explanation lies in a deliberately superimposed overlay of war game exercises being conducted by several governmental agencies on September 11th that inserted false blips into radar screens in the North East Air Defense Sector [NEADS], involved live-fly exercises with aircraft posing as hijacked airliners, and effectively confused and paralyzed all response by loyal interceptor pilots who would have seized the initiative that day, regardless of protocol, had they known where to go."

—MICHAEL C. RUPPERT,
from *Crossing the Rubicon: The Decline of the American Empire at the End of the Age of Oil*

Book Excerpt:
To the Brink of Hell:
An Apology to the Survivors
by Kelli Doyle
White House National Security Staff Advisor
(2002-2008)

Before I worked for the White House and long before my years with the CIA, I had to decide between majoring in history or international relations. I can still remember my first college professor trotting out the worn cliché, "History is written by the victors." Young and still impressionable, I believed it then.

I no longer believe it. In the war that is coming there will be no victors, only survivors.

It may be you to whom I write these memoirs. If you knew how it all began, then maybe you won't be so quick to repeat our mistakes. That I was there for many of these decisions allows me a unique perspective to shed light on what really happened.

It does not in any way exonerate me from the deeds.

Politics never interested me, but power . . . that was something different. To be counted among the elite, that was a goal I aspired to. Competition was in my blood. I was a two-sport athlete in college, our field hockey and lacrosse teams always ranked in the top twenty. For four glorious years my world consisted of practice, games, travel, more practice, class, parties, and maintaining my GPA so I'd be eligible to continue the ride.

Go Dawgs.

As my final year at the University of Georgia wound down, I developed a bad case of senioritis — a dreaded fear of graduating and having to enter the real world. What was I going to do?

Marriage was an option. My fiancé was a shooting star on the football team, but while I loved him dearly, he was going through his own trials and tribulations that only served to push our relationship onto the back burner. Law school was a possibility, but my ego, still fueled by competition, was demanding something out of the ordinary. When Career Day came, I moved from booth to booth, yet only one choice stood out among the rest, one I had never even considered: The CIA.

The Company was, and still is, the most powerful and secret organization in the world. Its budget remains hidden even from Congress, and few really understand the extent of its powers. It has its own mercenary army. It has its own corporations that influence wars and Wall Street. Enticed by my forthcoming degree in international relations (and three semesters of Arabic), the recruitment officer promised a training regimen that would challenge me physically, offering travel to exotic lands and an opportunity to serve my country.

That last part sealed the deal. I had competed in the Junior Olympics and world games and my soul was wrapped in the stars and stripes. Two weeks after graduating from the University of Georgia, I found myself in Washington, D.C., completing the exams necessary to receive my security clearance as a field officer. By fall, I had begun officer's training school. By the following spring, I was on "the Farm."

The Farm is Camp Peary, a military reservation located in York County, Virginia. The CIA and Special Ops use this heavily forested game preserve as a training facility. To free up the site's 9,275 acres, the Feds had to relocate two entire towns — Bigler's Mill and Magruder. The Farm has its own airport and is heavily secured, and with the exception of our after-hour get-togethers at Buck's strip bar and steak house, Camp Peary's activities are kept away from the public eye.

And for good reason. Among other things, the Farm is where the CIA trains its assassins. The program combines guns and wits with clandestine field training exercises, and for its female recruits a special treat — a jail cell interrogation that separates the GI-Janes from the Martha Stewarts. Being the former, I was able to "endure" and soon found myself fast-tracked for a battle looming in the Middle East.

The year was 1990.

The CIA does not make policy. Our job was to provide intelligence to the President of the United States and his policy makers, and once that policy is determined, our job was to execute it.

Yes, to the victors go history, but history and truth are two separate entities. I joined the CIA because I believed in what America stood for. I believed in the morality of truth. I could justify the coups on foreign governments and the tactics we used because, hey, we were the good guys, right? The end always justified the means . . . democracy's on the march. Let freedom reign.

It's hard to accept the truth. Lies don't shatter realities and dreams, only truth does that. And the truth was — the president lied.

All presidents lie. Roosevelt lied about Pearl Harbor. Lyndon Johnson lied about Vietnamese torpedo boats shooting at American ships in the Tonkin Gulf. Reagan lied about Iran-Contra. Clinton lied about his personal affairs in the Oval Office. I suppose even George Washington lied. (He probably never even owned a cherry tree.)

But it was the lies coming from the Bush-Cheney White House after the events of September 11, 2001, that led us to the invasion of Iraq and to a crossroads in Western civilization that will affect you and your loved ones and a billion more innocent people.

Did the U.S. intelligence community know Al-Qaeda's attack was coming?

Of course we knew. Bin Laden was on our radar since the first WTC bombing. Plus the FBI, CIA, and the White House received no less than a dozen warnings from foreign intelligence agencies that the United States would be attacked. German Intel specified the week of September 9. Russian President Vladimir Putin even dispatched a delegation to Washington, D.C., which included information that the World Trade Center would be struck by hijacked aircraft.

Not only were these warnings ignored, but no one would acknowledge having received them . . . even after Putin appeared on MS-NBC on September 15 detailing his warnings.

Wall Street investors certainly knew something big was going to happen. A day before the attacks, domestic and foreign investors placed an unprecedented number of "puts" (a leveraged bet a stock will drop) on the airlines and companies that would suffer devastating losses, in some cases over ninety times higher than normal trading. These financial transactions netted upward of $15 billion in insider trading that was halfheartedly investigated before they too were dismissed by investigators and the media, the latter manipulated by the Bush Administration, which were dictating which stories to run and which to kill.

Did we try to stop the attacks?

Yes, but we were prevented from doing so. FBI field agents in both Minneapolis and Phoenix who were close to exposing the plot were repeatedly and purposefully bottlenecked from taking action by a single supervisor — Dave Frasca — who would later receive a promotion for his actions. Then, on the day of the attacks, the joint chiefs, under Vice President Cheney's personal direction, scheduled and conducted five separate war game drills that purposely pulled interceptor jets away from the northeastern airspace corridor while deliberately inserting false blips on air traffic screens to simulate, of all things, hijacked airliners. Military jets that routinely intercept aircraft within minutes were delayed an unfathomable eighty minutes. Most never even entered the fray. While dedicated pilots and air traffic controllers desperately tried to determine what was real from what was staged, an FAA administrator "accidentally" destroyed the recordings of the day's tragic events . . . and he too was later promoted.

Those are facts . . . but only the tip of a dirty iceberg. Of course, none of that information was ever brought up in the 9/11 hearings.

While the public remained in fear, key members of Congress who opposed the administration's plans received packages of anthrax in the mail, the lethal spores later determined to have originated not overseas, but from labs used by the CIA.

One voice of opposition who refused to be intimidated — Senator Paul Wellstone — would conveniently die in a plane crash.

These "convenient coincidences" happened repeatedly throughout the events leading up to and following the activities of September 11th. Almost none were sufficiently investigated; almost all were cloaked in secrecy, stymied with retribution. Revealing passages in the 9/11 report were blacked out, and despite the biggest failure in intelligence history, no one has ever been reprimanded or punished.

Whether you prefer to believe in "coincidence theories" or "conspiracy theories," thousands of innocent American lives were sacrificed on September 11, 2001. But the real enemy was not Osama bin Laden and his Islamic radicals.

It was our addiction to oil.

Oil has gone from a cheap energy resource that spawned an industrial age, technological boom, and a population explosion, into a commodity that now determines foreign policy — and with it, the lives and deaths of millions of people. And yet it is a resource that is running out, the issue being one that has affected every president since Jimmy Carter.

So why don't we just replace oil?

Unfortunately, that's not so easy. Alternative energy resources have received lip service and scant investment, while trillions of our tax dollars continue to be invested in fossil fuels and military options that ensure our drills are in position to secure every last drop.

When it comes to oil and its suppliers, our foreign policy gets twisted like an Orwellian pretzel. In his first major speech after the events of September 11th, George Bush declared, "You are either with us or with the terrorists." That black and white stance turned multiple shades of gray after the Shi'ites gained power in Iraq and Hezbollah rose in Lebanon, threatening our chief oil suppliers — the Saudis (lest we forget, the hijackers' country of origin). In an effort to stymie the Shi'ites in both Iraq and Lebanon, the Bush Administration covertly began channeling billions of "rebuilding" dollars into Sunni resistance groups — otherwise known as Al-Qaeda.

That's right. Five years after they attacked the United States, the very terrorist organization we sought to eradicate was "hired" to quell a Shi'ite uprising unleashed by our own invasion of Iraq.

This memoir was not written to make a political statement or attack a political party. It was meant to expose the truth that surrounds our nation's addiction to oil . . . an addiction that funds our enemies, destroys our cities, and will soon lead to the annihilation of innocent millions.

"Men, in order to do evil, must first believe that what they are doing is good."

—ALEXANDER SOLZHENITSYN,
novelist and Nobel Prize winner

"The most honorable death is by killing. And the most honorable killing and the most glorious martyrdom is when a man is killed for the sake of Allah."

—HASSAN NASRALLAH,
Hezbollah Security General

"The White House deliberately pressured the EPA into giving false public assurances that the toxic air at Ground Zero was safe to breathe. This knowingly contributed to an as-yet unknown number of health cases and fatalities and demonstrates that the administration does consider the lives of American citizens to be expendable on behalf of certain interests."

—911TRUTH.ORG

"A child miseducated is a child lost."

—PRESIDENT JOHN F. KENNEDY

CHAPTER 9

Revolutionists Attack Saudi Air Base

Associated Press: December 16, 2011

RIYADH, Saudi Arabia—Rebels armed with explosives destroyed a squadron of F-15 fighter jets and two squadrons of Agusta Bell (AB) 205-S and 212-S attack helicopters housed at the Riyadh Airbase. Claiming responsibility for the attacks was *Ashraf*, a new revolutionary group that claims to represent the collective oppressed will of the Saudi people.

In a statement published by the underground newspaper, *Rai Al Nas,* one of the group's leaders said, "*Ashraf* opposes the hypocrisy of the Saudi monarchy whose Royals rob our citizens of our nation's God-given resources. *Ashraf* opposes the United States and other Western nations who keep the Royals in power because they seek to control Saudi resources. *Ashraf* also opposes radical Wahhabi clerics whose brutality has enforced the reign of terror unleashed by the Saudi monarchy. *Ashraf* is willing to negotiate the sale of the people's resources to Western nations once the seeds of democracy are sown in Arabia, but this can only be achieved by removing the Royals from their absolute power."

A Royal Saudi Air Force (RSAF) commander said that security would be beefed up at other military bases, and believed arrests were imminent.

Washington Dulles International Airport
Dulles, Virginia
December 16, 2011
8:25 pm EST

The refrigerated truck has been painted navy-blue with canary-yellow trim. Two-foot-high white-stenciled lettering identifies the purveyor as *Middle Eastern Delicacies*. There is an 800-number and assorted listing of food samples. The stolen license plate is from Maryland.

Omar Kamel Radi is the driver, Jamal al-Yussuf next to him in the passenger seat. Both men wear uniforms identifying them as employees. Each man wears a photo ID tag. Jamal grips a clipboard holding a work sheet detailing an extensive food order, called in by King Sultan's head chef. Despite the frigid air coming from the slightly opened windows, both men are sweating.

Omar stops at the airport security gate. He wipes a bead of perspiration from his heavy brow as he lowers the window for the guard. "Delivery. Hangar 12-D."

The guard shines his light inside the cab. "Shut off the engine and climb out. I'll need to inspect your load."

✦ ✦ ✦

An olive-skinned man dressed in an airport security guard's uniform watches the scene play out from his motorized cart parked sixty yards east of the gate. Shane Torrence, a veteran field operative of the Strategic Support Branch, lights a cigarette and then speaks into his walkie-talkie. "Food's here."

✦ ✦ ✦

Jamal al-Yussuf walks around to the back of the refrigerated truck, handing the guard the clipboard. Omar unlocks the back and yanks open the rolling doors. He extends and lowers the rear lift gate. A heavy scent of curry wafts out from the truck.

The tall Sunni climbs inside, followed by the guard.

There are two aluminum refrigerated storage lockers secured to the floor, each eight feet long, six feet wide and four feet deep, the huge cases on wheels. Omar pops the four sealed fasteners and raises the lid of the first, revealing enough food to feed thirty people. There are beef kebobs and chicken dishes, pastries filled with potatoes and meats, and an assortment of appetizers, sauces, and deserts, all wrapped in plastic sheeting.

The guard's mouth waters. "Looks good. Open the other one."

The Iraqi complies. Inside are two whole lambs, their bodies skinned and seasoned, wrapped in plastic sheeting.

"Gross. Close it up."

Omar re-seals the storage containers while the guard takes out his radio and calls for a security car. "It's Becker at twelve. I need you to escort a delivery truck to Hangar D."

The two deliverymen climb back inside the truck. The steel gate is retracted, allowing them entry onto the airport grounds. A white police car marked "airport security" leads them across the tarmac past rows of hangars until they reach building 12-D.

✦ ✦ ✦

SSB Agent Marco Fatiga watches the two vehicles approach the hangar that temporarily houses the Saudi 747. Like his associate, Shane Torrence, the Bronx native has been assigned to the two Iraqis as a "ghost."

A member of the Secret Service joins Marco outside the hangar. "Another delivery?"

Marco nods. "With these Arabs it's either food or women."

The truck is directed through the open hangar bay doors. A six-man Arab detail exits the 747. They off-load and wheel away the two storage lockers, while the Saudi head of security signs the work order and pays the tall driver.

"Wait here. Our kitchen staff will empty the containers

and bring them back out to you."

Twenty minutes later, the six Saudis wheel the emptied lockers out of the jumbo jet's cargo ramp. The two deliverymen join them as they load and secure the containers in the hold of the refrigerated truck.

No one bothers to search the empty lockers.

Marco Fatiga hovers close to Omar as he attempts to bolt the vehicle's rear doors. The former soccer goalie's hands are shaking, making it difficult.

The SSB officer steps in and secures it for him. "Better ease up on the caffeine, young man. You don't want to get into an accident."

The two men's eyes lock for a brief moment. The driver nods nervously and then climbs inside the truck. The airport security vehicle leads the purveyor off Dulles' grounds.

Forty minutes later, the truck pulls onto Interstate 66, heading west.

TIVERTON, ONTARIO
8:12 PM

The Steelback Canadian beer truck continues south along King Street through Tiverton, heading for Kincardine. The driver glances to his left at the Huron Wind Farm. Five massive 1.8-megawatt wind turbines dot the western landscape like giant white pinwheels. The former Air Force officer and CIA operative, now "freelancing" for members of the Strategic Support Branch, shakes his head. "Clean, free, and simple. Never had a Chinaman's chance."

◆ ◆ ◆

Michael "The Turk" Tursi was born in Hinton, West Virginia, an old railroad town nestled at the foot of the Appalachian Mountains where the Bluestone and Greenbrier rivers meet the New River. His mother, Mary, worked as an assistant principal and English teacher at the local middle school. His father, Patrick, was a police officer when he wasn't fulfilling his duties in the National Guard. For Michael, an only child, life was well regimented; homework and study the priorities, followed by church and little league sports. It was middle-class, apple-pie America, a lifestyle that suited Mike's parents but left their son wanting more.

Everything would change after the twelfth of June, 1977.

It was the last day of the school year. Mary Tursi was patrolling the halls, trying to bestow a fleeting sense of organization to the final moments of chaos when she came upon thirteen-year-old George Nathanial, a boy she had suspended a month earlier for bringing a hunting knife to school in a failed attempt to impress a would-be girlfriend. This time George had smuggled in something more lethal—a .25-caliber handgun he had taken from his grandfather's footlocker. George would later claim it was never his intention to shoot Mary Tursi, that he just wanted to show the weapon to his peers, but as they struggled for possession of the gun it discharged, fatally wounding the thirty-nine-year-old assistant principal.

When a teacher is killed, the aftershock ripples across the entire school district, creating a heightened sense of vulnerability that often takes years to subside. The effects on the victim's family, of course, are far more profound. To fifteen-year-old Michael, a young man raised to respect the law, the world suddenly made no sense. Bad things were not supposed to happen to good people . . . these were not the rules he had been taught to live by. For the next two years, Michael would spiral into a deepening state of depression, the onetime honor roll student failing his courses and quitting the baseball team, his father eventually resorting to having him home schooled just so he could attain his diploma. Psychiatrists were hired, drug therapies prescribed, but nothing seemed to help.

Desperate to return a sense of direction to his boy, Patrick persuaded his son to enlist in the United States Air Force. Three weeks later, eighteen-year-old Michael Tursi found himself on a bus, bound for Lackland Air Force Base in San Antonio, Texas.

Mike's first day began with his arrival on the base at one in the morning and ended twenty-three hours later the following night. Basic training is designed to separate the weak from the strong as recruits are torn down and then built back up. Physical activity is punishing, made worse by the mental duress. Enlisted men not cutting it can be sent home. Every so often a few opt to kill themselves rather than be shamed into quitting. During Tursi's eight weeks, his squadron experienced one attempted suicide and one that succeeded when a recruit took a nose-dive out a third-story window during morning formation.

Basic training teaches recruits the proper method to fight and kill. Mind games are mixed in with a physically demanding regime, adding additional stress. For Michael Tursi, training succeeded in restoring his competitive will to excel, and he quickly realized the Air Force could open doors—doors leading him away from the life of mediocrity he had always dreaded.

One day Tursi was ordered to an administration building where he was placed in a room with only a chair, desk, and a reel-to-reel tape player. A major informed him he was to listen to tapes, which included every language, and write down what he thought the speaker was communicating. It was a language aptitude test, and Tursi's scores were outstanding, warranting an assignment in Washington, D.C., as an interpreter.

He would opt instead for electronics.

After graduating basic training (bestowed with the nickname, the Turk) Michael was assigned to Sheppard Air Force Base in Wichita Falls, Texas, where he would spend the next fourteen months in training as an analyst technician for ballistic nuclear missiles.

✦ ✦ ✦

Tursi turns off the highway onto an access road leading into the Bruce Power Nuclear Plant. He stops the truck at the security checkpoint and waves to the approaching guard. "Paulie, how was the party?"

"I wouldn't know. Those events are strictly for the suits."

"Ah, who needs it, eh? Here, for you and the boys." Tursi reaches for the box of cigars on his passenger seat and hands it to the grateful guard. "Cubans, a gift from one of my regulars. I quit smoking years ago. Still, it's nice to be able to buy direct. Gotta love Canada."

"Unless you need a hysterectomy. My poor sister, she has to wait six weeks—"

"Yeah, that's too bad. Listen, I'm running late. Gotta pick up those empty kegs."

"Sure, sure. Go on through."

Tursi waves and enters the facility, heading for the loading dock.

❖ ❖ ❖

The Bruce Power Station, Canada's first privately owned nuclear plant, is composed of two generating plants, each holding four CANDU nuclear reactors. Short for CANada Deuterium Uranium, CANDU reactors use natural, unenriched uranium in their design, requiring deuterium oxide, or "heavy water" as both a coolant and moderator.

Uranium is a high-density metal believed to have formed during a super novae more than six billion years ago, when a star, ending its life cycle, collapsed in on itself and exploded, releasing radioactive decay and debris that eventually reached Earth. Uranium can be found in rocks and seawater and is the heat that occurs within the earth's crust.

The number of particles (neutrons) in the nucleus designate the different forms (isotopes) of uranium. When a uranium atom's nucleus splits apart, it releases a tremendous amount of energy. It also emits neutrons, which go on to split other nearby uranium nuclei, releasing more energy in what is called a fission chain reaction. Isotope U-235 (92 protons + 143 neutrons = 235) is used in nuclear fission because it yields an abundance of energy as heat when it splits. It is this heat that is used to make steam that drives a turbine in a nuclear reactor.

Of the two kinds of uranium found in nature, it is the rare U-235 isotope that is used in nuclear bombs. Natural uranium contains less than 1 percent U-235. In order to be usable in nuclear explosives, it must be enriched to 90 percent U-235 and only 10 percent U-238. The other fissile material used in nuclear weapons is Plutonium-239, a substance made by bombarding uranium-238 with neutrons in a nuclear reactor. Virtually non-existent in nature, plutonium is one of the most toxic substances known, inhaling merely a thousandth of a gram will cause massive fibrosis of the lungs. Ten pounds of U-235 or slightly less plutonium is all that is necessary to reach critical mass in a nuclear bomb.

For a CANDU reactor to operate with unenriched uranium requires the use of heavy water as a medium. Heavy water is water in which both hydrogen atoms have been replaced with deuterium. The production of a single pound of heavy water requires 340,000 pounds of feed water. Because heavy water can also be used to enrich U-235 into nuclear-grade uranium, production and distribution of heavy water is closely monitored.

The world's largest producer of heavy water? The Bruce Heavy Water Plant in Tiverton, Ontario.

◆ ◆ ◆

Tursi drives past the commissary and then rolls the big diesel until its left flank is lined up with the loading dock. Richard Weldon Small, the loading dock foreman, is waiting impatiently for him as he raises the vehicle's side gate. "There were . . . problems. My guy could only fill seventeen kegs."

"That wasn't our arrangement."

Despite the frigid temperatures, Small is sweating. "We did the best we could. There was less than an hour window."

Tursi looks over the twenty beer kegs hastily arranged on

five pallets. He walks to the fourth pallet and randomly selects a barrel. "Open it."

"We don't have time. My supervisor—"

Tursi unhooks a ratchet-like device from his belt loop and uses it to twist-open the keg. From his ski jacket pocket he takes out a ten-inch chemical analyzer and dips the metal end into the barrel's clear liquid content. Checks the meter: Deuterium.

"We've known each other six years. You don't trust me?"

"I don't trust anyone who's in a position to screw me." Tursi removes a thick envelope from his pants pocket. "Twenty thousand. Make sure your guy on the inside gets his, or you'll be looking over your shoulder the rest of your days."

Small leafs through the wad of bills. Then the two men roll the barrels onto the truck, securing them among the other ten kegs of beer.

Six hours and two rest stops later, Michael Tursi guides the beer truck across the Ambassador Bridge into Detroit.

"Those who would give up essential liberty to purchase a little temporary safety deserve neither liberty nor safety."

—BENJAMIN FRANKLIN

"FBI Director Mueller personally awards Marion (Spike) Bowman with a presidential citation and cash bonus of approximately 25 percent of his salary. Bowman, head of the FBI's National Security Law Unit, is the person who refused to seek a special warrant for a search of Zacarias Moussaoui's belongings before the 9/11 attacks. The award comes shortly after a 9/11 Congressional Inquiry report saying Bowman's unit gave Minneapolis FBI agents 'inexcusably confused and inaccurate information' that was 'patently false.'"

—DOUG GROW,
from "FBI Performs A Nasty
Little Sequel To Whistle-Blower Saga,"
The Minneapolis Star Tribune,
December 22, 2002

"A nation that is afraid to let its people judge the truth and falsehood in an open market is a nation that is afraid of its people."

—PRESIDENT JOHN F. KENNEDY

CHAPTER 10

Long Island, New York
December 17, 2011
7:12 am EST

Ace sits up slowly, immediately aware of the dull ache in his head. His stomach is empty and still a bit jumpy from having thrown up in the police car. The heat from the repeated jolts of electricity is a waning memory, but it has left a bad metallic taste in his mouth.

There are two other men in the holding cell. A heavy-set man in his fifties is lying on a bench, using his wrinkled sports coat as a pillow. The college student is on the floor, passed out cold.

Ace perks up at the sound of approaching footsteps. Using the iron bars, he drags himself off the floor just as the guard opens his cell door. Accompanying the police officer is a lanky fellow in his mid-forties, his tight, curly gray-brown hair matching his business suit.

Jeffrey Gordon, senior partner at Cubit, Gordon, & Furman, Attorneys at Law, greets his boyhood friend with a worried look and a quick embrace. "Bail's been arranged. Let's get you home."

"What about—"

Jeff shakes his head. "Not here."

✦ ✦ ✦

Ten minutes later they are in Jeffrey's car, inching their way through rush-hour traffic.

"But how can they just enter my home without a search warrant?"

"Patriot Act, section 213: Any federal law enforcement agency can enter your home or business, whether you are there or not, or whether they tell you about it or not, and use any confiscated evidence to convict you of a crime. It's all legal."

"It's fascism, that's what it is. What the hell happened to the Fourth Amendment?"

"It got bulldozed back in 2001. Section 202 states the Feds can read your e-mail, section 216 allows them to intercept your cell phone calls."

"Damn! How the hell could Congress pass—"

"Cheney and Ashcroft rammed it through before Congress even read it. The bill hadn't even been printed when the vote was called. The bottom line is the Feds can basically do anything they want, as long as they claim the suspect is part of an ongoing terrorism investigation."

"Terrorism? Jeff—"

"I know, I know. What about Kelli? Was she working on anything that would give the powers-that-be a scare?"

Ace thinks back to the night his wife was killed. "I don't know," he lies. "When it came to her job, Kelli never told me much. Jeff, how much trouble am I in here?"

"The FBI dropped the assault charge after I threatened to go to the papers with the whole funeral thing. But you have to be very careful. I've represented other clients targeted by the Feds, and paranoid is probably not a bad thing to be right now. Assume you're being watched 24/7, your phone lines tapped, your e-mail intercepted. In fact, just stay off the Internet until this thing blows over. And no financial transactions that look even remotely out of the ordinary. They'll have access to your credit cards, your bank accounts—everything. Hopefully this is just some leftover appointment from the Bush Administration being paranoid about crossing Kelli years ago. You certainly ruffled a few feathers at the funeral."

"Bunch of scumbags."

"Scumbags with power." Jeffrey turns onto the expressway and then looks at his friend. "I heard you lost your job."

"Yeah. Ruffled a few feathers there too."

"Do you need a loan?"

"Thanks, no, we're . . . I'm okay. It's just piling up a bit right now. To be honest, I'm more worried about the kids."

"Gay and I are coming by later. We'll bring Jesse and Rayna. Meanwhile, let me do some poking around and see what I can find out."

THE WHITE HOUSE
WASHINGTON, D.C.
DECEMBER 17, 2001
2:20 PM EST

Barack Obama, the forty-fourth president of the United States, sits impassively behind the thirteen-hundred-pound wooden desk constructed from timbers salvaged long ago from the British vessel, *HMS Resolute*. Obama is alone in the Oval Office, gazing absentmindedly out the glass doors that lead to the Rose Garden patio. The fourth heavy snowstorm this winter is set to hit the Northeast later this afternoon, and already two inches have fallen. The garden is blanketed in white beneath heavy gray skies, the forecast calling for ten more inches with temperatures dropping into the low teens.

People will die . . . happens every storm. Traffic accidents steal a few, a dozen elderly who can't afford to pay their electric bill will freeze to death.

Obama is two hours removed from his meeting with King Sultan bin Abdel Aziz, and he can still smell the man's overpowering aftershave on his lapels. But there is something else lingering in the Oval Office air. *What happens when the lights go out permanently? When the heat is gone? When the stoves don't work and there's no food to be had in all of D.C.? How long will it take before the people march on Washington?*

Barack Obama entered office with a mandate from the American people for change. Awaiting his administration was a mountain of challenges bigger than any world leader had ever faced: Trillion dollar deficits, collapsing banks, financial markets in ruin, the American auto industry threatening to go under, major corporations declaring bankruptcy, the housing market bottoming out, unemployment rising, two costly wars . . . and the threat of a nuclear-armed Iran and North Korea. Toss in the threat of a swine flu pandemic, and it was no wonder the President's hair was already graying. Repairing the damage was the equivalent of putting together a three-dimensional puzzle, the placement of each piece affecting the integrity of the entire structure. It meant campaign promises occasionally had to be sacrificed like pawns on a chessboard, a battle strategically lost to ensure a bigger victory down the road—the perceived hypocrisy destined to rile a group of constituents who were focused on their own set of priorities.

And sometimes there was a bigger sacrifice that had to be made, sometimes the truth had to be buried or altered in order to prevent an avalanche. Like the submerged mass of an iceberg, truth was the unseen threat that could sink the ship.

The truth about 9/11.

The truth about the world's diminishing oil reserves.

Proxy battles were being waged throughout the world, each one testing and evaluating the new administration's intent—while domestic rivals continued to press their attack against the President's policies for no other reason other than to position their party in the event he failed. Meanwhile, former President Bush and his trainer, Vice President Cheney, continued lobbing grenades from the sidelines in an attempt to rewrite recent history . . . and to diffuse illegalities surrounding their own legacy.

Despite Obama's efforts, problems across the globe are mounting, led by the hot spot in the Middle East. In Iraq, a hornet's nest of sectarian violence between Sunni and Shi'ite, spurred by Iranian mullahs and Islamic radicals, continues to be a thorn in the side of a budding democracy, preventing the President from significantly reducing the number of troops in the region. Having quelled its own democratic uprising, Iran and its desire to develop nuclear weapons (backed by subterfuge coming out of Russia and China) remains a serious threat to Iraq, Saudi Arabia, Syria, and Israel.

The situation eats at the President's ulcer every day. The on-going war in Iraq has dictated changes in U.S. Middle East policy, which now backs "moderate" dictatorial regimes in Egypt, Jordan, and Saudi Arabia, which are using their fundamentalist Salafis to spread the Sunni-Shi'ite conflict into Lebanon in an attempt to destabilize Syria. Meanwhile, brokering a peace agreement between Israelis and Palestinians that would lead to a Palestinian nation threatens to be derailed by a hawkish Israeli prime minister who makes a show of being dragged to the negotiation table, Hamas and Hezbollah's refusal to accept Israel's right to exist, and Iran's leaders, who continue to supply conventional weapons to both radical factions whose actions only hold their own people hostage.

The wildcard in this equation remains Saudi Arabia and its Royal dictators, who continue to play both sides against the middle in an effort to quell unrest both outside and inside their borders. While a nuclear Iran openly threatens the kingdom's borders, the House of Saud is rotting from within, its decay traced to decades of greed and abominable human rights abuses. Promises of open elections have dwindled into heavy-handed exploits generated more for public show than democratic change. The Saudi people, once determined to participate in the running of their own country, have festered in servitude, all hope of breaking the Saud family's monopoly on power dashed—at least as long as the Royals are backed by industrialized nations importing oil. The gap between the Saudi masters and the impoverished masses widens with each passing day, and within this vacuum of discontent Islamic Fundamentalism grows, fueled by the Iranian-led slaughter of Iraq's Sunni populace.

Having refused to "squander" its nation's profits on basic services necessary to build a modern economy, the House of Saud has chosen instead to subdue the will of its people. To deal with the Islamic threat, the Royals have resorted to bribing Muslim leaders, who in turn, have been utilizing these newfound financial resources to attack the West.

Meanwhile, there is a growing movement among Republicans in Congress to quash the Islamic extremists, with Neoconservatives like Dick Cheney, Karl Rove, and Fox News pundits beating the drums for an outright invasion of Iran. Military options have been secretly drawn up and discussed, but the President refuses to be pushed into another costly engagement—one he knows is fueled by the PNAC group's desire to control the Middle East and its diminishing oil supply.

In piecing together his three-dimensional puzzle, the President must defuse the situation in the Middle East by simultaneously withdrawing America's military presence in Iraq while guiding the United States to a fossil-free future that will drive a new green economy.

The question is how to get the dinosaurs in the financial sector to quietly go extinct.

The President smiles to himself. *Dinosaurs and oil . . . an appropriate metaphor. It'll probably take nothing less than another asteroid strike to allow society to move on.*

His thoughts are interrupted by his secretary's voice over the intercom. "Mr. President, it's 2:30."

"Thank you, Sophia." Straightening his tie, the former senator exits through his secretary's office and enters the Cabinet room.

Already seated at the conference table are his Chief of Staff, the directors of the CIA and Homeland Security, the Secretary of State, the Secretaries of Energy and Defense, and the Vice President. All rise as he enters to take his place at the open middle seat, his back to the bulletproof windows.

"Good afternoon. Hope everyone's keeping warm. As you know, King Sultan and I spent several hours together this morning discussing the situation in the Persian Gulf. The King assured me the recent unrest in Riyadh was an isolated incident and that tensions have dissipated. Unfortunately for the King, he's not a very good liar."

The Vice President forces a smile. "Mr. President, what was Sultan's reply to our offer?"

"The Saudis have agreed to increase oil production by one million barrels per day, beginning March first."

Applause and smiles around the table.

The President nods. "It'll be a nice boost for the economy and no doubt our poll numbers, but as usual, it comes with a price. On the one hand, Sultan claims civil unrest is of no great concern. On the other, he wants to utilize our resources to contain this new rebel movement, the Ashraf. The King claims Al-Qaeda is behind the group and wants the NSA's help in identifying and hunting down its leaders."

CIA Director David Schall smirks. "If Sultan's so worried about Al-Qaeda, why does he continue to allow its funds to pass through his banking system? As for Ashraf, we covered the group's activities in a daily briefing about six weeks ago. It's not a radical Islamic movement. In fact, it's a civilian-based democratic movement coming out of Jiddah, one gaining popularity among the foreign workers that run the Saudi oil fields. So far they've focused their attacks solely on Saudi Aramco sites."

"Which makes them a threat to our interests," states Howard Lowe, the Homeland Security Director.

"No argument," Schall responds. "However, this is not Al-Qaeda nor is it part of a Bedouin influence. We're dealing with a group that traces its descendants directly back to Muhammad. These are modern thinkers who oppose Wahhabi traditionalism as much as they do the Saudi monarchy. The movement receives financial support from Prince Alwaleed bin Talal, who's been openly critical of the House of Saud and Saudi Aramco for years. The Prince tends to be pro-American, though he's alienated himself in the past by speaking out for the Palestinians. Bachelor's degree from Menlo College. Completed his master's at Syracuse. In the past he's stayed clear of Saudi politics, focusing his energies on building a large international business called the Kingdom Holding Company. They're heavily invested in Apple, AOL, and Motorola and hold large stakes in a dozen major hotels. Forbes recently listed bin Talal as the fourth richest man in the world . . . behind King Sultan, of course. It was his donation following 9/11 that Giuliani turned down, but he's consistently contributed to many American institutions. If he's a radical, it's only in the context of opposing the House of Saud."

"Bin Talal's also invested heavily in entertainment conglomerates, including Rupert Murdoch's News Corp.," Director Lowe retorts. "That gives him a venue to spew whatever message he chooses across the globe."

"And what message is that? Human rights?" The President looks around the room. "Sounds to me like this Ashraf movement is one we should find ways to support."

"With all due respect, Mr. President," his Vice President counters, "that's incredibly risky. Iran's already favoring oil exports to China. If King Sultan learned we were supporting his enemies—"

"Sultan's supporting *our* enemies," Benjamin Simon retorts. The Filipino-American Chief of Staff looks across the table at Joe Biden. "You read last week's PDB. The majority of Al-Qaeda's funding, as well as other radical Islamic regimes, comes from corporations controlled directly by the House of Saud, or accounts originating from their central bank."

"Yes, as a counterweight to policies favoring the United States. The Saudis fear retribution. But if Sultan's inviting us in to take out this Ashraf movement, maybe we can use the opportunity to position nuclear warheads on our Saudi bases . . . counter the Iranian threat. Wouldn't you agree, Secretary Kendle?"

"I would." Joseph Kendle, Obama's Secretary of Defense runs a thick palm across his short-cropped reddish-brown hair. "We can't just sit on our hands while the Iranians aim their nuclear missiles at our military bases. If taking out a few Ashraf leaders allows us to accomplish that, I say do it."

"No." The President registers the acid reflux broiling in his gut. "Placing ballistic missiles in Saudi Arabia is extremely dangerous. The Muslims will perceive it as a prelude to Jihad. As for helping Sultan wipe out his enemies, here we finally have a group that might lead to a sea change in morality in Saudi Arabia . . . and our first response is to stamp them out? What are we promoting here, people? If the oil's really there, then someone's bound to sell it to us. Why not let it be a group that might finally institute some reform? Isn't that what Iraq was supposed to be about?"

After a moment, Patricia Moreau, the Secretary of Energy, speaks out. "It's certainly worth considering, Mr. President. At the same time, revolution means change, and change takes time. The Ashraf inhabit Saudi Arabia's west coast, but it's the Bedouin who control the east, and that's where the big oil fields lie. With the world economy still in recovery, the European Union's dramatic shift to the right, and instability in Iraq and Iran, not to mention Venezuela and Nigeria, can we really afford uncertainty in the Saudi kingdom at this juncture? The House of Saud has been in power a long time, and they're backed by the Bedouin. I doubt the Ashraf will ever control the Red Sea cities, let alone the entire country. And if there really is a revolution, that door swings both ways. Anarchy presents the Iranians with an opportunity to gain a stronger foothold in the region. Toppling the Royals now could lead to an Islamic onslaught."

"Bin Talal is a Royal, Secretary Moreau."

"Yes, sir. One voice among thousands. Maybe there are other princes willing to join him under the right circumstances, but it's unlikely. Let's face it, these Royals are pampered billionaires who have been known to kill their own. Bin Talal may support a revolution from a distance, but we've seen no indication he's interested in fighting for the crown."

A few nods of agreement.

The President is not ready to back down quite yet. "Tell me, what should the United States do if the streets of Saudi Arabia erupt in demonstrations shouting for democracy, as they did in Tehran back in 2009? We missed an opportunity back then. What should our response be if the Ashraf take Mecca and Medina? Muslim hatred toward the House of Saud rivals their hatred for the West. The climate in Saudi Arabia is percolating. How much longer can we afford to prop up the Royals?"

"With all due respect, Mr. President," the Vice President responds, "the House of Saud won't fall, not with our undivided support."

"Nixon and Carter said the same thing about the Shah of Iran." The President checks his watch. "I've got a call with the Prime Minister. We'll table this for now."

The cabinet members stand to leave. As the chamber empties, the President grabs his CIA director. "David, can I see you for a quick moment?"

"Yes, sir."

Alone with the President, Schall closes the door. "An interesting meeting, Mr. President. You toss bait quite well. Something's clearly going on."

"Plans within plans. Sultan was prepped."

"What do you need from me?"

"Pat Moreau's right. The last thing we need right now is Saudi Arabia caught in a power vacuum, but the extent of that threat is weighted by how much oil is really left in usable reserves. What I need is information . . . hard data, not the stuff coming from the D.O.E."

"Agreed. Ghawar and the undeveloped Empty Quarter hold the key."

"How do we find out what's down there? Who would know?"

"No one we can get to. However . . . I do know of someone who could help."

"Who is he?"

"I met him several years ago at a cocktail party. His wife introduced us. Name's Ace Futrell. Works for PetroConsultants, or at least he did until he went off the deep end at the Energy Hearings."

"Have your people reach out to him."

"Sir, it's . . . complicated. His wife was Kelli Doyle."

"Damn . . ."

"To make matters worse, Homeland Security opened a file on Futrell hours after Doyle was killed. If I back them off—"

"It'll send up warning flags to our Neocon friends."

"Yes, sir."

The President mulls it over. "Handle it. Personally."

"When you're drowning, you don't say, 'I would be incredibly pleased if someone would have the foresight to notice me drowning and come and help me,' you just scream."

—JOHN LENNON

"It is clear the U.S. authorities did little or nothing to preempt the events of 9/11. It is known that at least 11 countries provided advance warning to the U.S. of the 9/11 attacks. Two senior Mossad experts were sent to Washington in August 2001 to alert the CIA and FBI. . . . The list they provided included the names of four of the 9/11 hijackers, none of whom was arrested."

—MICHAEL MEACHER, MP,
UK Environmental Minister (1997–2003)
from "The War on Terrorism is Bogus,"
The Guardian,
September 6, 2003

"The men identified as the 9/11 ringleaders were under surveillance for years beforehand, on the suspicion they were terrorists, by a variety of U.S. and allied authorities—including the CIA, the U.S. military's 'Able Danger' program, the German authorities, Israeli intelligence, and others. Two of the alleged ringleaders who were known to be under surveillance by the CIA also lived with an FBI asset in San Diego, but this is supposed to be yet another coincidence.

—911TRUTH.ORG

CHAPTER 11

GARY LEE SCHAFER, DIRECTOR
RADICAL FUNDAMENTALIST UNIT
COUNTERTERRORISM AND MIDDLE EAST SECTION
FBI–HQ
DECEMBER 29, 2011

Director Schafer:

This e-mail will serve as a follow-up to communications originating from FBI-Chicago between 12/14 and 12/27/11. FBI-Chicago has confirmed suspect Jamal al-Yussuf has received deposits from a Cayman Island account totaling $112,210. Suspect Omar Kamel Radi has received deposits totaling $117,540. Over the last three weeks both suspects have purged their bank accounts of all monies. Neither suspect has been seen since.

We have received confirmation from the Strategic Support Branch (SSB) in Iran that indicates both suspects may have been recruited into Iran's Qods Force (Islamic Revolutionary Guard) sometime between December 2007 and April 2008. Photo surveillance confirms suspect Jamal al-Yussuf at Imam Ali Training base, located north of Tehran (Alborz Kouh Street) between April 2007 and December 2009. An SSB informant places suspect Omar Kamel Radi at Bahonar

Training Base near Karaj Dam in Tehran (Chalous Highway) between June 2007 and December 2009.

Immigration confirms suspect Jamal al-Yussuf arrived in the United States (New York) in February 2011. Suspect Omar Kamel Radi followed two months later (April 2011). Both suspects met up in late September in Aurora.

With this new information we are requesting:

• Electronic surveillance to relocate suspects.

• FBI monitoring of suspects' activities.

• NSA surveillance of suspects' cell phone activities.

Respectfully,

Adrian Paul Neary, Director
FBI–Chicago

Director Schafer rereads the e-mail transmission a third time, his pulse racing.

✦ ✦ ✦

Originally trained as a computer systems engineer, Gary Lee Schafer was recruited straight out of college by the Federal Bureau of Investigation to work in the National Security Division at FBI Headquarters. After completing his training at Quantico, Virginia, he reported to New York City to focus on criminal and intelligence investigations where he designed programs aimed at countering domestic terrorism and preventing the use of weapons of mass destruction against the nation's population and critical infrastructure.

What looked like a promising career would be sidetracked in 1993.

On February 26, a 1,200-pound bomb detonated in the parking garage beneath the World Trade Center. The explosion killed six people and injured over a thousand. Had the van transporting the bomb been parked a few feet closer to a main support pillar, the entire tower might have collapsed.

The FBI wasted little time in apprehending a suspect, Mohammad Salameh, who had foolishly been trying to collect a $400 deposit for the rented van. More plotters were quickly captured in what appeared to be a high-water mark for the FBI.

In reality, the FBI had failed to follow clues from an earlier case that could have prevented the attack. And it was their young rookie agent, Gary Schafer, who would blow the whistle.

Back on November 5, 1990, Meir Kahane, founder of the radical Jewish Defense League, was giving an anti-Arab speech at a New York hotel when El Sayyid Nosair, a thirty-six-year-old Egyptian immigrant, fatally shot the rabbi in the neck. Nosair was part of a cabal of Muslims who despised both Israel and Egyptian leader Hosni Mubarak. When Nosair's residence was searched, the police discovered paramilitary manuals, maps, and diagrams of buildings, including the World Trade Center.

Agent Schafer believed the evidence indicated a Muslim terrorist cell had planned Kahane's assassination, and more attacks were on the horizon. Unfortunately, Schafer's supervisors were loath to expand their investigation, looking instead for a quick conviction.

As Nosair's trial began, rioting took place outside the courthouse, with death threats made against the judge and lawyers. In an attempt to learn more about the Muslims, the FBI hired an informant, Emad Salem, a forty-three-year-old former Egyptian military officer, to assimilate himself within the group. Salem eventually became the bodyguard for Sheik Abdul Rahman, a radical Muslim cleric. The CIA, while in Pakistan to recruit Muslims to fight the Soviets in Afghanistan, had heavily subsidized Rahman in the late 1980s.

Incredibly, the jury found Nosair not guilty on the murder charge but guilty of possessing a firearm (the murder weapon that killed Kahane). Meanwhile, Salem continued his work as an FBI informant, sending information directly to Agent Schafer, for which he was paid $500 a week.

During the summer of 1992, Salem warned that the Muslim group was planning a major bombing in New York City. Agent Schafer reported Salem's information, but his FBI supervisors were convinced the informant was lying to save his job and decided to terminate his deal.

Six months later the World Trade Center was bombed.

After the attack, the FBI rehired Salem and promised him a million dollars to develop evidence of additional terrorist plots. Instead, Salem secretly recorded his conversations with FBI agents, which pointed the finger squarely back at Agent Schafer's bosses for failing to heed his earlier warnings. Many accused Schafer of instigating the tapings.

The FBI was doubly embarrassed when it was learned the contents taken from Nosair's apartment years earlier contained major clues that would have exposed the bombing plot.

Despite the fact that Muslim terrorists came close to killing thousands of Americans, there would be no Congressional investigation of the FBI's failings. Director Louis Freeh was praised, with several agents receiving commendations.

Agent Schafer, however, would suffer the fate shared by many whistle blowers, his promising career screeching to a halt.

Over the next sixteen years Gary Schafer had repeatedly been passed over for promotion, forced to sit back and watch while far less-accomplished agents had risen up the FBI ladder. Then, six months ago, Schafer ran into Jeff Anders, his old roommate at Quantico. Anders invited him on a diving trip to the Caymans, and soon the two were talking shop.

Like Shane Torrence and Marco Fatigo, the Strategic

Support Branch had recruited Anders after serving three tours of duty in the Middle East. Anders told Schafer he had helped the SSB establish an intelligence network in Iran. A domestic surveillance operation was under way, one that required a trusted pair of eyes at FBI-HQ. If Schafer was interested, arrangements could be made.

Anders set up a meeting between Schafer and Graeme Turnbull, a retired Colonel who had served in Iraq. Two months later, the director of the FBI's Radical Fundamentalist Unit unexpectedly decided to retire, and Gary Lee Schafer was offered the position, along with a substantial raise in pay.

✦ ✦ ✦

Steadying his nerves, Schafer answers the e-mail.

Director Neary:
CIA and U.S. Military Intelligence now estimates Iranian Qods Force recruits more than 30,000 foreign nationals per year, including non-mercenaries from Saudi Arabia, Bahrain, Afghanistan, Jordan, Iraq, and many European countries. At this juncture, the information your department has submitted to FBI-HQ does not justify the costly surveillance arrangements requested.

Continued monitoring of the suspect's bank transactions and use of identification should reestablish the subjects' new locations. Report progress immediately and directly to me.

G.L. Schafer, Director

Schafer rereads his reply several times, then clicks SEND. Shutting off his computer, he exits his office, informs his assistant he is grabbing a quick bite to eat, and then catches an elevator down to the lobby floor.

A fifteen-minute drive brings him to the library phone booth. He dials the memorized number, allows it to ring three times, hangs up, and then waits sixty seconds before calling back again.

"Speak."

"Chicago's on track."

"Understood."

The line goes dead.

"The September 11th families who fought for and gained an independent investigation (the 9/11 Commission) posed 400-plus questions, which the 9/11 Commission adopted as its roadmap. The vast majority of these questions were completely ignored in the Commission hearings and the final report. The membership and staff of the 9/11 Commission displayed awesome conflicts of interest. The families called for the resignation of Executive Director Philip Zelikow, a Bush Administration member and close associate of 'star witness' Condoleezza Rice, and were snubbed. Commission member Max Cleland resigned, condemning the entire exercise as a 'scam' and 'whitewash.' *The 9/11 Commission Report* is notable mainly for its obvious omissions, distortions, and outright falsehoods—ignoring anything incompatible with the official story, banishing the issues to footnotes, and even dismissing the still-unresolved question of who financed 9/11 as being "of little practical significance."

—911Truth.org

"We shouldn't be making deals. If somebody wants to deal, we issue subpoenas. That's the deal!"

—Max Cleland,
Georgia Senator and member of the 9/11 Kean Commission,
referring to a deal that was cut with the Bush White
House to allow a handpicked subset of commissioners
to be briefed on the Presidential Daily Briefings.
(Cleland later resigned from the Commission.)

CHAPTER 12

Montauk, New York
January 3, 2012
2:25 pm EST

A white fog hangs over Montauk Beach, the result of an unseasonable warm front meeting cold ocean. Ace, barefoot, dressed in shorts and a heavy mesh Georgia Bulldogs football practice jersey, tosses a football with his son, Sam. The eight-year-old, dressed in similar attire, insists on running deep post patterns. Each throw causes the former quarterback's surgically repaired left knee to throb. He ignores the pain, enjoying the game of catch.

After twenty minutes the boy tires out and heads back to the house to play video games.

Ace rejoins his daughter, Leigh, who has been watching from a sand dune, taking photos with her digital camera. "Get any good ones?"

"Not really, the light's terrible." She points to his left knee, the joint bearing two six-inch scars. "Does it hurt?"

"Nah."

"You were grimacing."

"Just stiff. It's fine."

"I bet it hurt when you tore it."

"Hell, yeah. This big three hundred-pound defensive tackle blind-sided me and my cleat got caught in the turf. Knee bent backward, they said they could hear it pop in the cheap seats."

"Ever wish you could go back in time, you know . . . to play again?"

"Not really."

"Come on, Dad. To relive your college days, big man on campus."

"That wasn't me."

"Mom told me stories. She said you were really good, and that you would have been drafted if you hadn't gotten hurt."

"She exaggerates. I was just a flash in the pan."

"What's that mean?"

"It means I peaked and fell." He looks at Leigh's expression; she's unsatisfied. "When I played in high school I was a backup, so when I went to Georgia. I knew I really had no chance of making the team, let alone starting. But I continued working out on my own, and in the next two years, I sort of grew into my body. Went from a 185-pound freshman to 220 pounds right before my junior year. I was in great shape. My arm strength really increased, and it caught the coaches' eyes during spring tryouts.

"Anyway, the first game comes along, and I'm listed as the third quarterback on the depth charts. Not too shabby for a big-time program. First quarter, first game and *bam* . . . our all-American quarterback goes down. Third quarter we lose our back up. I see the coach looking around, and suddenly I'm in the game. The noise is so loud, everything happening so fast, and we're down. Our receivers couldn't get open, so finally I took off running. I ran so fast I nearly ran out of my cleats . . . probably was scared out of my mind. But things started happening after that play, and I tossed a few nice passes for touchdowns. We ended up coming from behind, and all of a sudden I'm the next Kurt Warner."

"Who's Kurt Warner?"

"He played for the St. Louis Rams. Went from a grocery store employee to the starting QB for the Super Bowl champs."

"Wow, dad, so they could make a movie about you, huh?"

"Sorry, kiddo. Movies have happy endings. My career had . . . issues."

Leigh points to the narrow white scars that cut lengthwise along the inside of her father's wrists. "Those issues?"

Ace forces a smile. "Yeah."

"How come?"

He looks out to the Atlantic, its dark surface still blanketed in fog. He has never spoken to his daughter about his suicide attempt, never felt it was the right time.

"It's hard to explain. It was a confusing time . . . everything happening so fast. You have to understand, I really wasn't that good . . . no, that's not true. I was good, I just lacked experience. When my coach put me in, no one expected much, but when we kept winning, the pressure kept building, and all of a sudden we're playing in the Orange Bowl, possibly for the National Championship. That's big time. College football in the south . . . it gets crazy. It's not a pastime with these fans, it's religion. I couldn't walk through campus without being mobbed. I couldn't study, I couldn't eat, I couldn't think. I had students and fans and reporters and boosters hounding me day and night, everyone wanting a piece of me, offering gifts, money, women . . . like I said, it was crazy. By the time the Orange Bowl came around, I was a bundle of nerves, my hands were shaking so hard with adrenaline I could barely grip the ball. I fumbled the snap on the first play. Threw an interception on my second pass. The coach hung in there with me until halftime and then benched me. By that time the game was over."

Ace rubs at the scars on his right wrist. "Scholarship athletes tend to look down on us walk-ons, and I had replaced two popular teammates. It took all season to earn my teammates' respect, and I lost it in the first half of that game. The next few months were bad. I'd get threatening phone calls in the middle of the night, a few death threats . . . once someone even shot nails into my tires. Anyway, spring training comes along, and I'm still running with the starters. During our first scrimmage—non-contact for quarterbacks—my own defensive tackle pancaked me."

"That's how you hurt your knee?"

"Yeah. Guess the seniors were sending a message."

"That's terrible."

"Coach cut the guy, and the trainers helped me rehab, but it really screwed with my head. That spring I started having panic attacks. I'd lie down to go to sleep, and suddenly I couldn't breathe. The team doctor prescribed sleeping pills. Then the attacks started happening during the day."

"Where was mom during all this?"

"Busy with lacrosse. Whenever I mentioned the panic attacks, she'd just slap me upside the head and tell me to cheer up. You know your mom. We were young, immortal. The things I had to work so hard on . . . they came natural to her. Big-time athletes didn't have anxiety. She just couldn't relate."

"So what happened? Did you play football your senior year?"

"I tried, but the panic attacks kept getting worse. It was like . . . like being trapped in your own skin. I guess it was fear. The fear of failing. The fear of letting everyone down again. I handled it wrong, I know that now. I should have talked to someone . . . gotten on an anti-depressant. One night I just couldn't handle it anymore, so I decided to open a few veins and take a long hot bath."

Tears well up in Leigh's eyes. "Who found you?"

"Tet. Mark Tetreault. He was our tight end, my best friend. He saved my life."

"Tet? Is he the one who died on 9/11?"

"Yeah. He worked on one of the upper floors for a securities company. They lost a lot of people. The heat from the jet fuel . . . they say it was so hot, the flesh was probably melting. People were jumping from windows, but not Tet . . . he hung in there, no doubt trying to guide his coworkers to safety, only there was nowhere for them to go." Ace clears the emotion from his voice.

"Dad . . ."

"It was a long time ago, Leigh. You don't have to worry."

She snuggles closer. He puts his arm around her, squeezing her tight. For several minutes they listen to the sounds of the pounding surf.

Ace turns to his right. He tenses as he spots the man standing by the water thirty yards down the beach. "Leigh, go back to the house. I'll be along soon."

She turns and sees the stranger. "Who is it?"

"No one important. Go on."

She trudges over the dune, following a narrow boardwalk that cuts through the saw grass. Ace pulls on his sweatshirt and approaches the figure who is dressed in a black windbreaker, dress slacks, and matching shoes.

"Hello, Ace. Let's walk." CIA Director David Schall follows the shoreline east. "I want you to know I'm sincerely sorry about Kelli. She was more than a colleague, she was a friend."

"Who killed her?"

"Honestly, I don't know."

"You're the head of the CIA. Find out."

"Let's talk about you. Why did you spout off at last month's Senate hearings?"

"I don't know. Maybe I was tired of rehashing the same old crap."

"The President thinks you know a lot more than you're letting on."

Ace stops walking. "Is that what this meeting's about? Here I thought you were going to tell me why Homeland Security's got their collective heads crammed up my—"

"I can get you back into the game."

"And what game is that?"

David continues walking. "The President needs to know how much oil's left in the Saudi reserves. Assuming you had unlimited resources, could you find out?"

"By unlimited resources, you mean—"

"Unlimited."

"What's in it for me?"

"Your job back at PetroConsultants, with a raise. Two pay grades."

"Pass."

"And Homeland Security off your back."

Ace stops. "Are they your doing?"

"No. But your wife was making a lot of people nervous about something. Care to venture a guess?"

A wave breaks close to shore, washing over Ace's bare feet, soaking the CIA director's dress shoes and socks. "Damn it!"

"Okay, David. You want the Saudi info, I can get it for you, but here are my terms, and they're nonnegotiable. I want Kelli's assassin. I want his name and where to find him. Get me that, and you'll get your information."

"I can't do that."

"Of course you can, you're the damn CIA. You're the scumbags who start wars. And David, next time you instruct my attorney to have me meet you at the beach, at least wear sandals and jeans, huh? You look ridiculous."

"Not only did (FBI Supervisory Special Agent) Dave Frasca not share the information about Moussaoui to other appropriate intelligence/law enforcement authorities, he also never disclosed to the Minneapolis agents that the Phoenix Division had, only three weeks earlier, warned of Al-Qaeda operatives in flight schools seeking flight training for terrorists purposes! It is impossible to believe that Dave Frasca acted on his own, sitting on this information and not doing anything with it, unless ordered to do so. The Minneapolis FBI agents even tried to do an end run around Dave Frasca and notified the CIA's Counter Terrorist Center. The end result was that FBI headquarters' personnel (Frasca and unnamed higher ups) actually chastised the Minneapolis agents for making the direct notification without their approval. Going even further, Frasca 'undercut' the search warrant application by not adding information on Moussaoui's foreign power connections which he had promised Minneapolis agents would be included. He also made damaging changes to the text provided by Minneapolis agents thereby, according to one Minneapolis agent, 'setting this up for failure.'"

—Steve Moore,
from "9/11: Foreknowledge or Deception?"
Global Outlook
Issue No. 2
(Supervisory Special Agent Dave Frasca was later
promoted to Assistant Section Chief of the
International Terrorism Operations, Section I.)

CHAPTER 13

THE WHITE VAN CRUISES JUST BELOW THE SPEED LIMIT as it continues east on Main Street before turning south, entering a residential neighborhood. Magnetic signs on the vehicle identify it as belonging to a home improvement company in Decatur, Illinois.

Mike Tursi checks the time. He is forty minutes early, giving him an opportunity to check out the neighborhood before making his delivery.

◆ ◆ ◆

Michael Tursi was twenty-one when he arrived at Sheppard Air Force Base in Wichita Falls, Texas, to begin training as a Ballistic Missile Analyst Technician—BMAT for short. After fourteen months of intense training, the Turk knew every working part of an ICBM inside out. Upon graduating, he was ordered to take a thirty-day leave before reporting to Vandenberg Air Force Base in Santa Maria, California, for his course work and training in working with nuclear warheads.

Tursi's introduction at Vandenberg began with the viewing of classified films detailing the effects of thermonuclear radiation. The Turk and his classmates were horrified to witness the demise of American soldiers in the 1950s who, acting as "lab rats," had been stationed too close to the nuclear blasts. The lucky ones had been vaporized upon detonation, the rest had died slow, agonizing deaths from radiation poisoning.

With their minds now properly set, the training began. Simulations rehearsed every possible accident scenario, including the launch and retrieval of a real missile shot over the Pacific.

Following his graduation at Vandenberg, Tursi finally received his first official assignment—Little Rock Air Force Base in Arkansas. It was 1983, the height of the Cold War, and tensions among members of the "God Squad" were running high.

Little Rock was the real deal, home to dozens of ICBM silos containing Titan II nuclear missiles. After arriving at the base, Tursi was assigned a room and a silo crew. Each member of the Turk's team had to know the job of every other member in case a launch was required and a crewman was injured, dead, or had "flipped out" at the prospect of firing a weapon designed to kill millions of people. Training simulators were used to grade each individual and team, and the Turk's crew always graded out HQ (Highly Qualified).

Most nerve-wracking were alerts. Going on alert meant awakening at 4 a.m., arriving at squadron headquarters by 5:30 a.m., and then going through intelligence briefings before coding in. Each underground missile silo has a connecting subterranean site where the crews are stationed. In order to enter, a crewman had to call into the team already locked inside with the correct password and emergency code (the latter in the event something went wrong). Crewmen heading out on alert were heavily armed. Even the police had no authority over a BMAT on alert.

Arriving at the subterranean entrance, a solitary crewman would be allowed inside the outside portal to code in. Once inside, the replacement crew would complete a DSV (Daily Shift Verification) which meant physically going into the missile silo and inspecting critical parts of the ICBM, including the warhead. Working inside the silo, Tursi could actually feel the heat radiating from the nuclear warhead. As he moved deeper in the silo, the smell of fuel and oxidizer became overpowering.

While on alert, a BMAT crew would be sealed inside the missile bunker for a minimum of twenty-four hours. On one occasion, the cooling towers in Tursi's silo shut down, raising temperatures to critical levels, forcing his team to stay with the ICBM ninety-six straight hours before the system could be fixed. On that occasion an accident was avoided.

The Turk's crew would not always be so lucky.

ICBMs require maintenance. Propellant Transfer Service (PTS) was a routine that required a crew to change out the fuel and oxidizer from every stage of the missile. It was a dangerous procedure, for ICBMs possess very thin skins which can be easily punctured. Large, two-pound socket wrenches, attached by cords to the technicians' utility belts, are required to loosen the umbilical of the Titan II missile. As is usually the case, it is the smallest detail missed that often leads to the biggest accident.

Tursi's team was completing a PTS when a crewmen, having forgotten to attach his ratchet to his utility belt, accidentally dropped the heavy tool. The socket wrench fell into the silo, banked off the wall, and smashed into the ICBM, puncturing the missile's lower stage tank. Fuel gushed out of the Titan II, pooling at the bottom of the silo.

Michael Tursi knew an explosion was imminent, but he stayed with the warhead, quickly disconnecting electronics in the hopes of preventing the nuclear device from detonating when the fuel ignited.

As the Air Force Base went into lockdown and red alert, the emergency reached a critical stage, forcing Tursi's crew to evacuate the silo. Michael waited until the last possible moment and then sped away in an awaiting jeep. Minutes after he cleared the perimeter area, the fuel exploded, the detonation blowing the twenty-ton silo door half a mile away. Smoke and debris covered the area for miles in every direction, but the nuclear warhead didn't detonate.

Had it gone off, a substantial section of central Arkansas would have been vaporized and contaminated.

No press were allowed within ten miles of the base. Personnel living within the security ring either stayed inside their homes or were arrested on sight. By sunrise the warhead had been found, its casing wrecked, the nuclear device still intact.

No medals were handed out, the story spun, the real cause of the incident kept under wraps. Within the next five years the Cold War would end and the unstable Titan IIs phased out, pushing Michael Tursi out of a job. But his cool head had been duly noted by military intelligence.

Two days after leaving Little Rock, Arkansas, the Turk was recruited by the U.S. Intelligence community, his first assignment—the CIA.

✦ ✦ ✦

Michael Tursi drives past the street three times, circling back on different routes before finally following the road until it dead-ends at the cul-de-sac. The van is a rental, its Maryland license plate assigned to a vehicle owned by Dubai Ports World in Baltimore.

Tursi slows the vehicle, approaching a three-bedroom, single-story brick ranch house located on an irregular lot. A concrete driveway leads back to a three-car winterized garage the occupant uses as a workshop. The backyard is heavily wooded, part of the Shawnee National Forest. The brown-green waters of Deer Lake can be seen in the distance.

The home belongs to Professor Eric Mingyuan Bi.

✦ ✦ ✦

An expert in nuclear fission, now a tenured faculty member at Southern Illinois University, Professor Bi was born sixty-two years ago in Qingdao, China, relocating to the United States with his parents when he was ten. Eric Bi's father was full-blooded Chinese, a civil engineer who worked on many of China's hydroelectric dam projects. Bi's mother, Adzumi, was Japanese, her family hailing from Urakami, a suburb of Nagasaki, located on Kyushu, the southernmost of Japan's four mainland islands. Adzumi's father and uncles ran an import-export business at the harbor while she was growing up, their clan "recruited" by the Emperor's navy to organize supply ships during World War II.

On August 6, 1945, the Japanese Empire was felled when the city of Hiroshima was scorched from a "fire in the sky." Following the American's atomic attack, Adzumi's father immediately arranged passage for his wife and children to leave the island.

Three days later, at 11:02 a.m. on August 9, a more powerful nuclear bomb, code-named "Fat Boy," was dropped on Nagasaki. The primary target had been Kokura, but cloud cover had obscured the bomber pilot's vision. The weapon exploded directly above Urakami, vaporizing the town, along with the northern end of Nagasaki. Thirty-nine thousand people were wiped out in the blink of an eye. Twice that many lingered on for weeks from lethal radiation poisoning, Adzumi's father and uncles among them.

Adzumi was seventeen and resettled in China when Japan finally surrendered to the Allies. Fourteen years later, her husband moved their family to the States so that he could study earthquake engineering. An only child, Eric grew up listening to his mother's re-telling of those last, horrifying days of the war—stories that enticed the boy to learn how to harness such incredible power. After earning a master's and a doctorate degree in physics, Eric spent three years at the DOE's Los Alamos Nuclear Laboratory in New Mexico, mentored by Wen Ho Lee, a nuclear scientist who was later accused of stealing military secrets for China from tips sent in by anonymous officials.

Wen Ho Lee would later be exonerated, the suspicion of espionage now redirected at Professor Eric Mingyuan Bi.

✦ ✦ ✦

Tursi backs the van slowly up the driveway, parking within five feet of the closed garage doors. The Turk exits his vehicle carrying a small cardboard box.

Professor Bi exits from his kitchen, pulling on an overcoat. "You're early."

Tursi nods. "Let's talk inside."

Eric Bi keys open the side entrance to the garage, leading the Strategic Support Branch agent inside. A black Ford Explorer is parked in the middle space. A riding lawn mower and snow blower occupy another. Assorted tools hang along one wall. Nothing out of the ordinary, other than that the garage is heated and insulated.

Tursi hands him the cardboard box. The professor wipes humidity from his wire-rimmed glasses and then tears open the container. He removes the plastic-sealed packs of $100 bills.

"Two hundred thousand?"

"It's all there. You can count it later. You'll get the balance when I take final delivery. Let's see the colex."

Bi returns the packs of money to the cardboard box and then leads Tursi to a storage closet. He removes a wheelbarrow and rolls back the soiled carpet, exposing a wooden floor. Using a crowbar hanging behind the door, he pries loose three floorboards, revealing concrete steps that lead down into a basement.

The Chinese professor enters first to turn on the lights, and Tursi follows him below.

The room is almost a thousand square feet, its twelve-foot ceiling and windowless walls lined in lead-board, a lead-lined drywall. A 16,000-watt, propane-fed generator occupies one corner of the room, a lead container the size of a small washing machine positioned along a far wall next to a similar-sized plastic container. A biohazard suit is laid out across several folding chairs.

Occupying the center of the basement is an immense

object—a rectangular tank, six feet high and deep, ten feet long, composed of iron. Thirty baseball-size holes cover the left side of the tank, each hole bearing a rubberized doughnut housing. The top of the tank has been removed, revealing an internal metal sheath that divides the tank in half. The sheath is porous, bearing quarter-size holes. At the bottom of the tank are a series of heating elements, their insulated electrical wires running out of the tank, connecting with the generator.

A pipe runs out of the right side of the tank into two eight-foot-high centrifuges, one feeding into the other.

Michael Tursi peers inside the tank, looking confused. "I don't know, Bi, you sure this thing will work?"

"It will work. I guarantee it will work!"

"Okay, easy, just give me the Reader's Digest explanation."

"What you have here is a colex—a column exchange unit designed to convert, or enrich uranium-235 to uranium-238." Professor Bi points to the left side of the tank. "The U-235 fuel rods will be positioned in these holes, feeding unenriched uranium into the tank. The tank will contain the heavy water, along with a mixture of nitric acid, ammonium hydroxide, hydrofluoric acid, and fluorine. Heating elements will heat the water to precisely 250 degrees Fahrenheit, creating a chemical reaction, converting U-235 into uranium hexafluoride, or UF-6."

The physicist points to the two tall centrifuges positioned outside the main tank. "This first centrifuge will draw the UF-6 through the porous wall, separating enriched U-238 from the depleted U-235. This second centrifuge has two outtakes. The enriched uranium-238 will rise and be taken from this upper outtake and then stored in a lead tank until there's enough to cook. The depleted U-235 will be drawn out of this bottom outtake and stored in a separate cache. The process is repeated until there's enough enriched uranium to create our two packages."

"How long to do the job?"

"Each fuel rod should yield a gram of enriched uranium a day. Thirty fuel rods, thirty grams a day, figure about six months. How soon will you be delivering the fuel rods?"

"Soon enough."

"I need to stay on schedule."

"Just make sure everything else is ready."

Bi nods nervously, wishing the dangerous man was gone. "Come, I'll show you where to run the hose."

Tursi follows the professor back up the steps into the garage. Bi unbolts a four-inch rectangular cap situated along the bottom of the garage door. "Feed the hose through here."

The Turk exits the garage. Using his electronic key chain, he unlocks the van and opens its rear double doors.

Mounted to the floorboards is a 1,000-gallon polyethylene storage container filled with heavy water smuggled out of the Canadian power plant. Attached to the bottom of the container's faucet is two hundred feet of hose.

Tursi takes the free end of the hose and feeds it through the hole along the bottom of the garage. Inside the garage, Professor Bi takes up the slack. Several minutes pass and then Bi taps on the garage window, indicating he's ready.

The Turk turns on the valve, releasing the heavy water. Leaning back against the van, he lights a cigarette—never realizing his every movement is being recorded.

❖ ❖ ❖

In the two-story home situated directly across the street, FBI Special Agent Elliott Green works at a makeshift desk in the master suite, the windows of which face Professor Bi's home. Green, in his early forties, has spent the last two years assigned to a desk job at the CAC (Crimes Against Children) division at Springfield, Illinois. The agent's goal has always been to work in counterterrorism, but openings at FBI–Chicago are few and far between. Knowing his young agent was desperate for a change, Green's supervisor, a former cop named Charles Jones, had offered him an assignment in the field—a job originating out of the Department of Energy. Green had gladly accepted.

The "field work" turned out to be surveillance work on Professor Eric Mingyuan Bi.

Elliott Green has occupied the house across the street from the Asian-American nuclear physicist for two months, purchasing it through a bogus Florida corporation from its original owner, an eighty-two-year-old widow. To sweeten the deal and hasten her departure into a local seniors' facility, the company had agreed to buy the home with all its furnishings.

As much as Green enjoys his new "status," he also misses seeing his wife and six-year-old son. He hates the "old people" smell that lingers in the air, and refuses to sit on any piece of furniture or use any of the dishes collecting dust in the peeling sunflower-yellow kitchen cabinets. He lives exclusively out of the master bedroom, made fresh with a coat of white paint, new carpeting, bedroom suite, and home entertainment center, its flat-screen television linked to the closed-circuit cameras monitoring activities across the street.

After two steady months of surveillance, the FBI agent knows what time Professor Bi awakens every morning, knows what he eats for breakfast, his teaching schedule at the University, where he takes his lunch, and to whom he speaks with at school. So far, there has been nothing out of the ordinary to report, other than Bi spending long hours in his three-car garage, which doubles as a hobby room—until tonight.

Green watches the scene as it records and plays on his monitor. He zooms in on the short, stocky man's face as he reaches inside his van. After twenty minutes, the home improvement delivery truck's rear doors slam shut, the driver climbing back into the vehicle.

The van drives off—leaving Agent Green to his work.

"U.S. military sources have given the FBI information that suggests five of the alleged hijackers of the planes that were used in Tuesday's terror attacks received training at secure U.S. military installations in the 1990s. (Mohammed Atta) may have been trained in strategy and tactics at the Air War College in Montgomery, Alabama, said another high-ranking Pentagon official."

—*Newsweek*,
September 15, 2001

"You've just got to trust us. We are honorable men."

—Richard Helms,
CIA Director (1971)

Book Excerpt:
To the Brink of Hell:
An Apology to the Survivors
by Kelli Doyle
White House National Security Staff Advisor
(2002-2008)

The next 9/11 event will be a nuclear attack. In one hellish instant of inhumanity, millions of innocent Americans will be vaporized into dust. Worse off will be those who escape the initial blast. Blinded, their flesh scorched to the bone, they will lie in wait for hours and days, lingering in agony as they pray for the Angel of Death to take them.

If you happen to be living in a targeted city, then your days may already be numbered. Traveling on business? Visiting relatives? Life is a crapshoot. Take it from one who knows. Some of us get rich, others get cancer, and if that's God's will, so be it. But the events of September 11, 2001, and the more devastating attack(s) to occur have nothing to do with the Almighty . . . no, these deaths are part of a premeditated grand scheme being planned and financed by a moral minority convinced they alone have been blessed to carry out our creator's work.

I cannot give you the exact date of the attack, nor can I give you its location, but I can present you with the circumstances that have led us down this path of destruction . . . and what you can do to stop it.

* * *

To understand how we got to this point, we begin with a brief history lesson — call it the rise and fall of Petroleum Man. Petroleum, of course, is oil, and we're using it faster than we can pump it out of the ground. Oil fuels the economy, the economy fuels the military, and it was a combination of all three that gave birth to the three groups vying for control of the Middle East: The House of Saud, the Neoconservatives, and the Islamic extremists.

All three played a part in the events of 9/11, and all three will be involved when a nuclear detonation wipes out an American city.

Let's begin with the House of Saud.

King Sultan bin Abdel Aziz, the (anticipated) seventh ruler of Saudi Arabia, is the last surviving member of the "Sudairi Seven," the seven sons born to Hassa bint Ahmad Sudairi, the favorite wife of King Abdul Aziz bin Abdul Rahman Al Saud, better known as Ibn Saud. History books depict Ibn Saud, founder of the Kingdom of Saudi Arabia, as a natural-born leader, a man devoted to his faith, and a wise visionary who unified the Arabian Peninsula and used his nation's resources to benefit his people.

Ibn Saud was neither a unifier nor a wise man, nor was he even a descendant of royalty. Ibn Saud was a murderous brute whose family's rise to power came only because of a fortuitous relationship with an outside power; his wealth — an unearned find that bought him absolute power and fragmented a nation.

The history of the Arabian Peninsula dates back more than 5,000 years to several distinct Semitic tribes — ancestors of the Akkadians, Assyrians, Hebrews, and Arabs. Back then, religion among the Arabian tribes followed different forms of paganism, although many Arabs eventually converted to Judaism and Christianity. Then, in 622 AD, a man named Muhammad, born to the Banu Omar family, began preaching a new monotheistic religion which adhered to the teachings of Abraham and rejected idolatry. Forced to leave his home in Mecca, Muhammad and his followers consolidated their power base in Medina, and eight years later the Muslims returned in force to capture the city. Muhammad would die two years later, succeeded by his father-in-law, Abu Bakr.

Buoyed by Muslim conquests, Islam spread rapidly. Mecca became Islam's spiritual capitol, Medina its religious administrative and intellectual center. Over the next thousand years, different Muslim sects would battle for control of Arabia, all yielding to the rise of the Mongols and eventually the Ottoman Empire, which controlled the region into the fifteenth century.

In 1745, an upstart named Muhammad bin Saud, emir of the town of Dariya in the Nejd (central Arabia), joined forces with a spiritual leader named Muhammad ibn 'Abd al-Wahhab, who preached a violent puritanical interpretation of Islam. Over the next seventy years, the "Wahhabi" movement and the House of Saud would wage a jihad (holy war) across Arabia, only to be driven back in 1818 by the Ottoman Turks and their Egyptian allies.

The Sauds and Wahhabis retreated to Riyadh, which became their capital. In 1890, the House of Saud's puppet ruler, Abdul Rahman bin Faisal, was forced out of Riyadh, and the Saud family sent into exile in Kuwait.

In 1901, Abdul Rahman's twenty-one-year-old son, Ibn Saud, succeeded his father and set out to reclaim his family's land. A year later, Saud's army of twenty recaptured Riyadh by assassinating the Rashidi governor. Over the next several years, Ibn Saud conquered half of the Nejd, only to be turned back once more when the Ottoman Empire aided his sworn enemy, the House of Rashidi.

The outbreak of World War I would change Ibn Saud's fortunes, and with it, the destiny of the modern world.

British interests in the Arabian Peninsula had been growing since the late 1800s. By the eve of the first world war, Britain's leaders felt it necessary to deputize one of the four ruling Arab families in the hopes of gaining control of the region from the Turks.

Ibn Saud was neither educated nor linked to the descendants of Muhammad, making him the perfect puppet to fulfill England's needs. From 1911 to 1914, Ibn Saud used his new pipeline of British money and arms to turn his Ikhwan brotherhood — a sect of Wahhabi Bedouin — into a bloodthirsty mob. While rival Arab leaders attempted to modernize their people through farming and trade, the House of Saud practiced the ghazzu — violent raids on neighboring tribes. Encouraged by the British, Saud's ruthless followers burned thousands of people to death and beheaded others, displaying their spiked skulls at the gates of the city.

Women were enslaved by the hundreds and often given away to allies as gifts.

Working as England's exclusive enforcers, Ibn Saud invaded western Arabia, attacking the Hashemites and the other families. He captured the Jebel Shammar in 1921, Mecca in 1924, and Medina in 1925. Along the way his Ikhwan followers ransacked entire towns, slaughtering adults and children while murdering any religious leader who did not share in their strict Wahhabi beliefs. In an attempt to gain legitimacy, Ibn Saud went so far as to hire an Egyptian religious sheik to fabricate a family tree linking the Saud lineage to the Prophet Muhammad. In 1932, he formally named his newly conquered region Saudi Arabia and declared himself its king.

The Wahhabi Ikhwan were fanatics who served to keep the House of Saud in power. A cruel and backward sect, they had no tolerance for twentieth century innovations, nor the presence of non-Muslims in Saudi Arabia. Eager to force reform on others, the Ikhwan committed massacres that slaughtered upward of half a million people.

Though he would call himself a unifier, Ibn Saud had no interest in uniting the Arabian people. Unorganized and lacking a formal education, King Ibn Saud ruled his nation from a tent and spread his seed among thirty other tribes. He had dozens of wives, even more concubines and slaves, and often bragged that he had deflowered virgins by the hundreds.

The House of Saud ruled Saudi Arabia with an iron fist and kept the power among themselves. Provinces were run by members of the family. No outsiders were allowed to rule. To control the more advanced cities in the Hijaz, Ibn Saud founded CAVES — the Committee for the Advancement of Virtue and Elimination of Sin, enforced by his Wahhabi brutes. People were flogged in public for wearing perfume, jewelry, or Western apparel, and all men were required to grow beards. If a CAVES member wanted a woman for marriage, he couldn't be denied. The Hijaz legal system was abandoned, tribal law of the Wahhabi sect ruling the day. Backed by the Wahhabi clerics, British arms, and a monthly stipend, Ibn Saud continued to rule over his Bedouin police state.

And then, in 1933, everything changed.

Geologists had long suspected the eastern Arabian Peninsula possessed oil, but no one knew how much. Ibn Saud had granted the first oil concession to Britain in 1923, but little had been done with it. By 1928, the deal had been nullified and Standard Oil of California (SOCAL) entered the picture, purchasing the expired concession for a mere $250,000.

Eastern Saudi Arabia's oil caches are located in flatlands at very shallow depths, making them less costly to access, and the close proximity to waterways provided SOCAL a ready-made means to bring the fuel to market. With SOCAL's foot in the door, Harold Ickes, the U.S. Secretary of the Interior, began "lobbying" Ibn Saud with grant monies and other financial contributions, all of which went directly into the king's personal pocket.

In 1936, SOCAL assigned its concession to its subsidiary, California Arabian Standard Oil Company (CASOC), a Saudi Arabia operating venture that eventually became the Arabian American Oil Company (ARAMCO). By the end of World War II, ARAMCO was producing 300,000 barrels of crude a day, and the United States had officially replaced Britain as Ibn Saud's sponsor. But unlike Britain, which often dictated to its foreign oil suppliers how profits should be reinvested into the nation's economy and educational system, the United States made no such demands on the House of Saud. Of the $400 million received between 1946 and 1953, Ibn Saud gave almost nothing back to the common Saudi. Tens of millions of dollars were spent on lavish palaces. Expensive cars were driven until they ran out of gas and then left on the roadside to be replaced rather than refueled. Family members received huge monthly stipends, and bribery became the means to all ends.

The rich got richer, the poor . . . oppressed.

Always wary of his neighbors, Ibn Saud used oil profits to entice wars. Egypt was coerced into feuding with Syria, Syria with Iraq. It would be a practice continued over the next seven decades, designed to keep Saudi Arabia's influence over the region supreme.

Ibn Saud died at the age of fifty-two, leaving behind

one hundred wives, forty-two sons, fifteen hundred princes, a country with no infrastructure, built totally on nepotism, and a legacy of immorality. Under his "leadership," Saudi Arabia's citizens remained poor, uneducated, medically unfit, and under constant threat by their Wahhabi clerics.

The man who anointed himself king was succeeded by his eldest living son, Saud, a simpleton whose moral corruption surpassed even that of his father. Saud married more times than Ibn, had an insatiable appetite for the ridiculous, and was known to appease his sexual desires with young boys. He was finally replaced after being caught in a botched attempt to assassinate Egypt's President Nasser, who was gaining popularity in the region.

For their third king, the Royal House turned to Ibn Saud's second eldest son, Faisal, who, being more clever than Saud, knew better how to hide his reign's immorality from the public eye. Faisal bribed Arab newspapers to run phony stories about his accomplishments, and then, backed by the United States, used the country's wealth to encourage Yemen to oppose Nasser in Egypt, earning points with the Muslims.

Faisal's domestic policies continued to crush the will of his own people. Under the guise of reducing stipends to the Royals, he confiscated nearly 95 percent of all public lands, giving huge parcels away to family members, including an estimated $2 billion worth of tracts to his wife, Iffat. Faisal also encouraged members of his House to go into business for themselves, using oil to fund their corporations. To this day, Saudi government contracts cannot be won without a prince as a partner.

The United States knew full well about the unjust policies of the House of Saud, but America's newfound dependence on oil imports "encouraged" its leaders to look the other way. For his part, Faisal understood the delicate balance of maintaining both an Arab and Muslim identity while keeping the Middle East divided. After Egypt attacked Israel in 1973 and was beaten back once more, the king briefly won Arab support by shutting off oil supplies to the West. Faisal's own reign ended two years later when he was assassinated by a nephew, who was avenging his own brother's death (an execution ordered by the king for "religious reasons"). He was replaced by Crown Prince Khalid, whose first act as king was to appoint three of the remaining Sudeiri Seven: Nayef, Sultan, and Fahd (the latter deemed Crown Prince) to key ministerial positions. Relatives not of the Sudeiri lineage were denied posts. It was a coup among the House of Saud royals, and it created more bad blood within the family.

In 1982 Khalid suffered a fatal heart attack, and Crown Prince Fahd took over as king. Among western statesmen and foreign diplomats, Fahd had earned a reputation as being lazy and poorly educated. He was known to go on wild drinking and gambling binges, and his personal excesses remained unparalleled, even for the House of Saud. His palace cost $3 billion, he had a fleet of twenty-five Rolls Royces, five Boeing 747s, and his entourage traveled with two-hundred tons of luggage. His frequent trips to Spain cost up to $5 million a day, and he once gambled away $8 million in a single night in Monte Carlo. Under his reign, the House of Saud's top princes received payments of $100 million a year, with lesser family members taking in $4 million apiece. Fahd had more than 100 wives, countless prostitutes, and on one trip to Los Angeles, he and his party spent tens of thousands of dollars on Viagra. Under Fahd's rule, and despite the influx of hundreds of billions of petroleum dollars, the Saudi government ran massive federal deficits.

To counter these expenses, King Fahd created a new scheme to allow the Royals to siphon off billions more from their country's resources. Under the guise of "protecting its borders" Saudi Arabia began importing weapons, each arms deal filling the coffers of its Western sellers and lining the pockets of the Prince assigned to the deal as its broker or "fixer." Commissions routinely ran from the tens of millions into the billions of dollars, yet from a sense of practicality, were a waste of resources. The Saudi military lacked both personnel and the training necessary to handle this diverse cache of hardware, which, imported from the United States, France, and Britain, were often incompatible.

In the wake of the first Gulf War, the House of Saud purchased over one hundred billion dollars' worth of weapons, many of these sales arranged through (and profited by) the Minister of Defense and future king, Crown Prince Sultan. Skimming enough money to earn himself the title "world's richest man," Sultan's purchases included American F-15 fighter jets and British Tornados, Bradley Fighting vehicles and Chinese long-range ground-to-ground missiles. Sultan also commissioned the construction (through the bin Laden family) of military cities and bases that, to this day, remain virtually empty. Over two hundred naval vessels were purchased for the Royal Saudi Navy, including eight submarines, half-a-dozen frigates, nine Peterson patrol boats, and four corvettes, yet the navy's entire personnel would only amount to an average of twenty-one people per boat! Hundreds of military vehicles were delivered, then left to rot in the desert.

The hypocrisy of both King Fahd and King Sultan's military buildup was that neither ruler had any intention of creating a strong national military presence. While Saudi Arabia remains a country surrounded by potential enemies, it is the enemies within its borders — the oppressed Saudi people — that have always been the greatest threat to the House of Saud's monopoly on power. Despite the hundreds of billions of petroleum dollars that have rolled into the country, unemployment has reached 30 percent, the social security system remains unfunded, and the public works, including the electricity and phone companies are always in jeopardy of shutting down. As the economy moves closer to collapse, the Royals get richer and the people grow more rebellious.

But revolution in Saudi Arabia is not an easy conquest. Thousands of family members occupy key governmental positions, including posts in the air force as well as the ministries of defense. Because of the Royals' fear of being hijacked, only a Prince or a close family member can become a pilot. And while the House of Saud continues to profit from the billions spent on the military, the Royal family has always been loath to build an army capable of overthrowing its own regime, preferring to place its sophisticated weapons in the hands of its 35,000-strong Bedouin Wahhabi National Guardsmen, overseen by the Crown Prince. The Saudi army, with its smaller numbers, remains stationed along the outskirts of the country's major cities, further discouraging a revolt.

When revolt does occur, the Saudi reprisals are swift and abominable. Accused conspirators have been publicly beheaded, tortured, and even tossed out of planes. Those who strike for better wages have been imprisoned. Religious leaders have been executed. Journalists who report any anti-government sentiment simply disappear. Anyone can be arrested at any time for simply acting "suspicious." Requests by human rights organizations to visit detainees or investigate brutalities have been denied. Reports of prisoners having their fingernails and toenails torn off and other graphic descriptions of torture have been well-documented.

Yet the United States refuses to act, for as long as Saudi Arabia provides America with cheap oil, the House of Saud will remain in power. But America's military presence in the Gulf is a double-edged sword. Radical Islamic fundamentalism forbids a foreign presence in Saudi Arabia, bringing the House of Saud in direct conflict with its own Wahhabis National Guard. To appease the ulema, the Sauds have funded the madrassas — schools that teach radical fundamentalism and the hatred of Americans, Jews, and Christians. Radical Islam is thriving, and not just in Saudi Arabia. Iran remains the biggest threat in the region, with fundamentalists gaining footholds in Jordan, Kuwait, the Sudan, Egypt, Morocco, and Iraq.

And so it goes, this wheel of insanity:

Addicted to oil, the West continues to use its might to keep the House of Saud in power.

To stay in power, the House of Saud continues to support Islamic radicals or risk becoming their target.

To gain support for their movement, Islamic radicals have sworn to destroy the West . . . targeting Iraq and its Sunni population, while Saudi Arabia's own population, long kept under the thumb of its theocratic oppressors, cannot bring true democracy to the region as long as the House of

Saud receives the support of the United States.

For decades this wheel of conflicting interests has continued to turn, grinding over human rights and innocent lives as it rolls on, fueled by greed, driven by politicians empowered by an industrial world that uses a ledger sheet to determine civil rights from social wrongs. Add to this equation the estimated $850 billion the Saudis have invested in American corporations, and you have a powerful foreign leverage on the U.S. economy.

But what does the addict do when there are no more drugs to be had? What does the pusher do when the addict is no longer bound? The final pieces of the board are in play – a pawn, disguised as a king, being led into his final move by an unseen chess master . . . checkmating the end of civilization.

"The first hijacking was suspected at not later than 8:20 a.m., and the last hijacked aircraft crashed in Pennsylvania at 10:06 a.m. Not a single fighter plane was scrambled to investigate from U.S. Andrews Air Force Base, just 10 miles from Washington, D.C., until after the third plane hit the Pentagon at 9:38 a.m. Why not? There were standard FAA intercept procedures for hijacked aircraft before 9/11. Between September 2000 and June 2001, the U.S. military launched fighter aircraft on 67 occasions to chase suspicious aircraft. It is a U.S. legal requirement that once an aircraft has moved significantly off its flight plan, fighter planes are sent up to investigate. Was this inaction simply the result of key people disregarding, or being ignorant of the evidence? Or could U.S. air security operations have been deliberately stood down on September 11th?"

—MICHAEL MEACHER,
Former British Environmental Minister,
from "The War on Terrorism Is Bogus,"
The Guardian, September 6, 2003

"Bin Laden has been under surveillance for years: every telephone call was monitored and Al-Qaeda has been penetrated by American intelligence, Pakistani intelligence, Saudi intelligence, and Egyptian intelligence. They could not have kept secret an operation that required such a degree of organization and sophistication."

—MOHAMMED HEIKAL,
former Egyptian foreign minister

CHAPTER 14

THE UPPER WEST SIDE HIGH-RISE is located on 72nd street, offering most of its tenants an unobstructed view of Central Park. Jennifer Wienner's apartment is on one of the upper stories, a two-bedroom dwelling with hardwood floors, fireplace, and balcony, carrying a $6,000 monthly rental.

The former GOP political strategist is dressed in sweat clothes, seated on the floor of her master bedroom's walk-in closet, squeezed between three large cardboard moving boxes. She has already filled two of the boxes with purses and shoes, and is humbled by the amount of footwear and accessories she has accumulated over the years . . . and she hasn't even started packing her collection of boots. "That seals it, I'm definitely moving to Florida. From now on, it's strictly sandals."

The ringing doorbell signals yet another interruption. Cursing aloud, she makes her way out through the maze of boxes cluttering her bedroom and hallway, cringing at the pile of china that still awaits her attention on the dining room table.

Jennifer looks through the peep hole and opens the door. "Ace, what are you doing here?"

"I had a few errands in the city, thought maybe we could talk. Can I . . . ?"

"Yeah, sure." She lets him in, suddenly conscious of her

attire. "Give me a minute to change."

"You're fine."

"Are you kidding? I haven't even brushed my hair. Sit. I'll be right out." She hustles back to the bedroom.

Ace enters the living room. He manages to locate the four home entertainment center remote controls, but quickly gives up trying to figure out which device works the television. He powers on the flat screen by hand, the channel pre-set to CNN.

". . . the Avian Flu virus continuing its deadly spread throughout parts of Southeast Asia. On the political front, the Iowa Caucuses are set for later this week, followed by the New Hampshire Primary, yet it's still hard to predict which Republican candidate will emerge from the field of eight to challenge President Obama. Many consider Senator Crist as the early favorite, but his support for the President's programs may come back to haunt him. Another GOP favorite is Governor Prescott, who recently received the endorsement of Newt Gingrich. Of the six remaining candidates, only Senator Cubit—"

Jennifer returns, her ebony hair pulled back, her face revealing a touch of make-up. "Okay, now I feel human. So what's up?"

"Where's your laptop?"

"Probably buried under a pile of junk. Why?"

"Someone e-mailed me a video link today. I wanted you to see it."

She frowns and then leads him to her dining room table, where she locates the laptop beneath a stack of moving blankets.

"Go to YouTube and type in *Rockefeller Reveals 9/11 Fraud to Aaron Russo.*"

"Russo? The movie guy who ran for Governor of Nevada a while back? I thought he was dead."

"Before he died, he did this interview with Alex Jones."

"Ace, Alex Jones is a conspiracy wacko."

"Just play the video."

Reluctantly, she activates the interview. The late film producer and libertarian appears on screen.

"*The ultimate goal these people have is to create a one-world government, run by the banking industry . . . run by the bankers. And they're doing it in sections . . . the European constitution is one part of it. Now they're trying to do it in America with the North American Union. And they want to create a new currency, called the Amero. The whole agenda is to create a one-world government, where everybody has an RFID chip implanted in them . . . all money is to be in those chips . . . so there will be no more cash . . . and this is coming straight from Rockefeller what they want to accomplish.*"

"Ace, you came all the way over here to have me watch some conspiracy nut?"

"He's referring to Nick Rockefeller, an attorney who tried to recruit him into the Council of Foreign Relations."

"Ace, do you know how busy I am?"

"Shh . . . listen to this next part!"

"*Rockefeller told me eleven months before 9/11 that there was going to be an event . . . never told me what the event was going to be. And out of that event, we were going to invade Afghanistan to run pipelines from the Caspian Sea, that we were going to invade Iraq to take over the oil fields and establish a base in the Middle East and make it all part of a new world order, and we were going to go after Chavez in Venezuela. And sure enough, later, 9/11 happened. He was telling me we'd see soldiers looking in caves for people in Afghanistan and Pakistan and all these places, and there's going to be this war on terror, where there's no real enemy, and the whole thing is a giant hoax, but it's a way for the government to take over the American people . . .*"

Jennifer shuts it off. "So one of the Rockefellers is clairvoyant. So what?"

"Don't patronize me, Jen. You and Kelli rubbed elbows with these guys. I wanna know what the deal is."

"About what? The whole New World Order conspiracy?"

"No. About the CFR. Were they involved in 9/11?"

"Ugh." Grabbing a hand-woven Chamarras wool blanket, she returns to the den and curls up on the couch. Ace sits opposite her in a bamboo rocking chair. "Look, there are three elite think tanks in the western world: The Council on Foreign Relations, the Trilateral Commission, and the Bilderberg Group. Members of these organizations include politicians on both sides of the aisle— scientists, and yes, wealthy elite like the Rockefellers. Almost every president and presidential candidate are past or current members. The CFR dates back to the Woodrow Wilson Administration and the President's advisor, Edward House, who was probably a Marxist. House was instrumental is passing the Federal Reserve Act, which allowed a private central bank to create the U.S. currency instead of Congress. Naturally, the bankers made a lot of money from this act, so it's neither a coincidence nor a conspiracy that creating all-encompassing global financial institutions is a large part of the CFR agenda."

"What about the media?"

"What about them?"

"Are they members?"

"It's not like it's a secret. Go to their website, they list their members. Newspapers, television, major magazines. David Rockefeller's the Chairman of the Board."

"According to the late Aaron Russo, he's a Chair with an agenda."

"Everyone has an agenda. You had an agenda coming here. It doesn't mean you conspired to bring down the World Trade Center."

"If all these powerful politicians and bankers and the news media are members, why haven't I ever heard of these groups?"

"I think you just answered your own question."

"Tell me about the Trilateral Commission."

"Rockefeller and Zbigniew Brzezinski started it in 1970. Brzezinski believes in the whole one-world government deal. The Trilateral Commission was used to develop economic and defense relations between North America, Western Europe, and Japan."

"But these aren't governments? They're just . . . commissions."

"Commissions founded by the world's power brokers. These are the king-makers, Ace. No one gets to be president without their blessing. Take Jimmy Carter. How do you think an obscure peanut farming governor from Georgia became president? Better yet, look at Ron Paul. Back in 2008, the guy raised more money than any Republican and carried a message that appealed to younger voters. But he made two major blunders: He openly challenged the legality of the Federal Reserve Act, and he said he'd end the war as soon as he entered office. The CFR is run by the Federal Reserve banks, as well as the major corporations that profit from war. Before you could say 'blacklisted,' the media stopped speaking Ron Paul's name. They even kicked him out of the debate."

"You mentioned a third group?"

"Bilderberg. Basically another set of elitists with a globalist agenda, this one with roots in Western Europe."

"Obama?"

"Is he a member? I don't know. But his administration's filled with them, including Brezinski. Don't judge him too harshly—the guy's still alive. JFK decided he wanted to dismantle the CIA and he's six feet under." She smiles. "Oops, more conspiracy theory."

"Hypothetically, could a third party candidate, say a guy like this Senator Mulligan, ever win the Presidency?"

"And remain independent? Not likely. He'd have to be a billionaire. Even then, they'd probably recruit him or kill him. Like everything else in this life, winning elections essentially comes down to money. Money buys message. Message gets candidates elected. Not truth, not policies, not resumés or medals in wars . . . message. When it comes to casting their vote, the majority of Americans go to the ballot box believing they are voting for the candidate who best shares their own values or secures their needs. The reality is, most candidate's policies run counter to their own voters' interests. They get elected on sound bites and staying on message. Give me enough money to blitz the media and I could get Elmer Fudd elected, assuming he occasionally went to church and could lose the lisp."

"What if one of the candidates based their entire campaign on a radical plan to replace and conserve fossil fuels? I know Obama reversed a lot of Bush policies, but Congress made too many backroom deals, weakening his energy policy in order to cater to the GOP. What's needed now are sweeping changes, an economy based on green energy and conservation, an energy plan geared toward local utilities and alternative energy . . . even a new methodology of feeding people using organic farms and reinvigorating the soil, not these petroleum-based, steroid-enhanced industrial crop cities run by Monsanto. Instead of burning the village to save it, we shrink it down, making it more efficient. Think about it, Jen. No more dependence on the Middle East, no more bogus war on terror."

"Never happen, Ace."

"Why not?"

"You're messing with profits. The powers-that-be won't allow it. You expect these kings to sacrifice a room of their palace on behalf of the serf? Kings don't give a damn about serfs. Not in Saudi Arabia. Not in the West."

"Yeah? Well, there's an old saying: 'The people shouldn't fear the government, the government should fear the people.' "

"Will you be leading the revolt?"

Ace stares out the balcony window looking out over Central Park, its paths and bridges camouflaged beneath a fresh blanket of snow. From his vantage he can see the approximate spot where his wife was shot. Kelli's words come back to him now, as if her message had always been intended for this moment: *The only way we keep society from running off the cliff is with a radical change in course . . .*

"It's the reason I'm moving," Jennifer says, misinterpreting his expression. "I can't bear to look out there anymore."

He turns to face her, momentarily startled. In the light, and for the briefest of seconds, Jennifer is his wife's twin, albeit a dark-haired version . . . before the chemo.

"Ace, you okay?"

"The night Kelli died, she was trying to warn me about something. She said bad things were going to happen."

"Did you tell this to Homeland Security?"

"Before or after they tasered me? No, Jen, it didn't come up. For all I know, they could have been the ones who sanctioned her death."

"Easy."

"Did you know she was writing a book?"

"What kind of book?"

"A tell-all. She never showed it to me, but I imagine there's a bunch of people in Washington who weren't thrilled about it."

"And you think that's why she was killed? Come on, Ace. Dozens of former cabinet members and generals write tell-all books every year. None of them are sanctioned, as you put it."

"Kelli said there was going to be another attack, something far worse than 9/11."

"Islamic extremists?"

"It'll be made to look that way, but the Neocons will be pulling the strings."

"Kelli said that?"

"In so many words. She wanted my help. She wanted to expose the plot."

"How?"

"For the last six years, my PetroConsultant teams had been compiling new data about world oil reserves. Last month I told a bunch of senators that we may run out in five to seven years. But what if I'm wrong? What if the end's much closer than we think?"

"You're overreaching."

"Am I? Less than a year before 9/11, Dick Cheney began conducting all those secret energy meetings. Kelli was in those meetings. What if 9/11 and the Iraqi invasion were premeditated events, set in motion by the Neocons as an excuse to secure the last remaining oil reserves?"

"Here we go . . ."

"Just hear me out. Cheney has spent the last three years accusing the president of being weak on terror. What if he's not just attempting to defend his illegal policies? What if he has knowledge of another attack, manipulated by the powers no longer in power?"

"Ace—"

"If an attack occurred before the November election, who would win the presidency?"

Jennifer exhales. "Probably the GOP. But this is all nonsense . . . it's conspiracy theory 101, straight out of Alex Jones and Prison Planet. You're not a 9/11 conspiracy wacko, Ace. Stop thinking like one."

She jumps in her chair as he kicks over a box, sending books flying everywhere. "For once, Jennifer, can you just listen with an open mind?"

Jennifer grips the blanket, unsure. She's well-aware of Ace's past, how he snapped under pressure. *Kelli's murder. Losing his job. The arrest. In his state of mind, he's capable of anything . . .*

Ace takes a deep breath, calming himself. "My best friend died in the North Tower. He worked in one of the investment firms on the upper floors. Left behind a wife and three kids."

"I'm sorry."

"While he and his coworkers burned to death, the scumbags who knew about the attacks made a nice little profit from insider trading. That's why he was in so early that day, he was trying to catch up on all the paperwork from the night before. I don't believe in conspiracy theories, Jennifer, but the crap Washington fed us made no sense either. Remember golfer Payne Stewart? How is it that his private plane was intercepted by Air Force jets within minutes of wandering off course, yet four commercial jetliners were never intercepted, one of them managing to fly circles over the most guarded airspace on the planet before striking the Pentagon? The biggest screw-up in military history . . . and not one person lost their job? My friend's dead because a lot of people failed to act . . . or were instructed not to act, and now my wife's dead because of what she knew. You just got done telling me that the people in power will do anything to stay in power."

"I never said anything about killing people."

"How many people died because we invaded Iraq? A million? Killing people is what happens when you invade a country under false pretenses. Your cousin died believing it's going to happen again, and all of a sudden I believe her."

"I think you should go. I'm serious, Ace. Please leave."

"Fine." He heads for the door. "By the way, you're wrong about one thing. Not everything in this life comes down to money. It took cancer for Kelli to figure that one out."

He leaves—Jennifer slamming the door behind him.

"The contractor is not required to perform perfectly to be entitled to reimbursement."

—Rhonda James,
spokeswoman for the U.S. Army Corps of Engineers,
referring to Halliburton receiving nearly all of its costs
on a disputed $2.41 billion no-bid contract to deliver
fuel and repair oil equipment in Iraq.

"President Bush has named Barbara Bodine the director of Central Iraq. Many in government are upset about the appointment because of her blocking of the USS Cole investigation, which some say could have uncovered the 9/11 plot. She failed to admit she was wrong or apologize."

—Washington Times,
April 10, 2003
(Bodine was later fired for doing a poor job.)

"If Democrats were capable of handling the war of terror, then I ought to be singing on American Idol."

—Vice President Dick Cheney,
March 24, 2006

"Then the fourth angel blew his trumpet, and one-third of the sun was struck, and one-third of the moon, and one-third of the stars, and they became dark. And one-third of the day was dark, and one-third of the night also."

Revelation 8:12

CHAPTER 15

THE RESIDENTIAL AREA OF THE MADISON SQUARE–OLIVER section of east-central Baltimore City is thirty-two blocks of brick row houses situated on narrow streets and alleyways that date back to the early nineteenth century. It is primarily an African-American neighborhood, interspersed with schools, firehouses, the occasional stone church, and a few small businesses. It is an area teetering between urban blight and reconstruction.

Jamal al-Yussuf exits the corner convenience store carrying two plastic bags of groceries. He can feel the eyes of the locals telling him he does not belong. A harsh winter wind cuts through his fleece jacket, reminding him of the same.

A siren, wailing in the distance, sends his thoughts returning to Baghdad.

◆ ◆ ◆

Like many of his countrymen, Jamal was born into hardship. Iraq's war with Iran had been long and violent, stealing a cousin and two uncles, wiping out an entire generation of people. The American threat in 1991 had brought the terror home, followed by a decade of living on bare essentials.

But nothing could prepare Jamal for the violence to come.

Jamal was nineteen when Bush the son began openly

challenging Saddam. Being a Shi'ite, Jamal had no interest in fighting for the regime, but the military officers to whom he was assigned threatened to shoot anyone who would not stand up to the foreign invaders. Given a uniform and rifle, he had been sent to Safwan Hill, a military observation post several kilometers across the border. There were few professional soldiers among their ranks, the heavily trained Sunni guardsmen kept closer to Baghdad.

When the first American planes appeared Jamal grew very nervous, but there were no bombs, only a flurry of white papers dropping from the sky. The leaflets warned the Iraqi Army not to fight, that Saddam would be defeated, that it was better just to surrender.

Jamal didn't want to fight, but no one trusted the Americans. Bush's father had put Saddam in power, and then later had led the fight to oust the dictator, but had stopped short. It was no secret the Americans were coming to dominate the region and take Iraq's oil. Most Iraqis hated Saddam, but they didn't want the Americans there either. They simply wanted to run their own country themselves, free of outside interference.

Jamal was on duty one night when a deafening barrage shook the outpost—the U.S. marines were opening fire with their 155mm howitzer guns. Jamal dropped his gun and fled. Moments later, the observation post exploded in a huge fireball.

The night erupted into a living hell as American helicopter gunships swept in low to fire their missiles. Bombs exploded for hours on end, fires blazing everywhere. Jamal ran through streets covered in charred corpses and smoldering burned-out trucks, the soldiers' bodies having literally melted in the blasts.

This was not a fight, this was a massacre, and Jamal wanted no part in it. Shedding the remains of his uniform, he stole a motorcycle and rode back to Baghdad as machine gun fire ripped holes in the air and columns of oily black smoke rose from annihilated buildings. Survivors staggered into the streets.

Those still bearing limbs waved bloodied white flags.

Jamal returned to his family's house by dawn, but the war had followed him home. An exploding bomb had collapsed the roof, the debris crushing and killing his father. Jamal's mother was screaming—his younger brother was badly wounded, his gut torn open. Jamal picked him up and raced through battle-torn streets to the hospital, his hand all that was keeping the boy's organs inside his body. His brother would die before Jamal could get him medical treatment.

The next few days were a blur, the American planes always coming, the bombs always exploding in a world gone mad. There was no electricity, no water, barely enough food, and chaos everywhere. When the bombing would move off, Jamal and his cousins would take to the streets, looting stores like starving rats.

By the end of the week, the occupiers had arrived.

Iraq is a sectarian nation composed of Arab Shi'ites, Sunni, and the Kurds, who are Sunni but from a different ethnic background. Under Saddam's reign the Sunni elite had run the country, even though the Shi'ites represented 60 percent of the population. The United States' invasion upended that arrangement, and the Shi'ites moved quickly to try to gain power with their numerical superiority.

Compounding the chaos were Shi'ite insurgents from Iran, who saw an opportunity to inject their own fundamentalist influence in neighboring Iraq. Stability was further disrupted by Abu Mousab al-Zarqawi, al-Qaeda's leader in Iraq, himself a Sunni extremist. Then there were the wild cards—radical clerics like Muqtada al-Sadr, who ruled his Mahdi army of Shi'ites with a penchant for violence. As the U.S. military fought to maintain order in this maelstrom of competing national and international factions, the Iraq populace struggled to survive.

As Shi'ites, Jamal and his family were members of Iraq's poor working class. Talk of an American invasion had actually been welcome—until the opening hours of the attack when U.S.

bombs had killed three of their household. Devastated by these losses, Jamal and his family tried to cope in a city overrun by vandals, their new existence void of security and the simplest of comforts.

Months after the invasion, Baghdad's residents were finally placed on energy schedules that provided a scant two hours a day of electricity. On hot days, temperatures could reach a broiling 120 degrees. For those with generators, finding fuel became an even bigger problem. In a country possessing the second-largest oil reserves in the Middle East, people were forced to wait in long gasoline lines just to fill up. Yet the American militia and the government's elite always seemed to have fuel. Occasionally, Jamal and his friends were able to purchase gasoline on the black market, paying upward of twelve hundred and fifty Iraqi dinars for a liter, twenty times the cost from the days of Saddam.

The Americans instituted a 6 p.m. curfew, along with a driving curfew. Lacking electricity, Jamal's mother resorted to cooking meals on the kerosene heater. Baths were taken cold, the al-Yussuf home having no power to warm the water. Dinners were consumed by candlelight, and afterward Jamal would read to his younger siblings and cousins and then arise at four thirty in the morning to join his friends in gas station fuel lines often a kilometer long. It was always extremely cold, and many times the station would run out of gasoline before their turn. On good days they would ride over in Jamal's cousin's car, but on most days they had to walk.

Waiting in line, Jamal would hear rumors about the insurgency. Some were convinced the entire fuel shortage had been created by the Americans to limit the number of vehicles on the roads. Others believed local candidates running for political office were simply positioning themselves for the upcoming elections so they could supply gasoline at a later date and look like heroes.

Always present was the lure of Iranian insurgents who were offering upward of $500 U.S. dollars a month for local

Shi'ites to target police cars and American tanks with their rocket-propelled grenades. Jamal was tempted, but wary of their offers.

As the months turned into years, life in Baghdad showed sporadic signs of improvement. Still, there always remained a palpable sense of anxiety in the air, residents knowing that their momentary semblance of normalcy could be shattered the next minute by an explosion.

One morning, Jamal's family were walking down a trash-strewn road when they came upon a metal object protruding in the dirt. Two American soldiers took notice and within minutes the area had been cordoned off. As a crowd gathered, a demolition crew arrived, referring to the object as an IED (Improvised Explosive Device). Soldiers moved civilians back several hundred yards, and then the loudest blast Jamal had ever heard rocked their Baghdad neighborhood. Windows shattered, children screamed. But as the dust settled, Jamal could see that everyone was all right. As they passed the smoldering crater in the road, Jamal nodded thanks to two of the soldiers.

The elections brought a new kind of apprehension. Candidate lists were composed either of people affiliated with the Americans, led by the despised Ahmad Chalabi, or included tribal sheikhs whose sudden appearance in Iraqi politics threatened to turn their secular nation into one bordering on religious fanaticism. Adding to the Iraqis' disbelief—each election list had to be confirmed by Ali al-Sistani, an Iranian-born ayatollah.

Being confined within a city under the constant siege of armed foreigners who do not speak your language creates an uneasy feeling among locals. Many Iraqis believed that if an explosion didn't wound or kill them, the Americans or Iraqi security forces would. And there was always the dreaded fear of being dragged off to Abu Ghraib as a suspected Jihadist. Despite reported conflicts, Sunnis and Shi'ites had coexisted peacefully in Iraq throughout their shared history, often intermarrying.

But when the government is unstable and security is lacking, racial and religious groups tend to gravitate toward one another for protection, even if it means congregating with the extreme elements of a sect.

The lack of security always seemed to keep life teetering between the promise of democracy and the expectancy of chaos. One could take pride in witnessing the construction of new shops and residential areas, and yet just as prominent were government structures which remained bombed-out hulks.

Jamal's psyche was teetering as well, his thoughts dominated by the fear of losing more family members. As time passed, his outlook brightened. His cousins took to the streets to sell their wares and began earning a decent living, and Jamal even managed to get a construction job laying pipe for a new sewage project. Fuel lines gradually shortened, electricity remained on longer . . . life seemed to actually be improving.

Then, in late February of 2006, foreign jihadis, dressed like Iraqi police commandos, set off explosives inside the Shi'ite mosque of al-Askari. The golden domed shrine was one of Shi'ite Islam's holiest sites, and its destruction set off a frenzy of reprisals against Sunni mosques. Amid the violence, a group of Baghdad youths fired upon a U.S. Bradley fighting vehicle, disabling it. As children got caught up in the cheers, an American helicopter swooped in on the scene and fired—a hail of bullets killing the celebrating youth.

Two of Jamal's nieces were among the dead, and Jamal had born witness to the carnage. It was a reality-shattering moment, even worse than when he had carried his dying brother in his arms. Saddam's reign was oppressive, but it had held a tide of anarchy in check. Now the dam was breaking, the blood of innocent children was on everyone's hands, and Jamal al-Yussuf could no longer stand to be in his own skin.

He had to lash out, he had to do something . . .

Two days later, he found himself in Tehran.

❖ ❖ ❖

Four blocks north, two blocks east, and he is back at the brownstone row house with the dented black aluminum door hood. Trudging up the snow-covered cement steps, he keys in.

Jamal enters the kitchen and leaves the groceries on the chipped linoleum counter where he finds the note.

Tonight: 7:30 p.m.
Dundalk Marine Terminal
2700 Broening Highway

"By 2012 we will need on the order of an additional 50 million barrels [of oil] a day."

—DICK CHENEY, V.P.
(50 million barrels is equivalent to more than six times the current daily rate of oil produced by Saudi Arabia in 2006.)

"I'll admit it was . . . mixed signals."

—PRESIDENT GEORGE W. BUSH
referring to his 2006 budget, which cut $28 million in funding for renewable fuel research . . . after his 2006 State of the Union address called for a greater emphasis on alternative energy resources. Conversely, a single tax break in the Interior Department's 2006 budget awarded oil companies an estimated $7 billion reduction in rent paid to drill on public lands.

"Change is the law of life. And those who look only to the past or present are certain to miss the future."

—PRESIDENT JOHN F. KENNEDY

CHAPTER 16

Ace pulls himself up the staircase, his left knee sore from an earlier workout, his lower back stiff with arthritis. From the landing he can hear the teen girls giggling in Leigh's room. He heads for Sam's room and pushes open the door.

His son is asleep in the lower bunk, the lights out, the TV on. Hockey gear, ripe with sweat from tonight's two-hour practice, is strewn across the floor.

Better clean this up before Kelli . . .

Ace catches himself. He does that a lot, his mind not fully conditioned to his new reality—single parent. There is a part of him that still expects his wife to emerge from their bedroom in her favorite sweat clothes, or hear her voice complaining that "no one picks up after themselves around here," or hear her laughter as she converses with friends on the phone.

He looks down at Sam and sees Kelli's features in the boy's face. While Leigh takes after Ace—quiet, her world more internalized—Sam is outgoing like his mother, her personality living on in his. Both comforted and saddened by the thought, Ace covers the child with a blanket, turns the television off, and slips out of the room.

Following the giggles, he heads down the hall to Leigh's bedroom. He knocks twice and then peeks in on his daughter and her two friends. They are huddled around her new computer, laughing as they instant message another group of teens.

"Leigh?"

"It's all right, Dad, we know who they are."

"They're boys from our class, Mr. Futrell," pipes in Leigh's best friend, Olivia.

"Fine. Just remember what we talked about." Ace closes the door, grateful for the distraction provided by his daughter's friends. Leigh is internalizing her sorrow about the loss of her mother, and time has not begun to heal the wound. It is the adolescent's friends who have become the stabilizing force in her life.

He heads for his office and turns on the television, catching the end of the Knicks–Cavaliers game.

The office phone rings. Ace checks the caller ID— Jeffrey Gordon. "Hey, man, what's up?"

"I have a craving for ice cream. You in?"

Ace sits up, his adrenaline pumping. "Yeah, sure."

"Pick you up in fifteen minutes."

Living under the Homeland Security microscope, his phones tapped, his e-mail monitored, Ace has been forced to resort to code words, phrases, and his own "sleight of hand" in order to conduct business out of the specter of the federal eye.

Grabbing an old ivory-colored windbreaker jacket from a hook on the back of his door, Ace leaves his office, heads down the hall, and pokes his head in Leigh's bedroom. "Honey, Sam's asleep. I'm just running out with Uncle Jeff for a few minutes."

"Dad, what are you wearing?"

"What? It's comfortable."

"It's white. You're not a hundred. Wear the leather coat Mom bought you."

"Sure. Be back soon. Keep an eye on things, okay?"

Ignoring his daughter's fashion tip, he heads downstairs, zips up the lined windbreaker, and waits outside for his friend to pick him up.

✦ ✦ ✦

Four hundred and twenty-two miles directly overhead, moving in a static orbit high above Long Island is the Onyx spy satellite. Operated by the National Reconnaissance Office (NRO), one of sixteen agencies that make up the United States Intelligence Community (USIC), the satellite is as large as a bus and weighs upward of fifteen tons. The spy satellite possesses a 150-foot solar panel wingspan and wire-mesh radar antenna, all housed around its synthetic aperture radar (SAR), a pulse system that creates its own illumination, allowing images to be processed in day or night and in the worst weather conditions. Part of a highly classified stealth satellite program known collectively as the Future Imagery Architecture (FIA), ONYX was severely criticized seven years ago by members of the Senate Select Committee on Intelligence for its extraordinary price tag ($40 billion) and its inability to penetrate underground bunkers where Iran and North Korea house their nuclear facilities. Despite these objections, the program was funded by both the House and Senate appropriations committees.

✦ ✦ ✦

From his Sat-Lab at NRO headquarters in Chantilly, Virginia, tech officer Garret Matsuura watches a real-time video image being recorded of his subject, one Ashley "Ace" Futrell. The fourth-generation Japanese-American NRO employee had been assigned to Ace just over a month ago and has been coordinating the subject's activities with his opposite number at Homeland Security. Matsuura has no idea why his deputy director is so interested in the former PetroConsultant field manager, or why this particular case has been classified as 'UMBRA,' an unusually high top-secret designation for domestic surveillance of an American citizen.

Matsuura finishes off the remains of his dinner as his subject climbs in the passenger side of a Chevy Astrovan leased to Mrs. Gay Gordon, wife of the New York attorney who is a close friend of the subject. The computer identifies the driver as Jeffrey Gordon, the man who had contacted Futrell by phone twenty minutes earlier.

Satellite reconnaissance stays with the vehicle as it pulls into the parking lot of an ice cream parlor. The two men remain in sight by the store's side window and proceed to place their orders.

Matsuura yawns. *Ordinary people living boring lives. Skip the hot fudge sundaes and hit a strip joint or something, fellas. You guys are killing me.*

The two men return to the van with their deserts. After several minutes, the driver pulls out of the lot and proceeds north for three blocks and then turns into a Mini-Mart. While Gordon pumps gas, Futrell walks around to the side of the building to use the restroom.

✦ ✦ ✦

Ace yanks open the rusty metal door and enters the men's bathroom.

The CIA director is already inside. David Schall locks the door behind him and then hands Ace a manila envelope.

There are three photos inside, all black and white, taken from a telescopic lens. With trembling hands, Ace stares hard at the face of his wife's assassin.

"His name is Scott Santa, spelled 'S-a-n-t-a' but pronounced 'Shanta.' It's Russian. Moved to the States as a teenager, served in the Coast Guard as a radioman/crypto/Morse code operator before being promoted as a Boarding Officer where he held Top Secret Clearance. Served on two ships, a 210-foot medium endurance cutter out of New Bedford and a 180-foot buoy tender out of Homer, Alaska. The tender was the first vessel on the scene during the *Exxon Valdez* spill."

"Get to the important stuff."

"Twelve years ago he left the Coast Guard and took a job with the Vinnell Corporation. He was assigned to train the

Saudi National Guard."

"Vinnell? Wait . . . Vinnell's a CIA front."

Schall nods, partly from embarrassment. "You can imagine how this has piqued my own curiosity, and before you say anything, no, the CIA did not have your wife sanctioned."

"But someone obviously did. Where is he now?"

"We're not sure, though we suspect he returned to Saudi Arabia . . . after New York. What we do know is that he left Vinnell eight months ago. He does a lot of business in Jiddah and Riyadh, small arms, that sort of thing."

Ace removes his windbreaker, unzipping a hidden compartment in the lining. He tucks the envelope into the space, zips it closed, and then slips the jacket back on. "I suspect our paths may cross while I'm in Saudi Arabia."

"That's your business; let's discuss mine."

Ace reaches into his front pants pocket and removes several typed pages of notes. He hands it to Schall, who quickly reads through it.

"You're kidding, right? This is nothing short of a major military operation."

"Yeah, well, they don't call it the Empty Quarter for nothing. The Rub al-Khali covers 250,000 square miles. Did you think we were just going to set off a few firecrackers and take a seismic reading? It's also nasty out there, a trackless expanse of shifting sand dunes that gets downright frigid at night, often near zero."

"Isn't there a way to refine the search?"

"I did refine it. We're focusing only on the southernmost Saudi corner, close to the Kidan, Shaybah, and Ramalah fields. We're also sneaking a peek at what's left in the Ghawar, the largest oil field in the world. From those geological readings I should be able to compile a fairly accurate assessment of what's really left in the Saudi reserves."

The CIA director pockets the information. "You realize it'll take me months to have everything in place."

"I figured mid-April." Ace unlocks the bathroom door to leave—

—Schall grabs his arm. "You're not quite getting it, are you fella? The President needs this information now, not in three months."

"Then tell the President to ask King Sultan. Meanwhile, get Homeland Security off my back like you promised, or there's no deal."

Twisting his arm free, Ace pushes open the door and exits into the night.

"The main obstacles to investigate Islamic terrorism were U.S. oil's corporate interests and the role played by Saudi Arabia in it. All the answers, everything needed to dismantle Osama bin Laden's organization can be found in Saudi Arabia."

—JOHN O'NEILL,
FBI counterterrorism expert
(O'Neill was killed in the World Trade
Center attacks on 9/11)

"The 9/11 investigations made light of the 'Bin Ladin Airlift' during the no-fly period and ignored the long-standing Bush family business ties to the Bin Ladin family fortune. (A company in which both families held interests, the Carlyle Group, was holding its annual meeting on September 11th, with George Bush Sr., James Baker, and two brothers of Osama Bin Ladin in attendance.)"

—911TRUTH.ORG

"Possession isn't nine-tenths of the law. It's nine-tenths of the problem."

—JOHN LENNON

CHAPTER 17

Situated on forty-five miles of waterfront on the Patapsco River Basin, the Port of Baltimore dates back to the early 1700s when it became the official port of entry for England's tobacco trade with the colonists. Baltimore Harbor is now one of the United States' largest deep-water ports, its ninety-four piers loading and discharging up to 175 ships a day.

Jamal al-Yussuf works perimeter security at the Dundalk terminal main gate, checking identification and work orders of truck drivers making pickups and deliveries. By day he divides his prayer time between several local mosques, asking Allah for strength. He has joined a neighborhood gym and works out three times a week. He has made a few friends, but as per his training at Qods, will not allow himself to become close. Within three months he expects to receive his first promotion, enabling him to check cargo containers from foreign ports.

Until then he bides his time, making sure he is always punctual and respectful to his supervisors.

It is nearly eight thirty in the morning when he clocks out from his night shift, a long weekend ahead. He arrives home by bus forty minutes later, the white van with the home improvement sign already parked outside his apartment building. Omar Kamel Radi is in the driver's seat, dressed in overalls and a flannel jacket.

"Good morning, dog."

"What did you call me?"

"Dog. Among men of color, it is a term of endearment."

"It is an insult coming from the mouth of a Sunni. Do not address me in this manner again."

Jamal climbs in the passenger side. He attempts to recline the seat all the way back to sleep, but the two large storage containers anchored directly behind him make it impossible. Curling up against the door, he pulls his wool cap down over his eyes. "Do not wake me, Sunni dog, or I will cut you so your own mother does not recognize you."

Omar rolls his eyes and starts the van. He has a long drive ahead.

✦ ✦ ✦

Omar Kamel Radi was born in Haditha, a farming town of ninety thousand, located on the Euphrates River, one hundred forty miles northwest of Baghdad. While the Iraqi capital and its fortified green zone had paved the way to a new constitution, Haditha had been transformed into an insurgent stronghold. Here, it was the mujahideen who decide who got paid, what clothing people were allowed to wear, what music they could listen to—and ultimately who lived and who died.

At dawn, the Iranian insurgents would carry out public executions at the town entrance on the Haqlania bridge, nicknamed "Agents' bridge," a mortuary reference relative to the number of American agents who were beheaded. Small crowds would gather, each decapitation or disembowelment filmed, the DVDs distributed later that day in the Souk market.

That Haditha, once part of the Sunni triangle, fell to Shi'ite insurgents became one of the biggest failings of the American invasion. It was here that the Tawhid al-Jihad, the Iraqi chapter of Al-Qaeda, remained virtually unchallenged, and to even be suspected of aiding the Americans was to invite death. Like most people living in Haditha, Omar and his family were Sunni, and while they did not oppose the insurgents, they did not support them either.

On November 19th in 2005, all that changed.

It was just after seven fifteen in the morning. Four Humvees carrying U.S. Marines of Kilo Company were patrolling the residential area when a bomb went off, killing twenty-year-old Lance Corporal Miguel Terrazas. Five suspects—occupants of a taxi—took off running.

Perhaps it was the stress of dealing with an impossible situation, the seemingly endless tours of duty, or the repeated exposure to so much senseless bloodshed, but the killing of Miguel Terrazas caused the moral compass of the American soldiers to snap. Opening fire, the Marines gunned down the suspects and then inexplicably went on a rampage, moving from house to house, breaking in and destroying furniture while lining up men, women, and children for execution. When the killing spree was over, twenty-four Iraqis lay dead, nineteen of whom had been woken from their sleep at gunpoint. Among the victims were several young children . . . and Omar's pregnant wife.

The truth about the massacre would be hidden from the American public for months, though it incited riots in Haditha that would spread throughout Iraq. Sadly, shockingly, as horrific as the attack had been, it was all-too-quickly swallowed by the continued daily bloodbath of suicide bombers, beheadings, kidnappings, and unchecked violence that was claiming five hundred Iraqis every week.

But for Omar Kamel Radi, his world had shattered beyond repair. Weeks of grieving eventually settled into a cold, hard rage.

One day he ran into an old friend from school. After feeling him out, the friend told him he had joined a political resistance group receiving funding from Iran and had been sent to recruit him. The old Omar would have rejected the offer outright, but now everything had changed.

Three months after his wife and unborn child were laid to rest, Omar Kamel Radi joined Qods, an Iranian-based terror camp.

JIDDAH, SAUDI ARABIA
JANUARY 11, 2012
12:37 PM LOCAL TIME

The port city of Jiddah is located along the Red Sea in western Saudi Arabia in an area known as the Hijaz. Over three centuries old, Jiddah is now a modern commercial center, complete with an international airport and major roadways connecting it with other Saudi cities.

Many of the Hijazi who inhabit Jiddah are Ashraf Muslim—direct descendants of Mohammed. Each year tens of thousands of these pilgrims travel Jiddah's roadways on their journey to the holy city of Mecca. Living off the sea, working as merchants and traders, theirs is a lifestyle more westernized than their Bedouin cousins.

The tribal communities known as the Bedouin are scattered farther east in the Najd, an arid region of Saudi Arabia that contains Riyadh, the Saudi capital. Continue south by southeast and you'll eventually arrive in an uninhabited desert known as Rub al Khali—the Empty Quarter—home to the world's largest oil field: the Ghawar.

✦ ✦ ✦

The Red Sea Palace is a seven-story hotel located in Jiddah's commercial district. Scott Santa exits the hotel elevator and strolls through the grand lobby out into the Arabian sun.

Following a concrete walkway, the tall Russian-born assassin makes his way to the pool, every so often glancing at the digital display on his Casio watch.

Twelve thirty-nine . . .

Santa locates an empty lounge chair in the shade, angling his view so he can watch two Asian women in matching blue and white striped bikinis sitting by the whirlpool. He orders a drink from a waiter and checks his watch again.

Twelve forty-two.

Santa removes the cell phone from his pants pocket and powers on the device.

Twelve forty-four.

The phone rings once. "Go."

The American voice in his earpiece is amazingly clear, considering it is coming from half a world away. "He's coming. First week in April."

"Why the delay?"

"Unavoidable."

"It reduces our timetable considerably."

"Deal with it."

Santa smiles at the Asian women. One giggles. The other smiles back.

"Okay, I'll be waiting."

SPRING
2012

"The waves of a new Islamic Revolution will soon spread to the entire world."

—IRANIAN PRESIDENT MAHMOUD AHMADINEJAD,
2006

"We shouldn't fear the future, because we intend to shape the future."

—PRESIDENT GEORGE W. BUSH,
2006

"I look forward to a great future for America—a future in which our country will match its military strength with our moral restraint, its wealth with our wisdom, its power with our purpose."

—PRESIDENT JOHN F. KENNEDY

"At the new (global) decline rate of 9 percent we would need roughly eight million barrels a day of new (oil) production to offset decline. As one of the world's leading energy experts—who happens to also be the world's largest energy investment banker, Matthew Simmons—has said repeatedly in countless lectures, 'We need to find three new Saudi Arabias just to offset decline.'"

—MICHAEL C. RUPPERT,
An American Energy Policy

CHAPTER 18

Iran Arms Radar-Dodging Missiles with Nuclear Warheads

Associated Press: April 19, 2012

TEHRAN—Iran's military announced today that it has loaded nine of its Fajr-3 radar-dodging missiles with nuclear warheads. Each ballistic missile is capable of traveling 1,200 miles while avoiding anti-missile missiles. General Hossein Salami, the Air Force chief of Iran's elite Revolutionary Guards, was quoted as saying, "At the first sign of attack, the great nation of Islam will strike back against its sworn enemies, flattening Zionist cities and hostile Western military bases in Iraq and Saudi Arabia. Allahu akbar, God is great."

Press Secretary Kris Hamilton, himself a former officer in the U.S. Navy, was firm in the Obama Administration's response. "The President takes these latest threats very seriously. While it has never been the United States' intention to attack Iran, we will never hesitate to come to the aid of our allies in the region, nor shall we rule out the use of tactical nuclear weapons if we perceive a serious threat."

The U.N. Security Council issued warnings that Iranian aggression in the region would not be tolerated but, again, stopped short of sanctions.

MONTAUK, NEW YORK
APRIL 21, 2012
9:37 AM EST

"DAD, THE AIRPORT LIMO'S HERE!"

"Coming!" Ace shoves two more T-shirts inside his already overstuffed suitcase and forcibly zippers it closed.

Leigh hands him his passport. "Don't lose this."

"I won't. I'll only be gone eight days. Aunt Jen'll be here."

"Just do what you have to do, we'll be fine."

"Dad, the limo's—"

"Sam, I'm coming!" Ace gives Leigh a hug and then heads downstairs where Jennifer and his son are waiting. He passes his suitcase to the limo driver. "I'll be right out."

Sam gives him a quick hug. "Where are you going again?"

"Abu Dhabi."

"That's not a real place."

"It's in the United Arab Emirates. Look it up."

"Bring me back something?"

"For another hug."

The boy complies and then heads upstairs to play video games, leaving Ace alone with Jennifer. "Don't worry," she says.

"I always do." He hugs her. "Jen, listen—"

"We're family, Ace. Now go, before you miss your plane."

He leans in and kisses her on the lips, and then pulls away, embarrassed. "I'm sorry . . . force of habit."

She sees the confusion in his eyes and smiles as he half-trips out the door, hustling to the awaiting car.

CARBONDALE, ILLINOIS

The tank sits in the concrete bunker, humming softly. Protruding from the left side of the rectangular iron casing are thirty uranium fuel rods, taken from Iran's nuclear reactor.

Professor Eric Bi, sealed within a somewhat antiquated

environmental suit, carefully draws a wet powdery coffee-colored paste from the out-take located atop the second centrifuge. Gently, he empties the cache of enriched uranium into the large lead container in the far corner of the basement.

So delicate. So powerful. A force of nature, harnessed by man . . .

The physics professor returns the cache to the outtake and then empties the smaller outtake along the bottom containing depleted uranium into the plastic container for disposal.

Thirty fuel rods, each yielding a gram of enriched U-238 a day. Three hours of work a day tops, multiplied over six months time . . .

Eric Bi returns to the lead containment cache and uses his tools to knead the enriched U-235 residue into a thick paste—a paste he will eventually heat and solidify.

One-hundred and eighty days, three hours a day . . . that's five-hundred-and-forty hours of work . . . divided by 2 million dollars . . . that comes out to 3,700 dollars an hour. Not bad for a part-time job.

The paste becomes moldable like wet clay. Bi works it into one of the two golf ball-sized enriched uranium deposits he has collected, losing himself in thought.

Got to start working on the triggering mechanism. They want it wired into a cell phone . . . easy enough. Solder the wires from the phone's capacitor to the blasting cap. That should be enough to set off the C-4.

Bi's eyes glisten as he sets to work on the second deposit.

Sixty-seven years since Nagasaki. The last bomb ended a world war, the next will begin one. What would Mother say if she were alive? Would she be proud of her only child or ashamed? But this isn't about the past or revenge, Mother. It's about the future. This is to stop western domination, the lives of a billion and a half people at stake . . .

No, Mother, what I do now isn't for Japan . . . this is for China!

❖ ❖ ❖

Across the street, FBI Agent Elliot Green reads the morning paper as he finishes off his coffee and buttered raisin toast. The image of Professor Bi's garage remains a constant on the flat screen television, just as it has every morning for the last fourteen weeks.

The ringing cell phone shatters his morning routine. "Yes?"

"Mr. Green, are you available for Mr. Jones?"

Elliott tosses the paper aside. "Yes, of course."

A moment later, Chuck Jones, director of the FBI's Springfield office, comes on the line. "Elliott, sorry we haven't relieved you yet, but we've had a shortage of manpower."

"I understand."

"More important, the computer produced a positive match on one of our friend's visitors. I'm sending the file over to you now. I'll also be pursuing the matter with our friends in D.C. Let me know if there's any further contact."

D.C.? Green's heart races as he grabs his laptop.

The "visitors" had been three employees of a Decatur home improvement company. The "supervisor" who had arrived on the night of January 3 had sent two workmen back to Bi's residence two weeks later in the same white van. They had unloaded sheets of drywall, along with a pair of heavy-looking wooden crates marked "Shelves." Everything had been hauled inside the garage, the professor making a great show to the taller man where he wanted the work to be done.

The work had taken two hours . . . all of it concealed behind the closed garage door. When the men left, they had taken with them the old dry wall garbage, including the pair of now-empty crates.

Elliott Green had waited until Professor Bi had left for the university the following morning before peering in the garage window. A quick visual check had verified the interior walls had indeed been replaced by fresh drywall, along with a row of new cabinets. At the time he'd assumed the heavy cartons had simply contained the latter.

Green had sent the images of all three men's faces to FBI–Springfield for identification. After all this time, he had actually forgotten about the inquiry.

He opens Chuck Jones's e-mail and downloads the encrypted file.

Nothing on the two workers, but the foreman's face appears on screen, along with his identification:

Subject name: Michael Tursi

Graduated with honors: Ballistic Missile Analyst Technician—Sheppard Air Force Base.

Graduated with honors: BMAT—Advanced Training—Vandenburg AF Base.

Assigned: Little Rock, AR.: Titan II nuclear missiles. Honorary Discharge: August 1986

Current Whereabouts: UMBRA.

Elliott Green stares at the information. That Michael Tursi had extensive training in nuclear missiles was not as bothersome as the UMBRA classification—Above Top-Secret.

Whatever Professor Bi was working on in that garage, he had the support of at least one member of a branch in the intelligence service.

UCLA MAIN CAMPUS
LOS ANGELES, CALIFORNIA

Omar Kamel Radi walks through the south part of the UCLA campus, heading for the Student Activities Center. Although he occasionally attends lectures, he is not a student. He thinks often about enrolling, especially when he watches the varsity soccer team practice. He imagines himself playing goalie, and he daydreams about walking arm in arm with one of those blond American cheerleaders.

Omar's studio apartment is located within walking distance of the campus. He is amazed that students can afford such rents—an amount that would surpass three months' salary in Iraq. He could never afford the apartment based on his current job—working evening maintenance at the U.S. Bank Tower in downtown Los Angeles. But money is no longer a concern.

Days are easy for Omar, the campus offering a sense of peace he could never experience back in Nasiriyah. It is the night that tears at his soul, the time when dreams return him crashing back to earth.

Walking east on Manning Avenue, he pauses at a small gym to watch an aerobics class in session. The instructor, an athletic blond in her mid-thirties, leads a group of nine women and two men through a series of punches and kicks.

The class ends a few minutes later.

Omar enters the gym. He waits until the students leave and then approaches the woman. "You are very good. How much please . . . if I wish to train with you?"

The aerobics instructor towels herself off, her eyes taking in the tall Middle Easterner. "Classes are twenty dollars a session, but you have to join the gym. Is it just for you, or your wife too?"

"My wife . . ." Omar's eyes tear up. "She died six years ago. An automobile accident."

"Oh, gosh . . . I'm so sorry." She holds out her hand. "Susan Campbell."

"Omar al-Saddat."

"Saddat? Are you related to that Egyptian fellow?"

"You have heard of my great-uncle, Anwar?"

"Wasn't he assassinated?"

"Yes."

"Wow. Well, listen, I hope you join. I teach class every morning from 7:30 to 10:30, Monday through Friday."

"Thank you, Susan Campbell. I will see you tomorrow."

She offers him a good-bye smile and then grabs her gym bag and heads out the door.

Omar's heart seems to swell as he watches her go. He will spend the next six hours in the mall, shopping for workout gear, dress clothes . . . and new sheets and a matching comforter for his bed.

"There is enough oil (in the Gulf of Mexico) to fuel almost 85 million cars for 30 years."

—BARNEY BISHOP,
Oil Lobbyist

"Their predictive track record has been awful. In the land of the blind, reliable OPEC data is either untrusted or non-existent. OPEC should provide field by field production and well-by-well data, budget details and third-party engineering reports. The entire world assumes Saudi Arabia can carry everyone's energy needs on its back cheaply. If this turns out not to work there is no Plan B. Global spare capacity is now all Saudi Arabia."

—MATTHEW R. SIMMONS,
President of Simmons and Company International,
a specialized energy investment banking firm,
2006

"Dr. Colin Campbell, a senior oil geologist, retired oil executive and one of the most respected experts on Peak Oil wrote to this author recently about his new book *The Atlas of Oil and Gas Depletion* that he had worked diligently on and in which he was able to produce a reliable statistical picture of depletion patterns around the globe. He said that when it came to reserve numbers as presented by companies and nations, 'the only numbers that are certain are the page numbers.'"

—MICHAEL C. RUPPERT,
An American Energy Policy

SAUDI ARABIA OIL FIELDS

CHAPTER 19

Abu Dhabi, UAE
Middle East
April 23, 2012
7:56 pm Local Time

The landmass of Saudi Arabia dominates the Arabian Peninsula, its western shores stretching to the banks of the Red Sea, its eastern coastline meeting the Persian Gulf. While Iraq and Jordan border the kingdom's northern region, three smaller Arab nations form a "boot" around the Saudi southern border, separating it from the Arabian Sea: Yemen, Oman, and the United Arab Emirates (UAE).

The United Arab Emirates is located at the mouth of the Persian Gulf, wedged along the instep of the Saudi "boot." Considered one of the most modernized and liberal of all the Arab nations, the UAE is made up of seven independent states: Abu Dhabi, Dubai, Ajman, Fujairah, Ras al Khaimah, Sharjah, and Umm al Qaiwain. A Supreme Council of Rulers, composed of the states' seven ruling emirs, appoints the UAE's prime minister and cabinet.

Abu Dhabi is the capital and largest of the seven emirates. Its land mass, which includes almost two hundred islands, constitutes nearly 80 percent of the UAE. Oil was discovered here in the 1950s, and by 1962, Abu Dhabi had become the first emirate to export its black gold. Yet unlike Saudi Arabia, Iraq, and Iran, Sheikh Zayed, president of the UAE, reinvested his nation's wealth back into the development of his nation, transforming Abu Dhabi and its sister city, Al Ain, into vibrant westernized areas featuring sleek skylines, parks and gardens, superb roadways, and a modern international airport. The emirate of Dubai, meanwhile, became an entertainment and resort mecca, attracting celebrities the world over.

✦ ✦ ✦

It is dusk when Ace Futrell, carrying his leather briefcase, exits the air-conditioned lobby of the Baynunah Hilton Tower in downtown Abu Dhabi. By the time he reaches the curb, the humidity has adhered his long-sleeved denim shirt to his back.

A line of taxis occupy the entranceway. Ace heads for the last vehicle, its driver leaning on the hood of the car, reading an Arab newspaper.

"I need a cab."

"There are others available. I am on break."

"I'm heading for the race track and I'm in a rush."

The cab driver never looks up. "I have a tip for the fourth race. You would place a bet?"

"Agreed." Ace climbs in back, the Arab spewing expletives at other drivers as he hurls the taxi into traffic.

✦ ✦ ✦

An hour later the skyline fades against a golden-pink horizon as they motor west along the Abu Dhabi-Tarif coastal highway. On Ace's right is the Persian Gulf, its shoreline containing shallow lagoons that drain with each tide. Patches of coral are covered with pockets of mangrove, along with vast black mats of algae that resemble oil pollution.

On Ace's left, running inland, are the salt flats known as the *sabkha*. Beyond the salt flats are vast expanses of sand dunes that roll like cream-colored waves toward the southeast, driven by the prevailing northwesterly winds.

The sun disappears, yielding to a velvety night sky and cooler temperatures. In the distance, Ace can see patches of glowing light marking oil refineries in Saudi Arabia. A road marker indicates the Saudi/Qatar border is 12 kilometers ahead. The highway is empty, other vehicles few and far between.

Without warning, the driver stops the taxi in the middle of the road and turns around in his seat to face his American passenger. "Get out."

"Here? In the middle of nowhere?"

The gun appears, its barrel pointed at Ace's face. A wave of fear sets his skin tingling. "Cross the *sabkha* to the dunes." The Arab motions with the gun. "Move!"

Ace grabs his briefcase and climbs out. The taxi immediately executes a tight U-turn across the tarmac and races away, leaving its passenger stranded in the middle of an empty desert highway.

A cold wind blows in from the sea, churning memories of Montauk's shoreline and his children. *Get moving, pal. You're about a million miles from home.*

Zipping his windbreaker, adjusting his collar, he jogs across the empty highway, crossing onto the salt flats.

It takes him fifteen minutes to reach the first set of dunes. He begins climbing, cursing aloud as the course sand fills his shoes, the effort of managing the shifting incline registering in his surgically repaired knee. Gusts of wind whip at his back and howl in his ears, the sand tearing into his exposed flesh like shards of glass.

Reaching the summit, he looks out onto a desert that stretches as far as the eye can see. In the distance is a small oasis of light—the Abqaiq oil refinery, the largest oil and gas stabilization plant in the world. Located twenty-five miles inland from the Persian Gulf, Abqaiq can processes up to 13 million barrels of crude oil a day. Ace knows current production runs at only half that figure, which represents 80 percent of Saudi Arabia's daily output, much of it coming from the super giant known as Ghawar.

Spanning a thousand square miles, the Ghawar oil field

contains thirty pumping stations powered by six generators that transport crude oil through a network of pipelines to Abqaiq's Gas Oil Separation Plants. These "GOSPs" take the sour oil (crude containing hydrogen sulfide and carbon dioxide) and filter out the impurities. Once "sweetened," the crude oil is pumped to Ras Tanura, the main refinery and oil port on the Persian Gulf where it is readied for export. Besides being a refinery, Abqaiq functions as a small town, its population of 2,200 consisting of Americans, Saudis, and other nationalities. The compound is surrounded by a heavily guarded security fence, and only upper-level Aramco personnel and their dependents are permitted to live on-site.

Ace tears his eyes away from Abqaiq, focusing on the vast expanse of dark desert that lies before him. Somewhere out there is Ghawar, its secrets holding the entire world hostage.

Movement below . . . catching his eye. Ace looks down.

Resting in a gully like a giant black scorpion is the AH64-D Longbow Apache helicopter.

"At the current rate of growth in demand, China alone will consume 100 percent of the world's currently available exports in 10 years."

—Anonymous Oil Official,
October 2005

"Do you know the difference between estimated reserves, probable reserves, proven reserves, and ultimately recoverable reserves? They are accounting creations cooked up to value share prices and borrow money or attract investors. They have nothing to do with how much oil is in the ground. I have seen these numbers vary by as much as 300 percent for one field or region. Certainly the American media do not explain this. The truth about reserve numbers is that they are ledger entries more than honest scientific analysis. Oil companies have to pay taxes on reserves so they use smaller numbers when reporting those. But when it comes to reporting to stockholders and the media they use larger numbers to encourage consumers, boost the markets and inflate their stock price."

—Michael C. Ruppert,
An American Energy Policy

"My father rode a camel, I drive a Rolls Royce, my son flies a jet airplane, and his son will ride a camel."

—Arabian Proverb

CHAPTER 20

DRIVEN BY ITS TWIN 1,700 HORSEPOWER TURBO shaft engines, the Apache helicopter soars twenty feet above an endless flow of dunes, its nose down, tail high, flying like a wasp. The pilot, Lieutenant Master D.L. Garst, is seated in the elevated rear cockpit, his "smart" helmet, adorned with night vision sensors, linked to a rotating turret situated on top of the Apache's nose. As Garst moves his head, so moves the turret, its optical sensors transmitting the live video feed to a monocular lens positioned in front of the pilot's right eye. With his left, the pilot scans his interior display panels, which include a radar signal processor linked to a dome located on the mast above the airship's main rotor blades. The radar dome transmits millimeter radio waves in all directions, identifying and targeting any objects within range of the Apache warship.

As the military chopper races inland, the dunes turn a deep red-brown and begin rising like mountains. The dark color is a result of the sand's thin gray coating of clay which oxidizes into a rusty ferric iron within the arid climate.

Adjusting his swash plate, the pilot alters the blade's tilt, increasing his altitude while continuing his "nap-of-the-earth" flying. "Sir, we're approaching the northeastern tip of the Empty

Quarter. How you doing up there?"

Ace Futrell is seated in the forward gunner's cockpit, surrounded by enough weaponry to wipe out a small city. "Good . . . fine. What happens if we run into the bad guys?"

"We avoid them."

"Because I could fire a hellfire missile."

"That won't be necessary, sir."

"What about the Bedouin? They've been known to fire on aircraft."

"Sir, we're armored with Kevlar, thick enough to stop a 12.7 mm round. Just relax and enjoy the ride."

In the distance, Ace can make out pinpoints of light—pumping stations situated around Ghawar—the largest reservoir of oil ever to have existed on the planet.

✦ ✦ ✦

The origins of hydrocarbons that make up oil and natural gas began as algae, organic matter, and plankton that formed in the warm seas of the Jurassic Period tens of millions of years ago. This biomass slowly accumulated in stagnant sink holes, eventually settling in sedimentary rock. Through chemical reactions the biomass was converted into kerogen, a solid, waxy, organic substance.

Temperatures underground increase by fourteen degrees Fahrenheit for every thousand feet of depth, and it was at six thousand to fifteen thousand feet (the oil window) where kerogen-containing sediments, cooked over millions of years, "cracked" into oil. Natural gas, requiring greater heat and pressure, are often found in the same source rock deposits, only at greater depths.

Reservoirs of oil were formed and remain under tremendous pressure until tapped. As a well-bore punctures the cache, the pressure allows the crude to flow upward through pipes to the surface, the lighter oil flowing easier than heavier viscous oil. As oil is depleted, the pressure naturally eases, requiring water or gas to be injected into a reservoir to maintain production. Natural surface seepages can also occur, the LaBrea tar pits in Los Angeles, aided by tectonic activity from the San Andreas fault, being a prime example.

Of all the oil fields in the world, only four have ever produced over one million barrels of crude a day: The second-largest reserve, the Burgan field in Kuwait (downgraded after its collapse in 2005), the third-largest reserve, the Cantrell field in Mexico (downgraded after its collapse in 2008), Da Qing in China, and the Ghawar in Saudi Arabia, which produces more than the other three giants *combined*. Discovered in 1948, this mega-super giant, the largest of six fields that account for almost all of Saudi Arabia's production, is located in the southeastern quadrant of the Saudi Kingdom near the Empty Quarter, close to the Persian Gulf. Shaped like an elongated woman's stocking running north-south, the reservoir is 174 miles long and 12 to 18 miles wide, its tank consisting of two subparallel structural crests, separated by an oval-shaped saddle. Although it is a single field, it is divided into six sections. From north to south they are Fazran, Ain Dar, Shedgum, Uthmaniyah, Haradh, and Hawiyah.

Ghawar's production, which began in 1951, actually peaked in 1981 at 5.7 million barrels per day, a production figure later restrained for "market reasons." Since then, Aramco, the Saudi national energy company, has been forced to inject more and more seawater into the reservoir to force out the crude. This "water cut" surpassed 55 percent in 2004, meaning more than half the outflow from the super giant is now saltwater. It is estimated that Ghawar, a field responsible for 60 percent of all the oil ever produced from Saudi Arabia, is being depleted at a rate of 8 percent every year.

❖ ❖ ❖

The Apache sets down behind a quadrant of rocky escarpments and sand dunes, the natural barrier serving as cover for two camouflage tents and an Armored Medical Treatment Vehicle. The AMTV is a heavy battalion truck designed to treat injured soldiers under the protection of armor. Painted on its desert-camouflage hull is a red cross. Anchored to its roof is a satellite dish.

Ace climbs out of the forward cockpit, assisted by a corpsman dressed in desert fatigues. "Sir, Major Watkin is waiting for you in Ops."

He is led inside the main tent, which houses two portable generators that feed power to a series of computer stations. An Army technician sits at one post, tracking the approach of a low Earth orbiting satellite, while another tech keeps a vigil on his radar screen. Dominating the Central Command is a computerized GPS map of Saudi Arabia, guarded by a tall man in a khaki uniform, sporting a grayish-brown crew cut.

Major Matthew "Swatkin" Watkin began his career in the U.S. Army in 1994 as a combat engineer. The Virginia native has spent the last two decades in Kuwait, Afghanistan, Iraq, and now Saudi Arabia, coordinating military ground operations for the Strategic Support Branch with Kellogg, Brown, & Root. The Commander's attention is focused on the map and the walkie-talkie pressed to his ear, his eyes diverted from the main board as Ace enters the command post.

"Stand by, he just arrived." The Major wipes his palm across his khakis, ignoring Ace's extended hand. "You Futrell?"

"Yes, sir."

"Watkin, Matthew J. Congratulations, Futrell, you now occupy the bird's nest position atop my personal hit list. Been my displeasure to have spent the last three months coordinating this little covert adventure of yours, most of the time operating on nothing but a swag."

"Swag?"

"Scientific Wild-Ass Guess. You have any idea what you've put me through? Got a hundred and fifty men spread out over three thousand miles of desert, two dozen predator drones, and a GPS satellite circling somewhere over this godforsaken desert, all so you can collect a bunch of data. Three locations, seven hundred explosives, all set to detonate at ten second intervals . . . do I look like the choreographer of the freakin' Arabian Olympics?"

Anger courses through the blood vessels in Ace's neck. "This isn't a piss-hole we're peeking under, Major. It's a reservoir, the biggest in the world. Cut the explosives in half and you need twice as many receivers. As for being on your hit list, the whole damn world's on my hit list right now, so if you've got a better *swag* on how to accomplish what I've been ordered to accomplish without starting a jihad, my ears are open, Watkin, Matthew J."

"Still a pistol." The Major's face breaks into a broad smile. "Don't remember me, do you? South Carolina game. I sacked your scrawny ass twice on that final drive before you scored the winning touchdown on a naked bootleg. Practically spiked the ball on my friggin' head, you little prick."

Ace grins. "Watkin . . . Swatkin Watkin. Weakside linebacker, number 57. Nastiest cheap-shot artist in the Southeastern Conference. That last sack was an illegal hit. You practically drove your helmet through my sternum and out my ass. Still hurts every night when I get up to pee."

"Long as I made an impression." Watkin extends his hand. "Welcome to the magic kingdom, Ace, land of the crazies. Run by a Mickey Mouse ruler and his royal family of rodents. We've got about twelve minutes before our satellite makes its pass, just enough time for you to explain this whole setup."

Watkin leads him to the computerized map of Saudi Arabia's southeastern region. The Ghawar oil field appears olive green against the black desert, its profile ringed by darkened red pinpoints of light. Two more immense olive-green areas—irregular and oval shaped—occupy the Empty Quarter farther to the south.

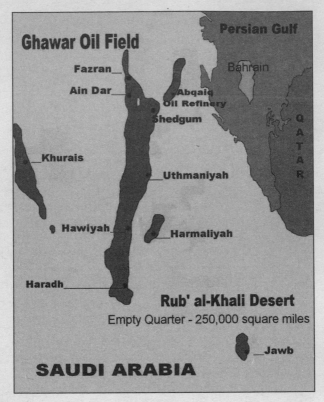

GHAWAR OIL FIELD

"Everything's in place as per your instructions. Two hundred explosives at the Empty Quarter sites, three hundred more at Ghawar. Deploying our teams over the Ghawar field figured to be the more difficult maneuver, but it turned out to be the easier of the two. We ended up disguising our guys in Aramco uniforms. Most of the blue collar stiffs working the fields are expatriates anyway, so who can tell. We stole two of their heavy utility trucks and dropped each man off at his post the moment it got dark. Had the charges planted and the geophones in place in under two hours. The Empty Quarter sites . . . they were the bitch."

"You sure the locations are set at the right intervals?"

"Every location was triangulated using predator drones, verified with GPS. Now maybe you'd like to explain how this whole damn thing's supposed to work."

"It's called reflection seismic survey. Essentially we're using the explosives to create a three-dimensional CAT scan of the geology using echolocation. The geophones measure the travel time of the seismic energy released by the surface detonations, sort of like tossing a stone into a pond and tracking the ripples. Seismic energy is refracted or bent in the subsurface and then reflected, the reflection producing a peek at the subsurface geology, creating a three-dimensional image. Data will be recorded by the seismographs, downloaded to the GPS satellite, and then downloaded to the main computer . . . which reminds me, I'd better set up my interface."

Opening his briefcase, Ace removes his laptop. He powers up the device and plugs his board into the larger main frame using several high-speed cables.

"And this'll tell us what's down there?"

"Assuming all goes well. My laptop will process the data, cross-checking the downloaded seismology with Ghawar's flow pressures, oil production, and oil and water ratios—information my team gathered over the last year. That should give us a pretty accurate assessment of how much crude Ghawar's got left in her tank. As for the Empty Quarter, there's either a vast reservoir of oil down there or there's not. Either way, we'll finally know."

The corpsman tracking the satellite calls out, "Two minutes."

"Acknowledged." Major Watkin pulls Ace aside. "The geophones are rigged to detonate two minutes after the array has been completed. We'll leave behind a bunch of outhouse-sized craters, not much else. However, it's possible our command center may experience some blowback."

"What kind of blowback?"

"From the good guys. Few years ago, when Al-Qaeda starting launching attacks on Aramco's refineries, the DoD decided to position a dozen of their SSB hit squads in the Saudi Eastern Province. Once the fireworks start, the Strategic Service boys'll be on Ghawar like bees to honey. Our presence can be justified, but the Saudis know who you are, and they'll quickly put two and two together. My orders are to wait until you download your report to our friends in Washington, and then get you the hell out of Dodge."

"Sixty seconds."

"What exactly are these SSB hit squads packing?"

"Enough SAMs to bring down an airfield of 747s. They'll shoot first with extreme prejudice and check the ID badges later."

"Nothing like working on the same team."

"Thirty seconds."

"Major, all units are clear of their targets and report a go."

"Tracking's a go."

"Radar's still clear."

"Ten seconds. Nine . . . eight . . . seven—"

Ace moves to the computerized board, his heart pounding.

"Five . . . four . . . three . . . two—"

On the "one" count, a pair of red lights flash "On" along the computer map's three target sites—another pair, one to the east and west of the first pair flash "On" ten seconds later . . . the sequence repeating itself every ten seconds, each successive explosion igniting a seismic wave front that causes the reflected subsections of the three subterranean geologies to glow green on the main computer board.

"Radar?"

"Still all clear, sir."

Raw data streams onto Ace's computer monitor, while

three separate images begin materializing like a slowly evolving MRI on the big screen. The detonations quickly complete the twelve-mile northern width of the Ghawar and then continue south along the reserve's eastern and western flanks.

"Major, I'm detecting activity at Abqaiq. Two helicopters, both Aramco."

Ace wipes a trickle of sweat from his forehead.

The Empty Quarter detonations continue circling their targets, the Ghawar field, with a third more explosives, materializing far slower on the computer board.

"Aramco choppers are circling Ghawar, Major. Forty miles out and closing."

Watkin winks at Ace. "No worries, just mouseketeers. It's the guys converging on us that we can't see that'll do the real harm."

"Two minutes."

The Empty Quarter targets complete their seismic surveys simultaneously, the Ghawar explosives still moving south. Ace quickly types in a series of commands, running an analysis of the raw data being downloaded from the main frame.

The last pair of Ghawar explosions converge upon one another, racing to meet at the southernmost tip of the field.

"Ace?"

"Got the first two images, Commander, just waiting for the big boy to finish."

"Saudi choppers closing fast. Fifteen miles."

The last set of explosives detonate along the Ghawar.

"Corpsman, is our pilot standing by?"

"Yes, sir."

"Mr. Futrell, the blitz is coming."

"Data's in. Computer's analyzing it now."

"Saudi choppers have closed to eight miles."

"Got it!" Ace hurriedly scans the completed report.

Ghawar Field

Tank: 277 billion barrels
Estimated recoverable: 75%
Total: 208 billion barrels

Empty Quarter

Tank: 310 billion barrels
Estimated recoverable: 65%
Total: 201 billion barrels

Combined proven reserves: 409 billion barrels

Major Watkin hovers over his shoulder. "So what's the verdict? Do I need to invest in a windmill or can I continue to enjoy my nudie channels on the satellite dish?"

Ace stares at the data, dumbfounded. "The Saudis . . . they weren't lying. The reserves are strong."

"Terrific," Watkin says, the sarcasm dripping. "Another twenty years in the desert, watching these towel heads spend our money. Download your report, and let's get you out of here, A-sap."

Ace encodes the information, transferring it to a secured file before he e-mails the report to David Schall at CIA headquarters. He unplugs his laptop, stows it in his briefcase, and then hustles after the Major to the awaiting Apache.

Watkin slaps him hard on the back as he climbs into the open forward cockpit. "Nice seein' you, fella. Remember me the next time you get up to pee."

Ace turns to respond, but the Major is gone.

Seconds later, the Apache lifts off, racing southeast over the desert dunes.

Ace lays his head back, closing his eyes. *After all these years, how could I have been so wrong? The Empty Quarter . . . sure, it was always an unknown variable, but the Ghawar? Saudi Aramco's been injecting five hundred million barrels of seawater into the carbonate reservoir since 2004 just to maintain enough pressure to draw out half that in crude. That seepage has to be flowing west, yet it's barely registering on the seismic survey. The original oil column was thirteen hundred feet thick. Six years ago it was less than one hundred fifty feet. How the hell can Ghawar possibly contain—*

Alarms sound within the cockpit, chasing Ace's thoughts as the Apache suddenly pulls into a steep vertical climb.

"Surface missile, fired at close range! Hang on!" The pilot activates the Longbow's jammer, its varying infrared frequencies confusing the inbound heat-seeking missile, buying them precious seconds as they soar east, then dive back to earth.

Ace grabs for the console, as two more missiles appear on his screen.

The Apache goes vertical, the sudden G-force pinning Ace to the back of his seat, the vomit rising as his stomach is squeezed in a vise, releasing him as they barrel roll and dive again, everything spinning in his vision, the dunes lunging at them like waves on an ocean, alarms rending the air, console lights flashing death knolls—

"No good! Gotta ditch! Hang on!"

Ace braces himself, his insides jumping as the Apache swoops low, skims a sand dune, and spins and smashes sideways into an immovable object, the impact jolting reality into blackness as the Kevlar canopy crumples around Ace Futrell like a crushed aluminum can.

"The Patriot Act was written before 9/11. Homeland Security and the 'Shadow Government' were developed long before 9/11, and plans for rounding up dissidents as a means for suppressing civil disturbance have been in the works for decades. 9/11 was used as the pretext to create a new, extra-constitutional executive authority to declare anyone an 'enemy combatant' (including American citizens), to detain persons indefinitely without habeas corpus, and to 'render' such persons to secret prisons where torture is practiced."

—911Truth.org

"Domestic policy can only defeat us; foreign policy can kill us."
—President John F. Kennedy

"Then I looked up. And I heard a single eagle crying loudly as it flew through the air, 'Terror, terror, terror to all who belong to this world because of what will happen when the last three angels blow their trumpets."

—Revelation 8:13

Book Excerpt:
To the Brink of Hell:
An Apology to the Survivors
by Kelli Doyle
White House National Security Staff Advisor
(2002-2008)

The next major terrorist attack will be a nuclear detonation. Can the death of millions of innocent people and another war in the Middle East be averted? To answer that, we have to understand how our role has changed in the politics of the Persian Gulf.

Prior to the Bush-Cheney-Rumsfeld doctrine, America's policy in the Middle East had always been about fostering stability to allow the oil to flow unimpeded. Stability required maintaining a balance of power between the Arabs and Muslims while the West and former USSR pulled at their proxies' strings. The Communists had Egypt and Syria, while Israel, being the lone democracy in the Middle East, became America's muscle in the region, Saudi Arabia our OPEC enforcer.

Storm clouds first appeared on the horizon when Egypt and Syria, equipped with Soviet weapons, attacked Israel on Yom Kippur in 1973. Initially caught off guard, the Israeli forces fought back, driving both invaders beyond the 1967 borders. It was a stunning defeat for the Arab world, and it placed the Saudis in a tenuous position among their Arab peers. To save face, the Saudis agreed to an American oil embargo.

Though the '73 oil crisis was artificially created, its effects staggered the U.S. economy. Long lines at the pumps forced Americans to consider alternative fuel sources. Solar panels were placed on the White House roof, gas mileage improvements enforced, conservation encouraged by the Carter Administration. It was a watershed event that could have changed the course of the world, but alas, the movement died when the Reagan-Bush Administration took office and the Saudis released a glut of cheap oil upon the market.

It was about this time that the CIA's puppet ruler in Iran — the Shah — was overthrown and replaced by Ayatollah Khomeini. Iran's Islamic fundamentalist movement changed the balance of power in the Middle East, encouraging other Muslim groups to revolt against the West . . . a direct threat to the Saudis.

Iran, with its theocratic Islamic fundamentalist regime, has always been enemies with Iraq, a secular Arab nation-state. Iraq was ruled by the heavy-handed Saddam Hussein and his pan-Arabist Ba'ath Party. Encouraged by the Carter Administration, backed by secret financial agreements with Saudi Arabia, Saddam launched an attack on Iran, a war which pitted the number two largest oil producer in the world against number three. As oil production declined, the House of Saud stepped up its own production, keeping prices down, prolonging the war.

Enter the Reagan-Bush Administration. The White House was torn over which side to support; Iran, whose fundamentalists had kidnapped American citizens, or Iraq and its brutal dictator. A prolonged war would serve to weaken both countries, but Reagan, who had publicly taken a stand to fight the Islamists, could not be perceived as aiding Iran. And so a covert strategy was devised, one that would allow the Reagan-Bush Administration to both funnel weapons to Iran through Israel and overthrow the left-wing government of Nicaragua by supporting the right wing rebels known as the Contras.

To fund this strategy, the CIA began trafficking drugs.

The U.S. House of Representatives had already voted 411 to 0 to prohibit any funding to the Contras, and the DoD and CIA were, by law, prevented from getting involved in any covert Contra operations. To circumvent this ban, the Reagan Administration used the National Security Council to "raise funding" for the Contras. These arrangements were overseen by Colonel Oliver North, who had established a working relationship with Manuel Noriega, Panama's drug baron. Over the next decade, the CIA transferred twenty-eight C-130 Hercules transport planes from the Department of Defense to the U.S. Forest Service, and from there into the hands of "private contractors" to move massive quantities of cocaine from Colombia, Mexico, Panama, and other drug-producing countries into the United States. Billions of dollars' worth of cocaine found its way into urban American neighborhoods like Los Angeles, the profits from which poured into the Contras . . . the victims of these immoral policies mostly Black and Hispanic kids.

Complicating this illegal arrangement was Saudi Arabia's King Fahd, who wanted to be paid off for his part of the equation with hundreds of Stinger missiles. Once more bypassing Congress, the Reagan Administration invoked "emergency measures" to settle its debt with the House of Saud.

To make these illegal payoffs, the CIA turned to the Bank of Credit and Commerce International (BCCI). Founded by a Pakistani banker, Agha Hasan Abedi, BCCI was an elaborate multinational corporation made up of an impenetrable series of holding companies, subsidiaries, banks-within-banks, and affiliates that managed to avoid audits and regulators. It had offices in more than fifty third-world countries, held key contracts with everyone from prime ministers and presidents to their wives and mistresses, and operated free of government control. In 1977, BCCI had begun exerting its influence in U.S. politics by purchasing the National Bank of Georgia from its CEO, Bert Lance, a close friend of President Carter. Using these fronts and shell corporations, BCCI covertly funneled money and arms. The bank had its own intelligence agency, and even its own paramilitary wing, known as the "Black Network." BCCI could provide the phony documents and letters of credit needed to purchase weapons, and it was through this international network of terror that the Reagan White House funded the Contras and escalated the Iran-Iraq war.

But there was one other covert operation that would make its impact felt in the Middle East and the rest of the world.

In July of 1979, President Carter had begun a secret campaign to provide military aid to the Mujahideen — Afghan rebels who were fighting the Soviets in Kabul. The Soviets took the bait and crossed the border into Afghanistan, and suddenly the USSR had its own Vietnam War. The House of Saud embraced this guerilla action, for it supported both Islam and the West against the atheist Soviets. When the Reagan Administration took office, the White House increased aid to these "freedom fighters," causing the Soviets to expend even more resources into the conflict.

The leader of these Afghan rebels? Osama bin Laden.

By 1983 things were not going well for Saddam and Iraq, whose army had resorted to using chemical weapons purchased from Western firms against the Iranians. To maintain balance and prolong the war, the Reagan Administration secretly began supplying Saddam's regime with helicopters, bombs, and howitzers — all in direct violation of the Arms Export Control Act. They also gave Saddam nuclear, biological, and chemical warfare suits, sophisticated guidance systems, and components for their chemical plants. As a result, by 1985 the war tilted back in favor of Iraq, causing the White House to respond in kind, this time selling more than five hundred TOW missiles to Iran.

In time the pendulum swung, and again the White House reacted.

In February 1986, the Reagan Administration arranged for the House of Saud to secretly sell Saddam British fighter planes, along with fifteen-hundred MK-84 bombs, each containing 2,000 pound payloads. But the Iraqis were ill-prepared to use their new gift, so the White House dispatched Vice President George H. W. Bush to the Middle East on a "mission of peace." The former CIA director (and future president) left for Jordan with two objectives: first, to supply military intelligence to Saddam so that he would use his air force to attack Iranian targets; second, to get Iran to release American hostages in exchange for 4,000 missiles. Within 48 hours he succeeded on both counts, and the Iran-Iraq war reached new levels of mass destruction.

Meanwhile, the House of Saud continued supporting the White House's covert operations. The Royal family, whose oil revenues had surpassed $115 billion a year, had on deposit more than $100 billion in U.S. financial institutions. America's banks were using this new-found leverage to lend money to other third-world banks. U.S. businesses soon took advantage, with companies such as AT & T, Proctor and Gamble, and IBM borrowing hundreds of millions of dollars. The arms trade between the two countries heated up, and the House of Saud purchased F-15s, Stinger Missiles, and C-130 transport planes — each sale yielding tens of millions in commissions to the Saudi Princes overseeing the deal. The rich were getting richer, the Iranians and Iraqis were dying, and the Saudi people were building up their hatred for the Royal family . . . and their American cosponsors.

In March of 1988, Saddam dropped chemical bombs from U.S. helicopters on the town of Halabja, an Iraqi town in Iranian-held territory, killing more than five thousand Kurds. It was not the first time chemical weapons had been used, but this time the Iranians rushed reporters to the scene and the world finally reacted. By August there was a cease-fire, and five months later, George H. Walker Bush took office.

The Iran-Iraq war had ended in a stalemate but had left Saddam with a million-man army, backed by sophisticated U.S. weaponry. President Bush continued using BCCI to fund the Iraqi dictator, allowing him to initiate chemical, biological, and nuclear weapons programs. In 1990, Saddam boasted that he had enough chemical weapons to consume half of Israel, a bold statement that finally forced Washington to react.

After providing Saddam with more than $5 billion in military aid, the puppet had become too powerful, and now it was necessary to bring him down a few pegs. Kuwait would be the bait.

Within days of the end of the Iran-Iraq war (and in direct violation of OPEC quotas), Kuwait began releasing more oil onto the market. The price of oil dropped, directly affecting Saddam, whose country desperately needed the money to rebuild its infrastructure. To compound matters, Kuwait was pumping the oil from the Rumailla fields, an area partially located in Iraq. Though it didn't need the money, Kuwait suddenly demanded Iraq repay an $8 billion loan Saddam had made during the war . . . all the while openly conducting ongoing meetings with the Iranian Foreign Minister and members of the CIA.

Saddam had no means to repay the loan, so Kuwait sold the debt notes at a huge discount, preventing Iraq from borrowing money on the international market. For the next sixteen months Iraqi officials attempted to settle their border dispute, but the Saudis refused to allow an Arab conference to convene. It was an old-fashioned squeeze play, forcing Saddam to turn to his one-time ally, the United States.

As Iraqi troops amassed along the Kuwaiti border, President Bush sent April Glaspie, the U.S. ambassador to Iraq, to meet with Saddam on July 25, 1990. Glaspie gave Saddam America's blessing to raise the price of oil, causing an inter-Arab dispute. When she asked the dictator what else he wanted, Saddam replied that his country's aim was to reclaim the Shatt al Arab, a region of Iraq that was now part of Kuwait. Glaspie's response was that, "The Kuwait issue is not associated with America." In essence, the United States had just given Saddam a green light to invade Kuwait.

On August 2, 1990, Iraq invaded Kuwait. In response, King Hussein of Jordan called a meeting of the Arab heads of state, hoping to avoid another war. Saddam agreed to withdraw 20,000 Iraqi troops from Kuwait, and it seemed a peaceful solution was at hand.

Enter U.S. Secretary of Defense Dick Cheney. On August 6, Cheney and his entourage met with King Fahd and his ministers, providing them with doctored satellite photos from the CIA and NSC that showed 200,000 Iraqi troops poised to attack Saudi Arabia! Cheney asked the King to allow American troops to land in his country. When Crown Prince Abdullah became alarmed, Cheney insisted Saudi Arabia was in danger of falling to an Iraqi-Yemeni-PLO invasion.

Four days later, the Arab heads of state, led by King Fahd and President Mubarrak of Egypt, mysteriously voted against mediating the Iraq-Kuwait dispute. The U.N. resolutions that followed only backed Saddam deeper into a corner.

Kuwait is far from a democracy. It is an oil-rich oligarchical Islamic regime run by the al-Sabah royal family, who, like the House of Saud, routinely violate the rights of its own citizens. Knowing that the American public would never support a U.S.-led invasion force to liberate another repressive regime, the Bush Administration turned to the public relations firm of Hill & Knowlton, who were paid $10.7 million by an organization calling itself "Citizens for a Free Kuwait." Craig Fuller, the firm's president and chief operating officer, had been George Bush's chief of staff when he was vice president to Ronald Reagan. After several failed attempts to register a blip with the American public, the firm fabricated a news story about how Iraqi soldiers had removed 312 babies from their incubators and left them to die on a hospital floor in Kuwait City. The firm even produced an eyewitness — a fifteen-year-old Kuwaiti girl, who testified at the October 10th Congressional Humans Rights Caucus. This "eyewitness" was actually the daughter of Saud al-Sabah, Kuwait's ambassador to the United States.

Over the next five weeks, President Bush used the baby incubator story no less than a half-dozen times in his speeches. The deceived American public changed its tune.

On January 16, 1991, President Bush unleashed

Operation Desert Storm, a war designed to "liberate" the monarchy of Kuwait.

Saddam surrendered on February 27. George Bush got what he wanted — Iraq had been removed as a threat to the House of Saud. But the President had stopped short of invading Iraq, a move that irked many Neoconservative members of his party, among them Dick Cheney, Donald Rumsfeld, and Paul Wolfowitz.

Meanwhile, Osama bin Laden had used America's annual $700 million stipend in military assistance to build a vast training facility in eastern Afghanistan. Bin Laden's army had swelled to twenty-five thousand strong, representing Islamic extremists from more than a dozen countries. Weakening Iraq, the most powerful secular nation in the region, created a vacuum that was quickly filled by bin Laden's Islamic fundamentalists, who opposed a Western presence in Saudi Arabia.

The United States' own foreign policy had indirectly given birth to Al-Qaeda — the base.

"Royal Dutch Shell shocked investors when it unexpectedly announced that it was slashing its estimate of proven reserves by 20 percent."

—*Washington Monthly*,
June 2005

"According to a restricted report issued by the authoritative industry newsletter *Petroleum Intelligence Weekly* (*PIW*), internal Kuwaiti records reveal that the nation's oil reserves are far below the officially stated amount of 99 billion barrels. The *PIW* report claims that Kuwait's remaining proven and nonproven oil reserves total about 48 billion barrels, or 51 billion fewer barrels than previously advertised. Another way of stating the matter is that the amount of estimated world oil reserves just fell by 5 percent . . . the equivalent of almost 20 months worth of total cumulative worldwide oil production and consumption, based on the current world oil use of about 84 million barrels per day."

— BYRON W. KING,
Energy Bulletin,
January 25, 2006

"Depletion of existing oil reserves is both pronounced and accelerating. In 2005 it was reported that 33 of the largest 48 oil producing countries had entered decline. Data compiled in 2008 showed that of the 50 largest oil-producing countries in the world, 42 had passed their peak and are in decline. In other words, nine more major oil producing countries passed their production peaks in the last three years alone. Indonesia, a founding member of OPEC, is now importing oil to meet its domestic needs."

—MICHAEL C. RUPPERT,
An American Energy Policy

CHAPTER 21

Paralysis. The kind that prevents movement yet still allows pain to seep into the nerves.

Blindness. A heavy darkness . . . filtered by shards of lunar light.

Silence. Unnatural . . . overpowered by the noise in his head, a terminal buzz, yielding to . . . blackness.

AFTERNOON

ACE BLINKS HIS EYES OPEN and gingerly moves his arms. He is in the Georgia locker room, lying on the training table, the team physician checking his vital signs, his head coach hovering close by.

"You all right, son? That was some hit you took."

"Got his bell rung good, coach. He's done."

"No. . . I'm okay, coach, I can play! Put me back in!"

"Put you back in? Son, haven't you caused enough damage?" The two men laugh, the sound echoing in his brain.

✦ ✦ ✦

"Huh!" Ace opens his eyes. He is in a subterranean room, lying on a bare mattress. Shards of sunlight filter through floorboards above his head, providing a dim, gray light. Relief floods into his psyche as he moves his arms—until he realizes they are shackled to the concrete floor.

His head has been bandaged. A dull ache greets him as he sits up, his eyes focusing on his Arab guard, seated in a folding chair. A machine gun rests across his lap, a cooler by his feet. The man offers a blank stare. Reaching behind him, he knocks on the closed door at his back.

Moments later, another Arab enters the room, dressed in a traditional white silk *thobe*. He is short and slender, with dark black hair and eyes, and an olive complexion.

"How are you feeling?" The English is smooth and eloquent, attesting to an American education.

"Who are you?"

Reaching into a cooler, the man removes a bottled water and tosses it to Ace. "You have a concussion and some minor bruises. The pilot broke his arm and was treated for secondary burns. He is being kept sedated in another room."

"What do you want with me?"

"That, Mr. Ace Futrell, really depends upon you." The Arab smiles at Ace's surprise. "Yes, I know who you are. I also know about your wife and children, your home in Long Island, your glory days in college, and your recent trouble at PetroConsultants. Your first reaction will be to assume I am with an intelligence agency, and I was, but my information comes to me firsthand, from a very trusted friend."

The Arab crosses the room and removes a blanket from a piece of furniture that turns out to be a combination television and DVD player. He presses play. An image moves into focus.

It's his wife! From Kelli's appearance, the video must have been taken within the last eighteen months, the chemo having just started to rob her of her hair and twenty pounds of muscle. She is seated in a living room—*their* living room—and the Arab is seated next to her, dressed in a sweater and jeans.

"Hi, hon. If you're watching this, well then there's a good chance that . . . that something bad happened to me and I'm no longer around. Before you jump to any wild conclusions or lose that famous temper of yours, let me introduce you to a friend of mine . . . a trusted friend. This is Ramzi Iskander Karim. Ramzi's family comes from Egypt, though he was educated in the States. Ramzi and I first met at Camp Peary. He joined the Company about the same time I did. That's right, he's CIA . . . sorry, ex-CIA. In a few moments Ramzi's going to share some very important information with you. I need you to trust him, Ace."

Kelli nods to Ramzi on the video, who takes his cue and leaves the room, offering her privacy.

The live Ramzi occupies himself in another section of the basement.

Kelli stares at Ace from the television screen. "This is hard. You live your life, you wish you could turn back the clock, undo certain things . . . make amends. I'm sorry, Ace. I'm sorry for not being there for you our senior year at Georgia when you were going through hell, I'm sorry for not being there now, for leaving you to raise Leigh and Sammy alone. Most of all, hon, I'm sorry I have to involve you in all this. If . . . if you had been in another profession, a football coach, a teacher . . . but the simple fact is, your business deals directly with everything that's been going on, and in order to stop something terrible from happening, I need your help. There are only a few people I trust these days, Ace, and Ramzi is one of them. Please listen to what he has to say and help him, if not for me, then for the kids."

She pauses, turning from the camera to wipe away tears.

Ace's eyes well up too.

"I've been involved in some bad things. The world can be an ugly place . . . sometimes you get swept up in that ugliness. You don't know how often I wish we had married right out of college. Things would have been so different. There's so much I regret, Ace, things that have festered in my gut the last six years . . . it's no wonder the cancer started there."

She chokes out a laugh. "You're probably saying to yourself, who is this woman and what did she do with my wife? Cancer and Kabbalah have given me a new perspective on life. I know you like to tease me about my Kabbalah classes, but it's what finally made me take a hard look at myself. Kaballah says it's our negative energy that separates us from God. What you went through at Georgia, the stress, the fear . . . it probably felt like you were in prison. I know my own choices imprisoned me. I believe now that each one of us are destined to accomplish great things . . . things that positively affect others. That's the key to escaping our prisons, Ace, to do godly things. Everything we say and do matters, every positive and negative action we do affects others.

"I've been involved in some bad things, and now I need to make them right. Ace, the world's moving down a very dangerous path. On one side you've got a growing sect of radical Islamists competing for the attention of the Arab world. On the other side you've got a group of radical hawks—capitalists who believe the only way to bring about change is through the barrel of a gun. Ego, greed, and self-righteousness . . . each side pushing the other, each side pointing the finger as they inch the world toward Armageddon. I know that sounds melodramatic, but I was a part of it, and now I want to do everything I can to change it."

She moves closer to the camera.

"Something bad's going to happen, sweetheart, unless we expose it and cripple the machine that feeds it. I've been actively working on solutions. Ramzi's a part of that. He needs your help. I told him you could do it. I told him how strong you are. You are strong, Ace, never doubt that. Things are going to get bad, but under every rock of discomfort is concealed an opportunity. All of us are God's vessels, Ace, we can do godly things. It's the fight of your life, but I'll be with you every moment. I love you, Ace."

The image goes blank.

Ace stares at the dark screen, emotionally drained. He wipes away tears, his insides trembling.

Ramzi returns and powers off the television. "She left her memoirs on a CD-ROM. You'll need to read it here. It's far too dangerous to keep with you while you travel. I'm sorry. I know this must be hard for you."

"Hard?" The words catch on the lump in his throat. "Why was Kelli killed? Who gave the orders? What the hell were you two working on?"

"In short, the prevention of World War III." Ramzi rattles a command in Arabic to the guard. The man unlocks Ace's shackles and then leaves the room.

"Ace, have you ever heard the term, '*shihadah*?'"

"No."

"Shihadah means God's blessing to those who die in the lesser jihad. The word jihad doesn't mean war but translates as 'striving' or 'struggle.' The greater jihad is the inner struggle to be a better person. The lesser jihad is defense of the community, whether by words or deeds. Some Muslims are so desperate to defend their community that they are willing to use terrorist tactics that are strictly forbidden by Islamic doctrine.

"When I studied in the States, I remember reading an account of the Hatfields and McCoys, two families whose rivalry turned into a violent feud. In many ways this rivalry reminded me of the Sunni-Shi'ite conflict—two sides sharing so much in common, at war not as much because of internal strife as external, exacerbated by a history of extremist violence. The Middle East remains divided by this strife, and the rest of the world chooses sides based on which nation supplies them with the most crude oil."

"And where do you stand?"

"I stand with the innocent majority, who seek merely to live in peace." Ramzi opens a bottle of water. Drains half of it. "My family was originally from Aswan, Egypt's most beautiful city, a small community set upon the southern banks of the Nile. My father owned a floating restaurant. Each day tourists in sailboats would arrive to dine on fresh fish and listen to Nubian music as the sun set. When I was nine, a group of radicals set fire to our barge, destroying everything we owned. One of my sisters was badly burned. My father's brother was a physician living in Mecca, and he invited us to move in with him while he treated my sister. And so we left Egypt and took up residence in the Kingdom ruled by Al Saud.

"My father was a devout Muslim. His family was part of the Al Hashem tribe, direct descendants of the Prophet Mohammed. These tribes are known collectively as *Ashraf*, individuals like my father are called *Shareef*. My father was a powerful businessman, but he was ill-prepared for what awaited us in Saudi Arabia.

"Despite western opinion, most Muslims are peaceful. Like any nation or religion, it is the radical elements that foster bad reputations. Throughout their history, the Wahhabi element of Islam has fiercely opposed anything they viewed as *bida*, a derogatory term that refers to any behavior that deviates from the fundamental teachings of the Koran. This puritanical view condemns anything considered western, including television, telephones, music, and movies. Yet it was this Neoconservative religious sect that was instrumental in creating the Saudi monarchy. It is their strong-arm tactics that keep Saudi citizens under control.

"What exists today in Saudi Arabia is an Arab identity held hostage by the hypocrisies of the Royals, who maintain dominance through the fanatical brutality of their Wahhabi clerics, who themselves have looked the other way while the Royal Family has trampled upon the Koran behind their palace walls, drinking, gambling, and womanizing. Control remains the key to power for extremists. This is why, instead of teaching the word of God, religious schools and mosques now teach hatred. In Palestine and Lebanon, in Iran and Iraq, the Jew is the devil personified, the United States his minion. Arab children are brainwashed from an early age. Hatred is the government's necessary ingredient to allow these oppressive regimes to maintain power within a closed society. This psychosis of violence is a distraction meant to temper the people's desire for freedom. ·

"After my sister recovered, my father, desiring to be close to the water, opened a restaurant in Jiddah. One day a Saudi prince visited our establishment, a man who had earned a reputation for deflowering virgins. The prince took notice of my twelve-year-old sister and sent one of his entourage to negotiate a price with my father. My father spit on the messenger and ordered the others to leave. A few hours later, our restaurant was visited by the '*mutawa*,' the Wahhabi religious police. My father was beaten, arrested, and taken to prison. To bring him home, my sister offered herself to the prince, who kept her in his palace for six months. My father was eventually released, having been abused by the Saudi torturer, Ali Shams, for nearly a year. He would live out his days bound to a wheelchair.

"When I was seventeen I joined the *Rai Al Nas*, an underground press that spoke out against the atrocities of the House of Saud. To be caught working for the paper meant certain death. Fearing his only son's beheading, my father arranged for my education in the States."

"So you joined the CIA to fight the Saudis?"

"I joined because I believed I could make a difference. I was wrong. The CIA is merely another tool of the West that enables the Royal family to maintain control as stewards of cheap oil. That stewardship will soon come to an end, bringing the world to a crossroads. Without oil the House of Saud will collapse, the question is—who will fill the void? The rise of radical Islam terrifies the Royals, but rather than stand up to its threat they have chosen to bribe its leaders, enabling them with money and weapons. Radical ideologies spread because the middle class has lost the will to quash them, or because the people are forced to choose between the lesser of two evils. To the common Arab, American fascism is far worse than Islamic fascism. Everyone knows the western invaders care only about stealing our oil. By invading Iraq, the United States chased the very people who would have stood up to Islamic fascism into their camp. And so the cancer spreads, from Iraq into Egypt and Jordan, from Saudi Arabia into Syria and Lebanon.

"Iran is the wolf at the door. While they would never challenge the United States or Israel in a conventional war, a new strategy appeared with the success of Al-Qaeda and the *intifada*. The strength of the Americans and the Israelis is also their weakness—they cherish life, while the terrorists do not. Hezbollah launches attacks while hidden among women and children, taunting the Israelis to attack so they may exploit the bloodshed to gain sympathy to their cause—which is not peace but the violent eradication of every Jew and every non-Muslim in the Middle East. Al-Qaeda plots their next acts of terror, sending a message to the world that Islam can fell a superpower with a small band of warriors using cardboard cutters and common household items.

"All that is about to change. Iran's decision to enrich its uranium opens a Pandora's box. There is a growing fear among intelligence agencies in Washington that Islamic extremists, supplied by Iran, will use suitcase bombs to unleash a nuclear holocaust in U.S. cities. Your wife was involved in a radical contingency plan—a preemptive nuclear strike whereby an American city would be wiped out by a terrorist cell, their success an excuse to crush the Islamic movement in Iran. Kelli helped set the contingency plan in motion and then she got sick. When Obama was elected and the Democrats took over both Houses, the Neoconservatives ousted from power saw the coming event as a means of retaking the White House."

"That's why Cheney has been openly predicting another attack . . . even going so far to state that it will be a nuclear weapon. And it was Obama's refusal to open up 'old wounds' by commissioning a new 9/11 investigation that emboldened his enemies. By allowing the guilty a free rein, Obama, Pelosi, Reid, and the Democrats have inadvertently given a green light to our worst nightmare."

"Now it is up to us to quell the storm."

Ace watches as Ramzi rolls back a Persian rug. Using two

razor-thin metal hinges, he works loose a slab of concrete from the floor and lifts it up, revealing a high-tech safe constructed within the foundation. Rotating the safe's retinal eye scan into place, he enters a combination and then presses his forehead to the device, submitting to the blue laser scan.

The safe verifies his identification and clicks open.

"We have two terror fronts that must be derailed in order to avert a nuclear holocaust. My role was to offer the Arab people a third choice—a true democracy, one that comes from within, in essence, a revolution. The *Ashraf* movement is that revolution— a true movement of the middle class and the poor, but it can only succeed by gaining control of the Royals' true weapons of power—Saudi oil and the fortunes they stole from the Saudi people."

The former CIA operative opens the lid of the safe and removes what appears to be a black CD-ROM case. "Are you familiar with a program called Promis?"

"No."

"Promis is the eye that sees everything. Its creator was an American named Bill Hamilton. Many years ago, Hamilton developed a computerized dictionary for the NSA that translated Vietnamese into English. Later, he decided to create a new program—something different, something that could track the movements of people around the world. He would fulfill this dream when he left the NSA and bought out a company called Inslaw, a nonprofit entity that developed software designed to cross-reference legal cases and court actions with potential witnesses and their families. By 1981, Hamilton had enhanced the system so that it could tap into virtually any computer network, searching utilities, telephone companies, airlines, and other services to track the location of a target by cross-referencing activities of a subject, their friends, relatives, and associates. Hamilton attempted to lease the program—Promis—to the Justice Department, but without much success.

"What Hamilton never knew was that the Justice

Department had secretly made copies of Promis and had distributed them to the U.S. Intelligence community. The CIA saw Promis as a means of tracking Mafia money laundering schemes, as well as using it as a tool to spy on Colombian drug barons. A copy of the program eventually ended up in the hands of Earl Brian, a man who had worked under Reagan when he was governor of California. Brian had contacts with Israel's Mossad. At the time Mossad was deeply embroiled over the first Palestinian *Intifada*. Brian was introduced to Rafi Eitan, an Israeli businessman who eventually took the Promis design to a far greater level. The new Promis became a disc that could be used in a personal computer, correlating data at far greater speeds. More ingenious, Eitan had a colleague equip Promis with a secret trapdoor—a built in chip that, undetected by the user, would allow Israeli Intelligence to monitor all on-going activities of its user host.

"Earl Brian's company, Hadron, was set up to sell the security program to foreign governments. Jordan was first to take the bait. Once installed at the military headquarters in Amman, Promis wired itself into a French-manufactured tracking system that the Jordanians were using to follow the activities of the PLO. Thanks to Promis, the Israelis could now track the PLO's leaders, which helped Mossad combat the *Intifada*.

"The potential usages for the Promis spy network were enormous, but Eitan and Brian's resources were limited. Enter Robert Maxwell, CEO of Degem Computers in Tel Aviv. Using the company's offices in South America, Maxwell began selling Promis to foreign governments and heads of state, including PLO Chairman Yasser Arafat. Almost overnight, Promis gave the Israeli and American Intelligence communities access to everything from Soviet-bloc military intelligence to the movements of thousands of terror suspects . . . to monetary activities involving banking and financial institutions across the world."

"What about bin Laden?"

"Ah, yes . . . bin Laden. An FBI agent, Robert Hanssen, had used his Russian contacts to sell Al-Qaeda the Promis program. Promis gave us access to bin Laden's movements and activities, but Promis also gave Al-Qaeda the ability to monitor our own investigations, as well as a financial tool to access its own money. Hanssen was later convicted as a spy, but the damage was already done."

"Then 9/11 . . . the White House must have known about the plot."

"Of course they knew. But the lies go far beyond the events of that day. Promis gave its owners access to all computer programs, as well as the means to alter data. All computers, Ace."

The blood drains from Ace's face. "The Presidential elections . . ."

Ramzi nods. "Voting machines tallied and controlled by computers, manufactured by companies that exclusively endorsed GOP candidates. Florida in 2000, Ohio in 2004. Ever wonder why these same swing states still refuse to mandate paper ballot receipts, despite the repeated controversies? The powers-that-be, in an attempt to maintain an edge, consistently block any and all election check-and-balances, their decisions backed by judges appointed by the same regime."

Ace lies down on the mattress, feeling dizzy. "If Promis gave Kelli access to everything . . . would that include Saudi Aramco's data?"

"Not just Aramco, but nearly every oil company and third-world national energy conglomerate, revealing the planet's true remaining oil reserves. Cheney knew back in 2000. It's the reason he refused to release details of his energy meetings. Of course, the CIA already knew Iraqi reserves had peaked long ago, Iranian reserves as well. Iran's posturing about going nuclear could have been derailed long ago. Initially it was a reaction to the United States covertly building military bases in Iraq. It's a prime example how one extremist reaction births an equal but opposite reaction."

Ace sits up. "When you found me in the desert, I had just completed a seismic survey. My data indicated Ghawar still has strong oil reserves, the untapped Empty Quarter too."

"Whose data? Who performed the tests?"

"The military."

"Which branch?"

"Strategic Support Branch."

"SSB is an organization established by Donald Rumsfeld and used by the Neocons to keep things from the prying eyes and ears of the other intelligence agencies. Tell me, how were the surveys conducted?"

"It was a massive military operation, involving hundreds of men, seven hundred controlled explosions. I don't see how—"

"You saw these men? You witnessed the explosions?"

Ace feels queasy. "No. All I saw were lights on a damn computer board. . . . Bastards, they set me up! There never were any explosions, were there? Just a bunch of rigged data they wanted me to send to D.C."

"And having sent it, you became expendable. Fortunately, the Bedouin are not as competent with their SAMs as their American counterparts. Who sent you to Arabia to gather data?"

"Schall, the CIA director. The President wants to initiate a new alternative energy policy, something with teeth. First he needed accurate data on the Saudi reserves."

"Instead, the puppet-masters led you to file a report that indicates the crude is plentiful. Who would benefit from such a fabrication?"

"The usual suspects. Oil companies. The Saudi Royals."

"Yes, but you are missing the true devil. There's another faction pulling the strings, the same group responsible for manipulating the events of September 11th."

"The Neocons?"

"Backed by the bankers. Once Iran falls under U.S.

domination, the remaining nations that harbor Islamic radicals will be next in line, beginning with the country that controls the only significant oil reserves left in the world—"

"Saudi Arabia." Ace shakes his head, overwhelmed by everything he is hearing. "Large Saudi reserves would justify funding an invasion . . . assuming the Royals were linked to this contingency plan."

Ramzi nods. "The threat from Iran has forced the House of Saud to trust the Neocons. Kelli believed the preemptive strike would occur shortly before the next presidential election, allowing the Republicans to once again use fear as their trump card."

"Where will the bombs go off? What are the target cities?"

"We don't know. Nor do we know how the weapons will be smuggled into the country."

"Why must they be smuggled at all? If these Neocons have access to—"

"The Neoconservatives are not the ones who will be pulling the trigger. Two Islamic radicals have been chosen as mules—puppets whose strings will lead back to Iran. The nuclear residue will be the key evidence—enriched uranium residue can be traced back to its original source. In this case, spent fuel rods used by Iran's nuclear reactor. Kelli was kept out of the loop as to how this might be accomplished."

"Okay, so we go to the FBI, have them seal the ports."

"There are 317 ports of entry into the United States. Homeland Security inspects a mere 7 percent of the cargo, and those are only the official ports. Yachts, cruise ships, private jets . . . even with Promis, it's impossible to pinpoint where and how the nukes will enter the country."

Ace feels the blood vessels in his left arm constricting from stress. "Okay, so what's the plan? While you're out trying to instigate a revolution, how do we stop these maniacs from taking out an American city?"

"Two ways. First, we expose the plot using Kelli's memoir.

We blanket the Internet and media and force it to become an election issue."

"You already said Obama and the Dems won't touch the issue, and the GOP will just spin anything we put out there as more conspiracy theory. Plus the mainstream media will avoid the story like the plague. No . . . what we need is an independent presidential candidate, one with the guts to expose the truth about oil and tie those facts into the threat of another terrorist attack, exposing the puppet masters before the event occurs."

"You know of such a politician?"

"Maybe. What's the second course of action my wife had in mind?"

"That . . . is a bit more tricky. We collapse the financial infrastructure of both the terrorists and the Neocon backers."

"How?"

"By using Promis. The program can tap into any computer, including those of financial institutions. Kelli used Promis to track the dirty money used by terrorist organizations. Days prior to September 11th and right up until the moment the first World Trade Tower fell, traders had been placing puts on stocks against companies involved in the attacks. You are aware of this, yes?"

"My best friend, Mark . . . he died servicing those transactions."

"Kelli used Promis to trace the activity, almost $15 billion of blood money that eventually found its way into the bank accounts of major corporations, financial institutions, Saudi Royals, Afghani drug lords, lobbyists, and even politicians. The combined assets of the guilty total more than a trillion dollars." Ramzi holds up the CD-ROM case. "Promis can access every penny in every account—that was Kelli's plan—to use these funds to finance the revolution. The data is stored on this Promis disk. Kelli said you had the means to set the plan in motion—a former teammate, I believe . . . one who had the level of sophistication necessary to access, harbor, and redirect the funds."

Ace shakes his head as another piece of his wife's puzzle drops into place. "A former teammate . . . one she helped parole. For someone battling for her life against cancer, she sure managed to pull a lot of strings."

"Kelli was indeed a force of nature, but do not let your guard down. What your wife has outlined is extremely dangerous. Kelli's former contacts in the SSB have already targeted you and your family. You cannot have Promis on you when you travel. Arrangements will have to be made to send it ahead to your contact in the States. So? Will you help us?"

Ace rubs the tension from his eyes. *Is this plot to nuke an American city really happening? If I get involved, it means placing the kids at risk. I'm already under scrutiny . . . the attack on the Apache means I've been deemed expendable. If I choose to be proactive, then maybe I can help derail things. If I do nothing, a nuclear suitcase bomb might actually wipe out an entire city . . . plus the people who want me dead will still want me dead. They already tried once, and they killed Kelli.*

"Before I agree to go through with this, there's something I want from you. There's a former CIA operative, a man named Scott Santa, Russian-American. He worked for Vinnell. I'm guessing he's still in the Persian Gulf. I want you to find him for me."

"Kelli's assassin?" Ramzi shakes his head. "This is very dangerous. It's better we handle him ourselves."

"No! It has to be me. I want to look the devil in his eyes as I take from him what he took from me."

"Ace, the man you seek is a trained killer, supported by various intelligence agencies. It is far too risky. Kelli would not approve."

"I wasn't asking her."

Ramzi sees the look in his eyes. "Very well. But you must understand, the Neocon machine . . . they also have Promis. You'll be watched and tracked every moment. You have children, they remain your vulnerable link. You will need to make arrangements to keep them safe. You cannot know where they will be taken. Do you understand what I am telling you? If you're caught, these people know how to acquire information."

Ace nods, his pulse pounding in his throat as he recalls Kelli's video-taped warning.

The fight of your life . . .

"If a nation expects to be ignorant and free, it expects what never was and never will be. The People cannot be safe without information."

—THOMAS JEFFERSON

"On September 10, 2001, Donald Rumsfeld announced a 'war on waste' after an internal audit found that the Pentagon was 'missing' 2.3 trillion dollars in unaccounted assets. On September 11th, this was as good as forgotten."

—911TRUTH.ORG

"Last year, [Ion Sancho, head of Leon County, Florida elections] discovered the supposedly impossible—that Diebold Election Systems touch screens and optical scanning machines had serious security flaws. Sancho challenged hackers to break into his voting machines four times. They always succeeded. Sancho raised alarms. Florida Secretary of State Sue Cobb, a Jeb Bush appointee, ignored him. And then they took away a $564,000 federal grant for disabled-accessible voting machinery."

—HOWARD GOODMAN,
Ft. Lauderdale Sun Sentinel
March 26, 2006

CHAPTER 22

GARY LEE SCHAFER, DIRECTOR
RADICAL FUNDAMENTALIST UNIT
COUNTERTERRORISM AND MIDDLE EAST SECTION
FBI–HQ
APRIL 24, 2012

Director Schafer:

I am forwarding surveillance footage submitted by Special Agent Elliott Green (155-16533-17) that confirms D.O.E. subject Professor Eric Mingyuan Bi (file # 112-11292-377) came in contact with an UMBRA-classified subject (Tursi, Michael R.) on 3 January 2012. The nature of this meeting appears to be the delivery and installation of drywall and garage shelving, most likely a cover story for transporting the contents of two large unidentifiable packing crates into suspect Bi's garage several weeks later. Keeping in mind that subject Bi is a professor of nuclear physics associated with two separate incidents of nuclear secrets espionage, I hereby request permission to conduct a FISA search of the subject's garage.

Charles Jones, Director, FBI: Springfield, Illinois
(155-63775-17)

Gary Schafer curses to himself. He rereads the e-mail a third time before hitting reply.

> Director Jones:
>
> Thank you for forwarding the surveillance footage. As you know, UMBRA requires special clearance far and above your current status. I will investigate the matter and take the appropriate measures. Please continue your diligent surveillance of subject Bi and report any and all new developments directly to me.
>
> G.L. Schafer, Director

Schafer hits SEND. He contemplates erasing the message, thinks better of it, and prints a hard copy to be filed in Eric Bi's folder. Then he picks up the phone and dials the extension of his assistant, Jim Leary.

"Jim, do me a favor and pull the file of Special Agent Elliott Green. I believe he's based in Springfield, Illinois."

BRIDGEVIEW, ILLINOIS
APRIL 25, 2012
8:44 AM CST

The village of Bridgeview is located just west of Chicago, its 3.6 square miles supporting an urban population of just over 15,000. Included among its populace is a large and active Muslim community.

Most of these families are simply seeking to maintain an Islamic identity. They send their children to school at a local *Madrassah*, where boys and girls are segregated while studying the Koran. Many worship at the Bridgeview mosque, which, over the years, has attracted members of the Muslim Brotherhood, a militant group that has often condemned American culture, praised suicide bombers, and prefers a more fundamentalist interpretation of Islam.

✦ ✦ ✦

The 2009 Chevy Trailblazer is parked outside the bank. Its occupant, Jamal al-Yussuf, is reading from the Koran . . . waiting.

A second vehicle parks nearby. Omar Kamel Radi knocks on the truck's passenger window. Jamal unlocks the door, allowing his fellow Iraqi entry. The two men exchange a quick embrace. "I can't believe I'm saying it, but it is actually good to see you. How are things in Los Angeles?"

"Good. The weather is beautiful."

"You are not smiling about the weather."

Omar nods. "I met someone, an aerobics instructor. She is blond and so beautiful. I told her I am a foreign exchange student from Cairo, studying engineering. I bought several text books. I even attend classes."

"This is very dangerous. If our sponsor knew—"

"My sponsor is a lazy dog. He leaves me notes on occasion, but I never see him."

✦ ✦ ✦

Parked in a van across the street from the bank are Shane Torrence and Marco Fatigo. The two Strategic Support Branch "handlers" have been eavesdropping on their subjects since the Iraqis first entered the United States nine months earlier.

"Hear that, Marco? Your boy thinks you're a lazy dog."

The side door of the van is yanked open. Michael Tursi hands each man a coffee and bag of doughnuts, saving himself the one in the cardboard carrier. "I see I missed our Muslims' happy reunion."

"Arabs," Torrence corrects, taking a bite out of a chocolate crème doughnut. "You've got your Arabs and your Muslims. These two are Arabs."

"You can be both, moron."

"Turk's right," Marco says, draining his coffee. "Now your guy, Shane, he's Shi'ite, definitely a Muslim. Omar, the kid I'm babysitting . . . Sunni Arab. Saddam was Sunni and he hated the Muslims. Turned out the whole reason he was posturing so much about weapons of mass destruction was because of Iran, not the U.S. He was more afraid of a Shi'ite invasion than anything we were going to do."

"Shut the hell up." Tursi snaps a fresh clip into his gun. "Read the damn dossier, Marco. You're Sunni converted to Islam. Far as I'm concerned, they're all bomb-toting towel-heads. Stay here. I'm taking a walk." He exits the van, slamming the side door closed.

Marco digs through his bag of doughnuts. "What's he so edgy about?"

"FBI caught him on surveillance tape back in January at Bi's house."

"Damn. Where the hell was Schafer?"

"He didn't know. It was a D.O.E. operation, nothing to do with counterterrorism. But you know the Turk. He won't sleep until he cleans up the mess."

✦ ✦ ✦

Back in the Chevy Trailblazer, Omar's good mood has festered into frustration. "You wouldn't understand, Jamal, you are Shi'ite. You are a simple desert people, disobedient to God. You are unbelievers who worship the teachings of Ali, the Prophet Mohammed's nephew. No Shi'ite will ever rule Iraq."

"And you are a Sunni dog," Jamal retorts. "Was Iraq better with Saddam?"

"Saddam was excessive in his cruelty, I'll admit, but Iraqis remain united only by the rule of the sword. And I didn't always despise your people. It was the Americans who divided us. The army they trained were all Shia and Kurd. No Sunni was permitted an officer's rank, as if we'd free Saddam from prison."

"If you believe what you say, why are you here?"

Omar stares out the passenger window at the bank. "The occupation won't last forever. When the Americans leave, the Iranians will move in. I refuse to see my country ruled by Islamic clerics."

"Yet you joined the Islamic Revolutionary Guard."

"What choice did I have? Haditha, Anna, Qaim, Rawa, Ramadi . . . all had fallen to Islamic rebels worse than the Taliban. The Americans have no idea who they are even fighting, so they shoot everyone. If it were not for the money being sent to my family, I would not be here."

"Is that the only reason you are here? Money?"

Omar turns to Jamal. "At first I wanted revenge, now I want something better for my family. Is that so bad? With money I send they could leave Iraq."

"Not me. If I die *shahid*, I will go to a place in heaven near God's other messengers. Is there a greater glory?"

Omar snorts a laugh. "You think Allah will let you enter heaven after slaughtering innocent women and children? You will not die *shahid*. You seek revenge for your father and brother, for your younger cousins. Revenge is not part of Islamic law nor martyrdom, no matter what Al-Qaeda preaches."

"The cleric who recruited me in Tehran, he said this assignment would strike a blow to the West's military agenda. For that I am prepared to die."

"Jamal, this does not have to be a suicide mission."

"*Shahid* is not suicide. Has kissing your blond American girlfriend made you a fool and a coward?"

"Cease your tongue and listen. When I was in Tehran I heard rumors that many of the Magnificent Nineteen were still alive. Mohamed Atta and Salem Al Hazni—"

"And Saeed Alghamdi, and the two Alshehris, yes, I heard this too! At Qods many asked about Atta's behavior, questioning whether he was truly a devout Muslim. We had read stories about his drinking, about visiting bars and strippers the night before the attacks. Our trainer confided to us, he told us Atta and the other planners . . . that these men were never even onboard the planes. They had been traveling on false passports, instructed the night before the attacks to get publicly intoxicated and to scream insults at the infidels so as to attract attention to themselves. We were told these men were no one's fools, that they had purposely allowed their driver's licenses to be photocopied, that they even used public library computers to send e-mail using unencrypted messages, all to leave false trails to the FBI."

"It's true!" Omar jumps in. "Their apartments . . . why would they leave behind ridiculous information about stealing planes, as if they wished to be caught? The authorities even claimed to have found Atta's passport in the World Trade Center rubble! Can you imagine? The American Press actually reported this, and the infidels swallowed every falsehood."

"It's true!" Jamal laughs with his comrade and then grows serious. "Omar, our sponsors . . . they instructed us to leave behind our own false trail."

"The laptop. Yes, I have thought about that too. And why must we drive two days to this town, just to wire money home to our families?"

The two men remain silent, deep in thought.

Jamal checks his watch. "The bank has opened. Do you wish to go first, or should I?"

"Go on, Shi'ite. Martyrs before rebels. I still have something to live for."

AMERICAN HOSPITAL—DUBAI, UAE
MIDDLE EAST
APRIL 26, 2012
6:13 AM LOCAL TIME

Starlight. It blinds . . . then fades. Blinds, then fades . . .
"He's coming to."
Ace blinks open his eyes. Through blurred vision he can

make out a gray room and a tall figure, hovering close by, checking his pulse.

"Ah, there we go. Good morning, my friend. My name is Gary Groves. I'm a physician here at the American hospital."

"I'm in the States?"

"Sorry, no, you're in Dubai. Nurse, bring the lights up, please."

The room brightens, forcing Ace to squint.

"The local police found you wandering close to the highway. Heat exhaustion, dementia . . . no identification. Can you tell us your name?"

"Futrell. Ashley Futrell."

"Well, Mr. Futrell, you've got a nasty head injury. Looks to be about a day old. You must have been wandering around out there for quite some time. Can you remember what happened?"

"I was . . . in a taxi. At night. I was heading to . . . to Aqua Dunya, to see the *Desert Pearl* cruise ship. I accidentally left my wallet at my hotel—"

"What hotel?" A Dubai police officer enters the room.

"The Baynunah Hilton."

"Continue."

"The driver got mad because I had no money. He pulled over to the side of the road. We were out in the middle of nowhere. He demanded I give him my laptop as payment. When I refused, we got into a fight. I don't remember much after that."

"What is your business in the Arab Emirates?"

"I'm a petroleum geologist, recently out of work. I came here seeking employment."

"I am sorry you had these troubles," the officer says. "Before you are discharged, I need you to fill out a police report."

"Yeah, sure. Then I think I'd just like to go home."

"In the aftermath of the Dubai ports dispute, the Bush Administration is hiring a Hong Kong conglomerate to help detect nuclear materials inside cargo passing through the Bahamas to the United States and elsewhere. The administration acknowledges the no-bid contract with Hutchison Whampoa, Ltd., represents the first time a foreign company will be involved in running a sophisticated U.S. radiation detector at an overseas port without American customs agents present. A U.S. military intelligence report, once marked 'secret,' cited Hutchison in 1999 as a potential risk for smuggling arms and other prohibited materials into the United States from the Bahamas."

—ASSOCIATED PRESS,
March 23, 2006

"The men who create power make an indispensable contribution to the Nation's greatness, but the men who question power make a contribution just as indispensable, especially when that questioning is disinterested, for they determine whether we use power or power uses us."

—PRESIDENT JOHN F. KENNEDY

CHAPTER 23

Operated by the Port Authorities of New York and New Jersey, John F. Kennedy International Airport (JFK) is located in the southeastern section of Queens County, New York City, in Jamaica Bay on 4,930 acres. The airport processes more passengers and air cargo than any port in the United States and handles the most international arrivals, between 150 and 160 aircraft a day. JFK's Contraband Enforcement Team processes six million parcels annually, confiscating huge quantities of counterfeit consumer products, undeclared currency, and illegal narcotics, averaging close to eight hundred drug seizures a week.

Like herded sheep, Ace and the other passengers from Emirates Airlines flight 201 file through customs, everyone weary from the fourteen-hour trip. Guessing at which domestic line is moving quickest, Ace takes his place behind a dozen other Americans . . . and waits.

Ramzi had set Ace free on a stretch of highway close to Dubai. They had gone over his story a dozen times, one they felt offered the best chance of avoiding an official U.S. inquiry. The Apache pilot would be taken to another medical facility two days after Ace's arrival in New York City and released.

The line moves forward as a family of five is led behind a Red Cross curtain.

Ace rubs his left arm, registering stress-induced catheter-like pain in his veins. *They wanted me dead . . . what happens now? Will the CIA believe I walked miles in the desert after the crash? Did Schall have anything to do with it? Will he simply accept my report on the oil fields, or does he plan on parading me in front of the Senate as a witness? Do they suspect Promis is being smuggled into the country?*

"Next."

Ace hands the female customs officer his passport.

"Anything to declare?"

"No."

She stamps his passport. "Second curtain is open. Remove your jacket and roll up your sleeves."

"What for?"

"Bird Flu inoculation. Next."

"Wait, why do I need—"

She points to a sign, giving him the tired look of someone who has answered the same question repeatedly for forty hours a week.

**Every person entering the U.S. is required
to be inoculated for Avian Bird Flu.**

"Next in line."

Ace moves to the second of six curtains displaying the Red Cross emblem. A nurse, identified by her badge as Beth Newman, directs him to an empty chair. "Afternoon. Where do you want it—arm or cheek?" She holds up a large hypodermic needle.

"Don't you have a pill?"

"Homeland Security says they're working on it. Sure would make my life easier."

"What's in that thing? How do I know it's safe?"

She hands him a flyer. "That'll explain everything. Now unless you want to go back to wherever country you flew in from, I'd take the shot. Arm or butt cheek?"

"As a symbolic salute to Homeland Security, stick me in the ass." Unbuckling his belt, he drops his trousers and ceremoniously flashes Nurse Newman his left butt cheek.

She jabs him with the needle.

"Ow! How bad is this flu threat anyway? Last time it was the Swine flu. Seems every few years it's a different pandemic."

"Potentially, this one is really bad. We've heard about a dozen recent outbreaks in Asia and Europe. Worst one was a small community in France. Killed about half the people infected. Tonight when you go to bed, you ought to thank God for the American pharmaceutical industry."

Ace buckles his pants and limps away, suddenly feeling uneasy.

CARBONDALE, ILLINOIS
3:47 PM CST

The abrupt knock startles Elliott Green from an afternoon nap. The FBI agent checks his watch, verifying Professor Bi will not be returning from his bowling league for another hour. He then heads downstairs, his gun tucked in the back of his blue jeans.

The television repairman is an olive-skinned Italian, dark hair. Five o'clock shadow.

Green opens the door. "Can I help you?"

Shane Torrence flashes the falsified FBI identification. "Only if you're Agent Green. Jerry Bobo, I'm your relief." He enters the house and looks around. "Smells like old people."

"Tell me about it." Green shuts the door behind him. "I wasn't expecting you until next Tuesday."

"I can leave."

"No, no, I'm more than ready." Green leads him upstairs

to the master suite. The bedroom is an oasis of electronics and dunes of dirty laundry. "Sorry about the mess."

"No worries." The SSB officer scans the room and sees the CD-ROM files. "Bet you're anxious to get home."

"You have no idea."

"Bring me up to speed and we'll get you on the road."

MONTAUK, NEW YORK
11:47 PM EST

The kids are in bed asleep, having survived their father's hugs and inquisitions about school. Now it is just Ace and Jennifer, alone in the family room.

"It's a nice night. Want to take a walk by the water?"

She smiles. "I would have thought you'd be tired of the sand by now. Just let me grab my coat."

✦ ✦ ✦

The moon is three-quarters and high, its glow filtered behind a haze of clouds. For a brief moment Ace is back on the Saudi desert, alone on the empty stretch of highway. His life, once a set routine of work, travel, and little league hockey games now seems to be leaping forward in quantum episodes of chaos, everything stemming from his wife's murder.

Four and a half months since Kelli died . . . is that even possible? Everything since the funeral . . . like some bad dream. When will I wake up? How can I even move past the grief when she's reaching out to me from beyond the grave, putting me on a road to who-knows-where? How do I know this nuclear scheme is even true? Because she said so on tape? Because some former colleague of hers showed me a CD-ROM, spinning it into some unverifiable tale of conspiracy? So maybe we are running out of oil, and yes, there is the possibility of a nuclear terrorist attack, but would Iran really have the guts to arm these guys? Is it really necessary to risk my life, to make Leigh and Sammy orphans? This mission of hers sounds like suicide.

Suicide.

The word shakes him to the core. After his attempt as a college student, Ace had awoken in a hospital room, his wrists bandaged, his arms strapped to the bed rails. He had bawled his eyes out, feeling alone and humiliated. Kelli was on a road trip, but Tet was by his side, always supportive, never judging. "Okay, Ace, so you screwed up. Forget about it. Just figure things out and move on. Remember what coach always yells when one of us goofs up: 'Bring 'em in, huddle 'em up, and focus on the next play.'"

Suicide . . .

Suicide was about dealing with fear and pain . . . it was a choice—the anguish of having to go on versus a less-painful alternative. Life and death. Now he was being asked to choose again . . . this time to risk his life and all he cherished in order to prevent the unthinkable—

"Ace, you okay? You haven't said a word."

He turns to Jennifer. "Yeah, fine. Actually, I did want to talk to you, but—" He looks around. The two of them are alone on the beach, exposed on the deserted shoreline. "Let's sit back here, by the dunes."

"Oh-kay." She follows him to the crest and sits next to him, their silhouettes now hidden behind sand and sawgrass. "So? What did you want to tell me?"

"This has to stay between us. What I'm going to say may upset you. I don't want you to react, just hear me out."

He tells her everything . . . from his meeting with the CIA director to why he was really in the Persian Gulf. He describes Kelli's video and Promis, and the future attack being orchestrated by the Neocons. She remains stoic through it all, her jaw muscles knotted behind clenched teeth.

When he is through, she continues staring at the ocean. "Jen?"

"What is it you want from me?"

"Your opinion, for one. You worked with Kelli—Butch and

Sundance. Is there any truth to what I've just told you?"

She chokes out a chuckle, wiping strands of dark hair and tears from her eyes. "I am such a fool. Here I am, thinking that maybe you wanted to be alone with me . . . you know, for other reasons. Instead, we're back to more of your conspiracy theories."

"You mean? Oh wow, I wasn't . . . I mean I could be—"

"Just forget it."

"No, Jen, listen. It's just my head's so screwed up right now and—"

"Shut up, just—" She looks away. "To answer your question, yes, there's some truth to it, but it's not what you think. Some of the more radical elements of the Bush Administration, Rummy's people, had talked with Kelli about it years ago. They asked her to identify key population zones in both Iran and Saudi Arabia. But it was just the usual war game stuff, nothing more."

"Targets for what?"

"Biological and chemical weapons mostly. Something that would wipe out a population—"

"And leave the infrastructure intact." Ace feels his left arm tighten again.

"It was just conversation, Ace. It happens all the time in the Pentagon. As for Kelli's video, remember your wife wasn't exactly stable these last few years. Dealing with cancer, the thought of dying, leaving you and the kids, and that whole Kabbalah thing . . . suddenly everything made her feel guilty about something. My advice . . . just let it go. Cheney's a loose cannon and everyone knows it. Keith Olberman should be thanking him for MSNBC's surge in the ratings. As for Iran, they know it's suicide to arm a terrorist organization with enriched uranium. As for this whole Peak Oil deal, it will work itself out."

"Work itself out? You still don't get it, do you? This isn't about long lines at the gas pump, or five-dollar-a-gallon prices. There is no substitute in place for oil. Zero, nothing. We should have committed to a different path a decade ago, probably two decades ago, but we didn't. Without oil, you can't grow enough food to feed the masses, let alone get the goods to market. You can't heat your home or drive your car. Without oil, our entire economy finally collapses. If the last tanker stopped shipping oil tomorrow, within months a million people would starve to death or die of medical complications in New York City alone. Transportation, electricity, the economy . . . the military. Your Neocon pals knew, Jen, after all, most of them worked in the oil industry. Peak Oil justified 3,000 dead Americans. And the dems . . . they're no better. There's a reason we're still in Afghanistan and Iraq, and it's not to uphold democracy. Maybe things would have settled down, only the economy tanked, and the greedy bastards who caused most of the world's problems weren't keen about dialing things back. Instead, they see an opportunity waiting out there in a One World Order. All they need is one final push, another 9/11, only a little bigger this time . . . one that amps up our retaliation and turns Iran and Iraq into an Exxon/Mobil station. How many innocent people will be incinerated this time around? Far fewer than the number of those who may eventually die after we run out of oil, which will tally in the billions. Call it ledger sheet logic. To these heartless bastards, it was a no-brainer."

"Stop! What you're saying . . . it's too preposterous. And President Obama would never allow any of this to happen."

"He won't be around. You watch. He'll be sacrificed, just like Kelli and Tet. Just like the Americans who died in those planes and in those buildings."

"Enough!" She walks away, following the path back to the house, leaving him alone with conspiracy theories that even he doesn't believe.

Way to go, schmuck. All she wanted was a little affection. Instead, you gave her the end of the world.

"They think they are absolutely right. That's one of the characteristics of fundamentalism—'I think I am right because I am close to God and anybody who disagrees with me is inherently wrong and therefore inferior."

—PRESIDENT JIMMY CARTER,
commenting about the fundamentalist Christian right.

"Halliburton has pulled off the impossible. They have actually done a worse job under its second Iraq oil contract than it did under the original no-bid contract."

—REP. HENRY A. WAXMAN,
House Committee on Government Reform,
commenting on a fifteen-page report by auditors
citing that Halliburton intentionally overcharged,
using hidden calculations to bill the U.S.
government in costs it never incurred.
(March 29, 2006)

"It's not the people who vote that counts; it's the people who count the votes."

—STALIN

CHAPTER 24

Christina Jordan, President Obama's campaign manager, hovers over her boss as his make-up artist applies fresh base beneath his eyes. "It's important we maintain a presence, Mr. President. The Republicans may be down to three candidates, but they're still getting around-the-clock media attention. We can't appear to be a lame duck while they continue their attack."

The President nods, his eyes closed, eyelids fluttering.

Christine pulls the make-up woman aside. "Roxanne, he looks washed out, like he just had chemo. Can't you fix that?"

Roxanne Dunlap, herself an ovarian cancer survivor, shoots Christina a nasty look. "He's sweating, Tina. I'm doing my best."

"It's the lights," the president retorts weakly.

"He was sick earlier," chimes in Mario Childress, the president's six-foot, three-inch, two hundred forty-pound Secret Service bodyguard. "Said he had a bad headache."

"I'll be fine."

"Of course you will," Christine says, fixing her dishwater blond hair in the mirror. "The gym's packed, the TV crews are set. A quick speech and we're in the limo and back on Air Force One in less than two hours."

"I don't know, Tina," Roxanne adds. "He didn't look so good before the make-up."

"There are twenty-seven district delegates from the Indiana State Convention expecting to see him, headache or not. This is a key swing state."

The President nods. His pulse is racing, his skin cool and clammy, and the dull ache is building again in his head.

"At which time you'll be introduced by Luke Messer. He's the executive director of Indiana's Democratic Party. He represents the 57th district. Luke's a sixth generation Hoosier, so I slipped in a few football references on your Teleprompter."

"Basketball," the president mumbles.

"Really? Anyway, Shelbyville's also the home of Thomas Hicks. He was the twenty-first vice president of the United States, under Grover Cleveland and . . . Mr. President?"

"Oh, hell—" Roxanne grabs Obama's head as it flops backward. In one motion, the Secret Service man swoops in and catches the President in his left palm while simultaneously activating an alert switch on his shoulder with his right hand. Pushing the make-up artist aside, he scoops the President up in both arms, gently lowering him to the floor as a dozen more agents rush the room, sweeping along with them the President's medical team.

ATLANTIC CITY EXPRESSWAY
NEW JERSEY
5:07 PM EST

The navy blue Chevy Astrovan weaves its way through a convergence of lanes near the Haddonfield exit as it merges onto Route 42–south. Ace glances at the mile marker, his adrenaline pumping. *Eight more miles. He'd better be there.*

He had begun his journey earlier that morning—a

seemingly innocent trip to the dry cleaners, followed by a stop at the shopping mall. He had parked in an underground garage, visited the sporting goods store to pick up a hockey pad for Sammy, grabbed a quick cup of coffee and a donut, and then had returned to the garage—to Jeffrey Gordon's car, the keys hidden behind the front passenger tire. While his friend drove out of the garage in Ace's Corvette, Ace had waited another fifteen minutes before departing the mall lot in the Gordon family van.

He had headed south, paralleling the New Jersey Turnpike before catching Interstate 95, continuing south through Philadelphia. The detour had added an extra hour, but he had no choice, knowing the turnpike's toll booth's fast-pass sensors would register Jeff's car, the information potentially received by Homeland Security.

✦ ✦ ✦

Ramzi's plan, to avert the next 9/11 by exposing it publicly, was not sitting well with Ace. If there was anything the Neocons had proven, it was that by controlling key factions of the government and media one could get away with even the most outrageous violations of code, conduct, and American law. The Constitution could be trampled upon with no repercussions. Bribery and ethics charges could be swept under the rug. Elections could be falsified, whistle-blowers ridiculed. The Vice President could even shoot a man in the face without having to submit to a police inquiry at the scene.

It was Promis's ability to track and move the bad guy's money that had ultimately committed Ace to the mission. With Kelli's data and Promis's access, Ace could play a global game of Robin Hood, using the world's dirty money to fund clean alternative energy resources that might ultimately avert the Big Rollover. For once, the guilty and greedy would have to pay for their crimes—in every sense of the word.

He owed that to Mark.

◆ ◆ ◆

Ace slows as he passes mile marker 37. *There . . . up ahead.* He blinks his lights at a car parked along the side of the road. A heavyset, bearded man in beige cut-off shorts and a midnight-green Philadelphia Eagles jersey steps out from behind the raised hood and waves at him for assistance.

Ace pulls over. "Need some help?"

"What was your first clue?" Kenneth Franklin Keene Jr. climbs inside the van, punching his former teammate on the shoulder. "Good to see you, Ace."

Ace drives off, the scent of tobacco and sweat pungent. "Life must be good. You really let yourself go."

"I was in prison, scumbag."

"I watch TV. Don't prisoners have access to weight rooms or barbells in the yard or something? You're supposed to be an athlete."

"That was twenty years ago, dog meat, and I was the friggin' kicker. And who are you to talk? At least I'm chillin'. You look like you ate stress for breakfast."

"You've got that right. Hey, put the cigarette away, it's not my car."

"You send me the freakin' Neocon version of Frankenstein's monster and I can't even smoke?"

"You sound frazzled."

"Frazzled? Dude, I passed frazzled a week ago. The only reason we're even speaking is because your old lady arranged my release."

"And here I thought you'd be salivating at the chance to make a big score."

"Money's fine if you're alive to spend it. Kelli was playing with fire. She must have tracked every drug deal, covert weapons sale, and money laundering scheme the Feds have dipped their wick in since '82. Heroin flowing out of Afghanistan, SAM missiles sold to the Sauds—name a terrorist organization and I'll show you how they got funded, what they bought, the trail of bank accounts the money passed through, and which Richie Rich the transaction made richer. This thing's a global spider's web of the nasty and powerful. You go public with it and they'll eat you for lunch."

"And my plan?"

Keene grins. "You mean to steal their money?"

"Blood money. We'd just be reappropriating it."

"Reappropriating. Good word. A lot of my cell mates were in for the same thing. Look dude, I'm a hacker. There's nothing to hack here. Kelli did that for us. But even with Promis, you can't just move a trillion dollars, not without sending off a million warning bells and whistles. This has to be done on the sly, bleed it quietly over weeks—even months—every transaction masked, every money trail erased. Plus you've got to set up bogus trails, create histories . . . everything to mask the money before you can move it into legitimate accounts without sending up any red flags. It takes a real artist to do that, an expert in COBOL."

"What's COBOL?"

"It's an acronym that stands for Common Business Oriented Language, the premier high-level computer programming dialogue of our time. Banks used to write all their code in COBOL, most financial institutions still do, especially in third-world nations where a lot of this dough is stashed. COBOL was also the first programming language mandated by the Department of Defense."

"I take it you have someone in mind?"

Keene smiles. "Oh yeah. The COBOL queen. Her name's—"

"Don't tell me—it's better I don't know. Can she do the job?"

"Dude, she's a python. Back when the Y2K deal was going on, she made a fortune writing code to protect systems. With Kelli's info and Promis as a delivery system, she'll create a COBOL worm that'll hack into every account and electronically transfer the funds through a matrix so complex

Magellan couldn't find his way home. Once downloaded into the mainframe at the National Commercial Bank in Saudi Arabia, we'll be able to—"

"Whoa . . . this has to be downloaded from a Saudi bank?"

"It's the perfect insertion point. The NCB's the biggest bank in the Middle East. At some stage almost every dirty dollar either originated there or passed through on its way to another financial institution. It's the central hub in almost every Al-Qaeda transaction funded by a Saudi prince and ol' King what's his puss, and we're talking hundreds of billions. Download the worm and it'll flow outward like the big bang—a million tentacles reaching into a million financial institutions, and we'll withdraw every dirty dollar . . . eventually."

"Eventually?"

"Again, steady progression. Just enough to keep the auditors busy without alerting the Feds."

"How do you plan to enter a Saudi bank and download the worm?"

"That's your end, Mister Hero Quarterback, not mine."

"You expect me to walk inside the biggest financial institution in Saudi Arabia, find my way to a computer terminal, and download a program?"

"It's our only real option. Maybe your old lady was going to do that, I dunno. You'll need at least twenty minutes on the terminal—thirty tops. Once the worm's in the system, there's no stopping it. Everything'll be time-released, with domestic monies staying in the States and foreign investments remaining overseas. That way we don't start collapsing economies . . . except, of course, in the states that sponsor terrorism. Those we'll flush down the sewer like turds."

"What's in it for you?"

"Kelli allocated $15 million, but my associate and I expect triple that fee or no deal."

"Forty-five million? For a programming job?"

"Do you have any idea what this entails? We're talking tens of thousands of man hours. I'll need to set up an entire organization—a legitimate company of illegitimate computer geeks who can be trusted to keep their mouths shut—not that we'll give them any clue as to what they're actually doing. But the reward still has to justify the risks, and the risks are death. Once the powers-that-be figure out that they're being systematically robbed, they'll come after us, guns blazing. Hell, let's call it an even fifty."

"What about seed money? You'll need to rent office space, purchase computers . . . I can probably get you twenty grand."

"See, dude, this is what I'm talking about. Move anything more than a few hundred bucks out of your account and the Feds'll be all over your ass. No, the money we'll use is already in a safe, hidden beneath the tiles under your clothes dryer. Combination is the day of the month that you, Leigh, and Sammy were born, in that chronological order."

Ace looks at Keene, dumbfounded.

"Kelli told me about it the day I was paroled. She didn't say how much, and I knew better than to ask, but she was obviously planning this for quite a while."

"Obviously."

"So where's all this blood money going, Robin Hood? Do you have a list?"

Ace reaches into his pocket, withdraws a hard diskette, and hands it to Keene. "The first $700 million needs to be dispersed into a series of 527 accounts accessible only to Kelli's cousin, Jennifer. The next chunk of change gets invested into alternative energy companies. After that, educational programs and charities across the board. I earmarked $4 billion for Lance Armstrong's Cancer Foundation."

"Damn. That should buy a lot of wrist bands, huh?"

"It used to drive Kelli crazy, even before she got sick, that the Pentagon could spend $70 billion every budget on Iraq while hundreds of thousands of Americans were dying each year of cancer. Pennies for people, dollars for war."

"This'll be like friggin' Christmas."

"The 9/11 Family Fund gets a nice deposit, along with the First Responder groups, and the VA program."

"I'm sure Mark's family will appreciate that."

"You'll see one more familiar name on the list. It sets aside $5 million in an account registered to Mitch Wagner. Make sure he can get to the funds without any hassle."

"Wagner? As in Wags, our old left tackle? What're you cutting him in for?"

"Wags doesn't know it yet, but he and his wife are going to be taking in my kids."

"Oh." For the first time Keene feels the weight of the conversation.

They pass mile marker 26, along with a sign indicating another five miles until the Frank S. Farley Service Plaza.

"Ace, there's something else. Kelli left you an encoded message."

"What kind of message? What did it say?"

"It was a map, some out-of-the way place up in Canada. She was pretty insistent you go."

"Go to Canada? What for?"

"She wanted you to find someone named Casper."

"Casper? This is a joke, right?"

"I don't think so. She used the term, 'on the souls of our children.' "

"This is nuts. Homeland Security's all over my ass. How did she expect me to cross the border without getting caught?"

"She, uh, left you a fake passport and driver's license. I printed and laminated everything . . . Stephen."

"Stephen?"

"Stephen Murphy. That's your new identity. You're a Canadian living in Melbourne, Australia, in the oil and gas safety business." Keene digs into his pants pocket, retrieving a plastic freezer bag containing the forged documents. "Your wife, she was really something, huh?"

"Unbelievable."

Ace follows the far left lane into the rest stop. "K.J., I'm really counting on you. If we do this thing, you can't screw it up."

"Hey, Cochese, I'm ice-water."

"You weren't against Tennessee."

"Blow me! It was a bad snap, and I still hit the goalpost from forty-eight yards. And who the hell are you to talk, Mr. Three Interceptions and a Fumble in the Orange Bowl? Just worry about how you're going to make it into that Saudi bank."

Ace parks. The two former teammates exit the car without informal good-byes, playing out their roles for any prying eyes. Keene heads for the gas station, Ace walks toward the main building to use the restroom.

A crowd has gathered around a television, their stunned expressions telling all.

"Again, if you're just joining us, President Barack Obama was airlifted to an Indiana hospital earlier this afternoon after suffering what doctors believe was a massive stroke. The President remains in a coma. The Vice President will be addressing the nation later this evening."

Ace stares at the monitor, the blood rushing from his face. *Those bastards . . . it's really begun.*

"I would like to call on the Arab world to enter into the world of peaceful use of nuclear energy with all speed and momentum."

—AMR MOUSSA,
Arab League Leader
March 29, 2006

"Today, a remarkable goal of the Islamic Republic of Iran's defense forces was realized with the successful test-firing of a new missile with greater technical and tactical capabilities than those previously produced."

—GENERAL HOSSEIN SALAMI,
Air Force Chief, Iran's Elite Revolutionary Guards,
commenting on the test-firing of a new multi-warhead missile not detectable by radar, capable of reaching Israel and U.S. bases in the Middle East.
April 1, 2006

"The world is very different now. For man holds in his mortal hands the power to abolish all forms of human poverty, and all forms of human life."

—PRESIDENT JOHN F. KENNEDY

CHAPTER 25

ACE GUIDES THE CORVETTE through the dark streets of his neighborhood. He turns left down his cul-de-sac, his pulse pounding as he spots the black sedan parked in front of his driveway. *Crap . . . they must've caught K.J. What if they made him a deal? Turn me in and he walks. Guy's on probation, I never should have trusted him!*

He slows, driving down the left side of the street. Lowering his window he positions the plastic baggy holding the fake passport and driver's license in his left hand. Approaching a neighbor's mailbox, he yanks it open and shoves the contents inside, all without braking.

Circling the cul-de-sac, he swerves around the sedan and parks in his driveway, his high beams momentarily blinding the CIA director, who is already approaching from the stone path that leads to the Futrell front door.

Ace's mind dials back to a distant memory—Kelli teaching him about facial expressions, body language, and eye contact. *Head position tells a lot. Don't tilt, and don't raise your chin. Look straight at your interrogator, and never look away, no matter what he throws at you.*

He keeps the headlights on a moment longer just to annoy David Schall and then climbs out of the low-slung sports car.

Glancing up, he notices Jennifer looking out from behind the curtain of an upstairs window, watching everything.

"Director Schall, don't you ever sleep?"

"Where were you today, Ace?"

"Gay pride parade, communist rally, the usual thing."

"Answer the question!"

Ace returns the man's glare. "Atlantic City. There's a sub shop on Arctic Avenue. You'd like it. It's called the White House. Unlike the place in D.C., these guys actually provide a public service."

"You expect me to believe that you took your friend's car on a six-hour jaunt just to get a sandwich?"

"Cheese steak, and they're the best on the planet. Rolls are brought in fresh every hour from a bakery next door." Ace reaches inside the passenger side open window and pulls out a heavy brown paper bag. A half-dozen two-foot-long hoagies and steak sandwiches are protruding out the top. "I'd offer you one, but I really don't like you."

"You took Gordon's car."

"Still tracking my whereabouts? I thought we had a deal." Ace moves closer, looking Schall straight in the eye. "Not that it's any of your business, but Jeff was entertaining an important client and was stuck with his wife's car, so I let him borrow mine."

"You're playing a dangerous game."

"Game? What game? I ran your little errand and almost got myself killed. Much to my surprise, it turns out there's plenty of oil in Saudi Arabia. Who knows, maybe I'll start working for Saudi Aramco."

"How'd you manage to cross sixty miles of desert?"

"I didn't. The chopper crashed. Next thing I know I'm in a Dubai hospital. Someone obviously pulled me from the wreckage. I assumed it was one of your guys."

"Ramzi Karim?"

"Who?" *Lock eyes, don't look away.*

"You're a bad liar, Ace. Karim's ex-CIA, he's stirring up a lot of trouble in the Persian Gulf. By now you know he was friends with your wife. Close friends. The kind that spent a lot of late nights together, or so I've heard."

"Screw you and your mind games." Ace pushes him aside and heads for the house.

"They found the Apache pilot, Ace. He was dead. Shot once in the heart."

Ace freezes.

"You're in way over your head, my friend. I'm offering you free advice. Be wise and take it. Find yourself another job, love your kids, and walk away from this mess before someone else you care about gets hurt."

Ace swallows back the bile rising up his clenched throat. He remains silent, the adrenaline coursing through his body causing every nerve and muscle to tremble. He refuses to move, waiting in silence as the sedan backs out of his driveway and pulls away.

CARBONDALE, ILLINOIS
MAY 7, 2012
10:12 AM CST

Elliott Green drives slowly past Professor Bi's home and parks his Subaru two doors down from the residence he has spent the last six months living in. Climbing out of the car, he removes his sports coat and hands it to his wife. "I'll only be a minute."

"Elliott, if we're late for the ceremony my sister will never speak to me again, which makes you a dead man walking." Carol Green tilts the rear-view mirror toward her and applies a fresh layer of lipstick.

"It was my grandfather's Swiss Army knife. I can't just leave it. Besides, I know my guy's routine. He won't be home for hours."

Green walks briskly past the neighbor's home and then cuts across the front yard of the stakeout house. He knocks on the door several times. Waits. Glances across the street at Eric Bi's home.

Something's different.

He knocks again and then locates the spare key under the planter and lets himself in.

"Hello?" No response. *Maybe he's sleeping?*

He hurries upstairs into the master suite, the bedroom door open. Bed, linens—no surveillance equipment . . . everything gone!

He races back down the stairs and out the front door. He dodges a car as he sprints across the street to Professor Bi's garage and looks in the window.

No cars. No tools. Empty!

Cursing aloud, he crosses the driveway to the side door leading into the kitchen. He peers inside and sees nothing.

Walking quickly back to his car, Green yanks open his wife's door and pops open the glove compartment.

"Elliott, what are you doing?"

"Stay here." A quick search produces the pick—a long, thin piece of metal that curves up at the end like a dentist's instrument. He locates the thin flathead screwdriver and pockets it, then grabs his gun.

"Elliott, don't do this! Remember what happened six years ago!"

Ignoring her, he hustles back across the street, his dress shirt already tinged with sweat. He tries the kitchen door, verifies it's locked, and then inserts the screwdriver into the keyhole. Applying torque, he offsets the lock's plug from its housing, opening a slight ledge that allows him access with the pick. Gently he feels his way in, prodding and lifting each pin pair completely into the lock housing, listening for the familiar *click* of the upper pin as it falls into place on the ledge in the shaft, popping open the lock.

Green enters, gun drawn. "Hello?" He moves from room to empty room, his pulse quickening.

The front door bashes open, Green greeting the blinding swath of daylight with the business end of his revolver. "Freeze!"

"Ahh!" Startled, Denice "Daisy" Webb spills droplets of scalding-hot Starbucks coffee across her bare arm, adding a voluminous breath to her already ear-piercing scream.

"Where's Bi?"

"Don't shoot!"

"Professor Bi, the guy who lives here. Where is he?"

"I swear I don't know. My husband, Ken . . . he bought the house a week ago from a realtor. Please, mister—"

Sold the house . . .Bi's gone! You blew it, dillweed. Green smacks himself in the forehead and lowers his gun. Looks around. "Okay, this realtor of yours, where can I—"

He screams as the hot coffee catches him flush in the face. Green drops the gun, panting in agony, and then looks up in time to see the 200-pound half-Italian, half-Choctaw Indian charge him like a bad-tempered Rhino.

"FBI! I'm FBI!" He fumbles for his ID and covers up as the irate woman delivers several body blows and a kneecap to his face.

FLAGSTAFF, ARIZONA

Located at a 7,000-foot elevation, the Northern Arizona community of Flagstaff is a small town surrounded by desert, nestled between ponderosa pine forests and the snowcapped peaks of the San Francisco Volcanic Field. At the center of town is historic Flagstaff, a grid of art galleries and restaurants, inns and country stores, made popular by an annual influx of tourists. The majority of Flagstaff's year-round population is settled within the borders of Interstates 17 & 40, the latter more commonly known as Historic Route 66.

The free-standing cinder block building is located on the east side of Flagstaff, not far from the Econolodge, the General Motors Auto Plaza, and half a dozen fast-food joints. Once a transmission shop, the facility has recently been leased to a private firm out of Tampa, Florida, though one would hardly know it based upon its boarded-up frontage and no trespassing signs.

A lone vehicle occupies the lot—a white van that has been parked around back every day for the last week. A magnetic sign identifies the owner's company as Smith Heating & Air Conditioning. The worker, an Asian man in his sixties, has been seen coming in and out of the building, occasionally picking up take-out food at the local diner. The only visible sign of a tenant preparing to move in are the brand-new security cameras mounted above the two locked entrances.

Professor Eric Bi is inside, working in one of the auto pits in a full radiation suit. The ceiling of the pit, once open to accommodate the lift, has been sealed at its floor level with half-inch thick lead sheeting. Two dehumidifiers are plugged into the pit's far wall, sucking moisture from the cool air. The trunk of a 1967 Buick Electra has been lined with lead, fashioned into a makeshift storage box.

Situated on a workbench before the nuclear physicist is a three-foot Plexiglas cube with built-in rubber gloves. Held upright within this cube is a putty-like ten-kilogram sphere, approximately the size of a large grapefruit. Over the next few months Professor Bi will use his tools to shape and smooth the ball of enriched uranium-235 and its twin, preparing the fissile material for its final destination among the rest of the components of the Mk-54 Special Atomic Demolition Munitions suitcase bomb—and their inception into the darkest chapter in the history of modern man.

SUMMER
2012

"As the details of the [9/11] plan are not yet fully known, it cannot be determined if Moussaoui has sufficient knowledge of the 747-400 to attempt to execute the seizure of such an aircraft."

—Harry M. Samit,
Minnesota FBI Agent, futilely urging his FBI
supervisor to act quickly against Zacarias
Moussaoui, one of the planners of the
September 11, 2001, terrorist attacks.

"FBI Supervisory special agent Michael Maltbie, who removed information from the Minnesota FBI's application to get the search warrant for Moussaoui, was promoted to field supervisor."

—Salon,
March 3, 2003

"Pasquale D'Amuro, the FBI's counterterrorism chief in New York City before 9/11, was promoted to the bureau's top counterterrorism post."

TIME Magazine,
December 30, 2002

CHAPTER 26

Lake George, New York
August 6, 2012
11:51 pm EST

LAKE GEORGE, A THIRTY-TWO-MILE-LONG WATERWAY located in the northeast section of New York State, was created at the end of the last ice age when glacial deposits dammed up two ancient rivers that flowed north to south through the Adirondack Valley. Ten thousand years later, the *Queen of the American Lakes* would serve as strategic real estate in the battles between the Algonquin and Iroquois Indians, the French and Indians, and the British and Colonists during the American Revolution. Where blood was once shed, vacationers now roam, with families enjoying the area's hiking trails, museums, beaches, waterslide parks, and personal watercraft rentals.

Ace and Kelli had been taking their kids to Lake George ever since Leigh was just an infant. Last summer's stay had been interrupted by Kelli's radiation treatments. With his wife gone, Ace had been hesitant to rebook the log cabin, concerned about how Leigh and Sam would handle their first family vacation without their mom. In the end he had relented, but decided upon a cabin along the shoreline rather than their usual rental on one of the lake's 245 islands. Leigh had lobbied to bring along a girlfriend, but Ace said no, opting to invite his in-laws instead.

Of course, Ace had apprised Bruce and Sharon Doyle of his plans weeks earlier. Convinced Ace had lost his faculties in lieu

STEVE ALTEN

of their daughter's murder, it was all they could do to keep from hiring a lawyer and demanding custody of their grandchildren. Jennifer had stepped in to reassure them that it was best just to humor him, and in the end they agreed, but only because they refused to take a chance with the kids' safety . . . just in case there really was something to their son-in-law's dementia.

As for Jennifer, her sudden change of heart regarding Ace's conspiracy theories had more to do, she claimed, with innuendo surrounding Barack Obama's sudden health issues, which had left the President in serious but stable condition. Confidential sources revealed that subtle security changes had been discreetly made in the White House's residential quarters, including a recent hiring within the pharmaceutical staff that oversaw Obama's blood pressure medication.

With a long recovery forecast, the First Lady decided her husband could no longer run for a second term. Vice President Biden was now running the country. After a week of deliberating, Secretary of State Hillary Clinton had turned down the offer to fill the Vice President's place on the party's ticket. She would challenge Biden at the Democratic National Convention.

On the Republican side, former Governor Ellis Prescott of Florida had secured the nomination, promising to lower the deficit by cutting government spending in half while restoring national security and opening up the country's wildlife sanctuaries to the oil companies.

Meanwhile, Senator Edward Mulligan of Pennsylvania had accepted the Green Party's nomination. With President Obama forced out of the race, a grassroots effort managed to get the third party candidate on the ballots of all fifty states. Lacking the financial means to mount a serious challenge, few "experts" felt he would match Ross Perot's voter record totals of 1992.

✦ ✦ ✦

It is the end of another busy day of activities at Lake George, their ninth together at the resort, and the lump Ace

Futrell has been registering in his throat all week has only gotten worse. Whether boating or fishing, or the three-hour hot air balloon ride, it has taken all his effort to maintain his emotions around his children. At one point Leigh had noticed her father tearing up, but he had covered himself with an anecdote about the family's first visit to the lake.

That night they had cooked the day's catch—fresh trout—followed by roasted s'mores by the campfire. Ace trembled when he had hugged his son and daughter good-night and then excused himself to read while they fell asleep in the cabin's loft.

Now it is quiet, just after eleven at night, and Ace finds himself standing on a mental precipice. Circumstances beyond his control seem to be forcing him to take the plunge—an act that potentially could prevent him from ever seeing his kids again. He continues to debate the matter internally, even as the ticking wall clock demands he make a decision, even as he carries his sneakers outside to the darkened front porch where Bruce and Sharon are waiting. His mother-in-law gives him a cold hug before returning inside.

Bruce waits by the porch steps while Ace slips on his shoes. "I parked the rental by the side of the road like you asked. Your travel bag is in the trunk."

"Thank you. Give the kids a few hours before you wake them. Make sure you remember the letter and money. Like we agreed, Jen will get the word out when things are safe. As far as my friend, just tell the kids he's a second cousin on my side of the family. Give him a three-hour head start, and then you and Sharon disappear, and I mean really disappear, someplace you've never been . . . never even mentioned. Be sure to mail your credit cards and licenses to that post office box like we talked about. Once you're on the road, use only your new IDs and—"

"And no e-mail or phone calls, we know. Can you at least give us a clue where you're going?"

"I can't. If all goes well, I'll be back in about ten days. But if things go bad—"

"If what goes bad?" Leigh is in her bathrobe, standing in the doorway behind the closed porch screen door. She steps outside, the rusty hinges creaking. "Dad, are you going somewhere?"

Ace breaks out in a cold sweat. "Honey, it's just a business trip."

"You're leaving now, in the middle of the night, without saying good-bye? Where are you going?"

"Shh, don't wake your brother. I can't go into detail right now, but—"

"You said if things go bad. What can go bad? Is this why you've been acting so weird?"

Bruce slips his arm around her. "Grandmom and I will explain everything. Come back inside—"

"No!" She pushes him away. "Daddy, you're scaring me. Where are you going, and don't lie. Does this have anything to do with what happened to mom?"

"Come here." Ace hugs his daughter, the words burning in his throat. "You have to trust me, okay? There are some things you're better off not knowing. Grandpop's going to tell you what he can. I want you to listen to him and do what he says, okay?"

She's sobbing now, afraid she'll never see him again. "You're coming back, right? You're not going to leave us?"

"I'm coming back, Leigh, I promise." He squeezes her tight and kisses her twice on the cheek. "Watch out for Sammy, okay?"

"Okay." She hugs him again and then heads inside.

Bruce squeezes Ace's shoulder. "They'll be okay. Do whatever it is you have to do."

The two men embrace, and Ace steps off the porch and disappears into the forest, cloaked by the night.

ELSMERE, DELAWARE
AUGUST 7, 2012
9:08 AM EST

Jennifer drives the rental car off the lot at the Philadelphia airport, following the signs leading her south onto Interstate 95.

At her request, the meeting had been scheduled at an off-site location, away from pollsters, volunteers, and the ever-watchful eyes of the television news crews. After a forty-minute ride into Delaware, she exits on Route 141 through the town of Elsmere. Following the faxed directions, she heads north on Kirkwood Highway, looking for a building with dark blue awnings. Five minutes later she arrives, parking in the private lot belonging to the law offices of Doroshow, Pasquale, Krawitz, and Bhaya.

The building is a half-century-old home renovated into office space. She leaves her name at the reception desk and finds a seat in the waiting area by an old stone fireplace.

"Ms. Wienner?" A spry Italian gentleman in his early fifties greets her with a warm smile. "Bob Pasquale. Did you have any trouble finding us?"

"No." She shakes his hand.

"Elsmere's a small community, but our clients prefer the location over downtown Wilmington. Everyone's upstairs in my office, if you'll follow me."

The law firm's founding partner leads her up a flight of steps, the second floor landing guarded by two plainclothes Secret Service agents. One searches her belongings while the other checks her for weapons using a sophisticated metal detector. Satisfied, they allow her entry into Robert Pasquale's private office.

Senator Edward R. Mulligan, the Green Party nominee for President of the United States, is seated on a leather sofa, his tie loose, shirt sleeves rolled up. He is listening to a large man with a shaved head, goatee, and Georgia accent rattle off figures about the southern Baptist vote. Two other "suits" and a lone woman feign interest as they feed off the remains of a breakfast platter.

The woman—Suzie Perlman—beams a huge smile as Jennifer enters the office. "Well, hallelujah, the cavalry's arrived. Senator Mulligan, this is Jennifer Wienner, although we always called her Sundance."

The Senator stands to shake her hand. "Thanks for flying in. This is our campaign manager, Silas T. Whitener." The bald man grips her hand with excessive force. "Cesar Diaz, our regional director—"

"Yes, we met at the convention in '08."

"My chief of staff, Aaron Coombs." Another big man with a kinder grip. "And you know our gal, Suzie. So?"

"So, we were a bit surprised when you called," Whitener says, motioning her to an empty chair. "Not sure what you can do to help us, but we'll be happy to listen."

Senator Mulligan chides him with a look. "What Silas means is we feel pretty good about the latest polls. For the first time, the major networks agreed to broadcast our convention."

"The latest polls have you at 22 percent."

"Which ain't too shabby," beams Whitener. "A good showing at the convention—"

"And you'll still come in third. Prescott and Clinton have ten times your war chest. Face it, your campaign's floundering. Unless you pull a rabbit out of the hat in the next few months, you'll be dead on arrival come November."

Whitener begins to retort, but Mulligan signals refrain. "Let's keep things in perspective, Ms. Weinner. We're still running as an independent."

"Then set the bar higher, because I play to win. I'm here because we're entering dangerous geopolitical waters, and the Neocons prefer force where tact is needed. America needs to steer the western world onto a new course. The question is whether you have the guts to see it through."

"I'm listening."

"The reason you still have slightly more than a snowball's chance in hell is because uniting the Democrats in Congress is worse than herding cats. America elected Barack Obama because they saw a man of vision. Unfortunately, when we needed radical changes, we got Republican-lite. For you to win, you need to carry a new message of hope to the American people, and that message is no more oil. They ask you about Iraq, you tell them we went in for oil, but since we won't be needing oil anymore, our boys and girls can come home, and anyone who refuses to allow our kids home is obviously not a patriot or a parent. Every time the Rove Rats toss another God, gays, or guns grenade at you, you'll repeat this exact phrase: 'This election's far too important to the future of our country to be caught up in the usual Republican horseshit.'"

Senator Mulligan looks around the room. "Horseshit? You really want me to use that word?"

"Yeah, I do."

Cesar Diaz shakes his head. "You'll lose the Christian right."

"You never had the Christian right. Let the American public see you as the no-nonsense guy you are, not the wimp these middle-of-the-roaders have turned you into. Speak your mind, but stay on message. When they ask you about Kyoto-III, you say we'll sign, even if China refuses. Then you force the Chinese to stand alone. They'll cave, believe me. They can barely breathe in their big cities. When the media corners you on abortion, you look them straight in the eye and say, 'I'm all for outlawing abortion, but only if we start doing a better job educating our teenagers about having unprotected sex. When they ask you about the war on terror, you go back to the energy message and how it's America's addiction to fossil fuels—an addiction fueled by oil pushers like Ellis Prescott and his running mate—that helped hijack our foreign policy. Simple message: No more addiction. We create a twelve-step program to wean us on green. In '13 we take our country back from the pushers and the self-serving politicians. You repeat that every day in every interview, and in every debate, and you'll win the White House."

Suzie Perlman claps.

Cesar Diaz is not as enthused. "What about money?"

"It'll come."

"How?"

"I know a lot of rich chipmunks who are afraid of seeing Dick Cheney stalking the West Wing again. Which brings me to my final point, and it's a deal breaker: You need to call the Neocons out. Every time Prescott brings up national security, you attack, questioning why the radical right seems to want there to be another 9/11. In fact, you question the official 9/11 report and say you'll commission a new investigation as president."

Jennifer looks around the room. The men appear dumbfounded, Suzie is grinning.

"Rich chipmunks, huh?"

"With deep pockets and lots of friends."

Senator Mulligan smiles. "When can you start?"

"Those who expect to reap the blessing of freedom must, like men, undergo the fatigue of supporting it."

—Thomas Paine

"Airplane black boxes were found at Ground Zero, according to two first responders and an unnamed NTSB official, but they were 'disappeared' and their existence is denied in *The 9/11 Commission Report*. U.S. officials consistently suppressed and destroyed evidence (like the tapes recorded by air traffic controllers who handled the New York flights). Whistleblowers (like Colleen Rowley, Sibel Edmonds and Lt. Col. Anthony Shaffer) were intimidated, gagged, and sanctioned, sending a clear signal to others who might be thinking about speaking out. Officials who 'failed' (like Myers and Eberhard, as well as Frasca, Maltbie and Bowman of the FBI) were given promotions. Accepting victims' compensation barred September 11th families from pursuing discovery through litigation. Those who refused compensation to pursue litigation and discovery had their cases consolidated under the same judge (Judge Hallerstein) and were dismissed."

—911Truth.org

CHAPTER 27

It had been a long night.

With heavy heart and force of will, Ace had left his children. Only the uncertainty of whether he would ever see them again outweighed the trepidation he felt about what lay ahead. Distracted emotionally, he quickly became lost as the cabin's lights were swallowed by the density and darkness of the forest. Eventually he did find the trail, but it was the wrong one and it left him out on the main road a good half mile from where his father-in-law had parked the rental car. By the time he had located the vehicle and had driven off the resort grounds onto Interstate 87 it was nearly one in the morning.

He drove in silence for the next several hours, traveling north on the Adirondack freeway, the Canadian border looming somewhere up ahead. At random moments his anger at his predicament became overwhelming, and his body shook with rage as he punched the steering wheel. He forced himself to regain control when he reached the Canadian border. Showing his phony license, he stepped out of his car when commanded for the vehicle search, the patrolmen using mirrors attached to long poles to see beneath the chassis. After a few benign security questions he was allowed to proceed through the checkpoint and onto Quebec's Autoroute 15, where he continued driving north to Montreal.

He arrived at the airport at daybreak, giving him a three-hour reprieve before the Air Canada flight departed for Halifax en route to St. Johns, Newfoundland.

✦ ✦ ✦

Designated one of the four corners of the world by the Flat Earth Society, Canada's northeastern coastline has two distinct landmasses—the island of Newfoundland, located in the Atlantic Ocean at the mouth of the St. Lawrence River, and its rugged coastal mainland, known as the Labrador Province.

Forming the eastern edge of Canada's "shield," Labrador is a 250,000-square-mile composite of granite heaved upward from sea and earth some 800 million years ago. Its dramatic coastline, covering more than 10,000 square miles, has been shaped by a succession of ice masses that have torn long finger-shaped gouges from its rocky mass. Continue inland and Labrador becomes an unfettered landscape of lakes, fjords, and deep valleys—one of the last great wildernesses on the planet. Three great mountain ranges cut across its expanse: the volcanic Kaumajet, the Kiglapait, and the mighty Torngat—the highest mountain range east of the Rockies. Boreal forests hold enough game to feed a small city. Further to the north the tree line ends, yielding to a vast wasteland known as the tundra—a place few humans have ever seen photos of, let alone ventured into.

That civilization has avoided this region is no surprise, for the weather is brutal, with extended winters escorted by coastal ice sheets and subarctic temperatures. The few people who do populate the area reside in six communities located on the harsh northeast coast, yet none of these outposts are linked by roadway, forcing travelers to rely on boats and planes in summer and snowmobiles and dogsleds in winter. Despite these brutal conditions, Labrador's population is the oldest in all of North America, their arrival predating Columbus by more than four thousand years.

Labrador's aborigines are known collectively as the Innu.

Nomadic tribes that migrated across the Bering Strait from Asia, the Innu eventually settled in Arctic North America and Greenland. The term Inuit means "real people, " Innu translates as "human being," and both native words are preferred over the more commonly used Eskimo or Indian references. Despite the diffusion of their population across the Canadian Arctic, the Inuit traditions have stood the test of time, with tribes still living off the land, tracking caribou in the winter, returning to the sea in the summer months to fish and hunt seals and whales. Migrating Innu reside in ice igloos or tents made of walrus and sealskin, their permanent winter homes constructed of stone or driftwood, framed in whalebone and covered with sod or moss. Adaptation into western cultures has been slow, but for the Innu living in Labrador, a need to have a say in their own future has forced them to acclimate into Canadian culture, with modern settlements established in Sheshatshiu, at the mouth of Goose Bay, and Natuashish, located on the northern coastline near Hopedale.

◆ ◆ ◆

It was after three in the afternoon by the time Ace's plane touched down in St. John's, the largest and oldest city in Newfoundland. From here Kelli's instructions were to fly on to Hopedale, a remote village located some five hundred miles as the crow flies up the northern Labrador coast. Exhausted from not having slept the last thirty hours, Ace booked passage on a 10:20 a.m. charter, then checked himself into a hotel for the evening.

◆ ◆ ◆

Ace lies in bed, staring at the clock . . . 8:35 p.m. The scent of cheap carpeting and musty bedding magnifies his despair. He yearns to speak with his kids, wishing he could reassure them that everything will be all right, but by his own design he has no way of knowing where they are or how to reach them. His eyelids flutter from exhaustion and his body aches, yet despite his overwhelming fatigue he cannot fall asleep, his mind refusing to cease its endless chatter.

What am I doing here? Kelli's dead, my life turned inside out as I chase shadows. What if Schall is right? What if I am being set up? What if it wasn't even Kelli on that tape? And what kind of father leaves his kids with total strangers eight months after their mother was murdered?

What if, what if, what if! This is insane—you're insane! You'll never make it into the Saudi bank, let alone download the Promis worm. The Saudis will arrest you, lock you away, torture you until you confess or die, whatever comes first. You'll simply disappear, but Leigh and Sam, they'll carry the burden of your bravado the rest of their lives.

I miss them so much, but I can't go home, not with Homeland Security just looking for a reason to arrest me—or worse . . . not with what's potentially coming down the pike. And who's this guy in Hopedale? Why is it so important that I find him? Does he know about the nuclear attack? Can he help stop it?

Go home to your family, Ace. Stop living the insanity that was Kelli's life.

Wake up, Futrell . . . you are the insanity.

"Shut up! Shut up, shut up, shut up!"

Ace tosses the pillow and claws at his hair, the room growing smaller, the walls closing in. "Get out, gotta get out . . . can't breathe!"

He's dressed and outside in less than a minute, gasping lungfuls of the cold night air. Down the metal stairwell and onto the street. He walks by the harbor, but it's way too cold, so he cuts through an alleyway, an inclined walkway leading to a pub, the Duke of Duckworth. Desperate, he enters, only it's a wall of people inside, strangers with lingering eyes, friends he'll never meet.

No good, keep moving . . .

Back into the night, trekking east again through downtown St. Johns, unable to escape the overwhelming feeling of emptiness. He turns down Military Road, his bearings non-existent, the hotel a figment in his exhausted state of mind. He is Alice fallen down the rabbit hole, swallowed by a strange city—a lost refugee in a bizarre land, his identity falsified, his soul diminishing with every painful step.

The church looms before him, stone and Roman Catholic. He staggers toward its three sealed portals, his mind frantic from exhaustion.

Locked.

Locked.

The last door creaks open, beckoning him entry into the house of worship. Ace has not been a believer for years, but there are no atheists in fox holes, and he is in it up to his ears.

The cathedral is empty, the lit candles rapidly diminishing.

He kneels by a bench. Lowers his head to his hands. Chokes out the words, "Give me strength," before collapsing face-first onto a pew.

✦ ✦ ✦

Son?

Ace opens his eyes. Morning light filters through stained glass windows. He sits up, having slept the last ten hours on the polished wooden bench.

The priest's face is tanned flush and weathered. "Son, you can't stay here. There's a mission . . . it's down the road."

"I know, Father. I'm on my way."

SPRINGFIELD, ILLINOIS

It is almost noon by the time Elliott Green arrives home from his meeting with Charles Jones, the Springfield FBI director. His wife, Carol, opens the door before he has a chance to key in.

"That was fast. Good or bad?"

He rolls his eyes as he pushes past her. "It's not enough that

I had to walk through that building listening to snickers about the broken nose and bruised ribs, what's worse was having to witness Chuck get reamed on speaker phone by Adrian Neary."

"The Chicago director? Why's he involved?"

"He heads up counterterrorism in Illinois. Frickin' Gary Schafer at HQ chewed him out yesterday, so naturally he tore a piece out of Chuck's hide."

"Wait . . . I thought Chuck sent a memo to Schafer about the UMBRA guy? How can they blame you for—"

"Blame flows downhill, Carol. The Department of Energy's pissed, Schafer's covering his ass, and Chicago's pointing the finger at Springfield for me being duped by whoever was posing as my field replacement. The long and short of it is that HQ's officially taken charge of the Bi file, and I'm off the case. Oh yeah, I also received an official reprimand that goes into my file for allowing the suspect to flee."

He heads for the kitchen.

She follows him. "If you remember, I was the one who told you not to break inside that house. If you had listened to me, your record would still be clean and I wouldn't have missed my sister's wedding!"

"You don't get it, do you? Bi's gone. He told the University his brother passed away, and he took a sabbatical to spend time with the family in Beijing. One problem: Bi has no siblings. Records show he never even left the country, which means whatever he was working on, he's still working on it, only now we've lost him . . . I lost him. Plus, he's got a spook with UMBRA clearance riding shotgun."

"He'll turn up."

"These guys are experts in nuclear explosives, Carol. Bi's mother's entire family bought the farm in Nagasaki, and I suspect he holds a grudge. If a dirty bomb goes off in some mall, guess who becomes the FBI poster boy for screw-ups?"

"Okay, so find him."

"Didn't you hear me? I'm off the case."

"Then take a leave of absence and find him on your own. You're good at tracking people down. Remember that pedophile, the one who set up shop as a child psychiatrist? He ran too, but you found him in Vancouver. Took you six weeks but you nailed him."

"Eight, and I had the Bureau's assistance. This time I'm shut out."

"Shut out? By who? Chuck Jones? Adrian Neary?"

"No, this one's coming from Director Schafer. The big cheese."

"And why would the head of the FBI's counterterrorism division give a rat's ass about you . . . unless he was afraid you might expose something he was involved in."

Elliott's eyes widen. "Yeah . . . that's true."

"Uh-huh." She heads into the living room. "I'll take that as a thank you."

ST. JOHNS/NEWFOUNDLAND COAST/
LABRADOR COAST/HOPEDALE

The twin engine charter bounces twice before gaining lift off the Torbay Airport runway, the easternmost airport in North America. Ace is one of only three passengers onboard, seated on the left side of the tiny aircraft, which looks like it has been flying since the days when Newfoundland was still a British colony.

His back is sore from having slept on the church bench, but the night's sleep has done his psyche a world of good. He is no longer worried about his children. He knows they are safe. His mind is now focused on the mission at hand.

The plane climbs to two thousand feet and then turns north, following the breathtaking coastline of Newfoundland on its way to Labrador and the village of Hopedale. Directly below is the Old Battery, a small community of weathered homes that seem to climb the sheer cliff face that rises out of the sea like a mountain. Moments later they are over Harbour Grace and Conception Bay, its blue waters teeming with sailboats. Farther east, the sea picks up a new-found fury as it crashes into Cape Bonavista, a plateau of rock that guards its lighthouse.

The plane climbs higher as the wind howls along its aluminum wings. Above the clouds, the occasional unobstructed view reveals a landmass carpeted in pine as they pass over L'Anse aux Meadows, the northernmost community in Newfoundland, an area once settled by the Vikings.

The coast of Labrador greets them at Henley Harbour, a waterway that sports icebergs in cooler months. By the time they are over St. Lewis, the cliff faces have noticeably flattened, the forests gone, the land still rocky but suddenly bare. Georges Cove, Bateau Harbor, Grady Island, Cutthroat Island . . . each territory takes them closer to the tundra as they continue their journey north.

The populace is also shrinking. Once home to thriving fishing communities, the northern coastal towns were cut to the quick back in 1992 with the cod moratorium. Smaller independent vessels have been replaced by larger corporate fleets capable of traveling hundreds of miles offshore in search of shrimp and crab. As a result, these once populated "outports" have become obsolete.

Ace tightens his seatbelt as the plane begins its turbulent descent. Somewhere in the distance is Hopedale.

◆ ◆ ◆

Located in Northern Labrador where large coastal bays open to the Labrador Sea, Hopedale was founded in 1782 as an Inuit settlement. Originally named Agvituk, an Innu-aimun term meaning "a place where there are whales," the name was later changed to Hopedale by Moravian missionaries arriving from Germany. Today the population numbers less than 650, 90 percent of which is Inuit, English their predominant language. The Innu call their Hopedale community Natuashish, which means beautiful. It is one of only two organized Inuit communities in Labrador, the other being Sheshatshiu, located farther inland and to the south at Goose Bay, home to the largest air force base in North America.

Ace grips his armrests as the plane's wheels skid across a small 2,500-foot gravel runway that seems to be diminishing all too fast. Miraculously, the plane stops before it meets sea, and moments later the outer door opens, venting the cabin with a blast of Arctic air that rocks the aircraft on its landing gear. Ace zips his leather coat and climbs down the steps, greeted by the low rumble of water riding against rock, the Labrador Sea sparkling before him beneath a cloudless blue sky.

The pilot empties luggage and mail from the hold. Ace grabs his bag, slings it over his shoulder, and heads out to the main road, a dirt path that winds around a rock-strewn field leading to Hopedale, a good mile in the distance. There are no cabs or cars, just two teens on bicycles, both Innuit females, possessing the familiar Eskimo-Asian eyes and jet-black hair, cherub cheeks, and warm smiles. Attached to each bike is a small sidecar.

"You are going to Hopedale, sir?" asks the younger of the two teens, who looks about Leigh's age. "My sister could give you a ride. Maybe you will give her a nice tip?"

Ace inspects the rusty sidecar, unsure. "You sure this thing will hold me?"

"Of course, sir. Very safe."

He climbs in, the sidecar sagging beneath his weight. The older sister struggles to gain inertia until finally they are cruising down a gentle slope toward Hopedale.

"Maybe you can earn a bigger tip. I'm looking for someone. His name is Casper."

The teen continues smiling and pumping the pedals but says nothing.

"It's a strange name, I know. Ever heard of him?"

Still no reply.

They reach the outskirts of a community whose dwellings appear to be straight off the set of a Hollywood spaghetti western. They ride past whitewashed wooden homes spread sparsely apart, and a church with a white picket fence. Situated on a boulder-strewn acreage is a modular schoolhouse resembling a series of warehouses. Ace can hear school children playing outside, their voices carrying over the flat expanse. They follow the sea, its rocky embankments supporting a colony of dingy one-room wooden shacks, some built so close to the water that their single occupants could fish out an open window.

Inuit are everywhere, the men repairing fishing lines or nets, others bringing in the morning catch from their small boats. Children play close to home while their mothers clean fish and skin seals. Some glance Ace's way, a few even wave.

But there are other native Americans in Hopedale who are not so preoccupied with chores. A few lay on stoops, passed out drunk, while others congregate in small groups, drinking and smoking. Some are teens, others middle-aged men and women. They gaze at him with vacant eyes . . . lost souls.

His teen driver brakes in front of a large, two-story building, a sign identifying it as the Amaguk Inn. "This okay? Ten dollars, please."

Ace climbs out of the side car, drops his bag on the dirt road, and pulls out his billfold. He hands her a ten-dollar bill and then shows her a twenty. "For you, if you can tell me who might know where I can find my friend, Casper."

"Ask the Chief. He knows everything." She snatches the twenty-dollar bill and rides off, kicking up clouds of dust. "*Qujannamiik!*"

"Yeah, thanks . . . thanks a million. Not even a receipt, huh?" Bag in hand, he trudges up four wooden steps and crosses a porch to the Inn's entrance.

It is more hunting lodge than hotel, the wood paneled walls covered in framed black and white photos, the scenes of dogsled teams, hunting parties, and fishing trips. The innkeeper, part Innu, part Canadian, is seated by a work bench, tinkering with a portable stove. Ace approaches.

The man never bothers looking up. "I'm guessing you're our Australian guest. Frank Nasuti, proprietor."

"Murphy. Stephen Murphy. From Canada originally."

"That right? What brings you home?"

"Home's Quebec, but a close friend spent some time in these parts. He bragged about it being the best damn salmon fishing he ever experienced. I was in St. John's on business and thought I'd fly up and hire his guide. Goes by the name of Casper."

"Don't know any Casper, but we can set you up nicely. How long you staying?"

"Not sure. Maybe a few days."

"Need a room?"

"That would be great."

"That's too bad. I only have twelve rooms, all occupied. Next time call ahead. What about food? You hungry?"

"Hungry? Sure."

"Dining room's open, but it's only for guests. Try Sylvia's take-out, down the road on the left. There's also the Big Land Grocery."

"Any other hotels in town?"

"No. But I have a friend whose wife died last winter. He'd probably share a bed with you."

"That's a tempting offer, but—"

"Think about it while you eat. You can leave your bag in the lounge."

Ace peeks inside the lounge where several older men are seated around a color television set. "Thanks, no, but I think I will grab a sandwich. Down the road, huh?"

"On the left."

Ace waves on his way out the door and steps into a sea of children, fourteen in all, ages eight down to three. Two women herd them away, smiling and apologizing, their words drowned out by the sonic boom of a squadron of fighter jets passing overhead, returning to the NATO base at Goose Bay.

The contrast in cultures is not lost on Ace, the new world overpowering the old, its influence gradually evaporating thousands of years of traditions. And yet soon, he knows, the pendulum may swing the other way, and it may be the traditional culture that survives.

Sylvia's Takeout is a small eatery with a few tables set up inside for summer hours. Ace orders a plate of fried chicken from a local girl working the counter and then takes the corner table, feigning interest in some of the brochures tacked to a bulletin board.

The man entering the premises is in his late fifties, tall, thin, and Caucasian, his gray-white hair pulled back into a ponytail, his beard and mustache grown heavy over a tan complexion. The maroon sweatshirt is so stained with grease that the college insignia is no longer readable. He doesn't enter the eatery as much as invade it, every step in his dust-covered army boots shaking the floorboards, every syllable renting the air.

"Duke, the usual! Chop, chop, son, I'm in a hurry. Make sure it's the fresh stuff too. You know I can tell the difference. Save that old crappola you've got frozen out back for the *takungartut.*" His gaze swings around to Ace, his eyes narrowing as if looking right through him. "Well, well, look what the cat dragged in. Fresh meat."

He saunters over, kicks out a chair from beneath the table, and sits on it backward. "Richard Lawrence, friend's call me Dick. Mechanic by trade, loner by choice. So who be you, *Gringo?*"

"Stephen Murphy. I'm in oil, the safety end of things. Decided to take a few days and see if the fishing's as good as they say."

"It's better. Got a forty-foot coastal with twelve hundred horsepower that sleeps five. Takin' 'er out as soon as I get my grub. You're welcome to join me; don't get to speak with the white man too often these days."

"I'd like that, but I sort of promised a friend I'd use his personal guide. Maybe you know him? Goes by the name Casper."

"Casper, as in the ghost? Sure I know him, only Casper's what the Americans call him. He's Inuit-Metis, part Aborigines, part European. Spends a lot of time up near Nain, the next community to the north. The man hunts whales and seals all summer and then heads inland when the weather turns to track caribou. Crazy mother, lives in igloos half the year. Not sure he'll have time to take you out fishing, unless you're after mammal."

"No, but just the same, I'd love to meet him."

"Consider it done. Hey, Duke, wrap my friend's stuff to go. He's coming with me."

"Thanks. By the way, that word you used earlier—"

"*Takungartut.* Means stranger. No worries, these people treat everyone like a friend. We're the ones that screwed 'em up. Forced 'em to join the twenty-first century. Canadian Provincial government made 'em political orphans. Started regulating their game, restricting their culture. Hell, these people were here long before our ancestors ever built their first boat. Took us a while, but we finally ruined 'em. Rob a people of their culture and you steal their soul. Introduce new gadgets and widgets and you give them the tools to hang themselves. Literally. Natuashish's not as bad, being a fairly new community, but Sheshatshiu, down by the air force base, now there they've got some serious challenges. Bad unemployment led to a feeling of being powerless. Innu aren't used to feeling useless, and there's nothing that attracts a fallen soul when he's down more than booze. We're talking major alcohol addictions. Kids see their parents losing it, they get depressed, and start sniffing gasoline. Lethal habit. Suicide rates among the Innu are some of the highest in the world. Things are gradually getting better, but it takes time . . . everything takes time, like our friggin' food! Hey, Duke, how about it? Before the sun sets this fall!"

✦ ✦ ✦

The Wellcraft 360 coastal offshore cruiser seats three plus the helmsman within its open cockpit, another six in the transom. Below decks is a full-service galley, a master suite, loft area, head, and engine room, which services the boat's twin Cummins Tw 600 horsepower engines.

Ace unties the bow and stern lines and then climbs aboard as Dick Lawrence pulls away from the dock, heading north along the Labrador coast. The bow bounces across a three-foot chop, the frigid sea spray catching Ace, chasing him to one of the cushioned pedestal seats next to his host.

"So," yells Lawrence, "what part of Canada you from?"

"Quebec. South side of Montreal."

"Know it well. Spend any time in Little Italy?"

Ace's pulse increases. "Not much over the last nine years."

"What do the French call it again?"

"Couldn't say. My family's English, we never *parle-vous'd* much, if you know what I mean."

"I hear ya."

Ace looks astern, the shoreline disappearing rapidly. "I thought we were following the coast up to Nain?"

"Casper never returns home until late. Thought we'd do some fishing. I know a great spot not far from here. You know, if we stayed on this heading, in a few hours we'd hit Greenland."

Ace smiles and nods, while alarm bells blare in his head. He holds on as the swells increase in size, bouncing the boat three-quarters out of the water.

"You think this chop is bad, you should be out here in winter. Huge waves, icebergs, and the cold . . . unbelievable. I've served time on freighters. Ice builds up on the exterior of the ship, and I mean thick ice, sheets of it. Conforms to everything, makes the vessel dangerously top-heavy, not a good thing in rough seas. My first time out, the captain hands us these heavy wooden mallets and tells us to start clearing ice. Imagine being out on deck in below freezing conditions, the wind howling, the swells twenty feet, and you have to smash apart tons of ice covering the bulkheads while you're slipping and sliding across the deck."

"Anyone ever go in?"

"Once in a while. Water's so cold it starts shutting down your organs in less than two minutes. One guy went overboard and it took us a few minutes to get back around to find him. By the time we fished him out, he was gone."

"What about in summer? How cold's the water now?"

"Good question." Lawrence slows the boat and then idles the engines, keeping the bow pointed at the incoming swells.

"This the spot?"

"This is it. Wait here, I'll grab the gear." Lawrence goes below.

Ace holds on as the never-ending swells rock the boat harder. *Kelli, what have you gotten me into now?*

Dick Lawrence returns, holding a length of heavy rope—and a shotgun.

"What are you doing?"

"You're a bad liar, son. I've got questions but not a whole lotta time, so here's how it's gonna be. You're gonna strip naked, tie this rope around you, and get in the drink while I ask you a few questions. Once you tell me what I need to know, you can get out. I figure you've got three to five minutes tops before you turn into bait."

"You're insane."

The shotgun blast echoes across the water as its payload kicks up sea. "You can take a dip with a bullet hole in you or without. Your choice."

Ace stares down the gun's smoking barrel and then unzips his coat and removes it. He kicks his shoes off slowly, his muscles quivering from adrenaline and the cold. The Arctic air bites into his exposed flesh as he strips off his socks and pants, peeling off his underwear and shirt.

Lawrence tosses him one of the ends of the rope. "Secure it tightly around your waist. I'd hate to lose you to a killer whale."

Ace loops the cord around his waist and below his armpits, hyperventilating as he ties the knot. His mind races, trying to prepare for the sudden shock.

"Okay, get in. Now!"

Ace moves to the rail. Swings one leg over the side and then the next. He hesitates a long second, eyeballs the gun still aimed at his head . . . and jumps—

The frigid sea jolts his body in spasms, driving the air from his lungs in a primordial yell as he fights to tread water a mere thirty-eight degrees Fahrenheit, his blood feeling as if it's curdling to lead as the agony of a thousand piercing needles courses through his scorching flesh.

"First question: What's your real name?"

"Acccceee Fuutrelll." His fingers and toes burn in excruciating pain, as if Neptune is soldering them with a blowtorch.

"Who sent you looking for Casper?"

"Mmmy wiffffe. Ke . . . Kelli Doyle."

"Where's your wife now, Mr. Futrell?"

"Deaddd. Mur . . . mur . . . dered." The blood flow to his extremities slows, his limbs moving in slow motion, his body sinking.

Lawrence tugs on the rope. "That was two minutes. It'll get easier as you go numb." Looking away, he scans the horizon, almost bored.

Ace's eyes grow wide, his teeth involuntarily chattering. "Isss thaaat it?"

"Who murdered your wife? Who do you suspect?"

"Agent." Ace is no longer certain his body is moving.

"You mean like a federal agent? Domestic or foreign?"

"Ff . . . foreign." His wheezing lungs can barely power his voice box.

"How do you know?"

"Long . . . story."

"Yeah, I bet it is." Lawrence checks his watch. "Six minutes.

You're strong. Most people would have passed out at the three minute mark. Thirty seconds."

Thirty seconds? Lawrence's voice echoes in his brain. *Thirty seconds. Thirty seconds. Okay, boys, time for two plays, three if we can get out of bounds. Come on, Dawgs, come on! Ace breaks the huddle. Stands over center. What's the play? Meat, you forgot the play! Screw it, just find the open man. Snap count? Can't . . . think. Hut . . . hut. . . hut . . .*

Dick Lawrence hauls Ace out of the water, his skin mottled and gray. He half-carries him below where hot steam is pouring from the open bathroom door. Carefully, he lays the naked man onto the shower floor, allowing the warm water to slowly revive him.

"Within the next half-century, it will be essential for the human species to have fully operational a flexibly designed, broadly equitable and internationally coordinated set of initiatives focused on reducing the then-current world population by at least 80 percent."

—J. Kenneth Smail,
Professor of Anthropology
Confronting the 21st Century's Hidden Crisis:
Reducing Human Numbers by 80 percent,
May 1995

"The nations of the world must develop a plan to reduce global population from nearly 6 billion to about 2 billion."

—David and Marcia Pimental,
Prof. of Ecology and Agricultural Science,
"Food, Energy and Society," 2000

CHAPTER 28

"HERE, DRINK THIS."

Ace takes the mug of cocoa from Dick Lawrence with both hands, his limbs still not fully his to control. He is dressed again, still shivering despite being wrapped under several wool blankets.

Lawrence had piloted the boat on to Nain, anchoring in a secluded cove. It is after seven in the evening, but the sun remains fixed above the horizon—Labrador's version of a summer Arctic night.

"Acute hypothermia. Condition becomes critical if the body's core temperature drops below ninety degrees. Body shuts down, dementia sets in. If I had to go, that's the way I'd do it."

"Don't let me hold you back."

Lawrence offers a half smile. "There are reasons I did what I did. First, I needed to find out what you knew. Second and more important, there's a microscopic tracking device floating through your bloodstream. I needed to shut it down."

"Tracking device? What the hell are you talking about?"

"The federal government's latest gimmick for violating our civil rights. Every citizen accounted for, every foreigner tracked. Americans too, if they make the White House hit list, which you obviously made."

"This is crazy! There's no tracking device on me!"

"Yeah, there is. They injected you with it when you went through customs at Kennedy International."

"Injected? No, that was a vaccine to prevent—"

"Avian Bird Flu. Sure it was. And you know this because you had the elixir analyzed, right? For someone who was married to a former spook, you really are naive." Lawrence takes the empty mug from him. "Total Information Awareness—TIA for short, another program brought to you courtesy of DARPA and the Evil Empire. Used to be a time when the Constitution actually protected the privacy rights of its citizens—of course, that was before the Patriot Act. But the Feds weren't satisfied with just being able to monitor your finances, Internet, e-mail, phone calls, and travel plans. No, they wanted to be able to actually get *inside* our biology. Enter the *Mu* chip, a tiny invader the size of a grain of sand. *Mu* allows the government to scan you, track you, and determine what hazardous materials you've come in contact with. The next generation *Mu* will enable Washington to eavesdrop on our very thought process. Exciting, huh?"

"The cold water . . . disabled it?"

"Yep. The chip's designed to embed itself within the wall of an artery. It's powered by your core body heat. Drop the core temperature below 93 degrees and you short-circuit the device. The Feds have been tracking you for months. They were using you to lead them to me. I'm Casper, by the way. The name was your old lady's idea. And I'm sincerely sorry for your loss. Your wife was a good soul. If not for her, I wouldn't be alive."

Ace lays his head back against the cushioned bench. He's exhausted physically and overwhelmed mentally. "Who are you?"

"Who I am is no matter. What I was, however . . ." Lawrence crosses the cabin to the bar and pours himself a drink. "I'd offer you one, but it's a fallacy that alcohol raises core temperature."

"Just answer the question."

"I was a microbiologist. I ran a lab specializing in antiviral vaccines. In 1997 we began extensive field work on Avian influenza, an infection which occurs naturally among birds. Wild birds carry the viruses in their intestines and infected birds shed the influenza virus in their saliva, feces, and nasal secretions. There are more than a dozen different subtypes of influenza, but the virus had never seriously infected people. Type-A influenza, however, is constantly evolving, and in 1997 we began receiving confirmed cases of human infection. The culprit was H5N1, a subtype that had crossed the species barrier to kill off 70 percent of those infected, the majority being once-healthy children and young adults. Scary stuff. Were H5N1 virus to suddenly gain the ability to spread easily from person to person, we'd be facing an influenza pandemic.

"Any hoot, in March of 2000 my research team was taken over by ARPA, the Advanced Research Projects Agency, a DoD initiative responsible for, and I quote, 'the direction or performance of such advanced projects in the field of research and development as the Secretary of Defense shall, from time to time, designate by individual project or by category,' unquote. ARPA, sometimes known as DARPA, depending upon whose ass sits in the Oval Office, decided they wanted my team to evolve the H5N1 virus. In essence, they wanted a strain that could actually cause the pandemic."

"What the hell for?"

"DARPA claimed it would assist us in finding a cure, should the need arise, but in a more evil sense, it also gave them the capacity to play God. Still, working with lethal strains is nothing new, and we certainly had ample facilities to contain the virus, but coming from the DoD, the request still sent shivers down our spines. Then, about a year later, our paranoia turned into real fear when microbiologists around the world began turning up dead."

"From the disease?"

"No, no, this was murder—targeted sanctions. The first one happened on October 4, 2001, less than a month after the 9/11 attacks. Air Sibir Flight 1812 left Israel, en route to Novosibirsk, Siberia, only the plane was shot down by what was later called an errant surface-to-air missile—the missile errant by about 100 miles. Everyone on board was killed, including five of the world's top microbiologists. About that same time two more Israeli scientists were murdered, supposedly by Arab terrorists.

"Eight days later, Benito Que, a cell biologist at the University of Miami, was found dead outside his hematology department. Police called it a mugging, even though Que didn't have his wallet on him at the time. Four days later, Donald C. Wiley, one of the world's leading microbiologists and winner of the 1995 Albert Lasker Basic Medical Research Award for his work on antiviral vaccines, was reported missing after attending a dinner at the Peabody Hotel in Memphis. His dead body was later found snagged on a tree near the Hernando de Soto Bridge. Investigators ruled it a car accident, even though his rental had been abandoned on the bridge with no structural damage."

"Damn . . ."

"Oh, it gets better. On November 23, Vladimir Pasechnik, a Soviet defector and expert on DNA sequencing, turned up dead outside his home. One day later, another air liner crashed, this one a Swissair flight. On board was Avishai Berkman, Amiram Eldor, and Yaacov Matzner—directors of the hematology department at the Ichilov Hospital in Israel, the Hebrew University School of Medicine, and the Tel Aviv Public health department. Two weeks later, on December 10, Robert Schwartz, founding member of the Virginia Biotechnology Association and the Executive Director of Research and Development at Virginia's Center for Innovative Technology, was found murdered in his home. Not even 24 hours later, Dr. Set Van Nguyen got his. Nguyen supposedly died after entering a refrigerated storage facility in Geelong, Australia, unaware that there just happened to be a toxic leak of liquid nitrogen inside. Feel free to Google any of these names . . . tell me I'm wrong."

"I think I get the picture."

"I'm far from done!" Lawrence snaps. "February 8, Victor Korshunov, head of the microbiology sub-facility at the Russian State Medical University, suffered a lethal cranial injury. Three days later it's Ian Langford's turn. British police claim they found nothing suspicious about the death, even though Langford's body was discovered crammed under a chair, his home ransacked, blood everywhere. Tanya Holzmayer was shot dead in Mountain View, California, on the 27th when she answered the door for a pizza delivery boy. That same night in another part of California, microbiologist Guyang Huang was shot in the head while jogging in a park in Foster City. Nineteen dead scientists in four months—all experts in the field of viruses. No arrests, everything kept out of the news and conveniently swept under the carpet. Coincidence or conspiracy theory—you tell me. Ah, but here's another coincidence. It turns out many of these biowarfare experts all worked for research facilities that received grants from—drum roll please—the Howard Hughes Medical Institute, a group long suspected of 'allegedly' funding black ops biomedical research for the CIA. And everything happening right after 9/11 . . . about the time militarized anthrax turned up missing at the biowarfare facility at Fort Detrick, Maryland, a complex whose security makes Fort Knox look like a 7-Eleven. If you remember, it was about that time the Bush Administration was trying to ramrod the Patriot Act down Congress's throat, only the Dems controlled the Senate by one vote, thanks to Jim Jeffords switching from Republican to Independent. There were two influential Democrats poised to thwart the Patriot Act— Tom Daschle and Patrick Leahy—and they were the only ones on Capitol Hill to receive packages of anthrax. The anthrax used in those packages was traced back to the Ames strain taken from Fort Detrick, yet John Ashcroft refused to follow up on that little piece of evidence—a strong-arm tactic so blatant that you would have thought the Mafia conceived it. But forgive me, after all, I'm just a conspiracy theorist."

"How does Kelli figure into all this?"

"Your wife was involved in the Neocon's next false flag event—a radical contingency plan to deal with the 'Big Rollover,' the end of oil. I know I'm preaching to the choir, but the Big Rollover is essentially a math problem. See, even with oil, the planet only has feeding and energy capacity for about two billion people. We manage now because four billion of our fellow human beings are slowly starving to death in Africa and Asia. That leaves about a billion or so of us lucky ones who get to lead the charmed life, only the rules change when the pumps run dry. Divide six billion into what little food and fuel resources are left after the Big Rollover, and you come up with approximately five hundred million people, give or take a few hundred thousand. No substitute for oil? No problem! We'll just sit back and systematically starve 5.5 billion people. Ah, but civilized folk, they don't just lie down with their kids and grandmas and friends to die. First they go crazy. Anarchy's a definite problem to the haves of this world, so we needed a contingency plan . . . just in case. When it comes to thinning the herd, you can't just drop a few dozen nukes or start a conventional war, not without gasoline, so what's the solution to global chaos? You guessed it—pandemic. Brought to you courtesy of DARPA—makers of the new and improved H5N1 virus."

Ace swallows the vomit rising from his gut. "The dead scientists?"

"Yep. They were the ones who would have found a cure. See, when you go to all the trouble to start a pandemic, the last thing you want are the Jonas Salks of the world running around curing your disease, so it's best you kill them off first. Kelli got to me just in time. Saved a few of my colleagues as well. Gave us new identities, kept us alive. If and when the pandemic finally strikes, a few chosen pharmaceutical companies will pocket another five billion dollars, and the powers-that-be will dole out the antidote . . . oh, but not all Americans will be saved. If you're a heterosexual, God-fearing Caucasian Christian who believes in Jesus—congratulations, your future looks bright. Black and Hispanic... not so good. Jew? For now, but only because the New Testament says we need Israel around to complete Revelation. Homosexual? Sorry, Brucie. According to Jesus' earthly disciple, Pat Robertson, God wants you dead, only God in this case is some sick Neoconservative capitalistic Grim Reaper who passed a law allowing him to inject you with a microchip designed to regulate your personal biochemistry. Ah, but in the end, guess who gets the last laugh? Yep, it's the man upstairs Himself, the Lord Almighty. See, those religious hypocrites who preach Jesus and love the fetus but hate stem cell research are still going to need fuel, and you don't think they'll be tapping into wind or solar do you? Nah, they'll use coal. Got to keep the wheels of commerce turning. One slight problem: Coal increases carbon dioxide levels, and despite George Dubuya and the fossil fuel lobbyists' claims to the contrary, Earth's atmosphere really has been teetering on the catastrophic fence when it comes to lethal levels of greenhouse gases. Add more coal, and the planet surpasses its critical absorption limit. Global warming becomes a runaway train. Arctic ice melts like it was in a microwave, and all that fresh water inundates the North Atlantic current, effectively shutting down the oceans' heat exchange system. North America and Europe become a winter wonderland, and we say bye-bye to the white man. But hey, no worries. The human race will go on, thanks to people like the Inuit and the Maya, aboriginal cultures that always respected the land and never needed electricity anyway. Poetic justice, huh? The white man steals the land from the Indians, exploits his resources, and modern man's reign ends in ignorance and self-destruction. What was it Jesus said? And the meek shall inherit the earth? Smart guy."

Ace pushes Dick Lawrence aside, barely making it to the toilet as he loses his lunch.

"The Army Corps of Engineers, rushing to meet President Bush's promise to protect New Orleans by the start of the 2006 hurricane season, installed defective flood-control pumps despite warnings from its own expert that the equipment would fail in a storm. The drainage-canal pumps were custom-designed and built under a $26.6 million contract awarded after competitive bidding to Moving Water industries Corp. of Deerfield Beach, Florida. MWI is owned by J. David Eller and his sons. Eller was once a business partner of former Florida Governor Jeb Bush in a venture called Bush-El that marketed MWI pumps. Eller has donated about $128,000 to politicians, the vast majority of it to the Republican Party, according to the Center for Responsive Politics."

—CAIN BUREAU,
Associated Press
March 14, 2007

"Remember JFK? When John F. Kennedy ran for president he had to convince the American public he would leave his (Catholic) religion in the pew. Today, politicians have to wear their religion on their sleeves . . . because 'Jesus knows who he wants to nuke.'"

—RANDI RHODES,
The Randi Rhodes Show,
June 6, 2007

"The Islamic-Fascists hate our freedom. They hate everything about us! How do you propose we deal with Iran?! You can't deal rationally with a religious group hell-bent on our destruction!"

—TODD SCHNITT,
The Schnitt Show,
June 6, 2007

CHAPTER 29

It sits on fifty-two acres in downtown New Orleans, a concrete and steel palace that, seven years earlier, had served as a refuge to thousands of people fleeing Hurricane Katrina. Now, beneath the repaired ten-acre dome that had nearly blown off in 140-mile-per-hour winds, thousands of independent-minded constituents congregate as one. The arena buzzes with excitement and anxiety as they await their candidate, hoping and praying he delivers the homerun their presidential campaign desperately needs in what most agree will be the most important speech of his political life.

From her perch in one of the press boxes, Jennifer Wienner opens her laptop, ready to chart Senator Mulligan's speech on a real-time polling program.

"My fellow Americans, I give you Senator Edward Randle Mulligan, the next President of the United States!"

Senator Mulligan steps out from behind the curtain, waving to his audience. He shakes hands with the VIPs on stage, hugs his running mate, six-term Congresswoman Cynthia McKinney, and then steps to the podium, allowing the applause to die down before he begins.

"The eighteenth-century English poet Edward Young wrote,

'All men think all men mortal but themselves.' Ladies and gentlemen, this election isn't about religious preferences or challenging abortion. It's not about gun rights or gay rights, which candidate goes to church more often, or who has the best smile for TV. It's not about living in a red state or blue state. It's not even about living in the United States. This election is about one thing: Survival. Our survival as a species and the world we want to leave our children. There are two choices that lie before us, two paths, two destinies . . . and one way or the other, your vote is going to make a major impact on deciding which course humankind ventures down. One choice leads to hope, the other oblivion. One leads to an independent, clean, thriving economy, and the other a planet teetering on global warming, foreign dependence, and unforeseen chaos.

"Our country, founded on the principles of liberty and independence, has been hijacked by two parties of self-serving politicians and businessmen who have used their influence to trample upon our civil liberties and sell our independence. We the people, caretakers of the present and guardians of the future, have remained all-too-silent while the unbridled power of the few has combined with the greed of the many to steal our hopes and dreams. Corporations, not voters, now shape our policies, the needs of a nation ignored. Members of Congress, entrusted and appointed by the American people to make laws that protect our family, have time and again voted in their own selfish, self-serving interests. Hardworking, dedicated Americans have watched in shock and disgust as the pirates of Wall Street have been allowed to pillage companies and steal pension funds that belong to you. Pharmaceutical companies have lobbied Capitol Hill to enact legislation that has allowed them to feast in windfall profits, while our sick and elderly must starve themselves just to afford their monthly medication. Companies like Monsanto now control seed stock and our food supplies, pumping our livestock with steroids and our crops with harmful pesticides. Twelve years ago our country was an economic bedrock, swelling with jobs and a surplus in our treasury, and now, three administrations later, we are generations in debt, our jobs outsourced, our retirement funds stolen, our nation bogged down in a war that maims and kills our sons and daughters while making its puppet-masters richer. Tonight I stand here before you and I say enough!"

A crescendo of applause.

Jennifer watches the pollster lines spike on her laptop. She types in a few notes.

"Back in 1973, the Arab world gave us a taste of what it means to be dependent on another nation or group of nations in order to fuel our cars and feed our masses, power our homes and drive our economy. Instead of seizing the moment, instead of investing our resources in technologies that would have led us to clean, cheap home-grown energies, our leaders let the moment pass, the oil addiction to manifest. If we could turn back the clock and take that high road, today there would be no war in the Middle East or threats of terrorism, today there would be no deficit and no global warming. Having sown our seeds in a new, green infrastructure, we would be reaping a fruitful harvest instead of maneuvering our armies in the desert to suck up the last remaining drops of Persian Gulf crude.

"For a moment, let us imagine the world that could have been, the changes I intend to enact as your new president. First and foremost, we shall enact a twenty-point energy plan based on conservation and alternative green energy programs. Instead of thinking nationally, we will strategize locally. In the sunbelt we'll turn to solar farms. Along the coast we'll build windmills. We'll invest in retooling our infrastructure and electrical grids, as well as a new rail system, paralleling the success of our friends in Japan. We will provide seed money for local farms, growing our food organically, restoring the soil, while investing in our communities.

"How will we pay for all these new programs? That answer is simple and long overdue: Within my first six months in office, I shall withdraw all American troops and private armies from Iraq, close our military bases, and begin a systematic withdrawal from Afghanistan."

Senator Mulligan pauses, the applause long and deafening.

"Imagine driving along our vast coastlines and seeing thousands of brand-new high-tech retractable windmills—windmills that will harness nature's unlimited fury to power our homes and businesses with cheap, affordable, clean electricity. Windmills whose aluminum and steel is forged by American workers, windmills whose turbines are constructed by American technicians, erected by American construction firms. And when my administration enacts laws that require all new construction to use solar panels, it will be the American worker who will assemble those photovoltaic cells and the American family that will benefit from clean, cheap, electricity. It takes leadership to turn this dream into a reality, and it takes a real commitment to change our infrastructure from a dependent, carbon-based economy into a lean, clean, and green society, and that is why I am here!"

Thunderous applause shakes the Superdome.

"My fellow Americans, vision is not enough. For you have heard the rhetoric before, but the intent was hollow, the action non-existent. It's not enough to talk the talk, we have to roll up our sleeves and make it happen. To change the world we must first change directions, and to change directions we must first purge our nation's capitol of all those elected officials who would stand in our way, all those beholden to the fossil fuel industry, all those whose candidacies are funded by the blood of our children. Over the next seventy-five days our campaign will identify those politicians who stand with us and those individuals who stand with the oil companies, and there will be no blue or red states—only green!"

Raucous applause. Jennifer smiles in satisfaction as the polling data spikes again.

"We know where Ellis Prescott and his cronies stand. We know where his campaign funds come from, which oil companies dole out the checks, which zealots fuel the vicious attacks broadcast by 527 organizations—organizations whose only strategy is to make up outrageous lies and repeat them over and over and over again until they blur the lines of truth. Do not allow their message of hatred to be the message of this election. Do not take your eye off the ball, ladies and gentlemen, when my opponents trot out the same old rhetoric of fear. This election is not about God, gays, or guns, nor is it about stealing votes from the Democrats. We salute the many years of service the Clintons have given to our nation, but now is not the time for more center of left politics or more fearmongering and corruption spawned by the policies of the radical right. Liberalism is not a four-letter word. It is a Jeffersonian means to guide this nation away from the archaic and abysmal economic and energy policy failures of both Democrats and Republicans. Tonight, we offer Americans another choice—a choice unbeholden to the oil companies and the military machine . . . free of the bickering that has handcuffed the last four years of the Obama Administration. The media will tell you we cannot win, but they are ruled by the biases dictated by their own corporate interests. Do not allow yourselves to be deceived by the devil who would steal your vote as quickly as he would steal your pension fund. Prepare yourself now for a war of words, for as the election draws closer, my opponents will become more desperate, and each of you must know the difference between what is truth and the snake oil being sold as truth."

The Senator pauses, waiting for the applause to die down.

"Speaking of snake oil, over the last few years, former Vice President Dick Cheney has been on a personal crusade to incite fear, predicting another terrorist attack that would somehow justify the illegality of torture and prove his administration kept our country safe. In doing so, Mr. Cheney fails to point out that the heinous events of 9/11 occurred on his watch . . . that intelligence warnings were deliberately ignored, and that a full investigation was made impossible after evidence was destroyed and key witnesses excused from testifying under oath. No one is above the law, Mr. Cheney. When elected, I shall appoint a non-partisan committee to investigate 9/11, and this time no stone will be left unturned. This time we shall flush out every snake and bring the guilty to justice."

A wild response. Cynthia McKinney offers an approving thumbs-up.

"To those of you who are amateur golfers, you know what a mulligan is." The Senator grins at the smattering of applause. "To those who don't, a mulligan is a term that means I screwed up and would like a do-over. My fellow Americans, as a nation we screwed up. The Democrats screwed up because we weren't as strong and decisive as we needed to be, and the Republicans screwed up because they allowed their grand ole party to be hijacked by radical elements of the right who suckle from the teat of a bigoted talk show host. All of us screwed up when we trusted that our leaders would not engage this country in a war under false pretenses. We screwed up when we trusted our government to build levies that would last and protect us in times of natural disasters. Now we must trust our hearts to decide which path leads to glory and which path leads to more lies and deceit, more pain and anguish, more dependence on third-world countries that do not especially like us. On election night your vote becomes the catalyst for change. No more red states, no more blue. Tonight I accept this nomination on behalf of all Americans who believe change is a verb, not a noun. The Green Party is that change!"

The three colored needles on Jennifer's monitor hit the upper reaches of the graph as the arena rocks beneath thunderous applause and the music of The Who's *I Won't Be Fooled Again* jump-starts the Green party.

ATLANTIC OCEAN
12 NAUTICAL MILES NORTHEAST OF PORTLAND, MAINE
AUGUST 26, 2012
4:28 AM EST

The moon's reflection splays across two-foot swells, rippling in the boat's bow wake. Ace stretches in the pilot's chair, grateful for the calm. They have been at sea a solid two weeks, following the Labrador coastline south through the Strait of Belle Isle, down past Quebec and through the Cabot Strait before hitting rough seas along the coast of Nova Scotia.

Dick Lawrence had used the time, elements, and Ace's subsequent seasickness in his training regimen. "When I dunked you, you were too focused on relieving the pain. It was too easy to extract the information."

"I had no reason to hide it."

"And if the Saudis capture you? If this plan of yours is to succeed, you have to believe in your alibi and hold out as long as possible."

"And how do I do that?"

"You have to train yourself to tuck your mind inside a place where they cannot reach you. You must dissociate your mind from the physical torture."

"The torture . . . besides waterboarding, what kind of things have you heard?"

"I won't lie, if these guys capture you, death may be your best option. The Chilean military, trained and financed by the United States, used to do barbaric things to their victims before they died. Electric shock or acid to the genitals, bayonets rammed into the anus, various body parts mutilated or punctured, toes, tongues, and ears cut off. Female prisoners were raped while members of their family were forced to watch, rats placed in their vaginas and into the mouths—"

"Stop!"

"I'm telling you these things to prepare you. You came to me with a cover story filled with holes. Your accent was wrong, your basic knowledge non-existent. You need to study, Ace. You need to know your new identity inside out. If someone yells 'Ace' from across the room, you have to be conditioned not to look. You have to become this new person. Because if they see through the ruse, the pain they'll inflict will be excruciating. They'll keep you alive, at least until they get what they want from you, which is why we need to prepare you. Beg to live and you're as good as dead. But if they see you want to die, they won't kill you. It's simple reverse psychology, but it tends to hold true."

The fear tactics had worked. Ace had studied, creating memories for his new persona, rehearsing what he would do at customs, how he would enter the Saudi bank, what he would say, how he would react. Knowing his false identity would never hold up under interrogation, he and Lawrence had come up with a legitimate reason why Ace would be seeking the help of a Saudi banker under false pretenses. The new alibi was stronger, and the training gave him confidence, just as it had twenty years ago on the football field. After two weeks he felt ready for his "bowl game."

◆ ◆ ◆

The horizon bleeds red as the sun moves closer to dawn. Gulls caw in the distance, the shoreline becoming visible again. They will arrive in Gloucester, Massachusetts before noon, giving Ace ample time to catch a taxi to Boston's Logan Airport. The reservation is under Stephen Murphy, his round-trip ticket to France. A hotel has been booked in Paris where he will stay for two days. Dick Lawrence's associates in Paris have scheduled a meeting for Ace with a French businessman who knows one of the branch managers at the National Commercial Bank in Riyadh, and a meeting with him will be set.

In five days, Ace Futrell will return to the Kingdom of Al Saud to kick off the biggest game of his life.

"A federal investigation into the bank accounts of the Saudi Embassy in Washington has identified more than $27 million in 'suspicious' transactions—including hundreds of thousands of dollars paid to Muslim charities, and to clerics and Saudi students who are being scrutinized for possible links to terrorist activity. The probe also has uncovered large wire transfers overseas by the Saudi ambassador to the United States, Prince Bandar bin Sultan. The transactions recently prompted the Saudi Embassy's longtime bank, the Riggs Bank of Washington, D.C. (PNC), to drop the Saudis as a client after embassy officials were 'unable to provide an explanation that was satisfying,' says a source familiar with the discussions."

—*Newsweek*,
April 12, 2006

"The Saudis are active at every level of the terror chain, from planners to financiers, from cadre to foot soldier, from ideologist to cheerleader. Saudi Arabia supports our enemies and attacks our allies."

—Laurent Murawiec,
Analyst, Rand Corporation

CHAPTER 30

Iran Threatens Retaliation through Hezbollah

Associated Press: August 28, 2012

As tensions in the Middle East continue to increase between the United States and Iran, Homeland Security experts have voiced growing concerns that Iran's newfound nuclear weapons capability could lead to an attack on American soil.

"We know Iran supports (Lebanon-based) Hezbollah, which has cells in the U.S., as well as Al-Qaeda," said Patrick Blanchard, Homeland Security Assistant Director of counterterrorism. "The Iranian government views the Islamic Jihad as an extension of their own state policies. Unlike the attacks of September 11th (2001), one- or two-men operational teams armed with a nuclear device could be deployed without much preparation."

Governor Prescott addressed these concerns in his speech yesterday in Cleveland. "We live in dangerous times. I think the American public understands and appreciates the fact that the Bush/Cheney Administration was tough on terrorism. I pray every day that our citizens will not have to pay the price for the lax years of the Obama Administration. As Vice President Cheney has repeatedly warned, closing Guantanamo was a dangerous mistake. As for the third-party candidate (Senator Mulligan), while investing in alternative energy resources is important, you don't get a mulligan when a nuclear weapon or a dirty bomb goes off. There is nothing more important to me than protecting our homeland. Come November, I believe most Americans will want a leader in the White House who best protects their family, not a candidate who cares more about the rights of terrorists or a man building windmills."

Washington, D.C.
August 29, 2012

FBI Director Gary Schafer pulls into the donut shop parking lot, checks his watch to verify he is still early, and then heads inside.

A half-block away, Elliott Green parks his car curbside. The suspended FBI agent has been shadowing Schafer's movements for the last eleven days. Today marks the first time the director has left his office during working hours, and Green doubts it is because of a sugar craving.

Minutes later, Schafer emerges from the donut shop with a coffee. Instead of returning to his car, he heads for the pay phone mounted on the building's exterior brick facing.

Bingo. Green's heart races as he aims a handheld parabolic dish the size of a small Frisbee out his open passenger window. The electronic surveillance device amplifies the collected sounds, concentrating them to the center of the dish where they are picked up by a sensitive microphone. Positioning padded headphones over his ears, Elliott simultaneously eavesdrops and records Gary Lee Schafer's call:

"It's me. What's your status?" (Pause)

Green grabs his camera with his free hand and adjusts the telephoto lens. Snaps a few quick pictures.

"Why the delay? (Pause) Yes, well now it does matter. The powers-that-be are debating moving up the date. (Pause) Because our friend is trailing in the polls, or don't you read the newspapers? (Long pause) Six weeks, nine at the most. Just be ready to mobilize. I'll call you next week with their decision."

Green gathers in his equipment as Schafer climbs back

into his car and drives out of the parking lot. He waits another thirty seconds before jogging over to the pay phone. He dials a number.

"Green, Elliott. Identification number 155-16533-17. I need the phone number and location of the last number dialed out from this payphone."

RIYADH KING KHALED INTERNATIONAL AIRPORT
RIYADH, SAUDI ARABIA
SEPTEMBER 1, 2012

The Air France commercial jet descends over endless brown desert, the steep escarpments of the Tuwaiq highlands rising along the periphery. In the distance is King Khalid International Airport, an oasis of concrete and glass spread out over eighty-seven miles of flatland.

Once a remote desert town, Riyadh has been transformed into the largest city in Saudi Arabia. The nation's capitol boasts two major universities: King Sa'ud University and Iman Muhammad Ibn Sa'ud Islamic University, as well as the most sophisticated medical center in the kingdom. Riyadh is also home to the Saudi Arabian Monetary Agency (SAMA), which functions as the country's central bank and investment authority.

The 737 jetliner touches down, then taxis to its designated terminal. Removing his briefcase from an overhead bin, Ace Futrell follows his fellow passengers through a carpeted air bridge and down an escalator into the corridor leading to customs and immigration.

Sunlight streams in through a great tiered roof composed of seventy-two curved triangular panels. Water cascades down tiled banks into a collection pool. Fig trees grow out of garden courtyards. Upward of seven hundred fifty thousand plants and three hundred varieties of trees, shrubs, and flowers have been imported to fill the airport's terminals, malls, and pavilions, as well as a mosque that can hold five thousand worshipers, and the

Garden of Eden effect is dazzling.

"Are you here on business or pleasure, Mr. Murphy?"

"Hopefully both."

The passport is stamped, the customs official sending Ace off to collect his belongings. The limo driver is waiting at baggage claim, holding a sign that reads "Stephen Murphy."

Twenty minutes later they are on the highway, heading for downtown Riyadh.

✦ ✦ ✦

"Why the hell are you calling me?"

Scott Santa feels satisfaction at having tweaked David Schall's blood pressure. "Our boy just arrived in Riyadh. I thought you'd want to know."

"What? Hold on . . . stay on the line." Santa hears the CIA director relocate to another room for privacy. "Are you certain?"

"You forget, I still employ people in customs. He's traveling under an alias, using a Canadian passport. The new security cameras scanned his face, the markers came up positive for an alert I had placed back in March. I told my contact to allow him through."

"What the hell for?"

"If he insists on hunting me, better I know where he is."

"He's a loose cannon! I suggest you—"

The Russian-American snaps his cell phone shut, cutting off the irate intelligence director. Seated in the lobby of the Intercontinental Hotel on Maazar Street, Santa watches with perverse amusement as Ace Futrell checks in at the front desk.

✦ ✦ ✦

"Welcome to the Hotel Continental, Mr. Murphy. We have you on the seventh floor. Your room charges have already been taken care of. Is there anything else I can do for you?"

"Yes, I was expecting a package."

The clerk searches under his desk, emerging with the

Federal Express package containing the Promis worm CD-ROM. "There you are, sir. Have a good stay."

GARY, INDIANA
SEPTEMBER 1, 2012

Located on the southern banks of Lake Michigan, twenty-seven miles from downtown Chicago, is Gary, Indiana, a city named after Elbert H. Gary, the chairman of U.S. Steel, though it is better known as the hometown of the musical Jackson family.

Mitchell Wagner, Ace's former college teammate, is the vice president of operations for the Gary Southshore Railcats, a minor-league baseball team competing in the Northern League, which operates in the Midwestern United States and the Canadian provinces of Manitoba and Alberta. Wagner escorts Leigh and Sammy Futrell into his office, his bay window overlooking right field of the U.S. Steel Yard, the Railcats' six-thousand-seat facility.

"I know it's not Yankee Stadium, but we still have a lot of fun. You can watch the games from here, or from our reserved seats behind home plate. What do you think, Sam? Maybe I can even put you to work as a ball boy."

"I wanna go home."

Leigh hugs her younger brother. "When can we go home?"

"Now, we've been through this. As soon as your dad feels good about things, I'll have you on the next plane to New York. Until then, let's all just make the best of it."

"What about school? We're supposed to start school in a couple of weeks."

"We'll hire a tutor. Again, I'm sure your dad will be home soon and—"

"And what if he's not?" Leigh's eyes cut into Wagner, who has been wavering himself of late about the legal guardian position Ace dropped on him out of the blue. "What if something bad happens? What if he never comes back?"

Sam tears up again. "I'm supposed to play peewee football. Me and Matthew Cubit already signed up."

"The Bears! I've got season tickets to the Bears." Wagner searches his top desk drawer for an envelope of tickets. "Sam, you and I could go, how about that? And Leigh, Mrs. Wagner could take you shopping. Have you ever been to Chicago? It's a great city, with cool museums and tons of malls. How about that?"

Sam wipes his face. "I don't like the Bears. I like the Jets."

"The Jets, huh?" Wagner looks frantically for his Chicago Bears schedule. "Hmm, we don't play the Jets this year. How about Greenbay or the Vikings?"

The boy sniffles.

"Hold the phone, how about the Giants? Look-ee here, Bears versus the New York Giants, and it's a Monday night game. That's pretty cool, huh? By then you'll probably be back home with your dad, but let's plan to go, all four of us. We'll spend the day in the city, and then it's Monday Night Football. You like the Giants, don't you, Sam?"

Sam looks at his sister, who nods.

"Beautiful." Wagner circles the date, wondering when the kids' father will ever get around to wiring the promised funds . . . or if he is even alive.

NATIONAL COMMERCIAL BANK
GHARNATA BRANCH, KHALID BIN WALEED STREET
RIYADH, SAUDI ARABIA
SEPTEMBER 3, 2012
10:27 AM LOCAL TIME

It was the first bank established in Saudi Arabia, founded in 1953, pursuant to a royal decree made by the late King Abdulaziz Bin Abdul Rahman Al Saud. With nearly 270 branches and total capital exceeding $1.6 billion, it is the largest, most powerful financial institution in all the Middle East.

Like most NCB banks, the Riyadh branch is laid out in four distinct sections. The main area includes a lobby complete with electronic services for clients to make deposits, withdrawals, or to pay bills. The second section is specifically for private banking clients, known as *Al-Weesam*. The third section is for individual client services, and the last segregates its banking services for women.

Ace enters the heavily air-conditioned building, the back of his shirt already drenched in sweat beneath his tan business suit. He leaves Stephen Murphy's name at the reception desk and then has a seat in the lobby, keeping his briefcase by his side. He is more excited than nervous.

Seventeen minutes pass before he is greeted by the branch's assistant manager, Mr. Ibrahim Al-Kuwaiz. A stocky man with graying goatee and bushy eyebrows, Al-Kuwaiz leads Ace back to his private office.

Ace closes the door behind them, his eyes immediately targeting the computer terminal.

"So, Mr. Murphy, I understand you know our friend and client, Mr. Daniel Pernini."

"More of a business associate, but Mr. Pernini speaks very highly of your bank, which is why I recently opened business accounts at your Paris branch. My company plans on expanding our operations in the Persian Gulf, but first I had a few issues to discuss."

"Such as?"

"First, if you could pull up my new account on your computer." Ace hands him a blank business check, the banking codes and account numbers appearing along the bottom.

Al-Kuwaiz enters his personal information into the computer to access the system and then types in Ace's banking info. "Hmm. Yankee Clipper Products. What is it you sell, Mr. Murphy?"

"You've heard of the New York Yankee baseball team? Well, we do it all. Souvenirs, programs—$200 million worth a year." Ace opens his briefcase and takes out a Yankees baseball cap. "For you."

"Most kind." The manager sets it aside.

"I have another gift; it's something very special. I want your opinion about it. It's very important. The bank manager in Paris tried it and loved it, but I find Saudi tastes to be different." Ace takes out a pack of chewing gum with a Yankee emblem. Removes a stick and hands it to Mr. Al-Kuwaiz. "This is a new flavor of gum. Chew it and tell me what you think."

"I am really not a gum chewer."

"But you are a businessman. A few quick chews and you'll have the freshest breath in the bank."

Al-Kuwaiz unwraps it. Hesitates, and then pops the yellow rectangle into his mouth, his thick goatee twitching as he chews.

As Ace watches, Al-Kuwaiz's eyes grow heavy, his jaws ceasing mid-chew. The gum is laced with Burundanga, a soluble powder better known in Colombia as Zombie Dust. Made from the borrachera plant, Burundanga has been called the world's most dangerous drug as it leaves its victims in a virtual coma, preventing the brain from recording any and all memory until it wears off hours later.

"Mr. Al-Kuwaiz?"

No response.

Ace removes the CD-ROM from the *John Lennon Greatest Hits* case, along with the Yankees' yearbook. Sliding his chair next to Al-Kuwaiz, he feigns reading the yearbook to the comatose manager as his eyes dart to the monitor. Casually, he leans under the desk, opening the computer hard drive's CD drawer. Quickly, he positions the CD-ROM containing the Promis worm inside and then closes the drawer.

A command appears up in Arabic. Using the mouse, he double-clicks on the prompter, his heart pounding as the timer bar pops up, signaling the worm is downloading.

Ace checks his watch: 10:38 a.m.

Referring again to the yearbook as if it was the Koran, Ace pretends to point out key passages to his Saudi Arabian zombie, silently urging the downloading bar to move faster—

—unaware that above his head, mounted in the ceiling behind a mirrored decoration, the bank's security camera is recording everything.

✦ ✦ ✦

Scott Santa enters the bank, wearing dark sunglasses and a beige Panama fedora. He smiles at the receptionist as he pretends to sign in, his eyes searching the registry, stopping at the name Stephen Murphy.

"May I help you, sir?"

"Yes, but first I must use the Internet."

The receptionist directs him to a vacant cubby along the far wall. "Help yourself."

✦ ✦ ✦

"And George Steinbrenner was finally forced to step down after he regurgitated a lung following the 2008 American League Championship loss to the Tampa Bay Rays. Years earlier, the Bronx Bombers had lost to another Florida fish-oriented expansion team, although it wasn't nearly as bad as losing to the Red Sox."

Ace checks his watch again: 11:14 a.m. His eyes remain glued to the bar code as it fills to 100 percent.

The monitor blinks off and then reboots.

"Well, it's been fun, but I really must be going." Ace pops out the CD-ROM. Slips it into the pages of the yearbook, grabs his briefcase, and exits the office as every computer terminal in the bank simultaneously reboots.

Moving through the lobby, Ace forces himself to slow down as he exits the bank—followed by his wife's assassin.

Ace leaves the bank entrance and turns right. He walks a block and rounds the corner as his fingers search the yearbook for the CD-ROM. Pausing, he forcibly steps on it, shattering it into a half dozen pieces. He picks up the shards, tosses all but one piece into a nearby trash receptacle, and hails a cab.

✦ ✦ ✦

He is back at the Intercontinental Hotel within twenty minutes, the adrenaline coursing through his body. His bladder tingles as he crosses the lobby to the elevators. The car loads, stops to let off other passengers, and then finally delivers him to the seventh floor. He keys open his room, rushes to the bathroom to urinate, and then changes out of the suit into casual clothes. He stuffs the suit into his bag, flings the remaining shard of CD-ROM out the open window and into the bushes below, and then grabs his bags and exits the room.

There are no cabs in front of the hotel. He signals to an attendant and waits, reminding himself to heed Dick Lawrence's advice. *Don't rush. Blend in.*

A taxi pulls into the hotel driveway. Ace waits for a middle-aged couple to climb out and then slides in back and slams the door. "Airport, please."

The taxi enters traffic.

Flight leaves in two hours. Get through customs, grab a sandwich, board the plane. Three hour lay-over in Paris, then it's on to the good ole U.S. of A. No, thanks, I was already inoculated for Bird Flu, and I had an allergic reaction. Now if you don't mind, I want to see my kids.

You'll get to New York by three tomorrow afternoon, hopefully in time to phone in the ad to the New York Times personals: Game over, final score 7–3. *Wags will call the phone booth at 7:30 eastern. Don't forget the all clear password. By Wednesday night, Leigh and Sammy will be back in my arms again . . . and then it's payback time.*

He hums a Diana Ross oldie. *Back in my arms again . . . so satisfied—*

"Sir, what airline?"

"Air France."

The driver lets him off at the international terminal. He makes his way through the Garden of Eden lobby and waits at the end of a long line at customs.

Twenty-five minutes pass. He grows nervous.

What if they find the bank manager before the drug wears off? Maybe you should have flown out of Jiddah? Or crossed the border into Israel? No, too dangerous.

"Passport please."

Ace hands the officer his passport.

"Thank you, sir. You've been randomly selected for a security check, please follow the officer to room six."

Random. Stay calm. Happens to me all the time.

He follows a customs officer into the brightly lit room.

It happens to Ace Futrell all the time—not to Stephen Murphy.

There are four of them. The Muttawa's beard is long, the religious cop's white *thobe* five inches too short. The other three men are Saudi police officers.

He never sees the fifth man, who clubs him across the back of the skull.

"You steal our wealth and oil at paltry prices because of your international influence and military threats. This theft is indeed the biggest theft ever witnessed by mankind in the history of the world."

—Osama bin Laden,
"Letter to the American People"

"President Bush and Vice President Dick Cheney authorized Cheney's top aide (I. Lewis Libby) to launch a counterattack of leaks against administration critics on Iraq by feeding intelligence information to reporters, according to court papers citing the aide's testimony in the CIA leak case."

—Associated Press,
April 6, 2006

"Extremism is so easy . . . when you go far enough to the right, you meet the same idiots coming around from the left."

—Clint Eastwood

CHAPTER 31

THE INDUSTRIAL PARK IS LOCATED off Grant Avenue, a main thoroughfare that runs past the Northeast Philadelphia commuter airport. Like the other office buildings in the complex, Unit-22 is a three-story affair, its brown-brick facing divided by the occasional narrow slit of rectangular glass that serves as a window.

The entire upper floor of Unit-22 has been leased to an entity calling itself the Johnston Foundation. Brochures describe the organization as a "united global effort to end suffering among children." There is a photo of a malnourished African child with a distended stomach on the front of the brochure and an address on the back where interested parties can send tax-deductible donations. The information lacks details about the size of the fund or who the foundation has helped.

Charles Wallace, known to his employees as CW, patrols the "Bullpen," seven rows of computer terminals eight rows deep. Each station is manned around the clock on eight-hour shifts, seven days a week by three rotating teams of computer technicians. "Starting pitchers" work the morning shift, creating new bank accounts in various financial institutions located in non-red-flagged countries throughout the world. "Middle relievers" work the afternoon shift, moving small deposits of seed money in and out of these accounts to create a history of activity. "Closing pitchers" work the night shift, stringing random sequences of accounts together before passing them on to "clean-up hitters" (located in another building) who eventually will arrange "donations" to a final recipient.

Attached to the base of each computer hard drive is a small black box the size of a cigarette pack. In the event of trouble, Wallace can press a programmed number on his cell phone, instantly erasing every file within every computer's data base.

On the first floor of Unit-22, two floors below the Johnston Foundation, is Brewer Travel. The agency handles just enough business to occupy its sole travel agent, Betti Fortier, a forty-year-old mother of four. Fortier enjoys the light hours and good pay, though she worries how long the owner can afford to keep the agency open. The slow business never seems to bother Lynn Brewer, who spends most of her time hunkered down in her private office at her computer, sipping diet vanilla Pepsi behind her closed Venetian blinds.

Brewer, a self-described "hyperactive, hard-rocking Irishwoman," is a former computer systems analyst who has spent the last decade bouncing between one missile defense contractor to another, always following the money. Though she has spent most of her last twenty years creating software programs to chase hackers, her specialty remains banking systems. For twenty-three days, the "COBOL queen" has been monitoring Promis, waiting for the spy program's worm she had designed months ago to come online.

At precisely 4:53 p.m., her computer "blinks."

"Well hello, gorgeous." She tosses aside the trashy novel she has been reading and rapidly types a series of passwords and commands.

The screen changes, revealing passages of streaming data.

Brewer smiles in satisfaction as she dials a number on her cell phone. "Mr. Keene? Lynn Brewer over at Brewer Travel. If you're still interested in booking that package to Maui you should do it soon, it looks like airfares are going up."

MABAHETH INTERROGATION CENTRE
RIYADH, SAUDI ARABIA

The cell is windowless. A bare bulb hangs from the ceiling, centered above a wooden table and folding chairs. Ace sits upright, his arms pinned painfully behind his back, his wrists handcuffed. His head throbs where the baton had struck his skull, his hair is caked with dried blood. His shoes and socks have been removed. His bare feet, shackled around the ankles, are propped up on the table.

A guard hovers behind Ace, leaning on a thick bamboo cane. The police interrogator continues to ask questions. "Who do you work for, Mr. Murphy?"

"I told you, I dabble in all sorts of ventures. Oil, a souvenir company."

"What was your business at the National Bank?"

"I'm starting a new product line in the Middle East. A friend recommended I move some of my assets into the bank. Is that a crime?"

"What did you do to the bank's assistant manager, Mr. Al-Kuwaiz?"

"Nothing. We were talking, and the guy sort of went dumb on me. Did he have a stroke or something?"

The interrogator nods.

The guard steps forward. He smiles at Ace—as he whacks the soft bottom of Ace's bare feet with the bamboo cane.

Ace jumps as he howls in pain, his body convulsing beneath him.

The investigator calmly continues. "You inserted a CD-ROM into the banker's computer. What was it?"

The bare bulb spins in Ace's blurred vision. "A video game, a sample of my wares. He . . . he asked to see it."

The guard pins Ace's legs to the table once more, the cane

slamming repeatedly against the bottom of his feet. Ace screams as the bones in his toes nearly shatter and his arches swell, the pain nearly yanking him into unconsciousness.

"We call this the *Falanga*. What awaits you will make this look like a woman's loving embrace. I want to be very clear here, Mr. Murphy. You are being charged with espionage. You have no rights, no lawyers, and the American Embassy will be given no information about where we will take you. No one will intervene on your behalf. There will be no trial. The penalty for espionage is death by beheading. At this juncture you have two choices: You can answer my questions now and spare yourself incredible human suffering, or you can continue to play the fool, in which case you will still give us the information we seek, only you will do it as you are being slowly dismembered."

Ace spits a mouthful of foamy saliva on the floor. "I am not . . . a spy."

The interrogator grabs Ace's hair and looks into his eyes. "Very well. This was heaven, Mr. Murphy. Now you are going to hell."

He nods to the guard. "Clean him up for transfer to Inakesh. I want him in Jiddah before dark."

✦ ✦ ✦

The ride lasts six hours. Ace sleeps through most of it on the van floor. They are heading west, following a two-lane highway across desert flat land. It is dark outside, darker in Ace's dreams.

Forcibly shaken awake, he sits up painfully in time to see the high walls of what looks like a palace. As they move closer, he can see the walls are cement, the palace a prison. Heavy steel gates retract, allowing the van to enter. Security lights cut through the desert night, escorting the vehicle as it makes its way around a circular drive to the front entrance of a rectangular three-story building.

Ace is dragged out of the van and led up granite steps

to the front doors of a massive stone building. Heavily armed National Security guards strip off his clothing. He is tossed a stained prisoner's uniform and then led down a flight of fourteen concrete steps to a basement corridor. Bare bulbs light a long hallway reeking of human sweat and feces. There are cells to his right and left; he is unsure if they are occupied.

They stop at the second to the last door on his left. The guard opens the cell, revealing a cramped four-foot-wide by six-foot-long chamber, the walls solid cement. A bare mattress is on the floor. There is a sink, its drain pipeless, aimed at a bare squat hole in the floor, the scent of waste from the crude toilet overpowering.

A large metal ring is bolted ankle-high to the interior wall nearest the door. The guard, a dark-skinned Bedouin built like a professional wrestler, opens Ace's left handcuff and recuffs it to the metal ring.

The Bedouin leaves, slamming the heavy cell door behind him.

Ace Futrell curls up in a ball on the mold-ridden mattress, fear causing his body to shake uncontrollably. He closes his eyes to the cold cell, illuminated by a single bare bulb dangling from the ceiling high above his head.

Sound slowly seeps inside a heavy silence. Vermin claws scrape concrete somewhere close by. Insects buzz his head. Whispers of Arabic filter through the barred rectangular portal in his steel door. Sobs of the condemned mix with the wail of the justifiably insane.

Ace has entered purgatory—what awaits him is hell.

"We had very, very good intelligence of the general structure and strategies of the Al-Qaeda terrorist organization. We knew, and we warned, that Al-Qaeda was planning a major strike."

—James Pavitt,
CIA Deputy Director of Operations

"Osama bin Laden did not comprehend that his actions serve American interests . . . If one looks at the map of the big American bases created for the war, one is struck by the fact that they are completely identical to the route of the projected (Afghan) oil pipeline to the Indian Ocean. If I were a believer in conspiracy theory, I would think that bin Laden is an American agent. Not being one, I can only wonder at the coincidence."

Uri Averny,
former member of the Israeli Knesset,
now a columnist for Ma'ariv.
February 14, 2002

Book Excerpt:
To the Brink of Hell:
An Apology to the Survivors
by Kelli Doyle
White House National Security Staff Advisor
(2002-2008)

The blueprint for 9/11, the Iraqi invasion of 2003, and the nuclear attack still to come all trace its roots back to two converging events: The coming oil crisis and the end of the first Gulf War.

In 1992, President George H.W. Bush was finishing up his first (and only) term in office when Undersecretary of State Paul Wolfowitz, a young Neoconservative, oversaw the drafting of a new policy statement entitled the "Defense Planning Guidance" (DPG). Coauthored by I. Lewis (Scooter) Libby, the document essentially provided details of how America should increase its military advantage across the globe to preclude the rise of another great superpower. The plan found its way into the highest offices of the Pentagon and was eventually "leaked" to the press, forcing then Secretary of Defense, Dick Cheney, to "soften" parts of the document. Allies named in the paper as potential rivals were none too pleased, and Congress labeled it "over the top." With an election year upon him, President Bush refused to implement it.

Bill Clinton won the White House and the DPG was subsequently buried by the new administration, which preferred to cut defense spending following the collapse of the Soviet Union.

Over the next six years, intelligence reports submitted by my department in the CIA-Persian Gulf division would eventually bring me into the fold of a hardline group of Neoconservatives, headed by Dick Cheney, Paul Wolfowitz, Richard Pearle, Jeb Bush, and Donald Rumsfeld, all members of an organization calling itself the "Project for a New American Century (PNAC)." Using the Defense Planning Guidance as its blueprint for America's future, the group created its own strategic military document, entitled "Rebuilding America's Defenses." Admonishing the Clinton Administration for its adherence to the 1972 ABM Treaty and for cutting military spending, the plan outlined a grand strategy that sought to exploit America's newfound position as the world's lone superpower. In order to thwart any future challenges as well as reduce the threat from attack by the rogue nations of Iran, Iraq, and North Korea — years later referred to by President George W. Bush as the "Axis of Evil," the report called for an immediate military build-up centering on upgrading and expanding our nuclear forces, developing space-based anti-ballistic missile defense platforms, repositioning our bases in the Persian Gulf, and increasing the battle-ready efficiency and sheer numbers of our deployed troops. According to the document, the United States should answer to no one, including NATO and the U.N., and had a responsibility to take a more permanent role in the security of the Persian Gulf.

In September of 2000, PNAC published a ninety-page report entitled Rebuilding America's Defenses: Strategies, Forces, and Resources For a New Century. Section V, entitled "Creating Tomorrow's Dominant Force," states, and I quote: "The process of transformation, even if it brings revolutionary change, is likely to be a long one, absent some catastrophic and catalyzing event — like a new Pearl Harbor."

Months later, aided by brother Jeb's governorship in Florida, which illegally disenfranchised forty thousand minority voters who shared similar last names with convicted felons, the GOP wrestled the election loose from Al Gore, and George W. Bush grabbed the White House.

Within months, Vice President Dick Cheney was organizing secret energy task force meetings involving some of the biggest players (and donors) in the fossil fuel and nuclear industry. My role was to supply maps of Iraqi oil and natural gas fields, as well as the locations of pipelines, refineries, and terminals. Of course, not everything involved post-invasion plans. Enron's Ken Lay urged the administration to weaken power plant pollution regulations while oil executives divvied up the Arctic National Wildlife Refuge as if it belonged to them.

But the subject that concerned almost every participant at these secret meetings was the Caspian Basin.

Following the collapse of the Soviet Union in 1991, major U.S. oil companies, including Texaco, Unocal, BP Amoco, Exxon Mobil, Shell, and energy powerhouse Enron, had doled out billions of dollars in investments (and bribes) to secure equity rights for oil and gas fields in the Central Asian nations of Turkmenistan, Uzbekistan, and Kazakhstan. The key to harvesting these yet-to-be quantified energy reserves, theorized to be worth upward of $6 trillion dollars, was to build and secure a pipeline across Afghanistan and Pakistan.

Afghanistan is a mountainous region, its chief export: heroin. At the time the country was controlled by drug warlords and the Taliban, which, aided by Saudi Arabia, took over the city of Kabul in 1996. Ten years earlier, Osama bin Laden and his guerilla regime had constructed a cave system throughout the mountains in order to battle the Soviets. The system was built by the Binladin Construction Group out of Saudi Arabia and funded in part by the CIA.

In December of 1997, Unocal officials met with Taliban representatives in Texas to finalize a $2 billion pipeline deal. One condition: The U.S. had to recognize the Taliban as the official government in Afghanistan. Despite the pleadings of Unocal's vice president, Congress refused, and a short time later Al-Qaeda bombed U.S. embassies in Tanzania and Kenya. The pipeline was quickly becoming a pipe dream.

Fast-forward to May of 2001:

Vice President Cheney released his national energy plan, which stated the U.S. had to seek "non-traditional supplies of oil" to meet our nation's growing needs . . . even in the face of foreign resistance. But drilling in the Caspian states was producing nothing near the projected oil and natural gas bounty U.S. companies had anticipated, while negotiations had completely broken down between Unocal and the Al-Qaeda-supported Taliban.

As referenced earlier, Afghanistan is the world's largest producer of the opium poppy used to make heroin. It is estimated $500 billion flows from poppy fields annually, the drugs ending up on the streets of the United States and other Western nations. The profits are washed through banking systems across the globe.

Plain and simple; Drugs finance cooked banking ledgers and the world's debt.

In early 2001, the Taliban decided to strike back at the economies of the West by destroying its own opium crop, and by late summer of 2001, the Dow Jones had plunged below 7,300. As the stock market fell, intelligence agencies the world over began warning of a pending Al-Qaeda attack on U.S. soil. German intelligence provided our Intel with the week the attack would occur. Putin sent a Russian delegation to the White House warning that the World Trade Center would be attacked by hijacked commercial airlines. Not only were these warnings ignored, but no one in the Bush Administration would acknowledge having received them . . . even after Putin appeared on MS-NBC on September 15 detailing his warnings.

On August 2, 2001, Christina Rocca, the State Department's director of Asian affairs, met secretly with a Taliban ambassador, but again failed to secure a pipeline deal. Thirty-five days later, planes struck the Pentagon and the World Trade Center, and PNAC had its new Pearl Harbor.

Afghanistan was invaded and the Taliban regime fell within months. One of the first acts of the CIA was to "liberate" many of the opium warlords who agreed to *"cooperate"* with U.S. troops who were advised to *"look the other way"* as production of Afghani poppy fields came back online. Within a year, heroin exports rose from a low of 180 tons in 2001 to 3,700 tons in 2002. By 2003, record levels of opium were being harvested, bringing in more money to Afghanistan than foreign aid. Hamid Karzai, a former employee at Unocal, became President of Afghanistan, while another Unocal representative, Zalmay Khalizad, took over as the Bush Administration's envoy to Afghanistan.

Months later, George Bush and his Neocon advisors — all members of PNAC — used a false trail of evidence to connect the events of 9/11 to Saddam.

Within a year, American forces invaded Iraq.

FALL
2012

"Then the fifth angel blew his trumpet, and I saw a star that had fallen to earth from the sky, and he was given the key to the shaft of the bottomless pit. When he opened it, smoke poured out as though from a huge furnace, and the sunlight and air were darkened by the smoke."

—REVELATION 9:1–2

"We will work to help Afghanistan to develop an economy that can feed its people."

—PRESIDENT GEORGE W. BUSH, April 2002
(The White House failed to fund Afghan reconstruction in its January budget proposal [an oversight fixed by Congress]. The Bush Administration later cut the State Department's $75 million request for continuing Afghan anti-narcotics efforts to $40 million.)

"Afghanistan is as unstable as it was before the American coalition went in. Right now . . . there is very little to show that things are improving."

—TAMARA MAKARENKO, Central Asian crime expert, University of St. Andrews in Scotland.

"The Pakistani intelligence agency ISI, creator of the Taliban and close ally to both the CIA and Al-Qaeda, allegedly wired $100,000 to Mohamed Atta just prior to September 11th, reportedly through the ISI asset Omar Saeed Sheikh (later arrested for the killing of *Wall Street Journal* reporter Daniel Pearl, who was investigating ISI connections to Al-Qaeda.) This was ignored by the congressional 9/11 investigation, although the senator and congressman who ran the probe (Bob Graham and Porter Goss) *were meeting with the ISI chief, Mahmud Ahmed, on Capitol Hill on the morning of September 11th!* About 25 percent of the report of the Congressional Joint Inquiry was redacted, including long passages regarding how the attack (or the network allegedly behind it) was financed. Graham later said foreign allies were involved in financing the alleged terror network, but that this would only come out in 30 years."

—911TRUTH.ORG

"There's nothing you can know that isn't known."

—JOHN LENNON

CHAPTER 32

THE TOWN OF PAGHMAN IS LOCATED in the hills outside of Kabul, its de facto ruler—Abdul Rabb al-Rasul Sayyaf—an ultra conservative Islamic fundamentalist with ties to extremist Saudi groups. Once a mujahedin leader who fought with the U.S. against the Taliban, Sayyaf has become a political force that is driving Afghani politics back into the stone age. To the West, he remains the key influence that led to a new constitution. In reality, it is his own lawlessness that is decimating the country. He has personally appointed most of Afghanistan's judiciary, while his subcommanders run extortion and kidnapping cartels in and outside of Kabul. A kingpin whose rule intimidates even President Karzi, Sayyaf enforces a strict Wahhabi doctrine of Islam, keeping women under the same restrictions as the Taliban he helped remove from power. To Western journalists he will often preach the virtues of democracy, while his men disrupt weddings where music is played and assault locals for listening to cassette players. Like the Saudi Royals, he lives a life of hypocrisy, his wealth affording him mansions, servants, and SUVs.

All that is about to end.

Sayyaf stumbles through the garden of his gated home in a daze, one bloodied hand loosely gripping the pistol, the other tugging at his thick black beard. The still-warm bodies of the dead and dying bleed in clusters throughout his estate, staining his Persian carpets, pooling on the white ceramic tile. Some are indentured servants who failed to escape his rage. Others were subcommanders whose loyalty he believed had been purchased long ago. Two of the dead are Pakistani—members of the ISI—dragged from their beds earlier in the day when news of the theft had first become known.

Everything gone—nearly $200 million—vanquished from bank accounts sworn to be untraceable. *Was it Karzi and the Americans? Was it the United Nations?*

He senses the military's presence before he hears the first jeep arrive. Within minutes they have surrounded the house. They will attempt to take him alive.

Sayyaf scoffs at the notion as he pushes open the rusted iron gate and confronts the armed forces, aiming his gun at the first commando he sees, the movement setting off a chorus of gunfire, the air whistling with bullets, his flesh rippling as it is torn apart, and his corpse dancing before collapsing in a bloody heap across his stone-paved driveway.

IJAMSVILLE, MARYLAND

Located thirty-five miles north of Washington, D.C., the Whiskey Creek Golf Club is a par seventy-two championship course that offers its high-end clientele dramatic views of the Catoctin Mountains as they drive pine-forested fairways to picturesque elevated greens.

Scott Swan's guests include James Raue and his eldest son, Adam—CEOs of a steel plant in Grand Rapids, Michigan, and Jeffrey Allen, an insurance lobbyist from Mitchell, Nebraska. The foursome are playing the back nine, teeing up on the twelfth hole—a long 455-yard par four that doglegs left.

The senior Raue is given the honor to hit first, based on his prestige, not his last hole. He takes an awkward chop, the ball slicing fifty yards before caroming off a tree. "Damn!"

"Take a mulligan," Scott offers. "You're entitled."

"Yeah, think I will. Doesn't make me a liberal, does it?"

The others laugh.

Scott's cell phone vibrates. The Tech-Well Industry executive snatches it out of the golf cart, walking away from the group to answer. "Swan. This better be important."

"It's Brian Westly, over at the bank. Is there something going on that I should know about?"

"Westly, I'm a little busy—"

"You transfer $448 million and you're too busy to tell me about it?"

Swan's heart skips a beat. "What the hell are you talking about?"

"This morning's electronic transfer. If you're purchasing more 747s for your Arabian pals, you certainly didn't need to liquidate so much cash."

"Westly, what the—" He pauses, he smiles and waves at the group, then turns his back and lowers his voice. "What transfer? I never authorized a transfer—"

"Four Carlyle privately managed investment accounts. Your password and authorization codes moved the funds."

"I never authorized any damn transfer! Call Carlyle—"

"I did. They're not exactly saying, but it sounds like their accounts are hemorrhaging too."

"You better find that damn money, Westly—"

"The money's gone. We tracked it to a private account in Greenland, where it stayed about two nanoseconds before splitting off into cyberspace. You'd better get in here, Scott. This is serious."

JIDDAH, SAUDI ARABIA

The girls are all Americans, seventeen in this particular lot. The majority are in their teens, the most precious barely eight. Having been drugged on and off since their arrival by private jet, they have been dressed in revealing Arabian outfits—to be paraded in front of a select group of Saudi princes—the high-end slave buyers among the Kingdom's elite.

While most nations have at one time or another participated in slavery, only Saudi Arabia and a handful of other Islamic countries continue the practice. President Bush waived all financial sanctions on Saudi Arabia for failing to do enough to stop human trafficking, and President Obama had not broached the subject during his first term in office.

And yet the Saudi slave trade remains common knowledge around Washington power circles, a tolerated "look the other way" crime that has been going on since King Fahd and his sons first ran child sex rings from their private mansions in Beverly Hills. Through a network of pornographers and pimps, American girls (and occasionally boys) are "recruited" through bogus modeling agencies or newspaper ads looking to hire dancers or women to work in escort services. Videos are taken of the subjects and then sent to potential Saudi buyers. Selected teens are later invited to hotels for "tryouts," while others are targeted for kidnapping from shopping malls and video arcades, fast-food joints and teen hangouts. The younger ones, bearing the higher price tags, must be lured away on their way home from school. Once taken, victims are hustled to airports and smuggled onto private Saudi jets (immune to searches) before the local police can even begin processing a missing persons' report.

Many child abduction organizations have refused to admit the activity takes place for fear of losing their federal funding. On the rare occasion a Saudi Prince or one of the King's nephews is caught in the act, a State Department official intervenes, releasing the Saudi national under terms of diplomatic immunity. If an international sex ring serving the Royals is busted, Washington allows those caught the freedom from criminal and civil prosecution by providing them with retroactive diplomatic immunity or State Department protection under the Foreign

Sovereign Immunity Act. Parents of abducted children become flustered and frustrated by the endless gauntlets posed by the State Department, which control all Saudi investigations.

The "Sauduction" of Washington . . . yet another deal with the devil to keep the oil flowing.

✦ ✦ ✦

It takes less than an hour for the young ones to be selected by their new masters. The "lucky" among them will end up as wives, Islamic law allowing a man to marry his slaves. But first, each Prince must make settlement with "the bank."

The banker, a "Bagowi" foreigner hired by the Royals to do their dirty work, tallies the first Prince's allotment and then accesses his bank account.

He accesses it a second time. Then a third. The banker turns pale.

The Prince, a second cousin to King Sultan, loses his patience. "What?"

"Your Highness, I do not understand. Your funds . . ."

The Prince stares at the screen. His account, which had earlier exceeded $782 million, has been drained to a zero balance. "Filthy son of a dog! What have you done with my money?"

"Your Highness . . . I swear I have done nothing!"

The enraged Prince grabs a knife from one of the palace guards and stabs the banker repeatedly in the neck and chest, the shrieking man's blood splattering across the polished marble floors.

WEST PALM BEACH, FLORIDA

The high-rise office building is located in the downtown area of the city on a stretch of land situated between the Atlantic Ocean and Intercoastal waterway. The headquarters of "Citizens for a Green Society," a 527 political organization, occupies most of the thirteenth floor.

From her corner office, Jennifer Wienner can see a haze of blue ocean in the distance. She rarely looks, her attention focused on the map of the United States stretched across one entire wall, its colored tacks representing Congressmen and candidates running for election. Green tacks designate politicians who have agreed to support alternative energy legislation (if their own campaigns receive 527 dollars from the CGS), blue are Democrats and Republicans who have yet to commit. Red tacks are the enemy—ultra-conservative right wingers beholden to the fossil fuel industry or Democrats who fear being anything other than centrists.

Jennifer stares at the map as she has done every day since her lease began in mid-August. On her desk are sixteen two-page scripts, each a sixty-second commercial spot waiting to be filmed. Taped to her wall is a triage list of targeted cities and the rates of local television stations who will air her spots. On the shelf by the window is a framed picture taken six years earlier of her and Kelli.

Not a day goes by that she doesn't talk to that photo. Not an hour goes by that she doesn't think about Ace, wondering what happened to him, wandering if he is still alive.

She curses silently at her cousin and then looks up as her assistant, Collin Bradley, knocks on her open door. Bradley is a former Capitol Police Officer she met years earlier when he was assigned to the Senate Chambers. Licensed to carry a firearm, Bradley doubles as her private security guard.

The big man is smiling. "The bank just called. They're receiving wire transfers. Hundreds of them."

Jennifer returns to her laptop and logs onto the Internet. She scans the company's bank account ledger.

The deposits are coming in rapidly, most in denominations between $20,000 and $50,000, though she counts at least eight in the six-figures. As she watches, the account balance surpasses $5 million.

"Contact Kreg Lauterbach at Ratio films in San Antonio. Tell him to start shooting those spots. Then get me the Fox and ABC affiliates in Cleveland." She winks at Bradley. "Looks like the Green Party's in business."

"The U.S. does not authorize or condone torture and has not transported detainees from one country to another for the purpose of interrogation using torture."

—Condoleezza Rice,
U.S. Secretary of State

"There's no question in my mind where the philosophical guidance and the flexibility in order to do so originated—in the Vice President of the United States' office. His implementer in this case was [Defense Secretary] Donald Rumsfeld and the Defense Department."

—Retired U.S. Army Colonel Larry Wilkerson,
former Secretary of State Colin Powell's chief of
staff, in regard to U.S. torture policy.
CNN.com, November 20, 2005

"I think it's very, very important that we have a clear understanding that what happened here was an honorable approach to defending the nation, that there was nothing devious or deceitful or dishonest or illegal about what was done."

—Dick Cheney,
on waterboarding

"It's drowning. It gives you the complete sensation that you are drowning. It is no good, because you—I'll put it to you this way—you give me a water board, Dick Cheney, and one hour, and I'll have him confess to the Sharon Tate murders. It's torture, Larry. It's torture."

—Jesse Ventura,
on *Larry King Live*, May 12, 2009

CHAPTER 33

His mind swims through feverish pools of delirium as the monsters continue to suckle and feed. He can feel their claws digging into the skin along his back, their weight pressing against his ravaged spine as their sharp rodent teeth tear off what little remains of his flesh . . .

❖ ❖ ❖

They had come for him in his dreams a dozen times before the two Bedouin guards keyed open his cell door. The smaller man had aimed his automatic weapon at Ace while the other had attached a set of leg shackles around his ankles, using a special tool to tighten the U-bolts. When he finished, the guard freed the handcuff connecting Ace's left wrist with the cell wall and then motioned a command for him to dress in the prison garb he had been using as a blanket.

Ace pulled the long-sleeved night shirt over his upper body, the heavy cloth material falling over his boxer shorts and down around his knees. Barefoot, he followed the two guards out of the cell.

Each step was cumbersome, the chain heavy, the slight slack in the metal cuffs digging into the flesh around his heels. As he limped past the row of cells, he caught glimpses of other prisoners looking back at him—dark, sunken, depraved eyes staring from behind the barred rectangular viewing holes in their doors.

Reaching the end of the corridor, Ace ascended the steps slowly, counting fourteen before he reached the ground floor and its blinding daylight. The bigger guard dragged him through the gated portal while two Mutawa—religious police—glanced at him with vacant eyes. A hot gust of wind tantalized his flesh as he crossed the yard, entering another building.

A sand-dusted tiled hallway ended at a heavy oak door. One of the guards knocked, waited for a muffled reply in Arabic, and then pushed Ace inside.

The chamber was the size of a small gymnasium, its concrete floor stained with sweat and blood. There was a garden hose connected to a faucet, and several grated drains. A stucco wall was adorned with leather whips and bamboo canes of varied lengths and thickness. An aluminum table held a tray filled with thin metal skewers soaking in rubbing alcohol, bloody residue everywhere. There were two chairs in the room, both anchored to the floor. One, positioned by the aluminum table and an IV stand, had thick padded arms and legs that dangled Velcro straps. The second chair was situated next to a series of car batteries and held one frightening feature—its seat had been cut out.

Laid out on a central work table was a series of bore needles used to inject fluids into body cavities. There was a pair of heavy pliers with flat ends—designed to remove fingernails, and a small stack of clean face towels. Assorted lengths of rope hung from hooks on another wall, along with a pair of wrist shackles that dangled from a pulley and winch rigged to the ceiling.

The sight of the torture chamber left Ace queasy. *Pre-game intimidation tactics. Don't even think about it.*

The guards pushed him through to another door, this one leading into the warden's air-conditioned office. Seated behind a cheap metal desk was a man in a khaki uniform, his head cleanly shaved, his salt and pepper mustache thick and bushy.

Behind him and off to one side stood the woman.

She was in her early thirties, a dark-skinned Arabian beauty blessed with high cheekbones and full lips, her long black hair hidden away behind a matching black scarf. Her physique, tall and trim, was cloaked in the traditional black burka worn by Saudi women. But it was her eyes that set her apart from anyone Ace had ever seen—fiery hazel-green eyes rimmed in golden flecks—blazing animal eyes that seemed to possess an inner rage.

Those eyes followed him as the two guards pushed him to sit in a folding chair positioned in front of the uniformed man's desk.

It was she who spoke, her English like velvet ice, carrying the slightest hint of a British accent. "This is General Abdul-Aziz. He is warden of Inakesh Prison. I am here to translate."

One of the guards wheeled a small aluminum table next to Ace's chair. From its single drawer he removed a lie-detector kit. Rolling up Ace's right sleeve, he forcibly positioned a blood pressure cuff around Ace's biceps while his partner strapped two rubber pneumograph tubes into place, one around Ace's chest, the other tight against his abdomen. Two finger-plates were clipped onto Ace's index and middle fingers, the galvanometers designed to measure perspiration.

Game time. Ace closed his eyes, willing himself to remain calm. No machine detects lies. A polygraph is simply a device that monitors significant involuntary physiological responses present in a person's body when that person is subjected to stress.

My name is Stephen Murphy. My name is Stephen Murphy. My name is Stephen Murphy—

The General rattled off a command in Arabic, ordering the woman to begin.

"Please state your name."

"Stephen Murphy."

"You are American?"

"Canadian."

"What is your occupation?"

"I'm in the oil business, among other ventures."

"Why were you in the National Bank?"

"I was arranging the transfer of assets." The rehearsed answers flowed easily, fabricated around multiple threads of truth. *With any luck . . .*

"What was on the CD-ROM you downloaded onto the bank manager's computer?"

"It was a video game, an idea I've been developing, part of the reason I wanted to set up shop in the Middle East. The manager wanted to see the game, only it never downloaded. Apparently it wasn't compatible with his computer."

The smaller guard monitoring the polygraph test said something to the warden.

The General nodded.

Before he could react, a thick palm clenched Ace by his throat, dragging him backwards over his chair and into the torture chamber.

Moving in from behind, a second guard lowered the shackles from the ceiling pulley and snapped them into place around Ace's wrists.

"Wait! Stop . . . I was telling the truth!"

Ignoring his pleas, the Arabs quickly stripped his prison garb and boxer shorts from his body.

Naked to the world, he stood before the woman, his arms outstretched above his head, his face flushed with humiliation. The hazel eyes seemed to absorb everything, yet her expression remained callous and cold. "All prisoners must learn that lies are poison, that only the truth shall release you from the agony that you are about to experience."

Heads turned as the torturer entered the chamber. He was a squat heavyset Bedouin in his late sixties, his long beard gray and curly, his eyes black and cold, like a shark. This was *his* chamber, and his very presence within its confines brought with it an air of danger, his every movement belying a performance that dated back decades.

He was the devil personified—a sadistic Arabian Grim

Reaper—and even the guards seemed intimidated.

His piggish dark eyes darted over Ace's physique, evaluating him. Turning to the far wall, the maestro selected a thick leather whip from its mount. Testing it with several expert flicks of his wrist, he ceremoniously removed his tunic, stripping down to a short-sleeved undergarment held tight around his paunchy waist by an elastic band. Grabbing a towel, he wiped off the whip's handle, refolded the cloth to his liking, placed it on the padded chair, and then nodded to the guards.

The shackles lurched to life, releasing a tsunami of pain—incredulous as it was instantaneous—as Ace was violently hoisted off the floor by his wrists, the agony in his arms and shoulders forcing the breath from his lungs. His vertebrae crackled as the muscles around his back and scapulae contorted in violent spasms, threatening to tear ligament from bone.

Through tears and screams, he rasped, "Enough! I'll talk! I'll tell you everything!"

The death merchant moved closer, his rancid breath overpowering as he spun Ace slowly around until he was facing a back wall splattered in dried blood.

Ace sucked in quick breaths, his tortured muscles trembling with adrenaline.

The whipped cracked air and flesh, Ace's scream exploding out his windpipe, sweat bursting from every pore as the skin was peeled away from his lower back. His body jerked in mid-air as the second lash pummeled his overstretched latisimus dorsi, shredding the flesh from his ribcage.

No more screaming! I won't scream again!

"Ahh!" He danced on the chain like a slab of raw meat, his splattered blood redecorating the back wall as again and again the whip came down—his screams receding into grunts, the grunts into mere wheezes . . . until finally there was just the crack of the whip.

The butcher stopped. He toweled himself off and spun his

prize around to face the others.

Fully conscious, Ace's eyes rolled back into place, his brown irises locking onto those of his tormentor. "That the best you got, fat boy?"

The two guards looked at one another, incredulous. The warden, wide-eyed, turned to his flustered sadist, who was already grabbing for another whip on the wall.

Ace spun himself back around, anger and adrenaline now fueling his resolve in this newfound game of wills, his mind detaching itself from the pain, his ego refusing to allow himself to succumb to unconsciousness.

Whap!

The new whip, lighter, carried a far deadlier sting and brought fresh tears to his eyes.

Whap! Whap! Whap!

Bring it on, you fat prick; you can't hurt me! I'm already dead!

Seventeen lashes later he passed out—only to be forcibly awakened by the shocking burst of cold water.

The sadist flung the empty bucket against the far wall, cursing in Arabic. The two guards shirked away.

The woman spoke, her voice clearly shaken. "Your name?"

The pain shook Ace's body. Through diminishing tunnel vision he could see the shadow of death dancing along the periphery of his fading light.

"Your name!"

"Ashley Futrell." It was his voice—unrecognizable.

"You are American?"

A nod.

"What is your occupation?"

"Petroleum geologist."

"Why were you in the National Bank?"

"Money . . . the Feds . . . threatened to take everything."

"The CD-ROM?"

"Assets . . . transfer."

The General barked out a slew of Arabic.

"General Abdul-Aziz says you are lying. He says you are a spy."

Ace stared at the warden through bulging eyes. "Tell the general he can blow me." The words sprung forth delirious fits of laugher—as the whip tore across his abdomen, barely missing his genitals. His body overtaken by convulsions, his mind fled the scene, repelling into blackness.

✦ ✦ ✦

Ace opens his eyes, chasing the monsters away.

He is back in his cell, dressed again in prison garb. His body is feverish and quivering. His stomach is nauseous, but he dare not vomit, dare not move, so afraid is he of disturbing the raw, open weight licking the wounds along his back like burning gasoline.

A wave of pain grips him again, dragging him under.

✦ ✦ ✦

"Drink this. It will soothe the fever."

The beautiful woman with the animal eyes is leaning over him, pouring the clear liquid into his mouth. Ace swallows and chokes and then drinks some more.

She removes a stethoscope from a concealed pocket in her burka and checks his heart beat. "You are lucky to be alive. No prisoner has ever remained conscious after so many lashes. Your strength angered Ali Shams. I must clean your wounds. This is going to hurt."

Carefully, she peels away the blood-soaked cloth from his back, wincing as she sees the extent of the damage.

"Let me die."

"If it is Allah's will. My orders are to keep you alive. If you die, I will take your place." From another pocket she removes a container of salve. Rubs some on her fingers.

His body convulses as she touches the cream to his back.

"I am sorry, but this must be done."

"Wait." Ace's fingers quiver as he positions his shirt sleeve inside his mouth and bites down.

The wave of pain jolts him off the floor and into a sea of blackness.

✦ ✦ ✦

Ace opens his eyes.

His head is resting in her lap. His upper body is wrapped in gauze. The rawness of the pain gone, replaced by a tremendous pressure, like a weight tugging against the open wound.

He sits up suddenly, crawls to the open hole in the floor and pukes—over and again until the convulsions have been reduced to dry heaves.

Drained, Ace curls up in a ball atop the bare mattress, his body shaking uncontrollably.

She curls next to him, her back to his chest, draping his arm around her waist. "For warmth."

Pressing his face against the nape of her neck, he passes out.

✦ ✦ ✦

Ace stirs himself awake. Many hours have passed. His fever is gone, and so is the girl. The pain is tolerable if he doesn't move. Carefully, he inches the half-empty bottle of water closer, sipping its remains. His empty stomach aches.

He hears someone outside his cell door. Keys jiggle in the lock.

She enters. "You have been unconscious two days. No one believed you would last." She kneels and checks his pulse. "Good. Your heartbeat is more regular."

"Are you . . . a doctor?"

"No, but I have received some medical training. Do you think you might be able to tolerate food?"

"Not yet." He sips more water. "What's your name?"

"Nahir."

"You're a beautiful woman, Nahir." Ace lays back again on

his side and closes his eyes. "Why is such a beautiful woman in such an ugly place?"

"If I am beautiful, then it is a curse. For many years my father was a chauffeur for one of the Royals—a Prince. At first the Prince was generous to our family, paying my father enough to afford a good life . . . to send me away to school. For three years I attended Cambridge University, studying premed. The summer of my junior year I returned home to spend time with my ailing mother. When the Prince saw me, he became enraptured and insisted I become his wife. The Prince had dozens of wives and even more slave girls, and I had a fiancé back in London. I told my father I did not want to marry the Prince. In response, the Prince had my father beaten and taken away to prison. I agreed to marry the Prince only if he released him.

"Several years passed. The Prince, who was very ambitious, decided to maneuver his way closer to the throne by poisoning his older brother. The assassination failed. As punishment, the Royals sentenced the Prince to ten years in prison. Royals do not go to prison, Mr. Futrell. I was chosen to serve his time.

"When General Abdul-Aziz learned I could speak English, he made me his official translator. That was three years ago. The warden has been most generous. I have a room next to the interrogation chamber to myself, and I am permitted free movement within the prison walls. On special occasions I may even take leave, as long as I am supervised."

"The guards leave you alone?"

The hazel eyes avert his gaze.

"And if I die, you die."

"Al Saud fears you for some reason. Why do they fear you, Mr. Futrell?"

Ace closes his eyes. "I really don't know."

"Over the course of two years (independent journalist Daniel) Hopsicker not only added information to what was known about (the 9/11 hijackers) military training, he also established that some of the hijackers associated with wealthy Floridians had both intelligence and Bush family connections. Hopsicker also confirmed that within hours after the attacks, Florida Governor Jeb Bush had a military C-130 Hercules transport fly into the Venice (Florida) airport where a hastily loaded rental truck, filled with the records of Huffman Aviation—where Atta, Alshehri, and others had trained—was driven directly into the plane. The C-130 immediately took off for parts unknown."

—MICHAEL C. RUPPERT,
Crossing the Rubicon: The Decline of the
American Empire at the End of the Age of Oil

"Ask not about things which, made plain to you, may cause you trouble."

—KORAN

CHAPTER 34

THE FRENCH RIVIERA, LOCATED on the Mediterranean Sea along France's southeastern coast, is one of the most luxurious and expensive vacation spots in the world. Known for its azure shorelines, gorgeous women and topless beaches, mega-yachts and exclusive marinas, and a nightlife that encompasses five-star restaurants and glamorous casinos—the French Riviera has become the destination of the ultra-rich and super-famous, many of whom congregate to Cannes each spring for the world-famous film festival.

Scott Swan maneuvers past couples dressed in tuxedos and evening gowns as he hustles along the Promenade des Anglais, following the waterfront street to the Hotel Negresco. Built in 1912, the pink domed palace still dominates the Bay of Angels, each suite individually decorated, reflecting the styles of the French Renaissance and Louis XIII.

The distressed CEO enters the grand lobby, passing beneath a monstrous chandelier originally designed for the Russian czar. Checking his watch, he opts for a quick pit stop and ducks inside the men's room.

September 11th . . . of all days to be meeting with these clowns.

The washroom is straight out of the Napoleonic era, the

wall lights made from helmets. He stares at a battle scene mural as he uses the urinal.

European decadence. Give me the Hawaiian Hilton any day.

Ignoring the attendant, he exits to the lobby and then catches an elevator to the penthouse floor.

Swan is greeted by two members of the French National Police. One searches him for weapons while the other checks his passport and then verifies his appointment via house phone. He is led to the double doors at the end of the hall, one of the most expensive suites in the hotel.

A member of the Saudi National Guard escorts him inside to a greeting area decorated in seventeenth-century baroque. Swan follows him through doors leading into a formal dining area.

They are seated around an enormous cherrywood table lit by a ten-arm cognac-finish chandelier. The walls are papered in satin-red, a gold-framed painting of Napoleon dominating one entire wall.

King Sultan bin Abdel Aziz is seated at the head of the table, dressed in a dark business suit, his head adorned in a white *ghotra*. His son, Prince Bandar bin Sultan, the ambassador to the United States, is on his right, the Saudi Finance Minister to his left. Swan is shocked to see the Finance Minister's left hand is gone, the remains of his wrist wrapped in bloody bandages.

Filling in the rest of the chairs are three generals, all dressed in uniform. Swan slides into the empty chair opposite the King. The man's skin tone is a pasty gray, his expression causing beads of perspiration to break out across Scott's forehead. Swan's contacts at the Carlyle Group have been sending him daily updates of civil unrest in the Saudi Kingdom, no doubt the reason the King has chosen the French Riviera to take an extended holiday.

"You are late, Mr. Swan. What have you to say?"

"My apologies. Our plane was delayed, extra security and all."

"About our money!"

Swan takes a measured breath. "The Carlyle Group is investigating the withdrawals. What complicates the matter is that all the appropriate passwords and codes were used, the monies routed into the Saudi National Bank before being dispersed. I realize $680 million is a lot of money, however—"

"Six hundred and eighty million! You think I'd waste my breath on such paltry sums!" Sultan turns to Prince Bandar. "Tell him!"

Bandar opens a folder, reading from a ledger sheet. "In the past twenty-two days, a total of $493 billion has been removed from Saudi accounts, a third of those funds from American institutions."

The blood drains from Scott Swan's face.

"Where is Mr. Baker? Where is Mr. Bush? Why are my calls being ignored? If I didn't know better, Mr. Swan, I'd say your country is preparing for an invasion."

"Your Excellency, please . . . I'm as shocked as you are by these circumstances. My own business accounts have been—"

"Do I look like a fool?" King Sultan stands, making his way slowly around the oval table toward his American guest. "In 2001, two days before September 11th, the Bush Administration shared with us a 27-page top secret document detailing battle plans for the invasion of Iraq. Does such a document exist for the invasion of Saudi Arabia?"

"No," Swan stammers.

"The thefts are having a measured affect on every financial institution in the kingdom," Prince Bandar states. "Saudi banks report losses approaching $500 billion. Seventy-three percent of these funds directly involve Royals, eighteen percent affect private corporations. The Bin Laden Group declared bankruptcy six days ago after $27 billion was transferred out of its holding accounts. Our economy has all but collapsed, if this continues—"

King Sultan hovers over Swan. "Three-quarters of a trillion dollars stolen without a trace, Mr. Swan. And yet the World

Bank remains quiet, the United States says nothing, and why should they? Wall Street has not suffered, at least not yet. So here is my message to Vice President Biden: The United States Treasury and the Department of Defense will immediately employ their joint powers to stop the purging of our accounts, while guaranteeing the return of every missing dollar to the House of Saud, with interest. If these conditions are not met by October 15th, OPEC will declare an oil embargo on the West, at which time we will demand the expulsion of all American troops from the Saudi kingdom, to be replaced with permanent military bases manned by the Chinese.

"If the House of Saud goes down, Mr. Swan, we will take you with us."

OVAL OFFICE, WHITE HOUSE
WASHINGTON, D.C.
SEPTEMBER 17, 2012

"These were not random accounts that were targeted," states Leonard Snyder, the White House chief economic advisor. "At least half the monies taken originated from commissions skimmed by the House of Saud on arms contracts. Patriot Missiles, F–15s, AWACS, Canadian Halifax frigates, French Helec torpedo boats, the British Yamama sale . . . as well as off-the-book deals that can be traced as far back as the Reagan years. The worm also raided the accounts of Hamas and Hezbollah, as well the satellite networks used by the Muslims to spew their hatred of Israel and the West. Naturally, the French and the rest of the European Union were quick to accuse Israel of masterminding the plot. They only backed off when it became evident that the Israeli banks had lost billions as well."

Homeland Security Director Howard Lowe chimes in. "Funds have been stolen, even after banks transferred holdings into new accounts under new corporate IDs. Whatever this worm is, it has the ability to lock onto its target and trace it through any computer-operational system. CEOs in the defense industry have become so paranoid that they're cashing out whatever they have left—bonds, pension funds—and that's sending a shiver throughout the entire financial community."

"I don't understand," Joe Biden snaps back. "How does a trillion dollars simply vanish?"

"It hasn't vanished," Snyder replies. "It's been electronically removed, its trail wiped clean, and then redistributed into who-knows-where. Whoever set this up was very clever about it. When they stole from Peter to pay Paul, they kept the transactions balanced, which is why most financial institutions are still intact. This was a very complex, well-planned operation. Can the funds be relocated? Doubtful, at least at this juncture."

David Schall kneads the pounding pulse in his neck as his mind races. *Promis . . . Futrell . . . it has to be—*

The Vice President glances at the CIA Director. "Director Schall, you have something to add?"

"Sorry, no sir. I was just thinking . . . whoever these thieves are, they've managed to target accounts used by terrorist organizations and drug cartels to launder money. The Saudi situation aside, maybe we can spin this into a good thing."

"Are you saying that the Carlyle Group . . . that the Haliburtons and the Brown and Roots of the world are terrorist organizations?"

"No, sir, of course not."

"Then let's get back to the problem at hand. Wall Street is taking a hit, but seems to be rebounding, the big emergency looming ahead is this potential oil embargo. Madam Secretary, how do you propose we deal with the Saudis?"

The tension between Biden and Hillary Clinton is palpable, the former New York senator and First Lady having been chosen over the Vice President to lead the Democratic Presidential ticket.

"Saudi Arabia is facing two major threats. Its economy is collapsing and the Royals are being threatened by its own populace. That leaves us two choices: We either negotiate a loan package or allow the inevitable to happen. Unless we catch these computer thieves, negotiating a loan package means nothing as the same thing could happen again. Allowing Saudi Arabia to collapse creates a dangerous power vacuum that will be contested by Islamic radicals, Iran, and the Ashraf. Since either situation leaves the Royals with the short end of the stick, we offer them an opportunity to remain in power as a puppet government while we stabilize their borders, inside and out."

"It'll never fly," Leonard Snyder says. "The House of Saud blames the United States for its losses."

"Let's at least negotiate the point," Howard Lowe says, turning to Joseph Kendle. "A lot can happen in thirty days, wouldn't you agree, General?"

"Yes, sir," the Secretary of Defense concurs, "I would."

FLAGSTAFF, ARIZONA
10:23 PM MST

Michael Tursi snatches the pay phone off its hook after the first ring. "Speak."

"The patient's in labor.

"So soon?"

"Her water broke early. Yes or no, is the doctor ready to deliver?"

"He's ready. I hear it's twins. Which hospital?"

"St. Mary's."

"St. Mary's is expensive. Who's paying the hospital bill?"

"It'll be taken care of." The line goes dead.

The Turk exits the phone booth, his heart racing.

❖ ❖ ❖

The electronic surveillance records the man's final words as Elliott Green pulls the small dish back inside his car. The rogue FBI agent has been staking out the Flagstaff phone booth ever since he arrived in Arizona on September 2, and tonight was the big payoff.

With the telephoto lens, Green snaps another close-up of Tursi's license plate as the car speeds away. He waits until the cloud of road dust settles before restarting his car, his mind replaying the conversation.

The patient's in labor . . . the attack must be imminent. "Wake up, Elliott. Don't lose this guy!"

He pulls out onto the road, accelerating after his suspect.

"Undercover investigators bought radioactive ingredients needed to make a dirty bomb and drove them into the USA past border security agents. When Homeland Security radiation detectors went off, the investigators gave Customs and Border Protection agents fake government licenses and receipts. Agents searched the cars, reviewed the documents and ultimately gave the undercover officers the OK to bring the material into the USA."

—*USA Today*,
March 28, 2006

"There are no permanent allies and no permanent enemies—just permanent interests."

—Lord Palmerston,
19th-century British leader.

"Change is avalanching upon our heads, and most people are grotesquely unprepared to cope with it."

—Alvin Toffler,
Future Shock

CHAPTER 35

There is no day and night in solitary confinement, there is only pain and depression—a physical emptiness that can break a man more than any inflicted wound. For Ace Futrell, loneliness has become a vacuum of immeasurable time, and though the welts from his first beating have gradually thickened and healed, his spirit continues to weaken.

Through feverish bouts of sleep he dreams often of his children, each reunion shattered by violence . . . a roadside bomb wiping out the inside of a shopping mall, a tidal wave striking their private beach, a tornado exploding their home into shrapnel. Kelli's presence is always there, but only on the periphery and never as his wife, and whenever he would try to focus on her features, her face would morph into Jennifer's.

He would awaken disoriented, sometimes screaming, his senses in chaos, assaulted by the around-the-clock noise of prisoners yelling in Arabic, cursing and banging on their doors, or the constant scent of human feces, some of it caked and hardened in the grooves of his concrete walls. At times he would hear whispers, his mind always wandering, and yet part of him was grateful to be in the cell . . . at least here he was safe. At least here he wasn't being beaten.

They fed him once a day, a bowl of rice and some unrecognizable meat. He could barely tolerate it the first week, but gradually he forced himself to eat.

He did not see the woman again until the sixteenth day . . . the day they came for him.

✦ ✦ ✦

She was waiting for him in the torture chamber, her hazel eyes cold and penetrating like their first meeting. Once more the two guards stripped him naked, this time placing him in the chair with no bottom so that his genitalia dangled below. His ankles and wrists were strapped tight. His limbs trembled.

His Angel of Death spoke as the sadist she had called Ali Shams reached under Ace's chair between his legs and doused his testicles with a wet towel. "I am going to ask you a few questions regarding your business in the Saudi Kingdom. A truthful answer shall not be punished."

A wave of nausea shook him from his groin into his throat, sweat oozing from every pore on his body as the metal clamps were attached to his genitalia.

"A lie, Mr. Futrell, shall bring with it terrible pain."

The warden entered. He sat down next to Nahir, watching from a folding chair.

Focus! Stick with the story. You have to hold out! Do it for Leigh and Sam! Do it for—

"What is your name?"

"Ashley Futrell." He felt lightheaded, dizzy, unable to catch his breath.

"What was your business in the National Bank?"

"Transfer . . . I wanted to transfer my assets into—

Ahhhhhhh!" *Daggers . . . flames . . . genitals . . . on fire . . . searing pain . . . so deep . . . white-hot . . . can't breathe!*

Off.

"Ughhh!" Vomit spewed from Ace's mouth across the cement floor, and then he flopped back in the chair, his sweat-soaked body sliding sideways within the restraints, his muscles in spasms, his nerves dancing uncontrollably.

He is jerked awake as the sadist drenches him with water from the garden hose.

Ace moans, rolling his aching head from side to side, his frayed nerve endings still smoldering, his twitching body causing his extremities to dance, his vision blinded by purple spots. *Stupid walk-on . . . they were toying with you . . . this is a man's game . . . you're just a child . . . you can't win, you can't fight back.*

"What is your name?"

His eyes flutter, the words chasing his mind through a feverish sea.

"What is your name?"

"Acefew. . . trell."

Your son, Sam, will be vaporized . . .

"Whuh?"

Leigh, too. We know where they live.

"Your business in the National Bank?"

Sam and Leigh will die a horrible death.

His eyes snap open. "What did you say?"

She is taken aback by his sudden ferocity. "I asked your business at the bank."

"You said something about my kids! What did you say?"

"I said nothing—" She glances at the warden, unsure.

"What did you say!"

The General grabs her by the arm. Commands her in Arabic.

"Mr. Futrell, what was your business at—"

"Blow me! You know what that means? It means crawl under this chair and suck on my dick! Go ahead, translate that to your General!"

Her eyes widen in fear.

"Do it! Tell him!"

The punch to his face breaks his nose but clears the fog from his head. He turns to Ali Shams and spits blood on the Arab's clean shirt. "Game on, asshole! That's right, smile, you prick! You think you scare me? I'm not afraid anymore! Death doesn't scare me! Pain doesn't—"

Ace's body jumps off the chair, the restraints threatening to tear loose from his arms and legs as the voltage seems to pin him in mid-air—his mind caught in the roll of a great tidal wave, his being held under, unable to breath, his body tossed about as it's ripped to shreds against the points of a thousand needles—

Off.

He collapses back in the chair, more dead than alive.

This time the hose fails to revive him.

The General yells at the woman. She hurries to Ace. Checks his pupils. Feels his pulse. Shakes her head no.

Ali Shams pushes her aside. Grabs a fistful of Ace's hair—

"*La!*" The warden instructs the enraged torturer to leave.

◆　◆　◆

The sea has calmed. He is floating on his back. The sun is bright, occasionally passing behind a cloud. He can feel its radiation warming his skin. Someone is speaking to him.

No . . . just let me float.

A wave tosses him, jerking him awake.

Ace opens his eyes.

He is back in his cell, lying on the mattress. His left wrist is handcuffed to the iron ring, his right arm is stretched out, palm up. The woman pins his forearm down with her bare foot as she inserts the IV needle. She tapes down the connection in his vein, anchors the intravenous bag to the sink, and then starts the drip.

Too weak to object, he lies back, registering a cool, calming sensation that eases through his bloodstream. "What is that?"

"An electrolyte solution."

He closes his eyes. "Just let me die."

"You are not a man who seems ready to die. You are a bull,

always ready to fight. You must back down. The next time Ali Shams will kill you."

"Good. Better to die up there than down in here."

"How many children do you have, Mr. Futrell?"

His eyes snap open, flashing a warning.

"I'm sorry, I meant nothing by it. I told you before, I too am a prisoner."

"It doesn't mean I trust you."

She stands over him, her hazel eyes portals of defiance. "When Ali Shams strips you in front of me, it humiliates you. I can see it in your eyes. Perhaps I can ease your embarrassment."

As he watches she removes her head scarf, allowing her long black hair to fall free. Loosening her burka, she steps out of her clothing completely naked, her taut, shapely figure wrapped in velvet mocha skin, her breasts small but firm, her left hand covering her groin.

Ace sits up, his heart racing in his chest.

She backs a step away and turns around slowly, revealing a swath of thick white scars crisscrossing her back.

"We are kindred souls now, yes?"

"Yes." Muscles quivering, he lays back again as she redresses.

"I hate Al Saud, Mr. Futrell. I hate what they have done to me, to my family, and to my people. Why does Allah forbid us freedom? Why does he bless the evil ones with power?"

"I don't know. The same thing seems to be happening in my country. The rich become more powerful, the poor get trampled upon, and the masses accept it all in stride."

"You are not a spy."

"No."

"Why—"

He takes a deep breath, fighting to focus through the pain. "My expertise is in oil. I was hired to check on the Saudi Aramco reserves. The men who employed me are very well connected. If I don't return to the United States before the presidential election, these men will issue a public report stating the Saudi reserves will be tapped out within five years."

"But this is not true?"

"No," he lies. "The reserves are healthy for now."

"And the bank?"

"A risky side trip. I was to receive payment in laundered funds from an associate in the Middle East. The transfer didn't work. Now I remain unpaid and in prison."

"These men you work for . . . they are well connected politically?"

"Yes."

"If I can get word to the American embassy, if I can get you out of Inakesh . . . you would take me with you?"

"Yes. Absolutely."

She pauses, debating the matter internally.

"Then I will help."

"Mailings of weapons-grade anthrax—which caused a practical suspension of the 9/11 investigations—were traced back to U.S. military stock. Soon after the attacks began in October 2001, the FBI approved the destruction of the original samples of the Ames strain, disposing of perhaps the most important evidence in identifying the source of the pathogens used in the mailings. Were the anthrax attacks timed to coincide with the Afghanistan invasion? Why were the letters sent only to media figures and to the leaders of the opposition in the Senate who had raised objections to the Patriot Act?"

—911TRUTH.ORG

"Richard Bergendahl (55) fights the war on terrorism in Los Angeles for $19,000 a year, one of the legions of ill-trained, low-paid private security guards protecting tempting terrorist targets. Bergendahl, who protects the fifty-two-story high-rise near the U.S. Bank Tower, said his training usually consists of a real estate manager reading security measures to him every few months. His building rarely has evacuation drills. Management's advice? 'Keep your coat buttoned. Keep your shoes shiny.'"

LARRY MARGASAK,
Associated Press,
May 30, 2007

CHAPTER 36

U.S. Bank Tower
Los Angeles, California
September 27, 2012
11:33 pm Pacific

Rising seventy-three stories above ground level, the U.S. Bank Tower, often referred to as the Library Tower, is the tallest North American skyscraper west of Chicago, and one of the top twenty-five in all the world. Years earlier, the public learned (after the fact) that the building had been one of the original infrastructures targeted by Al-Qaeda for the September 11, 2001, attacks, and was later a target of a foiled attempt in mid-2002. Security is tight for visitors entering the building, and businesses are advised to run background checks on all potential employees.

The maintenance company's security check on Omar Kamel Radi had been outsourced to a bogus corporation operated by Marco Fatiga's supervisor, Jeff Anders, at the Strategic Support Branch of the Department of Defense.

Omar changes out of his soiled uniform, inserts his time card, and clocks out. He then heads up to the main lobby.

Susan Campbell is waiting. "How was work?"

"Work is work." He kisses the blond aerobics instructor. "Perhaps I should shower before we go to dinner, yes?"

"Let's go back to my place. We can shower together." She takes his hand and they leave, strolling past Marco Fatiga, who has been watching everything.

INAKESH PRISON, SAUDI ARABIA
SEPTEMBER 28, 2012
7:45 AM LOCAL TIME

ACE AWAKENS TO THE CHAOS OF MEN ranting in the outer corridor. He scratches lice from his beard and then sits up painfully just as his cell door is keyed open. His guard, a large Bedouin named Hasan, unlocks his shackle and then tosses a pile of clothing at him—the business suit he had worn at the bank.

They're releasing me! Nahir did it!

He dresses quickly, his heart racing as he allows leg shackles to be placed over his slacks, his wrists handcuffed behind his back. But as he shuffles out of his cell, his moment of exhilaration is drowned in a wave of anxiety.

Three prisoners wait in the corridor, two men and a woman. All are dressed in street clothes, all on their knees, praying and begging their guards to allow them to return to their cells. The guards yell back, flogging them with bamboo canes as they drag them to their feet and herd them up the concrete steps.

Ace turns to the larger guard. Hasan is looking at him . . . grinning.

✦ ✦ ✦

Ace is led into the courtyard, the sun high in a cloudless blue sky, the heat stifling. The others have already been loaded into the back of an awaiting van. One of the guards cloaks Ace's head in a black *ghotra*, pulling it low on his face before fitting a blindfold tightly over his eyes.

Ace feels the strength seep from his body, forcing the guard to half carry, half drag him to the back of the van, shoving him roughly inside. Blind and on his knees, he uses his forehead to feel his way onto a bench, climbing up next to another prisoner as the vehicle accelerates out of the prison courtyard.

It is the female. She is sobbing, the men praying.

"*Marhaba.* Can anyone speak English?"

One of the men replies, "American?"

"Yes," Ace rasps. "Please, where are they taking us?"

"Today is Friday. Those selected on Fridays are taken to Jiddah for public execution. Today we are to die."

Ace slumps in his seat, each jolt from the uneven road banging the back of his head against the van's aluminum interior. Tears run down his blindfold to his neck, not because he is afraid to die, but because he is sad for his children. After losing their mother, after abandoning them . . . and all for what? Emotions well in his gut as he remembers their last night together at Lake George, hugging his son good night, promising his daughter he'd be back in a few weeks.

That was forty days ago, maybe more!

You lied to her. You lied to yourself.

He slams the back of his head against the van's aluminum interior, grinding his teeth as he curses his existence. *I knew better! I never should have left them! Why did I listen to her? I hate you, Kelli, I hate you! I hate you! I hate you!*

◆ ◆ ◆

The van stops. After a moment the rear doors open. He waits until his guard drags him from the vehicle, joining their small procession as they walk past interested onlookers watching from the parking lot. The muscles in his legs shake as he stumbles blindly up a set of stone steps. From the direction of the noise he can tell they are being taken to the center of a vast marketplace.

He recognizes General Abdul Aziz's voice bellow a command. His blindfold is removed, his *ghotra* pulled away from his eyes so he can see.

They are on a ten-foot rise situated in a crowded square. Across the street is a hotel, guests watching the festivities from private balconies. People are gathering quickly, joining the several hundred onlookers already present.

Twelve feet away, the executioner stands ready, his broad

steel sword polished and glistening. He is a big man with a thick mustache and goatee and dark psychotic eyes. His khaki uniform is stained in sweat, the white *ghotra* atop his head drenched as well. By the way he plays to the crowd, it is obvious he enjoys his work a little to much.

Please, God, do with me what you will, just take care of my kids, that's all I ask. With that, Ace closes his eyes, shutting down his thoughts as his body goes numb.

The General approaches, selecting the man seated on Ace's right. Two guards grab him by his arms, dragging him toward the executioner. The man falls to his knees as an Islamic judge—one of the Wahhabi clerics—uses a microphone to read the charges to the crowd.

The marketplace grows silent, the thick air heavy with an almost primordial bloodlust. People climb atop cars to see better.

The condemned man sobs, bowing his head to face Mecca.

Ace opens his eyes. He doesn't want to look but he can't help himself.

The executioner raises the heavy sword high above his head, then in one powerful downward arc plunges the blade through the base of the man's neck.

The crowd swoons, the first few rows splattered with blood as the body falls to one side, the head rolling to another.

Ace gags and looks away, his insides wracked by spasms.

More charges are being read. The woman on his left sobs against his shoulder. The General drags her to her feet, shows her to the crowd, and then shoots her twice in the head, spraying onlookers with a bloody mist.

The dead woman collapses in a heap by Ace's feet.

Chants fill the air. There are two prisoners left, and they want the American.

From his second-story balcony, Scott Santa reports the drama via cell phone to CIA Director David Schall.

Ace is dragged off his feet. His body is lead as he is dropped onto his knees before the executioner. All sound ceases. His muscles quiver uncontrollably.

He hears the crowd cheering, and suddenly finds himself whispering a Georgia Bulldogs cheer, "Go Bulldogs, go Bulldogs, go Bulldogs! Go Dawgs!"

The executioner pauses, unsure.

Ace chants louder, "Go Bulldogs, go Bulldogs, go Bulldogs! Go Dawgs!"

And then a woman's voice buzzes in his head. For a moment he imagines it to be Kelli, only the words are Arabic. In a daze he turns to his left.

Nahir is pointing at him, speaking rapidly to the General.

The executioner snaps out of his spell. He repositions Ace's skull. Shadows jump as the sword is raised overhead . . .

"I believe in God, but not as one thing, not as an old man in the sky. I believe that what people call God is something in all of us. I believe that what Jesus and Mohammed and Buddha and all the rest said was right. It's just that the translations have gone wrong."

—JOHN LENNON

"People who wear Christ on their sleeves and vote against helping people are the biggest hypocrites."

—CHARLIE MELANCON,
Louisiana Congressman (D)
after the House rejected funding to
repair New Orleans' levees

"Don't be afraid of what you are about to suffer. The devil will throw some of you into prison and put you to the test."

—REVELATION 2:10

CHAPTER 37

THE SCREAM SHATTERS THE NIGHT, startling Mitchell Wagner from a deep sleep. It takes the big man two full minutes to drag himself out of bed and join his wife in the guest room. By that time, both Futrell kids are crying.

Yvonne is in the girl's bed, hugging Leigh tightly to her bosom. Sammy is crying because his sister is so upset.

"What happened?"

"She had a bad dream. Take Sam downstairs for some milk."

"What did you dream?"

"Sammy, go with Uncle Mitch. There's fresh brownies in the refrigerator."

"What was it? A nightmare?"

Yvonne scowls at her husband—a silent command for him to leave.

Leigh looks up, her eyes red with tears. "Daddy's dead."

JIDDAH, SAUDI ARABIA

Nahir sits alone in the back of the van, her arms pinned painfully behind her back by the handcuffs. Her black head scarf loosens and she shakes it free.

The rear doors open—Ace Futrell tossed inside.

She waits until the vehicle accelerates down the road before she goes to him. "Ashley?"

"Nahir?"

Kneeling, she turns her back to him and works the blindfold free from his face with her fingers.

Ace looks up at her, choking back tears. "You saved me."

"As you will save me."

He sits up painfully, twisting within his shackles. Nahir bends down to him until their cheeks collide and their lips taste one another, setting off a frenzied kiss driven not by passion but a primal need simply to feel.

The van turns suddenly, shaking them loose. She moves to him again, only Ace turns away. Torn from the brink of an accepted death, he is emotionally spent, the waves of nausea still settling inside him. "Nahir, I can't. I'm so very grateful, but all I can see and taste is death."

"I need to feel you, Ashley, even if only for a moment."

"I can't."

"Would you rather be dead?"

"I am dead. I'm dead to those who care."

"I care."

"I know. What did you say to the general?"

"I repeated what you had confided to me in your jail cell. I knew this would affect him. Some say a revolution is close at hand, others believe an invasion. Those who serve the House of Saud fear retribution. I am not certain what the general will do next, but I am sure he will want answers. In the end, I may have done you a disservice. You may have been better off dead."

He moves closer, nuzzling her cheek. "I'm alive for now, and that's all that counts."

FLAGSTAFF, ARIZONA
OCTOBER 3, 2012
3:20 AM MST

The two white vans accelerate away from the EconoLodge parking lot, Shane Torrence and Michael Tursi in one vehicle, Marco Fatiga driving the other.

Elliott Green waits thirty seconds before exiting his hotel room to tail the two vans in his rental car.

The matching vehicles head through town, making a circuitous route before finally turning into the deserted parking lot of the former auto repair center, its three bay doors boarded up. Michael Tursi hops out of the passenger side of his van and unlocks the left and middle bays, allowing the two vehicles to enter. The Turk looks around and sees no one. Satisfied, he walks inside the garage, closing the two bay doors behind him.

Elliott Green watches through night glasses from the twenty-four-hour Mart across the four-lane highway.

Inside the garage, Professor Eric Mingyuan Bi emerges from his self-contained underground bunker in the far right bay, awkwardly ascending the ladder in his biohazard suit. "You're early. You said four o'clock."

Tursi ignores the remark. "Where are the twins?"

Bi removes his hood and gloves and then activates the right bay's lift. The lead plates that had sealed the subterranean hole have been removed, allowing the I-shaped lift to rise to ground level.

Strapped onto the iron support are three lead crates.

Torrence hesitates. "What about radiation? We're not wearing suits."

"The lead crates minimize the exposure. There's no danger," Bi states. "Give me a hand."

The four men pair up to remove the two 145-pound metal boxes and the third smaller box from the lift. The nuclear physicist releases the lids from the first two containers, revealing matching Army-green metal cases, each about the size of a small footlocker. A ten-inch cell phone antenna protrudes from the matching bombs.

Professor Bi smiles proudly. "As promised, two Special Atomic Demolition Munitions—SADMs for short."

Tursi drags one of the suitcases from its lead box and undoes the latches, revealing the bomb's contents for inspection.

Inside is a bell-shaped device, housing a smaller cylinder-shaped canister. Wires run from the head of this device to the back of a cell phone.

Professor Bi points. "The cell phone's battery connects to a blasting cap in the main canister. When you dial the phone number, the ring will send a power surge to the blasting cap, setting off the C-4 inside the main canister. That will blow one piece of the enriched uranium through another, starting a chain reaction that will end in a nuclear explosion."

Torrence looks worried. "What if we get a telemarketing call or a wrong number?"

"The cell phones remain off until you're ready to set the device. No one else has access to these numbers."

"Where's the cell phone numbers?" Tursi demands.

Professor Bi unzips his radiation suit and removes an envelope from his pants pocket. He hands it to Tursi. "My bank account and routing number. The moment my final payment hits the account, I'll call you with the cell phone numbers."

The Turk's face turns red with rage. "Why should we trust you?"

"The question is, why should I trust you? I've delivered the twins as asked. I've even included a third container of radioactive elements so you can leave your false trail. The success of this mission relies on both of us disappearing into the shadows. I want the mission to succeed. Remember, it was your people who wiped out mine. But I will not allow you to eradicate me, not if you want the twins to detonate." The Asian scientist's heart races, but he stands firm.

A tense moment passes as Tursi eyeballs the Professor, contemplating. "Tomorrow by noon. I'd better have those numbers within two minutes of the transfer."

"You will. Absolutely."

Tursi turns to Torrence and Fatiga. "Load up, we're out of here."

The four men carry the heavy cases to the vans, one SADM secured in the back of Fatiga's vehicle and the second suitcase nuke and the smaller container of radioactive parts in Torrence's van.

Tursi pulls Marco Fatiga aside. "I received confirmation from our people in Baghdad. They took out Omar's siblings this morning, the hit-men dressed as American soldiers. Word will be sent through the Muslim Brotherhood to your boy within a few days."

"That ought to teach him to fall in love in the middle of a mission."

Professor Bi tosses his radioactive suit into the right bay's hold. "I've rigged the pit with TNT and gasoline. I'll wait twenty minutes before detonating the evidence."

Tursi nods.

Torrence and Fatiga open the middle and left bay doors.

"One moment, please!" Professor Bi hurries over to Tursi as he opens the first passenger door of the Torrence's van. "The target sites . . . which ones are they?"

The Turk grins and says nothing.

"At least tell me what day the twins will be birthed?"

Michael Tursi climbs in the vans and slams the door. Shane Torrence punches the gas, accelerating backward out of the building, Marco Fatiga's van following seconds later.

INAKESH PRISON, SAUDI ARABIA

Ace Futrell's eyes bulge from their sockets, the veins from his neck.

Nahir averts her hazel eyes. "General Abdul Aziz has spared your life. Now he wishes to know who your contact was in the Persian Gulf."

Ali Shams pulls the rope tighter. Encircling Ace's neck, the cord cuts through his flesh and wraps around his arms, which have been pinned awkwardly behind his back before feeding through the overhead pulley. A second cord has been secured around the head of Ace's penis, preventing him from urinating.

His bladder is ready to burst.

His face is purple. Ace grunts through clenched teeth.

The tension is released. He gasps a breath.

"Your contact's name?"

"Santa," he rasps. "Scott Santa. Russian-American, lives in Jiddah, works in Riyadh. Release my bonds . . . I'll tell you everything."

Nahir translates. The General nods.

He falls to his knees as the ropes are freed. With trembling fingers, he turns his back to Nahir as he claws loose the cord tied around the head of his penis, releasing a blood-tinged urine that pools across the concrete floor.

"The General is waiting."

"He's taller than me, Caucasian, dark hair, thick eyebrows. Last time we met was in New York, right before Christmas. He worked for the Vinnell Group, trained the Saudi guard. He's on his own now, probably freelances for the CIA. I know oil, Santa . . . he knows everything."

"Former Vice President Dick Cheney warned that there is a 'high probability' that terrorists will attempt a catastrophic nuclear or biological attack in coming years, and said he fears the Obama Administration's policies will make it more likely the attempt will succeed. Cheney unyieldingly defended the Bush Administration's support for the Guantanamo Bay prison and coercive interrogation of terrorism suspects."

—Politico,
February 4, 2009

"The Joint Special Operations Command was a special independent wing of Special Ops, with no Congressional or departmental oversight. Established after 9/11, they reported directly to Vice President Cheney, who used them as an executive assassination ring, established to eliminate perceived enemies of the United States, both home and abroad. Under President Bush's authority, they've been going into countries, not talking to the ambassador or the CIA station chief, and finding people on a list and executing them and leaving."

—Seymor Hersh,
March 11, 2009

CHAPTER 38

"GOOD EVENING FROM TULANE UNIVERSITY in the revitalized city of New Orleans. I'm Katie Couric, and I'd like to welcome you to the first of the 2012 presidential debates between Secretary of State Hillary Rodham Clinton, the Democratic nominee, Governor Ellis Prescott, the Republican nominee, and Senator Edward Mulligan, the Green Party nominee. Tonight's debate will last ninety minutes, following the rules of engagement worked out earlier by representatives of the three candidates. Tonight's topics will focus on foreign policy and homeland security. All questions posed come from me and have not been discussed with the candidates. Each question allows for a two-minute response, a ninety-second rebuttal by the other two candidates, and, at my discretion, an extension of one minute for further discussion. As by rule, candidates may not direct a question to each other. The debate will end with two-minute closing statements. Senator Mulligan, the first question goes to you.

"Senator, it's been eleven years since Al-Qaeda's attack on U.S. soil. Since that time there have been three more foiled attempts to down our commercial jets and two bombs, one successful, that detonated aboard a subway train. Over the last two weeks the Internet has been riddled with excerpts from an unpublished memoir, written by the late Kelli Doyle, former National Security Advisor under the Bush Administration who was murdered back in December. The excerpts allude to a nuclear detonation on U.S. soil that would lead to an invasion of Iran. My question, Senator, is whether you give credence to these memoirs, and why you believe you would do a better job than Governor Prescott or Secretary Clinton in preventing such an attack?"

"Thank you, Katie. First let me say that all of us on Capitol Hill are concerned about the information as well as the associated accusations aimed at the Neoconservative movement. It's always been our greatest fear that a dirty bomb or biological weapon could fall into the hands of a terrorist, and any group or individual that would support such a horrendous scenario should be tried and hung for treason. As to the information itself, it's difficult to give credibility to any report whose author is not around to present the evidence. Ms. Doyle was a staunch Neoconservative herself, and this could very well be another fear tactic designed to sway our populace, and we've seen far too much of that from former Vice President Cheney since President Obama took office. Do I believe I could do a better job than my two fellow nominees in preventing an attack? Absolutely. The last two administrations talked the tough talk but refused to adequately fund security at our ports and borders. Osama bin Laden most likely died and was never captured, and the Persian Gulf remains a boiling pot that has only grown worse since we invaded Iraq. As President, my immediate goal will be to defuse these tensions; first by engaging in an exit strategy that will remove U.S. troops from what has essentially become a Sunni–Shi'ite civil war; second, I will move America's economy off our fossil fuel addiction once and for all. The invasion of Iraq had nothing to do with WMDs or 9/11 and more to do with a Neoconservative agenda that seeks to control the Middle East and its supply of oil. By invading Iraq, we only increased the threat posed by Islamic radicals, whereas immediately after 9/11 we could have used our goodwill around the globe to isolate these extremists. We've listened to the last two presidents talk about funding alternative energy during State of the Union speeches, yet nothing is ever meaningfully funded, and legislation dealing with significantly improving gas mileage standards and reducing global warming is always pushed into the future. Meanwhile, fuel prices continue to skyrocket and the oil companies continue to reap tens of billions of dollars every week. Well, I have a different agenda, and it's not to engage in endless rhetoric. Together, we will take the necessary steps to once and for all free our nation of our addiction to oil, and that, Katie, will make our country safer."

"Governor Prescott?"

"Katie, there's a simple reason our country hasn't suffered a major attack since September 11, 2001, and that's because the Bush Administration, backed by the support of a Republican House and Senate, passed legislation designed to go after the bad guys while keeping our nation safe. President Obama reversed many of these security measures, and he closed Guantanamo Bay. My opponents would argue that wire tapping and identity cards are nothing more than an invasion of privacy, that passage of the Patriot Act was an infringement on our right to live in a free society, and if you believe that, then on November 8 you should cast your vote for the Democrats, or waste it on the Green Party candidate. Personally, as a law-abiding citizen, I'm thankful the Republicans were in office at the time Al-Qaeda struck. As to these latest rumors, Kelli Doyle served her country honorably, but it's a little too convenient to pin this information on a dead woman, especially right before a presidential election. Personally, I believe the information was released by some 527 group with ties to the liberal wing of the Democratic party. When I read an e-mail that links a nuclear attack with a patriotic American like former Vice President Cheney . . . well, it just sickens me that members of our party and their families have to be exposed to such underhanded politics."

"Secretary Clinton?"

"As a former First Lady, Senator of New York, and having served proudly as Secretary of State under President Barack Obama over these last three years, I have seen first hand how diplomacy, backed by a strong commitment to national security, has kept our country safe without tarnishing our morality. As President, I would continue the Obama doctrine while strengthening our border security."

"Senator Mulligan?"

"The Governor accuses the Democrats of underhanded politics. When it comes to underhanded politics, Karl Rove wrote the book and the Republicans published it. As for the Patriot Act, I've yet to see a shred of evidence that indicates those laws prevented an attack or led to the capture of a single terrorist. What the Patriot Act has done is make a mockery of our Constitution. If the American public actually knew what was written into this far-reaching document there'd be a march on Washington. Simply put, the Patriot Act has legalized Gestapo tactics, allowing the federal government to investigate anyone for any reason, evidence be damned, and if you are investigated, there's even a clause that forbids you to speak about the investigation or face criminal prosecution. The fact of the matter is, the Patriot Act was passed before members of Congress ever had a chance to read it, and it has been used as a tool by the White House to monopolize its powers ever since. President Obama promised transparency in the White House when he was elected, and that never happened. The government continues to wiretap, operate in secrecy, and all of the Obama Administration websites detailing the trillion dollar stimulus packages were shut down within the first year."

"Governor Prescott?"

"Again, the Senator demonstrates the difference between a liberal view of the world and the actions necessary to protect our democracy from those who would attack us. The simple, frightening situation in the world we live in is that there is a sect of Islamic extremists who are ready and willing to strap bombs onto their bodies in order to kill us, and weaning our economy off oil isn't going to send them packing. I don't like it and you don't like it, but these radicals are out there. We know what they're capable of. We've seen their senseless killing and destruction. Add a rogue power like Iran enriching uranium for nuclear bombs, and you have a recipe for disaster. Remember, we have to rise to the challenge and be perfect every time. They only have to be successful once. The Patriot Act is an essential tool for going after the bad guys, end of story."

Smokey Hills, Kansas
6:49 PM MST

Special agent Elliott Green fills the Honda Accord's gas tank at the Exxon station, his bloodshot eyes focused on the white van progressing through the drive-through lane of the McDonalds across the four-lane highway. He contemplates a mad dash for the men's room, but the van is already at the pay window. *Cutting it too close . . .*

He caps the tank, returns the pump, and climbs back in the rental car, turning the radio volume up on the presidential debate.

Across the street, the van pulls out of the McDonald's drive-through onto U.S. Highway 83, continuing south, the FBI agent's vehicle remaining seven cars behind.

✦ ✦ ✦

Elliott Green has been tailing the van driven by Michael Tursi and Shane Torrence for nearly sixteen hours. After leaving the old garage in Flagstaff, the two suspects had driven east on Route 40 out of Arizona. By the time they entered New Mexico, Green had been on his cell phone with FBI–Phoenix.

Phoenix was not the closest FBI office to Flagstaff, but it

was the one Green trusted. Back in July of 2001, two months prior to the 9/11 attacks, Kenneth Williams, a senior special agent from the Phoenix FBI terrorism task force, had alerted FBI headquarters about a radical group of Muslims taking flight lessons in Arizona. Williams' memo to FBI Director Robert Mueller specifically mentioned the threat of hijacking aircraft. Williams' urgent request to institute a nationwide survey of aviation schools to discern a pattern was denied. During the subsequent investigation, Director Mueller would classify the document and refuse to show it to members of the Senate 9/11 panel.

Green gave FBI Phoenix the location of the boarded-up garage, along with the van's license plate. He also told them about FBI Director Schafer's phone calls to Michael Tursi.

As the van continued north into Colorado, zigzagging across local thoroughfares before reaching Route 70, the Phoenix director had phoned Green to report the garage had exploded and burned to the ground. Because Special Agent Green had been suspended, the Phoenix director was obligated to report the information to his own superiors.

It was late Wednesday afternoon when the white van crossed into Kansas. For a while it seemed they would remain on Interstate 70, until the suspects had exited on Route 83, heading south through Kansas's north-central "badlands."

Elliott is exhausted. He has not slept for more than two hours at a time in weeks, afraid he would lose track of Michael Tursi. He is running on caffeine, adrenaline, and fear . . . fear that a nuclear detonation is imminent, fear that one mistake at this juncture might cost the lives of millions of people.

He has replayed the telephone conversation between Director Schafer and Michael Tursi dozens of times while driving, desperate to break their code.

"The patient's in labor." *The attack is imminent.*

"Where?"

"St. Mary's Hospital."

"So soon?" *The hospital name must determine the date of the attack.*

"Yes or no, is the doctor ready to deliver?" *Professor Bi.*

"He's ready. I hear twins." *Bi has constructed two bombs, ready to be delivered to the target sites.*

Two vans, two bombs. To prevent the second he must stop the first.

◆ ◆ ◆

The urge to urinate becomes overwhelming. Elliott wiggles his legs back and forth, his bladder feeling ready to explode. He starts to pull over when the van suddenly turns left, heading east on Jayhawk Road.

They have entered a desolate valley known as Smoky Hills. The first area ever chosen by the U.S. Department of Interior as a national natural landmark, these mid-western flatlands date back more than one hundred million years to the Cretaceous Period when Kansas was covered by treacherous seas, populated by fifty-foot plesiosaurs and other prehistoric monsters. Now a fossilized desert, the valley contains towering chalk formations that reach heights of seventy feet, interspersed with incredible buttes and sandstone arches.

Elliott glances at the calendar he purchased three rest stops ago. *The patient is in labor . . . any holiday's coming up?* He checks the calendar again.

Halloween . . could be—wait, Monday is Columbus Day. Could it be that soon? What would St. Mary's have to do with Columbus Day? Christopher Columbus . . . 1492 . . . three ships. What the hell were their names? The Nina, the Pinta—

"Santa Maria! St. Mary's hospital! The attack is on Monday!"

He almost veers off the side of the road as the van turns again, this time heading south. Green follows, suddenly finding himself on a deserted stretch of road, the van and his rental car the only vehicles around.

Careful Elliott . . . He slows, but there is nowhere to hide.

Dust clouds roll up ahead as the van pulls off the road onto the shoulder.

Damn . . . did they make you? Too late, just keep going, double-back when you can.

Green shoves his electronic gear and the evidence incriminating Schafer under his seat and then accelerates past the van on his left, staring straight ahead, never noticing the gunman poised on one knee on the right side of the road.

A swarm of bullets bursts through the passenger side window, splattering Elliott Green's remains across the dashboard. The rental car veers off the left side of the road, continuing another sixty yards across the flatlands before coming to a halt.

Shane Torrence jogs across the tarmac, joining Michael Tursi. The two SSB officers approach the stalled vehicle, guns in hand.

Tursi opens the driver side door. Nudges the corpse back into its seat.

Torrence stares at Green's bloody face, the dead man's eyes still open in shock. "Aw, hell!"

"What? You know this guy?"

"It's the FBI agent, the one who was staking out Bi."

"Schafer?"

"Who else?"

"Incompetent bastard!" The Turk shoots Green's corpse four more times in the chest, sending Torrence backing away for cover.

"Easy, Turk!" Using the barrel of his gun, Torrence prods and feels along Green's clothing. Locates the cell phone in a pants pocket. Carefully extracts it, wiping the blood off with the loose end of the dead agent's tee-shirt. "We'll check his outgoing calls, see who he's been talking to."

"Yeah, good." Tursi looks around. The flatlands seem to run on forever, yielding to an occasional monument of rock.

He points southeast. "Send him out there while I change our license plate."

Torrence nods and then searches the ground. He collects several heavy rocks while Tursi returns to the van. From an envelope under his seat he removes a new license plate, this one registered in Ohio. Grabbing a screwdriver from the glove box, he removes the old license plate, swapping it for the Ohio tag, as Torrence restarts the FBI Agent's rental car and adjusts the steering wheel, aiming it for the open flatlands. Weighing down the gas pedal with the rocks, he puts the vehicle in gear, sending Elliott Green's remains bounding over a sea of desert for parts unknown.

"Where was the military? General Richard Myers [Acting Chair of the Joint Chiefs of Staff] and Mike Snyder [NORAD spokesman] both said no military jets were sent up until after the strike on the Pentagon [9:38]. Yet American Airlines Flight 11 had shown two of the standard signs of hijacking at 8:15. This means that procedures that usually result in interception within ten or so minutes had not been carried out in eighty minutes. That enormous delay suggested that a stand-down order, canceling standard procedures, must have been given."

—PROFESSOR DAVID RAY GRIFFIN,
The 9/11 Commission's Incredible Tales

"A report by Transportation Department inspector general Kenneth Mead said the manager for the New York air traffic control center asked controllers to record their experiences a few hours after the crashes, believing they would be important for law enforcement. Sometime between December 2001 and February 2002, an unidentified Federal Aviation Administration quality assurance manager crushed the cassette in his hand, cut the tape into small pieces, and threw them away in multiple trash cans, the report said. The manager said he destroyed the tape because he felt it violated FAA policy calling for written statements from controllers who have handled a plane in an accident or other serious incident."

—LESLIE MILLER,
Associated Press Writer,
May 6, 2004

CHAPTER 39

A STEADY BREEZE BLOWS IN from the open balcony doors overlooking the Red Sea. Scott Santa lies spread-eagled across one of the room's two double beds, finishing a joint, his eyes glazing over the live broadcast of the presidential debate. In the second bed are the Asian prostitutes, the two women curled next to one another like spoons. He turns the TV louder as one starts snoring.

A double knock. "Room service."

"About time." He puts the joint out, slips on his boxer shorts, and opens the door. The Saudi police bash their way inside, guns aimed at his face. "Down! On your knees!"

"American! I'm an American! My company works with—"

"Quiet!" One of the police strikes him with a baton across the back of his head.

The two naked women cower as their client is forcibly handcuffed and dragged out of the room.

ABQAIQ OIL REFINERY
SAUDI ARABIA
4:16 AM LOCAL TIME

"Tonight we change history! First we reclaim our nation's

stolen resources, and then the Arabian nation!"

Four thousand laborers, half of them foreign nationalists, cheer the live Internet feed of Prince Alwaleed bin Talal and their brothers-in-arms—members of the Ashraf movement.

Since 2005, Al-Qaeda and other Islamic extremist groups have launched a dozen unsuccessful attacks on the Abqaiq refinery, the most secure site in all of Saudi Arabia. Tonight's assault was a bloodless coup—the culmination of eight months of selling the revolution to workers who have always despised the House of Saud, combined with three weeks of working without paychecks due to "technical problems" at the National Bank.

Now, hours after the takeover, supporters have been streaming into the compound by the hundreds, many carrying weapons, cheering the arrival of the Saudi Army and their military vehicles.

In Saudi Arabia, it is the National Guard, made up of loyal Bedouin, that is entrusted with protecting the Royals and the kingdom's major cities. Far smaller, the Saudi Armed Forces are purposely positioned outside the major centers of government, making it more difficult for the soldiers to overthrow the King.

But keeping these disgruntled soldiers isolated made it easier for Ashraf's leaders to sway them to their side. With the successful takeover at the Abqaiq compound, the military has mobilized, sending dozens of long-dormant Bradley Fighting machines and armored personal carriers through the refinery's open gates.

Meanwhile, in a heavily guarded administration building, Ramzi Karim meets with the military advisors who are coordinating the revolution.

"The compound is secure," reports General al Jaber. "Seven wounded, nothing serious, all were members of the Interior Ministry. The American workers will remain locked down in their dormitories as we agreed. Aramco personnel harboring loyalty toward the Royals have been segregated from the group and placed under guard in the cafeteria."

Ramzi nods. "And the infrastructure?"

"All separation stations and natural gas plants are being rigged with explosives," states Mohammed Zayed, a disgruntled Saudi Aramco official. "Demolition teams are heading out to the pumping stations as we speak."

"Be sure the television crews film this when they arrive. Tell me about the military bases."

"Eastern Area Command reports Dhahran has been secured."

"Northern Command at Hafr al-Batin as well. Four Saudi pilots were arrested and the other Royals haven't shown up for duty since their bank accounts were purged."

Ramzi smiles. "What about the bases in Tabuk and Khamis Mushayt?"

"Northwestern and Southern Command Centers have been secured. But we knew the bases would not be a problem. How will the clerics respond?"

"They will wait and see."

"We still have the element of surprise," the General reminds him. "Perhaps we should consider making a move on Riyadh. With the king and his ministers in France—"

Ramzi shakes his head. "Move on Riyadh now and we invite the U.S. Armed Forces to enter the arena, and a direct confrontation is the last thing we want. The refinery may be our bartering chip, but this is only one battlefield, and there are things going on in America that must be resolved before we take the next step in the revolution. The last thing we need is to look like a regime of Islamic extremists. Let the Royals appear desperate. Our first goal must be to win the battle of perception among the Western media and the confidence of our own people."

BOCA RATON, FLORIDA
OCTOBER 6, 2012
7:40 AM EST

Jennifer Wienner drives south along scenic route A1A, the pristine aqua-blue of the Atlantic Ocean on her left, high rise condominiums on her right. She is happy about her campaign efforts, but far from satisfied.

The latest polls indicate Senator Mulligan has increased his lead over Secretary Clinton by a 39 percent to 35 percent margin, with Governor Prescott trailing at 21 percent, the remaining 5 percent still undecided. More important, the country clearly favors the immediate withdrawal of American troops from the Middle East as well as moving forward with a green energy plan.

But poll numbers mean nothing when dealing with a win-at-all cost GOP machine—one she knows is capable of pulling off its own "October surprise" at any time.

✦ ✦ ✦

The original "October surprise" dates back to the 1980 Presidential election when the release of American hostages from Iran would have all but guaranteed a reelection win to Democratic incumbent Jimmy Carter, whose administration was preparing to implement a second rescue attempt in the event negotiations broke down.

When the Reagan-Bush campaign heard about the rescue, it launched a major publicity blitz warning the public that President Carter was timing an "October surprise" solely to win the election. Meanwhile, former CIA director George Bush and other members of the Reagan team were secretly meeting with high-level Iranian and Israeli representatives in a hotel in Paris, forging an agreement that promised to award Iran with arms and spare military parts in return for agreeing not to release the American hostages until after the election.

On October 21, Iran publicly broke off negotiations with the Carter Administration, dispersing the hostages to several different locations in order to dissuade another rescue. Two days later, a planeload of F-4 aircraft tires arrived in Iran from Israel without the Carter Administration's knowledge. Reagan won the election and the hostages were released on January 21, 1981, only minutes after the Republican nominee was sworn in as President.

◆ ◆ ◆

Turning off A1A at Palmetto Park Road, Jennifer parks in front of a deli. Inside she orders a breakfast sandwich and a coffee to go and then walks back across A1A to an ocean-front pavilion to enjoy her food.

There are a dozen benches beneath the roofed structure, one occupied by a couple in their seventies, another by a scantily-clad female jogger tending to her miniature poodle. Teens mill about by the rail, watching surfers catch the occasional four-foot swell. Down the beach a yoga class finishes a sunrise meditation.

Claiming an empty bench, Jennifer eats her sandwich.

Twenty minutes pass.

"May I?" Without waiting for a reply, Kenneth Keene Jr. parks himself on the end of her bench, removes his bicycling helmet, and retrieves a bottled water and banana from his waist pouch. "Potassium break."

"You're late."

"There's a series of commercials running on Senator Downing at the top of every hour. It's like a friggin' soap opera. I just couldn't miss it. This last one reveals private medical records of his wife's abortion six years ago, only it wasn't his wife, it was an exotic dancer."

"I guess an elected official who rails against Pro Choice should make sure his own closet is clean."

"It just amazes me where they come up with this stuff. It's like . . . it's like they could read his mind."

"Anything on our boy?"

"Chatter. Nothing solid. We're shutting down soon. It's getting tight."

She stares at the ocean. "Before you do, I need you to locate someone for me. Name's Armond Proctor, goes by the nickname Dale. Caucasian, late fifties, a former sailor who worked explosives on offshore oil rigs for Dresser Atlas in Louisiana. Went to work for the NSA as a computer systems analyst in '94. Spent five years with the spooks before Diebold hired him. He disappeared during the 2000 election."

"You sure he's still alive?"

She stands, tossing him the uneaten half of sandwich. "He's alive. I want him found . . . before the election."

WASHINGTON MONUMENT, WASHINGTON, D.C.
OCTOBER 6, 2012
7:38 AM EST

The white obelisk tower is just over 555 feet, its image sparkling in the waters of the reflecting pool which runs west toward the Lincoln Memorial.

Scott Swan spots Howard Lowe seated on a park bench reading a newspaper. The Homeland Security director never looks up as the defense contractor moves within earshot, pretending to talk on his cell phone.

"I'm listening."

"I have information," Lowe says, "but it will cost you."

"Name your price. Sultan's desperate."

"Not from Sultan. This has to come from you. A deuce."

"Two hundred thousand? You're insane."

Lowe continues reading.

Swan swears at the phone. "Fine. Just tell me what you've got."

"We've tallied almost a trillion dollars in stolen funds. Most of it's dirty money, so the financial institutions are keeping it quiet, at least the ones in the West. In some of these other countries, bankers are turning up in body bags."

"How are the funds being moved?"

"Promis. Someone created a very clever worm. Remember Kelli Doyle?"

"The NSA staffer? I thought she was taken out."

"She was, but apparently not before she passed Promis off to her husband. Resourceful little prick. We had him twice and then lost him in Canada. His kids have gone AWOL. Seven weeks ago he turned up in Riyadh, in the National Bank."

"Dammit! Do you have any idea—"

"Yes."

"Can the process be reversed? Can the funds be traced?"

"Not without the worm."

"Where's Doyle's husband now?"

"The Saudis have him. They don't know who he is or what he's done."

"Just tell me where he's at."

"Inakesh."

"We have discovered how to hit the Jews where they are most vulnerable. The Jews love life, so that is what we shall take away from them. We are going to win because they love life and we love death."

—SHEIK HASSAN NASRALLAH,
Hezbollah leader
(The European Union has steadfastly refused to place
Hezbollah on its list of terrorist organizations.)

"We have not succeeded making our children love life. We have taught them how to die for Allah, but we haven't taught them how to live for the sake of Allah."

—ABD AL-HAMID AL-ANSARI,
Former Dean of Islamic Law, Qatar University, 2005

"They are a persistent bunch. They just keep coming at you when they have a good idea."

—STEVEN SIMON,
former White House National Security
official and author of "The Next Attack,"
Newsweek,
August 21–28, 2006
on Al-Qaeda and Islamic jihadists, after
their failed attempt to explode U.S.
commercial jets departing from London.

CHAPTER 40

Inakesh Prison, Saudi Arabia
October 6, 2012
Saturday

THE STRANGER'S FACE IS HARROWED AND THIN, the eyes sullen, sunken deep into their sockets. The hair is longer, grayed heavily around the temples. The mustache and beard remain unkempt, dark, with bizarre silver streaks.

Ace stares at his own reflection in the bathroom mirror and shudders.

The guard hands him the razor. Motions with the gun.

Take it easy, at least you survived another Friday. With a trembling hand, Ace shaves.

✦ ✦ ✦

Twenty minutes later he emerges, freshly showered for the first time in almost two months, his scarred wounds hidden beneath his now neatly ironed suit. Free from shackles, he is led through the courtyard and into a different administration building, one reserved for outside visitors.

Ace catches a heavy whiff of a familiar European aftershave a moment before he enters the small conference room.

A guard stands near the door, looking bored.

The warden watches from behind a two-way mirror.

Kelli Doyle's killer is seated at the far end of the table, smoking a cigarette. The man looks up at Ace and forces a smile. "There he is. Lost a few pounds, huh, champ? Bet you'll be glad to get back to the States."

Ace says nothing, but his eyes burn holes in the assassin's face, the adrenaline coursing through his body, setting every muscle to quiver.

Scott Santa's mouth twitches nervously. "I spoke with the Saudi police. They've graciously accepted your confession. I'm here to get you out. Be smart and in a few hours, we'll have you on a plane heading home to see Leigh and Sammy—"

At the mention of his children's names Ace is airborne, leaping across the table. He topples Santa backwards in his chair, his hands finding the assassin's throat, his thumbs puncturing flesh as they crush the man's windpipe.

OVAL OFFICE, THE WHITE HOUSE
WASHINGTON, D.C.
OCTOBER 6, 2012
SATURDAY 9:46 AM EST

Homeland Security director Howard Lowe enters the Oval Office, acting President Joe Biden already meeting with Joseph Kendle. The Secretary of Defense has laid out the latest satellite reconnaissance photos taken over Saudi Arabia.

Biden looks up. "You heard?"

"Caught it on CNN. Where's the Secretary of State?"

"Probably out kissing babies. What do these Ashraf rebels want?"

"A Royal-free democracy."

"Crazies."

"Sultan had me on the phone all morning. He's demanding we move in with U.S. troops or he'll cut off the oil—"

"Only Ashraf controls his biggest refinery," finishes the Defense Secretary. "We move in now and they blow up the entire infrastructure . . . it would take years to rebuild."

Howard Lowe flashes a harsh glare at the Defense Secretary. "Mr. President, it's Saturday. Go to Camp David. Let your new press secretary handle this. You've spoken to Sultan; his National Guard has stabilized the situation. We support our allies, blah, blah, blah, but there is no need to involve our military at this juncture."

"Good . . . good, and you're right, I do need the break. Some great games on this weekend. Redskins play the Cowboys."

Lowe nods. "Try to get some rest, sir. It's going to be a busy week."

DUNDALK MARINE TERMINAL
BALTIMORE, MARYLAND
OCTOBER 6, 2012
SATURDAY 11:25 PM EST

The 2009 Chevy Trailblazer enters the security gates, its occupant flashing his identification badge to the guard on duty.

Jamal al-Yussuf follows the access road back toward the river and then parks in the staff lot. He has been working the graveyard shift for the last two months.

Tonight will be his last at the cursed port.

The "delivery" had arrived two hours earlier in a white van parked beneath an overpass under Interstate 95. Jamal had lugged the heavy suitcase and duffle bag to his car, along with the copy of the Koran that his "contact" had left for him.

He selects a parking space close to his destination. He removes the duffle bag from the backseat, registering its internal heat as he slings it over his shoulder. He lights a cigarette to calm his nerves and heads for the open overseas pier.

The bright yellow shipping container had arrived last night. The gantry crane had lifted it from the cargo ship's hold, Jamal directing the operator to leave it in a row and space he knew would have little traffic on tonight's shift.

The steel container is forty feet long, eight feet high and wide, with a maximum cargo capacity of forty-four thousand pounds. It occupies the bottom position beneath a stack of four.

The authorities who will eventually track its journey will learn that it had originated from Tehran, loaded aboard an Islamic Republic of Iran cargo ship from the Imam Khomeini Port in the Persian Gulf. It was then relegated to a China-India service, making stops in Hong Kong and Singapore before reaching its first destination in the Philippines, where its shipping documents had been swapped for forged invoices. From there the container had traveled through the Panama Canal and gradually up the Atlantic coastline of the United States to its final destination in Baltimore.

Jamal verifies no one is around before unlocking and opening the container's door.

The inside is filled to capacity, cardboard boxes stacked to the ceiling on one side, long rolls of Persian rugs wrapped in plastic sheeting on the other. He begins removing the lightweight boxes as instructed, working his way to the center, where he finds the lead box, bolted to the floor. He unhinges the top and looks inside.

Empty.

Opening the duffle bag, Jamal dumps its contents into the lead box—wires, housings, plastic wrapping, metal brackets—everything covered in telltale radioactive residue.

He shuts the lid and leaves the cardboard boxes as instructed. Then he hurries to the edge of the pier and tosses the empty duffle-bag into the Patapsco River, watching it fill and sink.

An hour later he is driving north on Route 83 on his way to the Pennsylvania Turnpike.

VENICE BEACH, CALIFORNIA
OCTOBER 7, 2012
SUNDAY 11:15 AM PST

The Bohemian walkway is lined with tall palm trees, the late morning crowd pausing to enjoy the street performers and gawk at the scantily-clad women (and men) in bikinis, everyone soaking up the California sunshine.

Omar Kamel Radi holds Susan Campbell's hand as the couple strolls south on Ocean Front Walk. The green-eyed thirty-six-year-old aerobics instructor slips her arm around her steady boyfriend of two months and registers the contraction as he tenses up.

"Omar, is something wrong? You've been so quiet."

"I received word from back home. Two of my sisters were killed, shot by American soldiers."

"Oh my!" She stops walking. "How could something like this happen? Were they in Cairo?"

"Baghdad." He turns, wiping away tears. "I am not from Egypt, Susan, I am from Iraq. This bothers you?"

"It bothers me that you lied."

"People judge."

"I'm not judging. My cousin, he's over there now, fighting for your people's freedom."

Omar's eyes narrow, growing angry. "Freedom? Do you know what you are saying? Because I do not think you really know."

"Maybe we shouldn't talk about this right now."

"No, we will talk now!"

People turn to look. Susan walks away, Omar in pursuit.

"You know nothing about what we want, Susan! We never asked for your help or your freedom; we just wanted security. We just wanted to be able to live our lives in peace."

"Calm down."

"Maybe it was your cousin who shot my sisters, eh? Maybe he thought they were a threat?"

"Stop. Stop it right now. My cousin would never shoot a helpless civilian. Never."

"How do you know? Your military drops bombs that kill families. Is this the freedom you speak of? The Shi'ites take control of our city. They kill civilians. Is this the freedom you also enjoy? You know nothing about war. You are an ignorant woman with no hardship who . . . who dances, and drives her car, and surfs. What bloodshed have you experienced in your life to earn your freedom? What would you sacrifice to keep it?"

"I love my country—"

"You love your country? I love my country! What would you do, Susan, if foreign soldiers broke into your home and shot your parents? Would you smile at your liberators as they killed your little sisters? Or your grandfather, helpless in his wheelchair? Would you say 'Thank you' when the butchers offered you an apology and twenty-five hundred American dollars for each family member killed?"

Her eyes fill with tears. "Omar . . . I'm sorry, I didn't know—"

"No, what you mean is you did not wish to know. As long as it does not affect you, as long as you have gasoline to sit in traffic and cool your apartment, then the price of Iraqi freedom is affordable."

She reaches for him but he backs away, choking on his words. "I love you . . . but this cannot be. Too much has happened, too many deaths." He jogs several steps and turns, anger in his eyes. "Do you want to know what freedom really is, Susan Campbell? Freedom is the power to inflict justice upon your enemies. That is freedom."

He gives her one last look and takes off running down the beach.

WASHINGTON, D.C.
OCTOBER 7, 2012
SUNDAY 4:17 PM EST

"And the Cowboys recover the fumble on the Redskins thirty-five-yard line. And that should do it . . ."

The barflies boo, the crowd thinning out to avoid the late afternoon traffic.

Howard Lowe taps Gary Schafer on the shoulder. "Game's over. Let's walk."

✦ ✦ ✦

The two men stroll along the Tidal Basin around the Jefferson Memorial, the walkway lined with hundreds of cherry trees—a gift from the Japanese government that dates back to 1912.

The head of the FBI massages the tightness along the back of his neck. "When did our friend contact you?"

"Late last night. Gary, you should have told me about Springfield. The Colonel's orders were quite clear."

"Howard, I swear, I thought I had it under control."

"You didn't. Green contacted Phoenix and now they're involved, which means something has to be done, a sacrifice made to protect your office . . . and the rest of us."

"I'm listening."

The Director of Homeland Security pauses to pick a bud off a cherry tree. "Gary, do you remember the movie, 'Sophie's Choice?' Meryl Streep's character survived the holocaust. She was brilliant in the lead."

"Yes. She had to choose, right? Between two of her children."

Lowe nods. "One twin lives, the other dies. Contact our friend with your decision, and then save the child . . . personally."

"I share a deep disgust that those prisoners were treated the way they were treated."

—PRESIDENT GEORGE W. BUSH,
on torture in Abu Ghraib prison.
(Bush later threatened to veto an amendment to
the $450 billion Military Appropriations Bill
because it adhered to the Geneva Conventions'
prohibitions on torture.)

"In a memorandum dated 19 January, 2002, Secretary of Defense Donald Rumsfeld ordered the Chairman of the Joint Chiefs of Staff to inform combat commanders that 'Al-Qaeda and Taliban individuals . . .' are not entitled to prisoner of war status for purposes of the Geneva Conventions of 1949.' He ordered that 'commanders should'. . . treat them humanely, and to the extent appropriate and consistent with military necessity, consistent with the Geneva Conventions of 1949. That order thus gives commanders permission to depart, where they deem it appropriate and a military necessity, from the provisions of the Geneva Conventions."

—INTERNATIONAL LAW OF WAR ASSOCIATION

CHAPTER 41

"Do you understand what I am telling you, Ashley? This man is a friend of Al Saud. It is you who will be tortured to death, not him."

Ace is again in the death chamber. He is naked, his legs and arms strapped to the chair without the seat.

Nahir kneels next to him, pleading with him to confess. Instead he stares straight ahead, focusing not on the woman but on General Abdul Aziz, who is busy in his office with the two visiting princes and their entourage of bodyguards. The Royals are berating the warden, cursing at him in Arabic and demanding answers—and Ace can understand every word.

For nine weeks he has played dumb, the former petrol-geologist never letting on that he could speak Arabic. Now, as the Saudi Royals rattle on about stolen billions, he hears one word that tells him all is lost—one word spoken from the Royal's mouth—Promis.

They know. Someone got word to the Saudis and they know . . .

The muscles in his legs tremble within the leather strappings, each inhaled breath acrid with stress.

"Ashley, I have witnessed what Ali Shams will do. He will begin by tearing off each one of your fingernails and then he will work on your eyes. Tell them what they want to know and your death will be merciful."

They know what I did. What can I possibly tell them?

"Ashley, you have proven yourself twice, but the game has changed. Please, Ashley!"

They want their money back. They will torture me until they realize that the money is gone forever, and then they will keep me alive as long as they can—unless . . .

"They won't believe me, Nahir."

"Tell me, and I will make them believe."

Surround the lie with truth.

"The man I attempted to strangle—Scott Santa—he worked with my wife. Her name was Kelli Doyle. Before she was a national security advisor she worked with the CIA. She was murdered nine months ago. Scott Santa came to me and told me the men who had her killed were Saudi Nationals, members of the Royal Guard. Scott said he knew of a way to hurt those who hurt me, that if I downloaded a special CD program he had designed into a computer terminal at the National Bank in Riyadh that I would have my revenge."

"What was on the CD?"

"I don't know, he refused to say."

"You attacked him. Why?"

"While in prison I had time to think. I know now that he used me, that it wasn't the Saudis who had Kelli murdered, it was this man . . . this CIA assassin."

"Ashley, you are certain of this?"

He looks into her eyes. "Yes."

She leaves his side, hurrying to the warden's office. Knocks on the open door and speaks quickly, pointing at Ace.

The men listen intently. The General dials a number on his desk phone.

Minutes later, Scott Santa is led into the chamber, his bruised throat bandaged. "Now what? Prince Turki, good. Perhaps you could explain to—"

The guards force him to sit before the warden. One man fixes the blood pressure cuff around Santa's arm while the other attaches the remaining monitors of the lie detector machine.

"Prince Turki! Is this how you treat a friend? Prince Turki, *minfadlik*! *Minfadlik*!"

The warden slams his open palm on his desk. *"Ma ismok?"*

"Santa, Scott J. I am a U.S. citizen, subcontracted by the House of Saud to train—"

The warden cuts him off with a string of Arabic.

"His wife?" Santa looks over his shoulder at Ace, his expression falling as he hesitates to answer. "Yes, I knew her."

The guard operating the lie-detector nods as Ali Shams walks through the chamber and enters the warden's office, circling the proceedings like a predator in heat.

General Abdul Aziz asks another question.

The Russian-American stares at the rotund Saudi torturer, fear in his eyes as he spots the flathead pair of pliers in the man's left hand. "CD? What CD?"

The guard shakes his head.

Ali Shams smiles.

Ace's eyes widen as the sadist grapples with the Russian's left hand, separating the middle digit from the rest as he positions the tool, the flathead wrench biting down . . .

"Aaaah! You bastard, Futrell! You stupid—"

More Arabic from the warden.

"No . . . no wait! Okay, yes, I was in the bank that morning, but I had nothing to do with any plot to steal your money! No . . . no! Please—"

Ace turns away as the tortured screams reverberate in his eardrums.

◆ ◆ ◆

In Earth's four billion-year history, only one species has ever inflicted pain and suffering upon its own kind. Is this evolution? Intelligent design? If we were cast from the dye of our maker, does that make God a tyrant?

For the mother forced to watch her infant perish of

starvation, there is no God. For the family wiped out by religious fanatics, nothing can remain holy. For the mother of the soldier who loses his life in a battle unjust, no flag-draped coffin can offer her comfort.

For the many who find themselves facing inhuman abuse, only death is humane.

For Ashley "Ace" Futrell, there is no logic or hope, no more cause for prayer, there is simply the promise of relief that will come after a long, painful death.

As the room reverberates with Scott Santa's screams, Ace's mind races, searching desperately for a distant memory he can hold on to—a life raft in this sea of insanity.

He is in his backyard, as a boy. Tossing a football with his father, Brownie . . .

Older now . . . the strawberry-blond fifteen-year-old he met at overnight camp, his first kiss . . .

High school . . . his first real football uniform. That first game . . .

The thrill when he threw the winning touchdown pass . . .

The screams grow louder, shaking loose the memories.

School, think about school! High school . . . no, go straight to college, life at Georgia. Making the team as a walk-on . . . playing in that first game . . . the screaming fans . . . the two touchdowns! Meeting Kelli . . . love at first sight. Taking her to Tasty World, five-dollar giant margueritas at the Blind Pig . . . making love in the front seat of my old Chevy Malibu—

Men yelling. Arabic curses stealing his thoughts once more.

Focus on Kelli, you'll see her soon. Maybe we'll be young again? No cancer . . . no pain—

His eyes have been gazing at the aluminum table only inches from his left wrist, seeing nothing, seeing everything. Now, as Scott Santa's howls fill his ears, his vision refocuses on the tray and the sharp steel probes only inches away . . . six-inch skewers designed to inflict pain—or liberate one's soul. He stares at the three white scars running lengthwise down his left wrist, three white scars calling to him from the past.

Suicide . . . Do it, it's your best option!

With every last ounce of strength he wrenches and flexes his left forearm within its Velcro straps, gaining precious inches of slack . . . retracting and flexing until he can slip his wrist free! The rest of his arm remains taut against the chair but his fingers reach for the tray, straining to pull it closer, to snag one of those precious probes . . . his second and third fingers pinching one . . . losing it to the tray . . . touching another one . . . easy, Ace—

Got you!

His index finger maneuvers the skewer closer, his middle finger pinching the steel, palming it, pulling it back toward the chair.

Flexing his forearm, he gradually loosens the strap around his elbow, just enough to reach his throat . . . to plunge the instrument deep into his carotid artery.

The Russian screams again.

Do it! Lean forward and jam it home!

"It was a long time ago, Leigh. You don't have to worry . . ."

Ace freezes.

"I'm coming back, Leigh, I promise. Watch out for Sammy, okay?"

Ace weeps, unable to do it, unable to break his promise to his daughter.

Okay, baby girl, okay . . . maybe there's another way.

The screaming stops.

They're coming for you, hide the skewer!

He stares at the three white scars. Gritting his teeth, he maneuvers the probe within his hand, then forcibly pushes the sharp steel tip so that it penetrates the soft flesh below his wrist. Barely drawing blood, he uses the wrist strap as leverage to slide it deeper just beneath the surface of his skin . . . until the entire six-inch probe is embedded within his arm.

Ace tucks his left wrist back inside the Velcro strap and turns his arm palm-down as Scott Santa's bloodied body is carried out of the warden's office.

Now it is his turn.

One more shot, Ace. One more tick of the clock. God's giving you a chance to throw a Hail Mary . . . to get back in the game. All you have to do is survive.

"Tomorrow is zero hour."
"The match is about to begin."

—ARABIC MESSAGES,
intercepted by the NSA on September 10, 2001, and
translated on September 12.

"To commit mass murder on an unimaginable scale."

—PAUL STEPHENSON,
London Deputy Commissioner,
on the attempt by Islamic radicals to
blow up commercial jets over the Atlantic.
Newsweek,
August 21–28, 2006

"Then the sixth angel blew his trumpet, and I heard a voice speaking from the four horns of the gold altar that stands in the presence of God. And the voice spoke to the sixth angel who held the trumpet: 'Release the four angels who are bound at the Euphrates River. And the four angels who had been prepared for this hour and day and month and year were turned loose to kill one-third of all the people on earth . . .'"

—REVELATION 9: 13–15

CHAPTER 42

"Aruba, Jamaica . . . ooh I wanna take you to Bermuda, Bahama . . . come on pretty mama, Key Largo, Montego . . . baby why don't we go and snort some blow . . . way down in Kokomo!"

Michael Tursi laughs at himself, tapping away at the steering wheel to the Beach Boys' tune as he follows the airport signs to the rental car return. He smiles at the Avis attendant, offers his seat on the return bus to an African-American mother and her two young children, and says "good morning" to airport security.

Ninety minutes early for his flight to the Grand Caymans, he purchases a bagel, cream cheese, and a Philadelphia Inquirer, and then he sits and enjoys his breakfast at gate E–22.

After a few minutes, Tursi tosses the paper, his mind too cluttered, too excited to read. *Twenty-two million in the bank, and everything moving like clockwork. If only Rummy had listened to me ten years ago, there'd be a McDonald's on every corner in Baghdad by now.*

Like a kid on Christmas morning, he opens his laptop and accesses the Internet, needing to see his bank account one more time.

He types in his password and code and looks at the statement—

Balance: $0.00

"What the . . ."

He tries it again.

"Damn it!"

Heads turn.

Tursi is frantic as he simultaneously reboots the laptop and dials the bank's customer service number on his cell phone. He curses at the automated machine, punches in his account number when prompted, and presses zero over and over again, the sweat pouring from his body as a male service rep in India finally comes on the line.

"Good morning. How may I—"

"My account, I need to know the balance—right now!"

"I can help you with that, sir. I just need to ask you a few quick security questions."

He gives him his name, account number, his mother's maiden name . . .

"Thank you, Mr. Tursi, I see you have a zero balance in that account."

"What the hell are you talking about, Ghandi? Look at your records! Doesn't it show recent deposits totaling over $22 million?"

"Yes, sir. And a transfer this morning of $22,347,890, as per your instructions."

"I did not—" He lowers his voice as two police officers approach. "I did not transfer a dime! Not one dime, you stupid—"

The line goes dead.

Tursi curses. He dials Gary Schafer's cell phone number and hears the "line has been disconnected" message and nearly throws up his breakfast.

He hurries to the men's room. He takes the handicapped stall and washes his face, his hands quivering. *Think it through,*

Turk, think it through. Can't reach the Colonel, and he never would have screwed me . . . never. That leaves Schafer. Incompetent prick, he's covering his own ass, leaving me out to dry.

The Turk stares at his pale reflection in the mirror. "Game's not over yet, my friend. Not by a long shot."

Michael Tursi exits the bathroom and jogs to the airline counter a floor below to exchange his ticket for a new destination.

CHICAGO, ILLINOIS
12:15 PM CST

"What'd I tell you guys? Sue's the tallest T-Rex in the world."

Mitch Wagner leads Leigh and Sam Futrell into the Chicago Field Museum, leaving his wife, Yvonne, at the ticket counter to take care of business. "Sammy, what do you think? Pretty cool, right?"

"Yeah, if it was twenty years ago, before *Jurassic Park* came out."

"What? You don't want to even look around?"

"We've been here before."

"Twice for me," says Leigh."

Yvonne joins them. "Okay, we ready?"

"Now they don't want to go."

"What are you talking about? I just bought IMAX tickets. *Mission Deep: Mariana Trench.* It's supposed to be great."

"We saw it last year on a school field trip," Sammy says. "I told Uncle Mitch that yesterday."

"Yeah, well us old farts suffer from a disease called CRS . . . Can't remember sh—"

"Mitch!" Yvonne pats Sam on the shoulder. "Go with your Uncle Mitch and return these tickets while your sister and I figure out what we're going to do until the game starts."

LOS ANGELES, CALIFORNIA
1:45 PM PST

Susan Campbell enters her studio apartment, her blood sugar low from having taught four aerobics classes since seven that morning. She grabs a bottle of orange juice from the refrigerator, swigs several gulps, and then notices the note taped to the cabinet door.

Susan:

Forgive me, please. I should never have lost my temper with you. I have some important things I need to discuss. If you could meet me in San Diego at the zoo at 5:30 (at the gorilla house) I will explain everything and be most grateful. Pack an overnight bag, I have a special surprise.

I love you,
Omar

SOUTH BEND, INDIANA
4:37 PM EST

Shane Torrence steadies the steering wheel with one hand and drains the remains of his soda with the other, hoping the caffeine and sugar rush will provide him with a much-needed late afternoon jolt. The Strategic Support Branch officer is tired, having followed Jamal al-Yussuf in his Chevy Trailblazer over nearly twelve hours and eight hundred miles of driving, the last fifty on Interstate 80. Traveling west, the turnpike skirts the northern borders of Ohio and Indiana before circling into Chicago . . . the Windy City another two hours ahead in rush-hour traffic.

Torrence has two cell phones on him, the SADM's

detonator numbers programmed into both. He also has the number memorized, just in case.

Passing signs for South Bend, he instinctively rechecks his time line backward from zero. *We detonate at 8:11 Central. That's still three and a half hours, plenty of time to catch 65-South out of Gary, even in rush-hour traffic. Unless there's an accident. If there's an accident I'm screwed. But it'd have to be a really bad one, no movement for hours. What about the wind? If the prevailing winds are blowing south, then I could catch some radiation. Still, I'd be so far out by that time, at least to Indianapolis . . . that should be far enough.*

He accelerates, closing to within six car lengths of Jamal's vehicle.

Stupid bastard, I wonder if he actually still believes it's just a dirty bomb. Leave the car, then take cover and watch the show . . . if only he knew. Explosion should take out Masoud Ali Masoud and the rest of the Bridgeview Muslims . . . a little bonus.

Godless Islamic radicals . . .

SOLDIER FIELD
CHICAGO, ILLINOIS
5:05 PM CST

Doug Dvorak maneuvers his golf cart through the throng of tailgaters, keeping an eye out for any excessively drunk fans. The Aurora Police Area Commander has been working security at Bears games for the last three years, moonlighting for Homeland Security. He has never worked a Monday night game, but he's been told the expected 61,500-capacity crowd will be far rowdier than on Sunday games.

Plus there's an added bonus: President Obama and his family will be in attendance.

Tonight will be the first time Obama has been out in public since suffering a stroke. Wheelchair bound, his words still slurred, he is nevertheless recovering far ahead of his doctor's prognosis. Above all else, he is a Bears' fan.

Doug checks his watch: 5:15, still three hours to go before kickoff and the place is already a zoo. Accelerating the golf cart past rows of campers, he heads south to check on the Waldron Drive Parking deck, the traffic outside the stadium complex bumper to bumper.

U.S. BANK TOWER
LOS ANGELES, CALIFORNIA
3: 37 PM PST

The white van driven by Marco Fatiga enters the building's underground parking lot. The SSB agent follows the ramp down to the lower level and then backs into an empty space close to the row of trash bins. Shutting off the vehicle, he unlocks the rear doors and then walks to a silver Lincoln Town Car parked several rows away. He keys in and slinks low in the driver's seat, keeping vigil on the maintenance elevator.

Traffic getting out of the city's going to make things tight. Add another two hours to San Diego . . . could be cutting it close. Where the hell is he?

Fifteen minutes pass before the elevator doors open and Omar exits, pushing a four-wheeled trash bin. He tosses several trash bags into the dumpster and then guides the cart to the back of the white van. He looks around and then opens the rear doors.

A moment later, the Iraqi drags the heavy SADM out of the vehicle. He wraps it in a triple layer of garbage bags and then places it at the bottom of the cart, covering it with several full trash bags.

Omar wheels the bin to the service elevator and presses the button.

By the time it arrives, the silver Town Car is gone.

SOLDIER FIELD
CHICAGO, ILLINOIS
6:22 PM CST

Jamal al-Yussuf's pulse races as he exits the Dan Ryan Expressway onto Lake Shore Drive. He stares in wonderment at the massive stadium looming up ahead, its bright lights creating an almost halo effect in the darkening heavens.

Tonight I will die shahid. Tonight I will go to a place in heaven near God's other messengers. And though I will perish, my body will not rot or cool. Tonight, I will be taken to paradise where seventy-two virgins wait to service my every need for all eternity.

Ignoring the blaring horn of an irate driver, Jamal recites the Koran's Aal-e-Imran sura, verse 169. "Think not of those who are slain in Allah's way as dead. Nay, they live, finding their sustenance in the presence of their Lord."

✦ ✦ ✦

Two cars over, Mitch Wagner lays on the horn again as traffic slows to a crawl.

Yvonne shoots him a look. "What are you doing?"

"What does it look like I'm doing? I'm trying to park the damn car."

"I told you we should have left the restaurant earlier."

"Hey, I didn't even want to go. Plenty of great food in the ball park, I told you that."

In the back seat, Sammy looks over at his sister, feeling lost.

Leigh squeezes his hand.

U.S. BANK TOWER
LOS ANGELES, CALIFORNIA
4:25 PM PST

The maintenance elevator stops on the fifty-third floor. Omar pushes the cart out into the lobby, the top twenty floors only accessible from a different set of elevators.

"Hey . . . you!"

Omar turns, confronted by his supervisor, Cleve Wilson. "Where you been? I've been calling you on your walkie-talkie for twenty minutes. Get down to the real estate office on thirty-six. A fire extinguisher went off and made a mess of everything."

"Yes, sir." He pushes the cart back toward the maintenance elevator.

"Whoa, leave the trash cart here. They need you now!"

Omar nods. "Let me just park it out of the way." Without waiting for a reply, he pushes it down a side corridor toward the restrooms. He keys open a maintenance closet, digs through the bin, and hoists the heavy suitcase out, stowing it in the closet.

LOS ANGELES INTERNATIONAL AIRPORT
LOS ANGELES, CALIFORNIA
4:43 PM PST

The FBI Lear Jet touches down, brakes, and then taxis rapidly to an awaiting SWAT team helicopter. Moments later the door opens and FBI Director Gary Lee Schafer bounds down the steps.

Los Angeles FBI Director J.C. Rodriguez shakes his supervisor's hand as he leads him toward the chopper. "We've sealed off a two-block area. No one gets in or out. Sir, how certain are you—"

"We've been tracking the suspects for ten months, coordinating their activities with messages intercepted from Tehran. Had to wait until we knew when and where the bombs were coming in. They arrived in a shipping container two days ago, Port of Baltimore. Missed the suspects by twenty minutes."

The two men climb aboard the chopper, slipping headphones on to communicate as the airship lifts off.

"Sir, forgive me, but you're absolutely certain about the

detonation time? Because we can force a limited evacuation—"

"Six-eleven Pacific, 9:11 Eastern, and yeah, we're sure. We intercepted a communication about two hours ago between the two suspects. Besides, you'd need twelve hours minimum to evacuate L.A. in all this traffic."

"Yes, sir . . . but what about the second bomb?"

SOLDIER FIELD
CHICAGO, ILLINOIS
7:26 PM CST

Jamal al-Yussuf inches the Chevy sports truck forward, rolling his window down to speak to the traffic cop. "Please, I wish to park in here."

"Deck parking's full. Go down to the south lot."

"But I must—"

"South lot, that way! Move it, pal, you're blocking traffic."

Twenty feet away, Doug Dvorak stares at the driver of the Trailblazer, his skin tingling with the sudden rush of adrenaline. *Geez, it's him . . . the Iraqi kid!*

Doug takes three quick steps closer, the driver pulling back into traffic, continuing south on Lake Shore drive.

"Hey you, hold it!" Doug turns to the cop. "Where's he heading?"

"South lot."

Doug sprints back to his security cart, fumbling with his radio. "Central, this is Unit-One, Code Red! Suspect is a Middle Eastern male, mid-twenties, driving a black Chevy Trailblazer. Last seen moving south on Lake Shore Drive, possible destination is the South Parking Lot. Likelihood of terrorist activity is high, repeat high!"

Dvorak accelerates the golf cart south along a pedestrian walkway, his lights flashing, horn blaring.

"Unit One, Unit Seven, I'm moving toward the South entry. Stand by."

"Central, Unit One, contact Chicago PD! Get a bomb squad over to the south lot—"

"One, this is Seven. I'm at the Lake Shore gate. No sign of a Chevy Trailblazer. He must have bypassed the lot."

"Aw . . . hell!"

U.S. BANK TOWER
LOS ANGELES, CALIFORNIA
5:48 PM PST

Alone in the elevator, Omar checks his watch, cursing to himself. He is behind schedule, having spent the last hour cleaning up the mess on the thirty-sixth floor.

The elevator stops at the roof. Omar pushes the trash cart across the massive helipad, its perimeter outlined by a large glass "crown" that sits atop the tower, its lights illuminated at night. He hurries over to a series of satellite dishes anchored along the far side of the roof. He drags the heavy suitcase out of the cart—

"Evening."

Michael Tursi steps out from behind a satellite dish, the silencer on his gun pointed at Omar. "You're late."

The gun spits out three flashes of light, punching Omar in the chest. The stunned Iraqi looks down at the spreading crimson stains on his uniform, and then the dead man's legs fold beneath him as he collapses in a heap.

The Turk spits at the corpse. "Can't trust an Arab to do anything right."

SOLDIER FIELD
CHICAGO, ILLINOIS
7:56 PM CST

"All units, we have a Code Red. We are searching the immediate vicinity for a Middle Easterner, male, in his mid-twenties, driving a black Chevy Trailblazer. All police and stadium security personnel are to sweep the street-level parking lots and side streets within a five-block radius of Soldier Field."

Doug Dvorak is in the south lot, a half-mile from the south entrance of the stadium, watching a dozen cops double-time it on foot through rows of cars. *Something's wrong, they would have found him by now. Think! Assuming it is a dirty bomb, he'd want to take out as many people as possible, which means—*

"He must have doubled back closer to the stadium!" Dvorak guns the golf cart, racing north along Museum Campus Drive.

◆ ◆ ◆

The Chevy Trailblazer is double parked by a fire hydrant next to Soldier Field, the vehicle's grillwork pointed east, facing Mecca.

Jamal al-Yussuf checks his watch: 8:04 p.m. *Seven minutes . . .* He prays aloud.

◆ ◆ ◆

"Those four, right there, kids." Mitch Wagner points to the four empty seats. "Lower bowl, thirty-five-yard line. Not bad, huh, Sammy? Bet your old man would have loved these."

"Mitch!"

Sam's eyes tear up.

"Ah, geez." Wagner squeezes the boy's shoulder. "I didn't mean it like that, kid. I just know you're gonna see your dad again real soon. Hey, look up at the big screen. It's President Obama."

The crowd cheers as Barack Obama waves from his wheelchair, his family huddled behind him in the luxury suite.

◆ ◆ ◆

Ninety-six miles to the south, Shane Torrence pulls his car off the highway into a rest stop, preparing himself for a history-changing phone call.

◆ ◆ ◆

"Get out of the car! Now!" Doug Dvorak presses the barrel of his revolver against the driver's side window, aiming it at Jamal al-Yussuf's face.

The Iraqi stares at the police commander in disbelief, his mouth twisting into a half-snarl, baring his teeth.

Dvorak shoots out the window, splattering shards of glass across the front seat. In one motion he drags the suspect out of the car and onto the asphalt, handcuffing his wrists behind his back.

"Unit One to Central, I have the suspect. Museum Campus Drive, one-hundred yards north of Waldron." Doug scans the front seat, hoists the suspect onto his feet, and shoves him toward the rear of the SUV as a crowd gathers.

"Everyone stay back!" Doug yanks open the rear hatch. Grabbing the Iraqi by the back of his neck, he slams him face-first against the side of the truck, knocking him woozy, buying himself the freedom to crawl into the back of the vehicle.

Witnesses gasp. Several aim their cell phones to record the abuse.

Doug tosses several blankets aside, revealing the lead suitcase. Reaching inside, he slides the heavy SADM out of the rear gate.

"One to Central, I need that bomb squad here, A-SAP!"

"It's a bomb!" Word spreads, the nosey crowd quickly dispersing.

Dvorak leaves the bomb by the tailgate and then jams the barrel of his gun in the Arab's face. "Is it a timer or radio controlled? When's it supposed to go off?"

Jamal's eyes catch Dvorak's watch.

"Sonuva—" Doug knees the suspect in his face, breaking his nose, incapacitating him. He turns his attention to the SADM and unlatches the casing.

"God, help me . . . !"

8:09 . . .

The roar of the crowd rises out of the stadium, the Giants

kicking off to the hometown Bears.

Doug Dvorak scans the nuclear device. He sees the cell phone—

8:10 . . .

And instinctively powers it off.

U.S. BANK TOWER
LOS ANGELES, CALIFORNIA
6:09 PM PST

Michael Tursi drags Omar Kamel Radi's lifeless body aside. He opens the SADM and powers the cell phone off. Relatching the case, he drags it back to the trash bin as the thunder of rotors echoes across the rooftop in all directions.

The Turk looks up. The dark silhouettes are coming in fast from the southwest, the setting sun making it hard for him to see. "Move!" He muscles the SADM inside the cart and pushes it as fast as he can across the helipad, the suitcase nuke's unevenly distributed weight toppling the bin onto its side, spilling trash everywhere.

"Damn it!"

He reaches for the suitcase, but something bites him in the right hamstring. He tries to drag the heavy SADM, but suddenly he's lying on his face, blood pooling beneath him as the SWAT team helicopter lands, blowing garbage-filled trash bags across the roof like plastic tumbleweeds.

Minutes pass. A heavy boot rolls him over. He looks up to see a circle of faces, Gary Lee Schafer and Marco Fatiga among them.

The SWAT team members converse with the SSB agent, but Tursi can only hear the pounding of rotor blades. One by one they back away to examine the bomb, leaving only Marco Fatiga, who takes a knee by Tursi's face.

The Turk coughs up a mouthful of blood. "Why?"

Marco speaks into the dying man's ear. "Last minute call.

One twin lives, the other dies. Figured I'd play the hero. What the hell are you doing here?"

"Schafer . . . double cross. Stole our money."

Fatiga's face turns ashen gray.

The SWAT team demolitions expert carefully opens the metal case. "Sweet mother . . . this isn't just a dirty bomb, it's a nuclear device! It's wired to a cell phone. Everyone kill your radios, we don't want to set this thing off!"

"Wait! Let me handle it!" Marco Fatiga pushes through the crowd, and then, without looking, hits the power button on the cell phone . . . turning the cell phone on!

Gary Schafer looks down at Michael Tursi, who is grinning a blood-stained smile, the fingers of his right hand searching . . . hitting the preprogrammed number on his cell phone . . .

Startled looks as the cell phone on the SADM rings just once—stopping time.

"Then the seventh angel blew his trumpet, and there were loud voices shouting in heaven . . . Lightning flashed, thunder crashed and roared; there was a great hailstorm, and the world was shaken by a mighty earthquake."

—REVELATION 11: 15, 19

CHAPTER 43

LIFE. CONCEIVED IN AN INSTANT, BIRTHED in an instant, and in an instant we die, our lives those precious moments in between.

In the first millionth of a second that is the SADM's conception, a spark from the bomb's ringing cell phone detonates its C-4 plastic explosive, unleashing a speed-of-light chain reaction that blows a small portion of enriched uranium into a larger volume of U-238 . . . birthing ten trillion calories of energy in an intense, blinding flash of light five thousand times brighter than a Palm Desert noon-day sun. Asphalt melts and paint burns off walls, metal buckling until fission's first official breath, an inhaled gasp a millisecond later that captures every molecule of air over a twenty-mile radius. Trees and telephone poles uproot, windows shatter in their frames, as downtown Los Angeles is inhaled into ground-zero's vortex, becoming a purple-gray mushroom cloud whose heart glows bright red as its core superheats into a fireball—a mass of hell so hot that it briefly reaches two hundred million degrees Fahrenheit, five times the temperature of the sun's core.

Fission's "afterbirth" is an electromagnetic pulse, the EMP created when the nuclear explosion's gamma radiation strikes air molecules and dislodges "free" electrons, producing strong electric and magnetic fields that damage every electronic system they come in contact with, including the commercial passenger jets landing and taking off only miles away at Los Angeles International Airport.

✦ ✦ ✦

"Ladies and gentlemen, this is Captain Primosch speaking from the fight deck. We are beginning our approach into Los Angeles. Clear skies, calm winds, and a temperature of seventy-two degrees. It's been our pleasure having you on board this afternoon. Thank you again for flying USAirways, and we hope to see you again real soon. We should be on the ground shortly."

High school teacher Holly Owen adjusts her seat, stealing a glance at the nervous flier next to her. The Asian man has been sweating profusely since their flight had taken off from Phoenix, but now he looks positively pale.

"Sir, are you all right?"

"Huh?"

"We're almost in L.A., just a few more minutes."

Professor Eric Mingyuan Bi looks at the petite woman, fear in his eyes. "I was foolish, I should have flown out of San Francisco, but there was a three-hour layover."

She looks at him, puzzled, and then shrugs it off, returning her attention to grading papers.

From his vantage in the cockpit, Ian Primosch and his First Officer, Robert Slack, have a clear view of the Pacific coastline. LAX is due east, its runway in sight, the city of Los Angeles nestled farther north below the San Gabriel Mountains—

FLASH!

The explosion of light ignites the sky a brilliant white, instantly blinding both pilots, who clutch their eyes, their damaged retinas completely fried. A second later the 727 is jerked sideways as if caught in hurricane-force winds. Captain Primosch gallantly fights the controls he can no longer see, somehow managing to activate the automatic pilot, never knowing the nuclear blast's electromagnetic pulse has already crippled his aircraft's electronics.

Power shuts down.

For several long seconds the commercial jet glides in a vacuum of silence, and then a chorus of screams fills the cabin as the massive plane falls nose-first from the sky like a wounded bird.

✦ ✦ ✦

Infancy. It began in the second millionth of a second as a thin shell of high-pressure gas formed before exploding into a fireball over half-a-mile in diameter. Vaporizing the U.S. Bank Tower down to a thousand-foot crater, the growing monster expands outward at 750 miles per hour, a conflagration of wind that combusts every object within a two-mile radius—save only the strongest concrete structures—into superheated dust. Farther out, cars are blasted into the air like leaves on a windy day, torched into mini-explosives as the wave of hell ripples outward at the speed of sound, overtaking the USC campus and Koreatown, Dodger Stadium and Hollywood in temperatures so hot that it burns buried coffins and the remains of their dead.

Pedestrians on the Miracle Mile, blinded by the flash, scream in agony as their hair bursts into flames and their charred skin peels away from their bones. Further down Le Brea Avenue, the ancient tar pits combust, belching thick, black smoke that turns day into night. Vehicles backed up on the Interstates are heaved one over the next like flaming dominoes.

Dexter Khan and his wife, Brenda, are sitting in traffic on Santa Monica Freeway when the couple from Trinidad and Tobago are instantly engulfed in fire, their vehicle hurled off the highway, along with ten thousand other passengers and five thousand cars—everyone cremated before their vehicles strike the scorched earth.

Seconds pass into minutes as fission enters its childhood, fueled by vast amounts of thermal energy. Entire neighborhoods ignite. Beverly Hills and Watts, UCLA and Cal State, Sherman

Oaks and West Hollywood . . . and tens of square miles in between—all engorged infernos. As these enormous volumes of superheated air rise, cool air is drawn in from the Pacific, creating a pumping action that revs up hurricane-force winds, further intensifying the firestorm. Structures collapse, adding more flammable material to the already spreading holocaust that is the Los Angeles nuclear inferno.

Back at LAX, a stunned P.J. Walther looks out from the remains of his control tower 277 feet above a tarmac that is now on fire. Bay windows he had been gazing out only seconds ago have been blasted into shrapnel, everything around him smoldering. The FAA air flight supervisor has lost most of his hearing, yet his ears still ring every few seconds as commercial jets that had been lined up on runways and by gates detonate in a cascade of powerful explosions that reverberate in the black, smoke-clogged air. Walther's skin feels heavy and hot—his state of shock numbing him to the fact that his flesh has been engulfed in third-degree burns, charred black beyond recognition. His coworkers lie dead and dying on the floor.

He will join them before the day is done.

Miles out, a safe distance from the weakening EMP, the rest of LAX's incoming aircraft have broken from formation, their pilots engaging emergency procedures, climbing their jets to higher altitudes as they race away from the ominous mushroom cloud now rising like a malevolent genie on the eastern horizon.

In Venice Beach, surfers have been blasted backward off their boards by a superheated matrix of molecules that now include the subatomic remains of hundreds of beach-goers. Surfer Theron Turman is underwater, having been tossed aside by his wave seconds before the blistering wind had struck. He surfaces now to a scene out of a *Terminator* movie, the shoreline littered with charred bodies, the promenade and surrounding infrastructure a blazing inferno, the eastern horizon billowing clouds of black smoke.

Bill Douglas and Angela Wong Douglas, cofounders of World Tai Chi and Qigong Day, had been leading their local gathering of two-hundred practitioners as part of a massive annual "global healing event" when the inferno had roared in from the east. So fast was the blast wave that it had melted flesh from bone while the husband and wife team were still "grasping the bird's tail." So hot was the inferno that it has actually transformed the sand into swaths of glass, preserving the activists' feet and ankles within the molten material—a haunting memorial to those who wished for peace.

On Santa Monica Pier, Sharon Harris-Hill had been looking out to sea when the sky had illuminated its lethal white. She had screamed in horror as the big commercial jet had plunged into the Pacific only a half-mile away. Her last thought—that terrorists have used rockets to shoot down planes, and then the mother of three had turned in horror to see a mushroom cloud rise fifty thousand feet above downtown Los Angeles, a second before a wall of hot gas, propelled by gale force winds, had blasted her sideways into the sea, collapsing the pier beneath her like kindling.

❖ ❖ ❖

Two hours south of Los Angeles, Susan Campbell waits at the San Diego Zoo's gorilla house. She has been looking for Omar for over an hour, and now her initial excitement about the getaway is turning to anger. She tries his cell phone again . . . still no answer . . . unaware that the nuclear storm clouds on the horizon contain the remains of her boyfriend.

❖ ❖ ❖

Moments have passed into minutes, the fission beast now approaching adolescence. Since its creation twelve minutes ago, more than a million people have been incinerated. Now the blast wave has dissipated and more than a million tortured souls lie in agony along death's periphery. Many are blind. All suffer a tortured existence, their flesh having been transformed into a quilt of festering blisters and bleeding sores. For these victims there will be no relief. Everything around them is a wasteland of radioactive debris. Help will not arrive, medical personnel hesitant and ill-equipped to enter the radiation zone. Badly burned, their organs laced with radioactive particles, the luckiest of these living dead will drift back and forth in a coma-induced state until death finally relieves them from their sentence.

And now the first hour passes, moving the nuclear genie into adulthood. Frightened Southern Californians who had been well beyond the blast wave venture out of their homes to gawk at the atmospheric maelstrom, only to be caught within its purple rain — radioactive particles of pulverized dust and debris that descends from the heavens— a fallout that will burn their skin and scorch their eyes as its toxins are inhaled into their lungs. For these unfortunate souls, death will come within twenty-four to seventy-two hours. For others, cancer will eat them slowly away during their dramatically shortened lives.

Ground zero is ash.

Los Angeles is a dead zone.

The fission monster has struck America. Its legacy—a radioactive lifespan that will languish for decades to come.

"The government consists of a gang of men exactly like you and me. They have, taking one with another, no special talent for the business of government; they have only a talent for getting and holding office."

—H.L. MENCKEN

"President Bush, who used specious claims about a nuclear threat to launch his disastrous war in Iraq, agreed to a deal—in blatant violation of international accords and several decades of bipartisan U.S. policy—that would enable India to double or triple its annual production of nuclear weapons."

—BOB HERBERT,
New York Times
March 11, 2006

"I would characterize current U.S. nuclear weapons policy as immoral, illegal, militarily unnecessary, and dreadfully dangerous."

—ROBERT MCNAMARA,
former Secretary of Defense,
Foreign Policy Magazine
May/June 2005

"No snowflake in an avalanche ever feels responsible."

—UNKNOWN

CHAPTER 44

Jennifer Wienner is in her office, reviewing a new series of 527 commercials when her assistant, Collin Bradley, barges in, shuts off the DVD, and turns on CNN.

"The nuclear device exploded at 6:14 Pacific, just eight minutes ago, wiping out most of downtown Los Angeles."

Jennifer goes numb. "No . . ."

"No word yet from acting President Biden, but CNN correspondent Teri Smith is standing by at the White House. Teri, is the President aware of the explosion?"

The red-haired reporter looks as if she's been crying. "Katherine, we've received word that the President has been informed of the attack, that he and his family are being moved to a secure facility, and that he will be addressing the nation as soon as he learns more."

"Any indication whether this was Al-Qaeda?"

"The only thing we're being told is that this was a terrorist strike, most likely involving foreign nationals, and that—"

"Teri, stand by . . . we're getting a report out of Chicago that a second terrorist strike may have just been foiled. Bill West is in Chicago . . . Bill?"

The correspondent is an island of calm amid chaos as tens of thousands of football fans stream out of Solder Field. "Katherine, this story is still unfolding, but here's what we know so far. At approximately 5:30 this evening local time, a Homeland Security officer recognized a suspect wanted for questioning by the FBI. The suspect is a Middle Eastern man in his mid-twenties. The officer chased down the man's vehicle, apprehended the suspect, and deactivated some kind of explosive. We are not being told whether the device was a nuclear device, only that it was safely deactivated. As a precaution, the Monday Night Football game between the Bears and the Giants has been postponed, but the crowd began dispersing almost immediately as word of the Los Angeles attack hit the Internet."

"Bill, I want you to stand by. Joining us via satellite from his home in San Diego is CNN terrorism analyst Dr. John Rogers. Dr. Rogers, you're two hours south of Los Angeles. Were you able to see the explosion?"

"No, I was inside my office at the time, but a few of my neighbors saw the mushroom cloud. Right now, if you look behind me, the northern horizon is covered in black smoke from fires that are burning out of control. With the prevailing winds moving out of the northeast, we'll be evacuating, heading as far east as possible to escape any nuclear fallout."

"Doctor, we've just learned that Chicago averted what looks like a similar attack. Are our cities under siege?"

"I hadn't heard about Chicago, but wow . . . if that's true . . . then yes, it's possible." The analyst suddenly looks pale, unnerved.

"Sir, over the last month the Internet has been rife with blogs and anonymous reports predicting this attack, pointing the blame squarely at the Neoconservative movement and its influence in the Middle East."

"Katherine, I think it's a mistake to assign blame before we know the facts. At this juncture, our first responsibility is to make sure our cities are secure, that our ports are being checked—"

"With all due respect, shouldn't that have been done back in 2001?"

"Yes, absolutely. Experts have been preaching this for years, but Congress repeatedly failed to address the situation or adequately fund port security, preferring to focus their attention on the war in Iraq. Tonight, it seems, we paid dearly for that shortsightedness."

"Last question, Dr. Rogers, and I know you have to leave . . . any idea how large a nuclear device this was, and how many people may have perished in the blast?"

"Until we can inspect the devastation, there's no telling how large this bomb was, but as a basis of comparison, the device that was dropped on Hiroshima was a fifteen-kiloton bomb, the one that followed on Nagasaki twenty kilotons. Twenty kilotons would be the equivalent of twenty thousand tons of TNT. Compare that to our modern-day hydrogen bombs, which yield fifty million tons of TNT, and you realize the potential danger of nuclear war. Based on the damage we've seen, I'd put the Los Angeles blast within the Hiroshima range. Keep in mind, those were air blasts, the bombs dropped from a plane. This was clearly a surface blast, the effects and concentration of radiation totally different. As for the number of dead . . . untold millions."

BLUEMONT, VIRGINIA

The helicopter transport carrying acting President Biden, Homeland Security Director Howard Lowe, and Joseph Kendle, the administration's hawkish Secretary of Defense, soars west over the town of Bluemont and Virginia Route 601. In the distance, landing lights illuminate, guiding the chopper toward the fenced-in compound.

This is Mount Weather, a top-secret military base located forty-six miles outside Washington D.C. Managed by Homeland Security, the eighty-five-acre compound contains a subterranean city equipped with private apartments and dormitories, cafeterias and hospitals, a water purification and sewage plant, a power plant, a mass transit system, a television communication system, and even an underground pond. While no member of Congress has ever publicly claimed knowledge of the facility, many senior House Representatives are, in fact, tenured members of this subterranean capital's "government-in-waiting." Nine federal departments have been replicated within the facility, as well as five federal agencies. Secretly appointed Cabinet-level officials serve indefinite terms, without the consent of Congress and far from the public eye, their purpose—to govern the United States in the event of an all-out nuclear assault.

The helicopter touches down. Biden's party is escorted through a security building and then loaded aboard an elevator that descends into the bowels of the facility.

Biden's eyes are rimmed red with emotion. He knows his family is safe, housed in another part of the subterranean city, and the Obamas are on the way, along with the rest of his cabinet. Although he has not had time to dissect the situation, he also knows the world has changed on his watch, and his response to the crisis will have rippling effects.

He barely nods to the MPs as he steps off the elevator, allowing Director Lowe to lead him to Mount Weather's equivalent of the West Wing and its Oval Office.

Joseph Kendle closes the door behind them.

The acting President snaps, "I want to know who perpetrated this mess—was it Al-Qaeda? A domestic terrorist? Or was it some false flag event, concocted by those Neocon Nazis, like the Internet's been forecasting?"

Kendle and Lowe exchange looks. "Sir, preliminary reports indicate there were two terrorists, both trained, financed, and armed by Iranian Qod forces. Our experts are examining the particle residue from the Los Angeles detonation, along with the enriched uranium in the captured bomb. If the uranium traces back to Iran's nuclear reactor, then it was a terrorist attack, sponsored by Tehran."

"And if that's the case . . . then what?"

"Then you go public. You connect the dots . . . and we

demilitarize Iran, once and for all. We change the world, sir."

"Change the world? Like Bush and Cheney changed the world? Have we learned nothing from 9/11?"

The General snaps, "With all due respect, sir, preliminary estimates from Los Angeles say as many as two million people may be dead. Add to that another million who were exposed to the fallout, plus the radiation and destruction of one of our major cities."

Lowe jumps in. "Sir, we're dealing with militant Islamic regimes that control significant world oil reserves, who are defiantly supplying terrorists with suitcase nukes. We need to act decisively now, before any more bombs go off in London or Tel Aviv, or a dozen more American cities, collapsing our economy."

"Director Lowe's right, sir. You can bet Clinton and Prescott will be demanding a military response, as well as the American people. We either control the variables on our watch, or be held accountable on theirs."

The President looks around the windowless room. "I hate this place. At least let me address the nation from the real Oval Office."

Lowe shakes his head. "We're under attack, we follow protocol. The last thing we need is another *My Pet Goat* incident. The American public needs to see a man in charge of his faculties and his nation. A President who follows proper procedures is a man in charge. They need to see your strength."

Biden nods. "Okay . . . I'm doing better." He looks at Kendle. "Brief me on Operation Freedom Reigns."

"Yes, sir."

SAUDI ARABIA

On hands and knees, Ace crawls across the desert, delirious with fever, close to death. The sand burns his swollen feet and blisters his fingers raw. The merciless sun scorches the flesh on his exposed back, his left forearm sizzling as if doused in acid.

He finally collapses and rolls over on his back, the pain unbearable.

"Futrell . . . "

No . . . just leave me to die already.

"Futrell!"

✦ ✦ ✦

Ace opens his eyes. He is back in his cell. His right hand is heavily bandaged, throbbing in pain, the nails of his middle three fingers having being torturously torn off with pliers.

"Futrell? I know you're still alive, I heard you moaning."

The man's voice is coming from behind the concrete wall.

"Go to hell."

"We're in hell." Scott Santa is lying on a mattress in the next cell. Both of his hands are bandaged, the empty socket where his left eye had been now plugged with bloodied gauze. "I didn't murder her, Futrell."

"I was there, I saw you." Ace examines his left forearm. The probe is still there, concealed beneath his skin. Gritting his teeth, he gingerly begins pushing it back out through the wound.

"Listen to me . . . she paid me to do it! It was part of her plan . . . a set-up . . . to get you to carry the ball over the goal line. Her words."

Ace freezes, his pulse jump-starting. "You're lying . . . she wouldn't do that!"

"She was dying, Futrell. The cancer had spread to her brain. She only had days—maybe a week. She wanted her death to have meaning. She wanted it to motivate you . . . to provoke you into finishing what she had started."

"No!" Ace tears the skewer free from his flesh and rolls painfully onto his knees, shouting at the wall. "She wouldn't use me like that! I don't believe you!"

Scott Santa closes his remaining eye, feeling dizzy. "Think it through. She knew how to get to them, how to defeat them.

She arranged everything. Promis. Ramzi. Her own death. She even pulled strings years ago to move you up the chain of command at PetroConsultants."

"What . . .?"

"You didn't know this? Ha!" Santa breaks into a fit of coughing as Ace slumps down to his knees. He strikes the back of his head against the concrete wall, recalling how he had "miraculously" landed the promotion at PetroConsultants, how it was Kelli's idea to apply, that he never wanted to travel that much in the first place but she had insisted, the opportunity too good to pass up.

Random thoughts rush through his mind. "Her cousin . . . Jennifer . . . was she involved?"

Santa moans. "Butch and Sundance. They planned everything."

Tears of anger roll down his cheeks.

"Women, huh? Cunning as cats, and just as vicious. Got to hand it to them . . . they got you to play along, and you did. Because of you, the House of Saud's collapsing, but in the end, everything will still play into the Neocon's agenda. Iran will be carpet bombed with chemical weapons, wiping out the extremists' hives while leaving the oil, and the Saudi fields will be ours for the taking."

Ace is too weak, too drained emotionally to answer.

"You and me . . . we're worse than dead. They'll keep us alive, torturing us like this for weeks. The fat one . . . he's good at his work. And the girl . . ." Santa's voice trails off.

"What about the girl?"

The CIA agent mumbles something before he slips back into a pain-induced unconsciousness.

Ace stares at the steel pick for several long moments. Finally he wipes the blood off the instrument and sets to work on the cell door lock.

"The political mind is the product of men in public life who have been twice spoiled. They have been spoiled with praise and they have been spoiled with abuse. With them, nothing is natural, everything is artificial."

—PRESIDENT CALVIN COOLIDGE

"To those who scare peace-loving people with phantoms of lost liberty, my message is this: Your tactics only aid terrorists."

—ATTORNEY GENERAL JOHN ASHCROFT

"Only a respect for the law makes it possible for free men to dwell together in peace and progress . . . Law is the adhesive force in the cement of society, creating order out of chaos and coherence in place of anarchy."

—PRESIDENT JOHN F. KENNEDY

CHAPTER 45

PRESIDENTIAL ADDRESS
OVAL OFFICE, MOUNT WEATHER
OCTOBER 8, 2012
11:17 PM EST

"AND IF WE'VE LEARNED ONE THING since September 11, 2001, it is that terrorists know how to use America's freedoms as weapons against us. Tonight our enemies targeted the populations of two major cities. Thanks to our intelligence community and the heroics of an alert member of the Illinois police department, one of those attacks was averted.

"It wasn't nearly enough. We should have done more to prevent this catastrophe. When it comes to fighting our enemies, there can be no mercy. I promise you, we will find out who was behind today's acts of evil and those perpetrators shall be punished. Until then, our priority must be the security of our nation. As such, I have raised the terror alert to Code Red. Until further notice, all U.S. borders and ports will remain closed, all containers opened and checked. All flights have been grounded. A state of martial law is now in effect, which includes a 10:00 p.m. nationwide curfew. The military will be establishing roadblocks on major U.S. highways, all vehicles subject to search and seizure. Finally, as per National Security Presidential Directive 51 and Homeland Security Presidential Directive 20, I am canceling the scheduled November 8 national elections until an acceptable level of security can be reestablished. As patriotic

Americans, I know Secretary Clinton, Governor Prescott, and Senator Mulligan will accept and support these measures so that we may move forward, as one nation, in the days and weeks ahead, to ensure the safety and welfare of all Americans. Thank you, and God bless the United States of America."

WEST PALM BEACH, FLORIDA

Jennifer Wienner tosses her desk clock at the television, shattering the plasma screen and sending her assistant ducking for cover. "Damn Neocons!"

"Take it easy, boss." Collin Bradley picks particles of glass out of his hair.

"Those Neocon bastards manipulated every angle. They set the whole thing up."

"You got the word out. The media won't let them off the hook."

She turns to him, venom in her eyes. "You don't get it, do you? It doesn't matter who's in office anymore. By triggering the nuke before the next election, they forced the United States to settle the Iranian issue, once and for all. Biden won't back down, and neither will Clinton. And Prescott is just another Neocon stooge."

"Okay, so we organize Mulligan and the Dems . . . we march on Washington."

"Those things only work in an open society, Collin. The Executive Orders Biden just rattled off, they're emergency powers, established by Bush, that allows the President to essentially bypass the Constitution and do anything he wants. You think post 9/11 was bad, that was nothing. This time dissenters won't be booed at their podiums, they'll be arrested and moved to secret detainment camps. By week's end the White House will present its gift-wrapped package of lies to the American people, and long before those fires in California are ever put out, we'll have chemical bombed Iran and declared war on a billion Muslims."

She shakes her head in disbelief. "We're witnessing history, Collin, the end of Democracy . . . the birth of the United Corporation of America."

FBI–Chicago
Chicago, Illinois
October 9, 2012

The bullet-proof limousine parts the crowd, its police escort leading the vehicle down a ramp to the underground garage.

FBI Director Adrian Neary greets Homeland Security Director Howard Lowe with a warm handshake. "Howard, I'm glad you're here. As you can see, word got out that we're housing the suspect and it's all we can do to control the crowd."

"We'll move him to a more secure facility as soon as we can. This is Special Agent Shane Torrence. Agent Torrence is on loan to us from the SSB. He had been tracking the two suspects' whereabouts, coordinating with Director Schafer."

Neary shakes Torrence's hand. "I was real sorry to hear about Gary."

Torrence nods. "Sometimes life comes down to a matter of inches. The last report we had was that LA SWAT had shot the suspect on the roof, that they had taken him down. Gary had coordinated the arrest, he wanted to be there in person."

Lowe squeezes Torrence's arm. "He died a hero. Let's make sure it wasn't in vain."

Neary leads the two men inside. "The arresting officer's waiting upstairs in my office. The suspect's in a holding cell. We can move him to an interrogation room—"

"Not necessary," says Lowe. "Agent Torrence will see the prisoner while I speak with Commander Dvorak."

✦ ✦ ✦

Doug Dvorak is waiting in Director Neary's office, wearing his dress uniform. He has not slept in more than thirty-six hours, and the adrenaline rush of the last twelve has been replaced by waves of fear—what might have been—as he stares at the gruesome scenes on TV.

Satellite reconnaissance using thermal sensors cuts through the heavy smoke to reveal ghostly shots of ground zero. A massive crater is visible, its heat signature still radioactive-hot and glowing. Three square miles surrounding the crater have been pulverized to dust, the remains of steel girders and concrete skeletons all that is left standing in this petrified urban forest. Helicopters dropping pond-size caches of water are focusing on the still-sizzling Le Brea tar pits, while forestry planes drench the periphery thirty miles out, attempting to stop the spread of fires.

Perhaps the most frightening images come from the MASH units that have been set up in gray zones—intermediate areas between the blast site and the surviving population. Medical personnel sealed within self-contained radiation suits are treating thousands of shocked and dying men, women, and children, their numbers so overwhelming that they are being lined up in rows along scorched lawns and fed IV drips of morphine and Sodium Pentothal—an anesthetic that also minimizes the effects of radiation. When a CNN camera focuses on a burnt child, Doug turns off the television, unable to handle any more.

What kind of world do we live in . . . what kind of maniacs—

"Commander Dvorak?" Director Neary enters the office with his guest. "This is Howard Lowe, Director of Homeland Security."

"A pleasure, commander. Please sit." He nods to Neary, who leaves the office. "What you did . . . your country owes you a great debt. We'd like you to join us in Washington where the President will be awarding you the medal of honor."

Doug breaks into tears.

"I know. . . it's hard to think about such things when we're dealing with so much death, but your presence would help us heal."

Doug nods.

"I need to ask you a few important questions . . . about Jamal al-Yussuf."

❖ ❖ ❖

Heavily armed FBI agents stand guard at a security desk checkpoint. Shane Torrence's weapon is confiscated, his body scanned using a metal detector wand. A closed circuit TV monitor reveals the interior of a holding cell, a man lying face down on a cot.

An FBI agent leads Torrence down a short corridor to the cell door. "The drugs we shot him up with initially made him talkative. Told us about his training in Iran, started to mention something about working with a sleeper cell in Baltimore, and then he clammed up. We were ready to administer more drugs when Washington put a stop to everything."

Torrence nods. "We find it more effective to use the same questioners in an interrogation. The suspect actually forms a bond."

"Understood." The FBI agent leaves. Torrence pulls up a chair. "Jamal, rise and shine."

Jamal sits up. He is dressed in an orange prisoner's jumpsuit. No shoes or socks. No belt. The cot is anchored to the floor. The sink lacks a mirror.

"Seventy-two virgins awaited you in paradise, Jamal. You had it all. You were so close to paradise, but you failed."

❖ ❖ ❖

"And you're certain the suspect said nothing?"

Dvorak rubs at his eyes, trying to remember. "My focus was on the bomb. By the time I deactivated it, Chicago PD had arrived. We secured the suspect and sealed off the area. There was no time to question him."

Director Lowe smiles . . . relieved. "You did well. Go home and get some rest. I'll have Director Neary make arrangements to fly you into Washington on a private jet."

◆ ◆ ◆

Jamal moves to the bars, standing only inches away from Torrence. "How can I still die *shahid*? Tell me!"

"You die *shahid* by preventing the Americans from questioning you, from turning your words into lies."

"I want to die. Will you help me?"

Torrence stands, using his body to shield his actions from the closed circuit TV camera. He tears at the lining of his suit, his fingers extracting an empty hypodermic needle. He passes it through the bars. "Wait several hours, and then fill the needle with air and shoot it into your vein. Do it several times, and then shove the needle deep inside your mattress without the camera seeing you.

"When you open your eyes, you'll be in paradise."

OVAL OFFICE, WHITE HOUSE
WASHINGTON, D.C.

King Sultan bin Abdel Aziz and his son, Prince Bandar, sit uncomfortably on one sofa, facing President Biden's new Secretary of State, Richard Diefendorf. The former Arizona prosecutor and United Standard Oil executive flashes a false smile at his guests. "Your Highness, what has always separated the Saudi Kingdom from the rest of the Arab nations has been your ability to remain flexible during times of strife. It's been this flexibility that has allowed our two nations to serve each other so well as business partners over the last seventy-plus years—"

Sultan cuts him off with a wave of his hand. "The House of Saud has been robbed of nearly a trillion dollars. Rebels control our largest refinery, further paralyzing our economy. Revolution is being whispered on our streets. What kind of business partner allows these things to take place? I am here at your President's request, but my patience is worn thin. If the United States will not remedy this situation, the Chinese will."

Diefendorf continues. "Your Highness, the United States is not responsible for the illegal transfer of assets that have affected your nation as well as ours. Seven of our top fifteen defense contractors have been victimized, along with a dozen of our largest financial institutions and countless private businesses. Every intelligence agency is working on the problem, as well as our banks. What we are proposing will bring financial aid to your country while allowing the Saudi monarchy to remain in power for generations to come, without fear of a hostile Islamic invasion."

"Go on."

"The United States will retaliate for the Columbus Day attack by bombing Iran's military installations, terrorist training camps, and nuclear sites. We will also target and kill the Ashraf rebels currently controlling your refineries. The nature of these strikes will not harm the infrastructure. Saudi Aramco will then take over Iran's oil fields, reselling the oil to the United States at $35 a barrel."

Prince Bandar's eyes widen.

"In exchange for a $100 billion loan, 70 percent of which must be directed to the Saudi economy, the House of Saud will guarantee 80 percent of its current natural gas and oil reserves to the United States. The term of that loan and contract will extend twenty years, with negotiated ceilings placed on pricing."

Diefendorf sits back and waits, the offer on the table.

Sultan shakes his head, his cherub cheeks twitching with emotion. "You steal our money, you steal our oil, and in exchange you offer us a twenty-year lease on our kingdom?"

The Secretary of State runs a manicured hand over the knot that highlights his cleanly shaven scalp. "With all due respect, Your Highness, we have not taken your money. We have purchased your oil and made you billionaires. We have sold you

STEVE ALTEN

advanced weaponry, allowing your royal agents to pocket billions more in illegal commissions. Furthermore, we have stood idly by while your monarchy has suppressed even the most basic of human rights from your own population, while your treasury funds radical Islamic groups that attack our people. What we offer you now is not a twenty-year lease, but a final solution that will remove Iran from the Middle East equation—the last challenge to your sovereign rule."

Prince Bandar speaks to King Sultan in Arabic. "This is an insult. Let the Chinese court us, the offer will change."

Diefendorf leans forward, his expression all business as he responds in Arabic. "The offer will change, Your Excellency, but not how you think. The moment you meet with the Chinese, our intelligence services will release evidence that implicates the House of Saud in supplying the uranium fuel rods used in the bomb that destroyed Los Angeles. We'll recognize Ashraf's leaders as the founders of a new Saudi democracy while you and your family are criminally charged with conspiring in the deaths of millions."

Diefendorf sits back, enjoying the look of shock on the two Arabs' faces. "Decades more of decadence, or a public execution? Think it over, Your Highness. But the President addresses the world in six hours, and I will have your decision before you leave this room."

INAKESH PRISON

Sweat pours from Ace's face as he continues probing the cell door's keyhole with the steel skewer, unsure what he is doing, the dead bolt refusing to budge. After twenty minutes he stops, his right hand throbbing from the effort.

Don't give up . . . if you can't pick the lock, then find another way out.

He reexamines the heavy metal door, focusing on its three hinges.

Maybe . . .

He looks around his cell, searching for something he can use to strike the steel probe like a hammer. But there is nothing, not a rock or loose chunk of mortar, just the defecation hole and the sink.

He walks to the sink and then unceremoniously jumps in the air and lands on its rim with his buttocks, his weight tearing the porcelain bowl nearly free from the wall. Cold water sprays from a lone iron pipe, all that is keeping the dangling sink from crashing to the floor. Grabbing hold of the pipe with both arms, he tugs. Meeting resistance, he lays down beneath the sink on his back and presses his bare feet against the porcelain bowl, popping the sink free.

The basin now rests on his belly, water trickling out the severed pipe. Leaving the sink on the floor, he returns to the door and peers out the barred window.

Looks. Listens. All clear.

He returns to the sink, raises it above his head, and drops it on the cement floor.

The bowl shatters into a dozen pieces.

He selects a baseball-sized chunk with a flat edge, checks the corridor again, and sets to work on the middle hinge, placing the steel pick along the open bottom of the pin, tapping it from below with the chunk of porcelain.

Rusty with age, the hinge refuses to yield, and then slowly, gradually, the pin's head separates from the top of the hinge. A dozen more strikes and it pops free!

Ace's heart races with adrenaline as he moves to the lower hinge. He strikes it again and again, the pin rising from the hinge—

"Futrell!"

The Russian-American's voice startles him.

"What are you doing?"

"Carving my initials for posterity. Keep your voice down." Ace continues striking the lower pin until it too pops free. He sets to work on the remaining upper hinge, all that separates him from escaping his cell.

"Futrell, take me with you!"

Ace ignores him. He taps at the pin, inching the head loose.

"You'll need my help! I can get us to safety."

Ace frees the top pin. The heavy door wobbles, now held within its frame only by the dead bolt. Pressing against the loose side, he pushes the door open, catching it before it collapses into the corridor.

Scott Santa watches from the barred window of his own cell door. "Outstanding. Now free me."

Ace carries the door back into his cell. He checks the corridor again before approaching Santa's cell. "I have no key, and even if I did, why should I help you?"

"You're not free yet. Two have a better chance than one. And I can get us to Ramzi."

Footsteps! Someone descending the stairs at the end of the corridor!

Ace hurries back to his cell. He stands the door within its frame, the fingers of his left hand holding the cut-out window's bars to maintain its balance, his right hand gripping the chunk of porcelain like a weapon as he crouches, ready to spring.

The footsteps grow nearer. The guard pauses at his door. He presses the brass key into the lock—

Now!

Ace pile-drives the door into the guard and clear across the corridor, registering a heavy *thud* with the contact. Flipping the door over, he rears back to pound the Arab with the chunk of porcelain–

"Nahir?" She is dressed in her black burka and matching head scarf, her broken nose gushing blood from the blow.

Ace sits her up. "Nahir, are you all right?"

"You don't have time for this," Santa whispers urgently. "Grab her key and free me!"

"Shut up!"

Nahir's eyes open, the woman still woozy. "Ashley?"

"Nahir, we're getting out of here."

The hazel eyes refocus. "How did you escape?"

"I'll explain later. Where are the guards? Are they posted upstairs?"

Nahir regains her feet, backing slowly away from Ace.

"Futrell, don't trust her. Can't you see she's with them?" Santa's face is pressed to the bars.

Ace stares at Nahir's hazel eyes, suddenly predatory . . . nervous. "Nahir?"

She matches his gaze and then turns and runs.

"Stop her!"

Without thinking, Ace winds up and throws the hunk of porcelain—a fastball that smashes dead-center into the back of Nahir's scarfed head. She goes down as if shot.

"Well done. Now get the key."

Ace lifts the fallen door. Finds the key and frees Santa. "How did you know?"

"It's an old trick. Using females to gain a prisoner's confidence."

Ace kneels by Nahir and verifies she's breathing. "She's coming with us."

"You're insane. We'll be lucky just to make it to the courtyard."

"I said she's coming."

"Fine, play your game of Sir Galahad if you wish, but if she comes to, be prepared to silence her . . . or I will."

Lifting the girl over his shoulder, Ace carries her to the end of the corridor. Santa signals for him to wait while he climbs the steps to take a look.

The Russian returns a moment later. "Luck may be on our side. It's dark out—must be late. There's only one guard posted at the gate, which has been left open. Another guard is making his rounds. He's two buildings over. That gives us three to five minutes tops. There are several vans parked about fifty paces from this building, but they're out in the open, with no way to reach them other than crossing the courtyard. Any ideas?"

✦ ✦ ✦

Ace stands by the prison block's entrance facing the courtyard. He is dressed in Nahir's burka and black scarf, the woman's loose-fitting garment a foot too short and skintight across his broad shoulders, chest, and arms. He waits until the guard enters the next building over before emerging from the shadows. Hands tucked deep in the burka's pockets, head bowed, he walks toward the van, trying to stoop as he moves, hoping to conceal his bare feet and exposed calf muscles.

He is halfway to the nearest vehicle when a large man in a nightshirt exits from his quarters on the opposite side of the compound.

Ali Shams lights a cigarette.

Ace continues walking, trying to look small and inconspicuous.

The torturer sees him and calls out in Arabic, "Nahir, come here, I need you to walk on my back!"

Twenty yards . . . Ace pretends he cannot hear the sadist.

"Nahir, you little bitch! Do not ignore me!" Ali Shams staggers toward the two vans. "Nahir!"

Ace picks up his pace. He reaches the nearest van and opens the driver's side door—

"You pigeon-brain whore! What are you doing?"

Ace checks the ignition . . . no keys. He checks the sun visor, the seat, the floor . . . nothing.

"Do you wish to be beaten?" Ali Shams is ten paces from the van's passenger side door when he realizes something is not right. "What is this?"

Ace flips open the ashtray . . . and grabs the keys! He climbs in and starts the van.

"Hey . . . *hey!*"

Shifting into drive, Ace presses his bare foot to the gas pedal, the van's rear tires kicking up dirt as he executes a tight U-turn and races back toward the prison block. He slows down as Scott Santa jumps out from the shadows, dragging Nahir's semi-naked body with him. The Russian tosses the girl through the open cargo door and then leaps inside as Ace accelerates back across the compound, the prison yard suddenly flooded with light.

Ali Shams runs toward the prison entrance. He yells at the guard to close the main gate. The van's headlights switch on, the left beam illuminating the fat Arab's nightshirt as he runs. Ace swerves after him, jamming the pedal to the floor as he bears down on his torturer.

Ali Shams turns around just as the van's grill plows into him doing fifty miles an hour, the front bumper rupturing his internal organs and crushing his rib cage before impaling him as a hood ornament. The guard, who has a dead-on shot with his AK-47 assault rifle, freezes.

The van veers toward the startled guard and then swerves out the open prison gate, bashing through the perimeter chain link fencing.

Ali Sham's mouth vomits a stream of blood and vomit across the windshield before the corpse slides off the hood, only to be dragged twenty feet more before being released . . . and run over by the van's left front tire.

Ace grapples with the wheel as the vehicle crushes the sadist's skull, popping the front left shock in the process. Steering free of the dead Arab's body, Ace accelerates down an asphalt road to the main highway, heading east.

"A democracy cannot exist as a permanent form of government. It can only exist until the voters discover that they can vote themselves largesse from the public treasury. From that moment on, the majority always votes for the candidates promising the most benefits from the public treasury with the result that a democracy always collapses over loose fiscal policy, always followed by a dictatorship. The average age of the world's greatest civilizations has been 200 years. These nations have progressed through this sequence: "From bondage to spiritual faith; From spiritual faith to great courage; From courage to liberty; From liberty to abundance; From abundance to selfishness; From selfishness to apathy; From apathy to dependence; From dependence back into bondage."

—ALEXANDER FRASER TYTLER,
from *The Decline and Fall of the Athenian Republic*,
published in 1776

"Let us not seek the Republican answer or the Democratic answer, but the right answer. Let us not seek to fix the blame for the past. Let us accept our own responsibility for the future."

—PRESIDENT JOHN F. KENNEDY

"All dreaded it, all sought to avert it . . . and the war came."

—ABRAHAM LINCOLN

CHAPTER 46

"MR. SPEAKER, MEMBERS OF CONGRESS, my fellow Americans: On September 11, 2001, the enemies of freedom committed an act of evil against our country and everything we stand for. Thus began the war on terror, a war that has cost us the lives of thousands of American men and women and almost a trillion dollars—a war we cannot afford to lose. And now all of us know why. Four days ago, on a day set aside to honor the courageous explorer who discovered our great nation, our enemy struck again. Four days later, as the world sits in shock, I come to you tonight with answers.

"The two men involved in the Columbus Day atrocity were radical Islamic jihadists who were recruited out of Iraq and trained for their deadly suicide mission by members of Iran's Qod forces. Jamal al-Yussuf arrived in the United States sometime in early February of 2011, Omar Kamel Radi followed a few months later. The two met up in late September of 2011 in Aurora, Illinois, where they were instructed and financed by Iranian sleeper cells. These well-connected cells enabled Jamal al-Yussuf to obtain a security job at the Port of Baltimore, while Omar Kamel Radi moved to California to work maintenance at the U.S. Bank Tower in Los Angeles—ground zero.

"Let me repeat: The two men involved in the Columbus Day massacre were recruited and trained by Iran's Islamic Revolutionary Guard, known as the Qods Force. Iraqis were specifically chosen over Iranian nationals because they come from a land now liberated from oppression, allowing them to enter the United States without causing suspicion. At the Qod terrorist training camps, these men were brainwashed by their Iranian trainers into believing the death of millions of innocent Americans would serve their people. While they trained, the Iranian government that supported their mission commissioned two nuclear devices to be built using enriched uranium-238 taken from spent nuclear fuel rods.

"We have in our possession the unexploded device that was captured in Chicago as well as radioactive debris from the bomb that destroyed Los Angeles. In both cases, the enriched uranium used in these nuclear suitcase bombs matches uranium taken from Iran's nuclear reactor. We now know these suitcase bombs, or SADMs, arrived in the Port of Baltimore on October 5. We have found the container they arrived in and the bomb's radioactive residue. We have traced the overseas shipping container to a port in Iran. There is no doubt who was behind the attacks. Any prosecutor who even glances at the evidence would tell you that this is an open and shut case. And we have all seen news footage of the Iranian people rejoicing in the streets of Tehran as downtown Los Angeles burned.

"Over the last seven years, Iran's President Mahmoud Ahmadinejad and the Supreme Leader that supported his tainted reelection in 2009 have openly and blatantly defied the world's will by developing nuclear weapons. Moreover, Iran's leaders have threatened to use them against Israel, America, England, and our allies in the Middle East and in Europe. And now the minions of their evil have struck.

"To the majority of peace-loving Arabs and Muslims sharing our world, I wish to convey that we respect your faith, that many of our own law-abiding citizens follow the teachings of Islam. But hatred holds no place in Islam any more than it does in Christianity and Judaism, Buddhism, or any of the other practiced religions. Hatred rarely begins as a boiling pot. It is instead a simmer that heats up when communities fail to stand together against oppression. Radicals have hijacked the teachings of Mohammed. What we ask of moderate Islam today is to condemn the radical elements of your culture that led to the heinous events of October 8, to direct your intolerance not to the freedoms that come with an open society but to those who force you to live in fear.

"Tonight we are honored to have with us Commander Douglas Dvorak of the Aurora Police Department. Commander Dvorak and the Homeland Security agents operating out of Chicago saved millions of lives when they caught Jamal al-Yussuf only minutes before he could detonate his nuclear device. Commander, we are honored to have you with us."

The cameras turn to an embarrassed Doug Dvorak, who waves from his seat beside the First Lady and his young son, Simon, as he receives a sixty-second standing ovation.

"To all Americans, I ask you to continue to support the victims of this tragedy with your contributions and your prayers. I ask for your patience in dealing with the restrictions that remain in effect. While martial law will eventually come to an end, there will still be delays and inconveniences that will accompany tighter security.

"Our economy was rebounding well before October 8, and it will be strong again. To that effect, we are honored to have with us King Sultan bin Abdel Aziz of Saudi Arabia and his son, Prince Bandar. The King has agreed to jump-start the United States' economic recovery by selling America oil at a substantially reduced rate—at least until we can overcome the setbacks of the Columbus Day attack. Thank you, King Sultan. You are a true ally and friend."

The King offers a half wave to the applauding crowd.

"Finally, to the nation that plotted and executed the murder of two million of our people, I issue this decree: Citizens of Iran, your self-appointed leaders and mullahs have led you astray, your acquiescence to their iron rule has empowered them to take you down a dark path—a path that will lead to your own destruction. Rise up now against your oppressors or suffer the consequences of their actions."

The chamber rocks with applause.

"What was discussed in the Energy Task Force meetings under Dick Cheney in 2001? Why is the documentation of these meetings still being suppressed? Is Peak Oil a motive for 9/11 as an inside job?"

—911TRUTH.ORG

"A previously undisclosed meeting last year of President Bush's most senior national security advisors was the highest-level discussion about how to rewrite the Cold War rules. . . . Among the subjects of the meeting was whether to issue a warning to all countries around the world that if a nuclear weapon was detonated on American soil and traced back to any nation's stockpiles through nuclear forensics, the U.S. would hold that country 'fully responsible' for the consequences of the explosion."

—DAVID E. SANGER & THOM SHANKER,
The New York Times,
May 8, 2007

"Now we have a problem in making our power credible, and Vietnam is the place."

—PRESIDENT JOHN F. KENNEDY

CHAPTER 47

Majority of Americans Favor Nuclear Strike

Associated Press October 13, 2012

A recent poll found an overwhelming majority of Americans favor a nuclear strike on Iran in response to the terrorist attack on Los Angeles.

"Iran trained these people, Iran sent the bombs, and as far as I'm concerned, Iran deserves to be nuked," said Lynn McDonald, a teacher in Houston, Texas. "I know there are innocent people in Iran . . . families, but you can't just sit idly by and allow your government to support these kinds of atrocities."

Iran Will Launch Nuclear Missiles If Attacked

New York Times, October 14, 2012

TEHRAN—Following acting President Biden's speech on Capitol Hill, Iranian President Mahmoud Ahmadinejad responded by threatening to launch nuclear missiles at Israel and Saudi Arabia if attacked. "The great nation of Islam was not responsible for the devastation in Los Angeles. If the United States thinks they can create new lies to justify another invasion as they did in Iraq, then they are making a grievous error. At the first sign of an attack, we shall launch nuclear-tipped Shahab missiles at the Zionist cities as well as the American Green Zone in Baghdad.

Israel's Prime Minister has responded to the Iranian threat by stating that Israeli Defense Forces were updated two years ago with the Arrow 3 theatre ballistic missile defense system, and that the first Iranian nuclear missile fired, whether successful or not, would lead to a "significant response."

Code-named Homa or Fence, Arrow 3 is deployed in two batteries, one near Tel Aviv and one to the south of Haifa. The anti-missile missile system has successfully completed sixteen intercept tests. Iranian forces are believed to be in possession of a dozen operational nuclear missiles, with Israel's nuclear arsenal numbering well over two hundred.

AL UDEID AIR BASE
QATAR
OCTOBER 17, 2012
7:22 PM LOCAL TIME

The Al Udeid Air Base in Qatar is the forward headquarters of U.S. Central Command (CENTCOM), the Unified Combatant Command military group responsible for rapid deployment of U.S. forces in the Middle East, East Africa, and Central Asia.

CENTCOM's commander, General Mike Tristano, began his military career in the U.S. Army's Special Forces. Unlike the President and Secretary of Defense, the battle-tested General feels the invasion plans for Iran are far too ambitious, especially when his combat troops are already so overextended. He knows a nuclear strike option for Iran is on the table, but he has yet to be briefed.

Tristano enters his war room, joining his chief of staff, Major General Ben Serviss, his deputy commander, Vice Admiral Brandon Herbert, who is overseeing naval operations in the Persian Gulf, and Major General Cynthia J. Zizzi, the director of ground operations and the highest-ranking female officer in the armed forces.

Detailed maps of the Middle East line the walls of the chamber. Facing the conference table is the room's centerpiece—an eight-foot-high, multilayered transparent digital display board, offering CENTCOM real-time data of friendly and hostile troop movements, air support status, atmospheric weather conditions, and the location of the super-carrier, USS *Ronald Reagan* and her battle group, now steaming northwest through the Persian Gulf.

The General takes his place at the head of the table. "Do we have an updated target list?"

"Yes, sir." General Zizzi types in a command on her laptop, a revised target list appearing on the computerized map, broken down by category.

General Tristano removes his hat, massaging the tension building along the back of his neck. "I'll be blunt, people. We're still being kept in the dark by the Secretary of Defense, and it's got me pissing mad. Air strike, nuclear strike . . . no one's saying. But this whole operation reeks of 2003, the White House jumping in with both feet before thinking things through."

"Kendle spent time in Iraq. He knows full well we don't have the manpower to police another hostile nation."

Vice Admiral Herbert concurs. "This is death on a massive scale, any way you slice it. Even if we don't go nuclear, bombing a nuclear reactor with conventional weapons is still a dangerous venture. General Zizzi, you spoke with Los Alamos. What did the eggheads have to say?"

"They agreed saturation bombing, or even a lone Tomahawk strike on Iran's nuclear installations could create a Chernobyl-like radioactive cloud. The Indian Ocean is still experiencing its monsoon season. Even a small storm would draw radioactive fallout southeast over India's coastal cities. Calcutta, Rangoon, Dhaka, Mumbai, Chennai, and Colombo would all be exposed, with the higher humidity leading to even more adverse effects.

Obviously, things get worse if Kendle persuades Biden to order a tactical nuclear strike on Tehran. Radioactive fallout could affect both Pakistan and India, even moving into China, Russia, and as far east as Japan. Musharraf's government is already in trouble in Pakistan. A nuclear strike would ensure his demise, and his replacement would most likely be an Islamic radical. That would provoke a military response from India. We're also bracing for a major Shia retaliatory attack in Iraq, once the invasion begins."

"General Serviss, how certain is INTEL that we've targeted all the Shahab missile sites?"

"At this juncture, confidence is only running at 75 percent. The Shehab-III has a maximum range of eight hundred miles. If they manage to launch, their most likely targets are Camp Doha base in Kuwait, Al Seeb airbase in Oman, any number of targets in Saudi Arabia, and the Israeli cities of Tel Aviv, Eilat, Haifa, Beersheba, and the nuclear complex at Dimona. The Israelis have the ARROW defense system, but the other sites remain exposed. Oh . . . and of course, our site here in Qatar."

"What about the Chinese?"

"I think we have to expect some response. Iran is China's second largest source of imported Middle East oil. They also use the Iranian terminal for the export of natural gas from Turkmenistan. A large-scale invasion would likely spell the end of NATO as well."

"Damn politicians. Let 'em all rot in hell." General Tristano checks the local time: 8:12 p.m. "I'm scheduled to speak with Defense Secretary Kendle again at twenty-one hundred hours. We'll reconvene then."

The CENTCOM senior staff exits the chamber.

General Tristano grabs the Admiral's arm, wanting him to remain behind. "What have you heard, and don't bullshit me, Brandon, we go back too far."

"I spoke with Fisher, the *Ronald Reagan's* CO. A supply ship made a delivery earlier this morning, Kendle's orders."

"What kind of delivery?"

STEVE ALTEN

PERSIAN GULF
OCTOBER, 17, 2012
10:28 PM LOCAL TIME

The United States Aircraft Carrier *Ronald Reagan* (CVN-76) plows through the gulf at a steady fifteen knots. A thousand feet long, displacing ninety-seven thousand tons, the steel fortress towers twenty stories above the waterline, its hulking presence on the Arabian horizon foreshadowing death.

Escorting the carrier are sixteen combat ships, ten support ships, and two *Los Angeles*-class attack subs. Two 567-foot Ticonderoga-class warships flank the boat, each equipped with the Aegis Theater High Altitude Air Defense (THADD) program, a highly sophisticated battle-management system designed to shield the carrier from attack. The two Ticonderogas are also equipped with Tomahawk cruise missiles—long-range projectiles capable of destroying targets up to a thousand miles away.

Captain Scott James Fisher, the carrier's commanding officer, has spent most of the last twenty-four hours in the ship's Combat Information Center (CIC), the carrier's nerve center. Within this dark, heavily air-conditioned chamber, dozens of technicians focus their attention on tactical computer screens, monitoring the carrier battle group's position, the surrounding defense zones . . . and the electromagnetic emissions emanating from hostile forces in the area.

The Captain appears a rock on the outside, but his thoughts are back home with his family—his parents and sisters, residents of Ventura, California . . . all missing.

Commander Tony Ordonez, Fisher's executive officer, weaves his way between computer stations, carrying sealed orders. He hands the encoded message to his skipper.

Fisher glances at the note. "Assemble the senior officers."

Ten minutes later, the CO joins his senior staff in a small conference room adjacent to the CIC. The evening's target list has been divided geographically, each area assigned a sortie.

"We're a go. First wave of sorties launches at zero-three hundred hours. Second wave six hours later. Questions?"

"Second-wave payload, skipper . . . is it a nuke?" Commander Ordonez asks the question everyone wants to know.

Fisher hesitates. "Officially, the decision is being held back while the bureaucrats continue haggling at the U.N., but my sources tell me a nuclear option for Tehran is off the table. The repercussions from the radioactive fallout are just too risky." Fisher looks into the faces of each of his senior officers. "We're going with chemical weapons, VX nerve gas. The rebels who captured the Saudi refinery will get the first taste at oh-three hundred."

The senior officers nod, everyone's adrenaline pumping.

Fisher bows his head. "What happened in Los Angeles, what nearly happened in Chicago . . . it affects all of us. Nobody likes war, gentlemen, but when attacked, when the enemy brings bloodshed to our homeland . . ."

The Captain looks at his men, tears mixing with the fire in his eyes, "Tonight, we teach our enemy a lesson—paybacks are a bitch."

ABQAIQ OIL REFINERY
SAUDI ARABIA IRAQ
1:07 AM LOCAL TIME

For weeks the Saudi National Guard has taken up positions outside the fortified gates of the Abqaiq refinery, squaring off against a well-armed platoon of Ashraf freedom fighters. Not a shot has been fired, the impasse ensured by explosives the rebels had planted around the refinery's highly flammable pipelines and storage tanks.

Inside the compound, Bradley Fighting machines and Abrams tanks—stolen from the House of Saud's own military depots—stand guard over the perimeter fence, the administration buildings, and dormitories. The revolution, which had been gaining momentum, has lost support since the nuclear attack in Los Angeles, an event that has enabled the House of Saud to paint the Ashraf rebels as just another violent terrorist organization.

✦ ✦ ✦

A reflexive jerk awakens Ace from a restless sleep. For several long seconds he searches his surroundings until he recognizes the infirmary.

Nine days have passed since Ace, Scott Santa, and the Saudi woman escaped Inakesh Prison. They had raced east on the highway to Riyadh before pulling off at a petrol station to switch vehicles. Santa had hot-wired a car while Ace restrained Nahir.

By dawn they had arrived at the outskirts of the oil refinery.

Ramzi's men had interrogated Nahir. Santa was right—she had been lying. Years earlier she had been arrested by Saudi officials for her involvement in a vodka smuggling ring (alcohol is illegal in the kingdom), earning her scars from a public flogging. Her father, General Abdul Aziz—the Inakesh warden—had managed to commute her jail sentence in exchange for her work at the prison. They had made an especially effective team—Ali Shams the sadistic torturer, and the beautiful and compassionate Nahir Abdul Aziz providing a shoulder the prisoner could lean on while confessing his sins. Even the Friday execution had been a ruse, everything designed to win Ace's trust.

She remained in the compound under lock and key.

Day by day, the worst of Ace's physical wounds had begun to heal. He is now able to keep down solid foods, and the intravenous drips have fought off an infection and fever that had developed after three of his fingernails had been torturously extracted.

What has been slower to heal are his emotional wounds, his mind unable to escape the horrors of the last two months.

He rarely sleeps more than a few hours at a time, the deeper, non-rem stages leading to terrifying night terrors that cause him to wake up screaming.

Adding to his mental burden are the scenes of devastation being broadcast from Los Angeles, along with the sobering realization that his children could have suffered or even perished had not the second bomb been defused in Chicago. Despite his efforts, despite the torture he has had to endure, his wife's worst fears are coming true—America is under siege from within and the Neocons once again pulling the strings on U.S. foreign policy. An attack on Iran is imminent, the Asfraf rebellion all but over.

He checks the time: 1:22 a.m. Unable to sleep, he laces up the khaki army boots the rebels had given him, slips on the matching jacket, and heads outside.

The moon is full, high over the desert plain, its luminescence casting an eerie light upon the armored vehicles in the compound. It takes him several moments before he realizes something is amiss—the Saudi National Guard is gone!

✦ ✦ ✦

Ace locates Ramzi Karim in the basement of one of the administration buildings. The Ashraf leader is with his military commanders, discussing the National Guard pullout. Scott Santa is there as well, the CIA agent chain smoking and listening in, a makeshift "pirate's patch" now covering his empty left eye socket.

"The Guard's withdrawal means the American attack will come tonight," Ramzi restates for Ace's sake. "We need to be prepared."

"They will not bomb the compound," one of the younger rebels responds. "The Americans cannot afford to lose the refinery."

"While they may not use explosives, Khaled, they will strike using chemical or biological agents. Thousands of families—

women and children among them—remain in Abqaiq's dormitories. If we stay in the compound they will wipe us out."

"We have a dozen functional biohazard suits," an army general reminds him. "Give the suits to my squadron, and we will maintain a vigil at the gates. The rest of you—lead the exodus into the desert."

Ramzi nods. "Khaled, organize the evacuation. You must leave before dawn. I will remain behind with the General."

"Wait." Ace limps toward the group. "So maybe you'll survive this attack, but it won't change a thing. You're running low on food, and the House of Saud has obviously made a deal with Biden. How long do you think you can hold out?"

"The longer we hold out, the stronger we become in the eyes of our people. Rebellions only succeed when the will of the populace rises as one. We were close once. The American attack may yet serve to win us more support."

"Martyrs don't lead rebellions, Ramzi. If you want to take back your country, you have to do it now, by exposing the truth behind the attack on Los Angeles. We have to connect the dots for the media. Incriminate the Neocons and we give the American public what they need to start their own rebellion."

"Ace, the lies are far stronger than any evidence we could produce. These people don't play by the same rules, they'll do anything to stay in power."

Anything to stay in power . . .

A seed of thought takes root. Ace closes his eyes, his mind fighting to reel in a distant memory. *Anything to stay in power . . . where had he heard that statement before?*

Jennifer . . . that day in her apartment!

"And if 9/11 was the biggest intelligence screw-up of all time, how come no one ever lost their job? My friend's dead because a lot of people failed to act, and now my wife's dead because of what she knew, and you just got done telling me that the people in power will do anything to stay in power."

"You want to know how the Neocons win, Ace? They begin

with the message, a lie they can sell. Message gets candidates elected. Not truth, not policies, not resumés or medals in wars—message."

"Ramzi, we don't need evidence, we just need to drive home the right message. Kelli's murder, the money trail, the nuke linking Iran to the attack . . . get me in front of the news media. I can sell this!"

"It won't stop the invasion."

"No, but it will force the American media to raise the issue. It will cast doubt on who's really to blame. After 9/11, everyone was afraid to question Bush, and those who did were publicly disgraced—branded traitors. But if we come out in force now, playing up on what we've already disseminated over the Internet—"

Ramzi looks at his commanders. "Where are the news crews?"

"Gone. The National Guard forced them to leave the area."

"I think I know a way we can bring them back."

"An 'emergency response exercise' is scheduled to take place at 9 a.m. the morning of 9/11, involving the simulated crash of a small corporate jet plane into a government building. The exercise is to be conducted by the National Reconnaissance Office (NRO) in Chantilly, Virginia—just four miles from Washington Dulles International Airport, from which Flight 77 took off, and 24 miles from the Pentagon. The NRO draws its personnel from the CIA and the military. The exercise is to involve the jet experiencing mechanical problems and then crashing into one of the four towers at the NRO. In order to simulate the damage from the crash, some stairwells and exits are to be closed off, forcing NRO employees to find other ways to evacuate the building. However, according to an agency spokesman, 'as soon as the real world events began, we cancelled the exercise.' After the attacks, most of the agency's 3,000 staff are supposedly sent home."

—Associated Press,
August 21, 2002

"There will always be dissident voices heard in the land, expressing opposition without alternatives, finding fault but never favor, perceiving gloom on every side and seeking influence without responsibility."

—President John F. Kennedy
Speech for Dallas Texas,
November 22, 1963
(Never delivered)

CHAPTER 48

THE SHERIFF'S HELICOPTER KICKS UP a twister of limestone dust as it lands near the camper. Deputy Caleb Kennedy-Smith allows the air to settle before exiting the chopper to join the two couples gathered by the base of a limestone rock.

The wrecked Honda Accord's grill is buried deep into the escarpment. The deputy looks inside at Elliott Green's decaying remains. He grimaces. "All right, who called this in?"

One of the men, a heavy-set biker, raises his hand. "Me and the wife were out riding when we saw the car. I told her not to touch anything, but she might have left a print or two on the door."

"Okay, sir, wait by the camper. I'll take your statement in a minute." The deputy speaks into his radio. "Base, this is 902. I'm out at Smokey Hills, approximately six miles north of Jayhawk Road. We've got a dead body. Caucasian male, mid-forties. Multiple gunshot wounds. Gonna need the FBI in on this one."

ABOARD THE *RONALD REAGAN*
PERSIAN GULF
1:37 am LOCAL TIME

Captain Fisher is in the armory, a high-security chamber

located in the bowels of the aircraft carrier. As instructed by the secretary of defense, the CO is personally overseeing a handpicked weapons crew in the fusing and loading of dozens of specially-made binary chemical bombs. Once finished, the canisters will be loaded onto the freight lift, designated for the sortie scheduled to bomb the Abqaiq oil refinery and its rebel extremists.

Hundreds more of these weapons of mass destruction line the armory, waiting to be dropped on another target—the population of Iran.

Abqaiq Oil Refinery
1:43 am Local Time

The blast sends shock waves rippling throughout the compound, igniting night into day in a fiery explosion that can be seen and felt for miles. Secondary detonations follow like exploding dominoes as pockets of liquid natural gas ignite, dispersing fiery mushroom clouds into the heavens.

Six men, all dressed in biological suits, watch the fireworks from one of the compound's golf course fairways. Ramzi removes his hood to speak with Ace, "You can feel the heat even at this distance. Imagine if we detonated the entire refinery."

"This'll do for now. What about that call?"

Ramzi digs through an exterior pocket and hands him a cell phone. "Remember, the NSA is monitoring everything. You've got about three minutes before they intercept the call."

Ace dials the overseas number.

◆ ◆ ◆

"Hello?"

"Jen?"

Jennifer Wienner nearly drives off the side of the road. "Ace! Thank God! Are you all right? Where are you?"

"Saudi Arabia, the Abqaiq Oil Refinery. Jen, listen carefully. Where's Mulligan?"

"He's meeting with members of Congress. Cheney's been

on TV all day, demanding Biden take out Tehran and the mullahs responsible for LA. No decision yet."

"What time is it there?"

"Almost nine."

"Contact Mulligan. Have him call a major news conference for ten o'clock. Tell him I'm going live within the hour to present criminal evidence against the Neocons, linking them to the attack on Los Angeles. Then call our boy in Atlantic City . . . hello? Jen? Hello?"

The line goes dead.

ABOARD THE *RONALD REAGAN*
PERSIAN GULF
2:54 AM LOCAL TIME

Having been debriefed, teams of pilots exit their squadron ready rooms, joining the controlled chaos of the four-and-a-half acre flight deck—the most dangerous piece of real estate in the world.

Lieutenant Rudi Anger climbs inside his F-35C Joint Strike Fighter (JSF), a stealthy $28 million killing machine designed with the latest cutting-edge avionics, propulsion systems, and firepower. The panoramic cockpit is alive with a matrix of liquid crystal monitors, all linked to the lieutenant's helmet-mounted display.

As the pilot moves through his checklist, a munitions crew loads a dozen of the special binary bombs into two parallel bays located in front of the JSF's landing gear. A mechanic signals the pilot to start his jet's engine. The cockpit is closed, the fighter's surface given a final check. Hand signals warn crewmen about the jet's hot exhaust while the flight deck handler signals the "all clear."

Seconds later, the JSF launches vertically into the night. At five hundred feet the afterburners kick in, hurtling the killing machine west toward Saudi Arabia.

ABQAIQ OIL REFINERY
2:57 AM LOCAL TIME

The CNN crew is first to arrive.

Field reporter Rebecca St. Croix is on her first stint in the Middle East. Her cameraman, Larry Kelly, is doubling as her director, his younger brother, Sean, their sound man. As Larry films the blaze, the gates of the compound open, and they are greeted by Ramzi Karim, still wearing his biological suit.

"My name is Ramzi Karim. I am a former member of the CIA and one of the Ashraf leaders. I have with us an American citizen who has evidence that a Neoconservative faction was involved in the plot to blow up Los Angeles and Chicago."

Rebecca's grey-blue eyes widen. "Where is he? Will he allow us to interview him?"

"Yes, but it must be a live interview. Can you arrange this?"

Before she can respond, Larry Kelly is dialing his cell phone.

◆ ◆ ◆

Ace, dressed in his biohazard suit, enters the administration building basement where Nahir Abdul-Aziz is being held in a locked meeting room. Keying open the dead bolt, he unlocks the door.

She is seated in a padded chair, the burka having been replaced with an oil worker's orange jumpsuit. Her long hair is braided, hanging free behind her back. The hazel eyes soften as he enters the room.

"Ashley . . . are you here to kill me?"

"No."

"You understand, there was nothing I could do. Saudi women have no power, marked women like myself are a scourge—"

"I understand."

"Inakesh is a terrible place, I too was its prisoner—"

"I said I understand. Nahir, for whatever reason, you were

the one who kept me alive, the one who nursed my wounds. In the middle of the insanity, you were my only beacon of hope. For a while, a part of me actually, well—"

"Love?"

"I don't know . . . maybe."

"It was part of the illusion, Ashley. Trust me, I am not worthy of your love."

"People can change."

"I am not so sure."

"If that's true, then civilization may already be over." He hands her the key. "I came to release you. Ashraf's abandoning the compound, American fighters are on the way. You can follow the others into the desert, and then it's up to you."

"And you?"

"I'm staying here. News reporters are on their way. I'm going to try to stop a nuclear holocaust."

"If it's all right, I will stay with you." She squeezes his hand and then looks up as Scott Santa enters the room, wearing a biohazard suit.

"Conspiring with the enemy?"

"What is it you want?"

"A word. Alone."

Ace nods to Nahir, who leaves.

"Think about what you're about to do, Futrell. Think about the repercussions."

"I have."

"No, I don't think so." Santa circles the conference table, his lone eye irritated and red, twitching nervously. "You're about to announce to the world that members of a conservative political party planned the Columbus Day massacre in order to justify the bombing of Iran."

"The world needs to know the truth."

"The truth? You don't know the truth! Do you even understand what this conflict is about?"

"Oil."

"Oil is nothing but a byproduct. This is about two different ideologies—one an open society promoting freedom and commerce, the other a closed society dominated by religious fanatics who kill indiscriminately in order to control their own populace. These people live to die, Futrell. They've been taught to hate since birth. It's all they know. You can't rationalize with terrorists who have been convinced that blowing up innocent people is their ticket to paradise."

Santa pauses. "Listen."

Ace hears a low rumbling sound . . . bombs exploding in the distance.

"It's begun," Santa says. "Tonight we cut off the head of Islamofacism. Make your little speech and you dishonor the deaths of those Americans whose sacrifice will lead to a greater good."

"Not every end justifies the means. What kind of democracy allows its president and advisors absolute power to wipe out entire populations because they alone decided it was the best course of action?"

"This isn't about democracy. It's about war . . . the war on terror."

"There is no war on terror! The PNAC lunatics dreamed that up to take over the Middle East and perpetuate their military regime. There are innocent people out there, families who have no interest in your rules of conflict or your idea of democracy. They just want to live out their lives in peace. These are moderates who want a civilized existence—it's the actions of our empire that pushes them to accept radical Islam. Obama was right. Winning their hearts is the key to defeating radicals. We should be supporting their efforts, not slaughtering them."

"In war, innocent people sometimes die. What history honors is the cause."

"What cause? Capitalism? Is that your justification for slaughtering millions?"

Santa shakes his head. "You know nothing about the real

world. Millions die every year. We just ignore the headlines. They die of war and abuse, they die of starvation and disease. Americans ignore their plight, filing it away as another global cause allocated to celebrities. My family's roots trace back to Russia, to the time of the czar. You have no idea what it means to live under an oppressive regime. I served in the Company, the CIA, for twenty-six years. What you call murder we called liberating societies. And that's what we do tonight. Yes, the cost is high, but if we do nothing, then the cost is a hundred-fold. Think it through! The world is filled with oppressive regimes . . . Islamic radicals who won't hesitate for a moment to wipe out as many westerners as they can. What happens when a nut like Ahmadinejad or his Hezbollah goons actually launch a real WMD, not some ten kiloton suitcase nuke, but a fifty megaton warhead. Maybe they'll wipe out Israel—maybe the entire island of Manhattan! What will you say then?"

Ace loosens the upper catches on his Racal suit. "I agree there's a real threat, but we're making it worse. By invading Iraq, we forced Muslim moderates to choose sides instead of helping us isolate the extremists. Today's actions will signal the official start of a holy war that will only end with the destruction of civilization. Violence never truly stops violence—only peace can do that."

Santa sneers. "Peace? Peace is an illusion. This is good versus evil, a black and white issue, and those of us who see the world for what it is cannot afford to wallow in a liberal's shades of gray."

Ace steals a glance over Santa's shoulder, then returns to stare at the man's cold eye. "Before my wife was killed, she told me the Neocons hired her to plan a nuclear attack set up to appear as if the Iranians were responsible. The Los Angeles bombing . . . it was a false flag event, just like 9/11. Wasn't it?"

"False flag indicates government involvement. Corporations move the world, Futrell, not governments. What you label Neocons are the world's movers and shakers, the ones determined to control events before the events control us. The first Bush agreed to demilitarize Saddam, but he refused to finish the job. Clinton refused as well. After that, we stopped asking. If you want to move the flock, invite the wolf. September 11th was designed to change the rules of engagement. The Columbus Day attack was set up to crush the nuclear threat in Iran. Without state support, fanatical Islam will fall."

"And the House of Saud?"

"When the time is right."

"You left out Venezuela."

The Russian-American's eye widens, and then he offers a wry smile. "Like warfare, oil is a catalyst—a means to an end. Chavez's nation will be labeled the linchpin in the war on drugs. He too must be controlled."

"You mean like the drug lords the CIA control in Afghanistan? See, the problem with your theories is that in attempting to control the monster, you become one. Convinced the end justifies the means, you sell drugs in New Orleans to finance the Contras, assassinate leaders of foreign nations— trading one oppressive regime for another, and you never hesitate to make deals with the devil. Well, guess what? You've become the devil. You and your fellow hypocrites don't give a damn about democracy. The only cause you truly understand is money. Money and power."

Santa reaches inside his jacket, retrieving the 9mm semi-automatic. "Your wife once shared the same ideals as the PNAC, did you know this? It was the cancer that changed her perspective. It made her weak—a bleeding heart liberal. I took great pleasure in putting her out of her misery."

The agent aims the gun at Ace's head—his good eye exploding in a blast of blood and bone fragment as the bullet tears through the back of his skull.

Ace turns to Ramzi, still aiming his weapon from outside the meeting room door. Nahir and the CNN film crew are with him, all in biohazard suits. "Geez, Ramzi! Think maybe you were cutting it a bit close?"

Ramzi re-holsters his weapon. "His rants made for a better interview."

The CNN cameraman continues to film, his sound man nudging the female reporter, who is still in shock. The woman regains her composure. "Mr. Futrell, Rebecca St. Croix, CNN. Sir, could you tell us who this man was?"

Ace takes a breath, fighting to collect himself. "His name was Scott Santa. He was the CIA-trained assassin who murdered my wife, Kelli Doyle, a former national security advisor under the Bush Administration. The two of them were involved in a Neoconservative plot to allow terrorists to use a nuclear device on an American city so that we could disarm Iran. My wife documented everything. We're sending some of the evidence over the Internet to the major media outlets. Biden needs to stop listening to the Neocons in his cabinet before those lunatics coerce him into starting World War III."

❖ ❖ ❖

The Joint Strike Fighter soars over the desert, racing for the burning infrastructure in the distance. The jet's Lockheed Martin electro-optical targeting system (EOTS) configures its multiple targets, its undercarriage yawning open . . . ejecting its payload.

❖ ❖ ❖

Ace, Nahir, Ramzi, and the CNN crew instinctively look up as bombs explode three hundred feet over the oil refinery . . . bathing the small city in VX nerve gas.

"Officials at NORAD have stated when the hijackings first occurred they initially thought it was part of the Vigilant Guardian drills running that morning. Despite some confusion, once Flight Eleven struck the World Trade Center at 8:45 a.m., everyone should have known this was not a test. . . . Scrambling aircraft simply means providing an Air Force escort to survey the situation. This has nothing to do with shooting down an aircraft. Such scrambling procedures had occurred sixty-seven times in the year prior to 9/11. The concept of this simple standard operating procedure failing from 8:28 a.m. when Flight Eleven made an unplanned one hundred-degree turn to the south, until 9:38 a.m. when the Pentagon was struck, is inconceivable without a military order. Such an order, or multiple orders causing 'confusion,' may have been scripted into the war game scenarios that morning. We do not know if this is the case, and it seems the 9/11 Commission doesn't want to know."

—MICHAEL KANE
Elephants in the Barracks:
The Complete Failure of the 9/11 Commission

"Our most basic common link is that we all inhabit this planet. We all breathe the same air. We all cherish our children's future. And we are all mortal."

—PRESIDENT JOHN F. KENNEDY

Book Excerpt:
To the Brink of Hell:
An Apology to the Survivors
by Kelli Doyle
White House National Security Staff Advisor
(2002–2008)

The Neocon's solution to disarm a nuclear Iran meshed with another global concern appearing quickly on the horizon — the end of oil.

When it comes to the human ecosystem, energy is everything. Societies ultimately succeed or fail based upon their ability to process energy. That the planet's population explosion coincided with the industrial revolution is no mere coincidence. The two are intrinsically tied together, a result of the impact of fossil fuels — specifically oil.

A quick but vital lesson: It is oil and its byproducts that allow machines to complete tasks formerly performed by human or animal muscle power. A century ago, horses and humans had to live off the crop they farmed, the capacity of land they could work quite limited. It was the advent of gasoline-powered vehicles and their introduction into agriculture that suddenly enabled industry to plow, plant, and harvest massive acres of land quickly and economically, making it possible for 2 percent of our population to feed our entire country . . . allowing civilization to expand.

Industrialized farms rely on oil. It's used in fertilizer and pesticides, and it's the diesel that powers farming equipment on a massive scale. Without gasoline, goods cannot be transported by truck to central collecting and processing points, or perishables distributed to cities and remote areas. Without oil, we could not populate vast regions of our own country. Imagine living in desert states like Arizona or New Mexico, or the cold northern areas in Minnesota and Wisconsin without energy to cool and heat our homes, feed the populace, or supply goods and other services. Oil makes it all possible.

What most people fail to realize is that it takes energy to get energy, gasoline to drill an oil well, electricity to manufacture a photovoltaic solar panel. Can we replace oil? Not for transportation. Nuclear power is expensive and creates dangerous radioactive waste. Wind, while an effective alternative source of electricity in some regions, cannot push a truck carrying perishables to market. Photovoltaics, long underfunded, remain expensive. Hydrogen is not an energy source. It is an energy storage medium, and the production of hydrogen requires fossil fuels. Natural gas is running out, and again cannot mobilize an economy.

The harsh reality: When it comes to energy production and profit ratio, nothing competes with the economics of oil — the primary reason America has failed to invest in other alternative energy resources. Combine that fact with the all-powerful fossil fuel industry, which uses its billions in profits to leverage politicians, and you have a steep mountain to climb in order to effect quantum change.

That cheap oil is running out is no great secret, though economists will debate endlessly into the night as to the exact year the last economically affordable drop will be drained. Controlling that last drop had always been at the crux of the Neocons' "Project for a New American Century," but the sudden realization that Iraqi oil reserves (and others) had been greatly exaggerated forced the radical right to readjust its plans . . . and ponder another harsh reality:

How many of us can actually exist on this planet at the same time without fossil fuels?

The law of unchanging energy supply states that a

growing economy must eventually consume more energy than it can produce. World oil reserves peaked back in 2005 and consumption is soaring, effectively burning the candle at both ends. The effects are already being felt. More than three billion people worldwide are malnourished and living in poverty. Grain production and arable land per capita have been declining steadily since 1984, along with fish production and fertilizers essential for food production. Inversely, water, air, and land pollution has increased, along with global warming. As the U.S. National Academy of Sciences has pointed out, humanity is approaching a crisis point.

For decades, Earth's carrying capacity had been artificially increased because of an abundance of oil — oil that supported industrial agriculture and technological advances in key sectors, including transportation networks, medical care, and sanitation. With our primary energy source running out faster than anticipated, our leaders are faced with a sobering reality — at current reserves, there are simply too many people living on our planet to feed and house everyone.

Here's the basic math: Six billion of us exist today, and that number must be reduced by roughly 66 percent over the next two decades or severe famine, induced by the end of oil, will do it for us.

That's four billion people who must be strategically eliminated to avoid anarchy.

And so society's gluttons came up with their own contingency plan, one they didn't exactly publish on their website. Instead of conserving energy and weaning America and western society off fossil fuels, the world's elite decided to seek out alternative methods to selectively "thin the herd" while allowing their entities to make even more money.

The two most effective ways to reduce population centers are pandemic and war. As I type this passage, genetically manipulated epidemics are being developed in government-controlled labs, along with cures that will be selectively administered by key allies in the pharmaceutical industry. As for those annoying scientists who might potentially "cure" a future pandemic — many of these individuals have already been "eliminated."

After the occupation and resultant struggles in Iraq, and faced with the reality of America's depleted armed forces, a New Republic Doctrine was created. In essence it states, "the most cost-effective way to invade and control a foreign land is to initially employ methods that will radically reduce the populace while preserving the country's infrastructure."

Translation: Instead of invading a hostile third-world nation with troops, use tactical chemical weapons to destroy the will of your enemy . . . and its people.

When it comes to systematically murdering hordes of human beings while leaving buildings and oil wells intact, there is nothing quite as lethal or effective as a chemical nerve agent. Nerve agents are toxins designed to disrupt the transmission of cholinesterase, an enzyme nerve cells use to clear themselves of acetylcholine, the chemical that causes muscles and glands to contract. By inhibiting cholinesterase, the muscles of the diaphragm will contract uncontrollably, leading to death by suffocation.

The most lethal family of chemical agents ever created is the V-series — ten times more toxic than sarin gas. VX is the worst of the lot — an odorless, colorless, oily agent that does not wash away easily. Even a small dose of VX on the skin or inhaled will cause severe convulsions, respiratory paralysis, and death within several minutes.

Because VX is so lethal, the Defense Department must deploy it in binary bombs — canisters designed with separate chambers, each holding the two VX chemical precursors. When fired or dropped at elevation, the bomb's acceleration causes the partition within the capsule to break, the VX nerve gas mixed as it races toward its intended victims.

The end of oil.

A nuclear Iran, led by an extremist with an agenda.

The threat of radical Islam, fueled by a hatred of Western society.

A Neoconservative agenda, backed by elitists seeking a one-world government.

The variables of destruction are all in place, the game of chess coming down to its last fatal moves, checkmating the end of our civilization as we know it.

"The President has the power to seize property, organize and control the means of production, seize commodities, assign military forces abroad, call reserve forces amounting to 2.5 million men to duty, institute martial law, seize and control all means of transportation, regulate all private enterprise, restrict travel, and in a plethora of particular ways, control the lives of all Americans. Most of these laws remain a potential source of virtually unlimited power for a President should he choose to activate them. It is possible that some future president could exercise this vast authority in an attempt to place the United States under authoritarian rule. While the danger of a dictatorship arising through legal means may seem remote to us today, recent history records Hitler seizing control through the use of the emergency powers provisions contained in the laws of the Weimar Republic."

—SENATORS FRANK CHURCH (D-ID) AND
CHARLES McMATHIAS (R-MD),
September 30, 1973

"Vice President Dick Cheney vigorously defended a secret program that examines banking records of Americans and others in a vast international database, harshly criticizing the news media for disclosing an operation he called legal and 'absolutely essential' to fighting terrorism."

—NEW YORK TIMES,
June 24, 2006

"We shall be judged more by what we do at home than what we preach abroad."

—PRESIDENT JOHN F. KENNEDY

CHAPTER 49

SENATOR MULLIGAN STANDS BEFORE THE PODIUM, fists balled in anger, as the CNN live feed featuring Ace Futrell and Scott Santa is abruptly cut off . . . seconds before Ace was interviewed!

The Green Party candidate turns to address the hastily gathered group of reporters. "The Internet rumors were true—the attack on Los Angeles was a false flag event, perpetrated by the radical right. Tonight, I call on all members of Congress to join me in an emergency midnight session on Capitol Hill to investigate charges that members of this administration and the Bush Administration were directly involved in the Columbus Day attack. Tonight I call on Congress to take back control of our nation before our military commits mass murder!"

AL UDEID AIR BASE, QATAR
3:51 AM LOCAL TIME

CENTCOM's commander, General Mike Tristano, listens to Vice Admiral Brandon Herbert as he barks orders over the video speaker phone at Captain James Fisher aboard the Air Craft Carrier, *Ronald Reagan*.

"Exactly how many of these binary bombs did the Secretary of Defense order the supply ship to bring onboard, Captain?"

Fisher's complexion seems to pale over the monitor. "Sir, just over three hundred."

General Tristano swears under his breath. "Captain, under my direct order, no more VX bombs are to be loaded aboard any aircraft, is that understood?"

"Sir, Defense Secretary Kendle has already issued orders to the contrary."

"Captain, the Secretary of Defense is under suspicion of treason," the Admiral shoots back. "If the Secretary of Defense contacts you, you will refer him to me, is that clear?"

"Yes, sir."

"Major General Zizzi, what's the status of the Phase I targets?"

"Nuclear targets have been destroyed and the Iranian Air Force has been immobilized. Fourteen sorties are now on approach to terrorist training camps."

"Captain Fisher, you will complete Phase I of the mission and then await orders from CENTCOM."

"Yes, sir."

WEST PALM BEACH, FLORIDA
11:35 PM EST

Jennifer Wienner is watching CNN on her cell phone when her assistant calls out from his office, "Jen, turn on CBS, they're breaking another story!"

She changes the channel to a live scene at FBI Headquarters in Chicago where Director Adrian Neary is being grilled by the press.

"The suspect, Jamal al-Yussuf, was found dead about two hours ago. Preliminary autopsy reports indicate it was a heart attack."

"Sir, the suspect was only in his late twenties. How is it possible—"

"As I said earlier, we are investigating all possibilities, including foul play."

"Did anyone visit the suspect prior to his death?"

Neary contemplates his answer carefully. "I'm sorry, I can't comment at this time."

"You just did!" Jennifer hugs her assistant as he enters the room. "It's happening, Collin! It's all coming down like a house of cards!"

Collin Bradley's expression gives her pause as he hands her the phone.

CAPITOL HILL,
WASHINGTON, D.C.
12:12 AM EST

The police presence is enormous, officers and Homeland Security arresting any dissenter so much as wearing an anti-war T-shirt. The media are kept at bay—no cameras allowed within a quarter-mile of the Capitol Building.

Inside, a deeply shaken Senator Joseph Mulligan looks out upon an empty chamber as an aide hurriedly approaches. "Seventeen Democrats, three Republicans—that's all that showed. Homeland Security arrested every one of them, sir."

The doors burst open, three armed Homeland Security agents making their way toward them from down the center aisle.

"This is a sad day," Senator Mulligan says. "A sad day for democracy."

"Senator Mulligan, we are placing you under arrest, the charges—treason. Under the statutes of the Patriot Act, you are not entitled to counsel. You will be detained until further notice."

AL UDEID AIR BASE, QATAR
4:22 AM LOCAL TIME

The MPs enter, their guns drawn.

General Mike Tristano looks up from his desk, his

blood pressure boiling. "What's going on here? Holster those weapons!"

"I'm sorry, sir. You're under arrest."

"Arrest! Under whose orders?"

"The President of the United States."

ABQAIQ OIL REFINERY
6:47 AM LOCAL TIME

First light unveils a landscape of death—thousands of bodies, the dying gasping final breaths their lungs cannot breathe, the poisoned nerves of the deceased still twitching.

Cloaked within their protective garments, the CNN crew moves carefully amid the fallen as they film the heart-wrenching carnage: Locals . . . fathers and sons, mothers clutching infants . . . part of an exodus that began a blink in time too late.

Ace hyperventilates behind the plastic hood of his biohazard suit as he staggers through the refinery, his insides emotionally ravaged, his anger raging at the senselessness of an act that he was utterly powerless to prevent. Nahir is by his side, wearing Scott Santa's biohazard suit.

Ramzi Karim stumbles from one body to the next, sweeping suffocating children up in his arms, carrying them inside a building, the act of desperation far too late against the man-made toxin.

More news crews arrive on the scene, all wearing protective biohazard suits. Within hours their shocking images will appear on news networks across the globe.

OVAL OFFICE, WHITE HOUSE
WASHINGTON, D.C.

Acting President Biden sits behind his desk, wringing his hands as he watches the cable news broadcast of Abqaiq. "How bad is this?"

"Bad." Jim Miller, Biden's new Press Secretary mutes the television's sound.

Defense Secretary Kendle enters. "CENTCOM's back under control. I was forced to arrest General Tristano."

Biden is livid. "You can't just do that without clearing it with me! This entire process has got to slow down."

"Tristano was insubordinate, he cancelled Phase II."

"What's Phase II?" asks the Press Secretary.

"Our response to Los Angeles," Lowe replies. "Destruction of key Iranian population centers."

"Destruction how?"

"VX nerve gas."

Jim Miller winces, the former Olympic baseball player suddenly wondering why he accepted the press secretary job in the first place. "Mr. President, with Senator Mulligan's arrest, with these images of dead children coming out of Abqaiq, I strongly advise you to put this attack on the back-burner."

"Out of the question." Defense Secretary Kendle stares down the Press Secretary, a man half his age. "I have sixteen warships in the Persian Gulf—"

"Which succeeded in destroying Iran's military bases and nuclear installations. Threat over, mission accomplished. Stop the war now and we win in the arena of global politics. Slaughter tens of millions of Iranian civilians and we declare open war on a billion Muslims."

"Enough!" Kendle spits. "You're the Press Secretary, you're not here to dictate policy. People a lot more experienced than you have devoted the better part of their careers working on a game plan—"

"To do what? Invade Iran by neutralizing its populace? It's all over the Internet—kill the radicals and take the oil. Brilliant plan! Well, it didn't work in 2003, and it—"

"Quiet!" The Homeland Security director points to the television, turning up the sound.

It's a CNN report, broadcast live out of Phoenix.

FBI Regional Director Marc McDuff is speaking at the podium. "Coordinating the investigation with agents in Kansas, we were able to identify the body of FBI agent Elliott Green. Agent Green had been involved in an ongoing investigation of a nuclear physicist, Professor Eric Mingyuan Bi. After searching the vehicle, FBI agents recovered recorded telephone conversations made by Agent Green of FBI Director Gary Lee Schafer and a yet-to-be-identified terror suspect. It should be noted that the director was in fact on the scene in Los Angeles just prior to the detonation of the nuclear weapon on October 8, and was killed in the attack."

Joe Biden stares at the television, his heart palpitating, his skin bathed in a cold sweat. His entire political career has been dedicated to preserving liberties and protecting the rights of the "little guy," now he has allowed himself to be swept up in a lynch-mob mentality where revenge supercedes the Constitution, might equating to right.

"Mr. Secretary . . . call back the sorties."

General Kendle's face flushes red. "Sir, you have no idea—"

"Do it now! Director Lowe, release all detainees, and then I want your resignation on my desk within the hour. Yours too, General. Mr. Miller, schedule a press conference for nine a.m. I'm calling for a full investigation of the Columbus Day massacre, and this time, the committee will have full subpoena power."

"It would be a terrible disservice to those Muslims who are liberal, who are democrats, who are modern, who want to live a civilized life . . . to throw them in with the barbarians, because they are on the right side, and more than that, they have a great deal to offer in the war against militant Islam."

—DANIEL PIPES,
Middle East Forum Director

"But we're all capable of savagery. In that regard, there is no difference between 'us' and 'them.' We all retain the essence of our humanity that allows us to kill at all. No one suggests that we not kill the enemy. The difference lies in what our systems are constructed to do and how they perform when called into duty. The difference lies in the quality of the cage in which our monsters reside during the off season. The difference lies in the willingness to look, to see, to judge and to act when monstrous subjects are at hand. These are not differences made real by the existence of a Geneva Convention, but differences made real by the structure and behavior of the US military and its civilian oversight."

—SEYMOUR HERSCH,
May 17, 2004

"If we cannot now end our differences, at least we can help make the world safe for diversity."

—PRESIDENT JOHN F. KENNEDY

FALL
2012

CHAPTER 50

The monstrous 247-foot Galaxy C-5 transport circles Dover Air Force Base on its final approach before landing. Ace Futrell is seated in the upper deck, along with sixty-two wounded soldiers and a cargo lined with the flag-draped coffins of the dead.

The last seven days have been a whirlwind of intelligence briefings and backroom deals, the U.S. military action in the Persian Gulf called off after succeeding in destroying Iran's nuclear facilities, along with its military bases and suspected Qod training centers. After around-the-clock negotiations, the U.N. Security Council announced a cease-fire, with Iran's mullahs agreeing to clamp down on all radical Islamic sects and cut off all military and financial aid to insurgents in Iraq. Iran and Syria also agreed to cease all military aid to Hezbollah and other terrorist organizations, with the United Nations "vowing" to keep the offending nations to strict timetables.

At least that was the "official" story.

In the wake of the Abqaiq massacre, the Ashraf movement had spread, leading to waves of demonstrations in Jiddah and the eastern provinces. The Royals continue their hold on power . . . but only for the moment.

Back at home, all "political detainees" had been released, the nation's red alert status reduced to orange. Acting President Biden has delayed the November election in lieu of a full investigation of the Columbus Day massacre.

As for Ace, he has made his own deal with the powers-that-be, agreeing to quash Kelli's memoir in exchange for his life back. Should an "untimely death, disappearance, or act of God" claim his life or that of a family member, then Ace's "merry men" will release the information via the Internet.

And so he finds himself returning to the States, his mind still in a state of shock over what has transpired. He cannot conceive of the devastation in Los Angeles. He grapples with his wife's involvement in the plot. At times he despises her, and at times he wonders if her efforts may have changed the world. Physically, mentally, and spiritually burned out, he no longer cares about oil or politics, the chaos going on in the world, or the wreckage of his life. He no longer wonders why he was spared from the torture chamber at Inakesh, or why he is still alive. When he looks in the mirror, he is bewildered by the person staring back at him.

Nahir is a fading memory. Freed from her existence at Inakesh Prison, she had decided to relocate to India where her mother's family resides. Ace had let her go, deciding it was best to close that chapter of his life.

✦ ✦ ✦

The military transport taxis across the runway, coming to a halt at one of the open hangars. Ace gazes out the window at the crowd—families and loved ones of America's wounded and dead.

He has journeyed through hell, but for so many, the journey continues.

He thinks about his children, wondering how he can get in touch with them after such a long absence. Will they recognize him? Will they forgive him?

The black government-issue limousine rolls to a stop beyond the crowd. Ace sees David Schall exit the vehicle, the CIA director walking toward the C-5 transport, accompanied by two heavily armed MPs.

So that's the way it's going to be . . .

Nine months ago Ace had stepped off a plane in New York, a man in full, anxious to see his wife, blissfully unaware of the storm gathering on his horizon. Now the storm has struck and passed, leaving everything that was his life in shambles.

How do I pick up the pieces?

Stepping out of the plane into the sunshine, he looks out at the crowd, at the widow who awaits her husband's remains, at the children who will go on without their father, at the father who has lost a son. At the combat veteran who has sacrificed a limb . . .

He pinches away tears, feeling ashamed.

David Schall greets him as he steps off the ramp. "Walk with me."

"Do I have a choice?"

David Schall sees the glazed-over stare. He dismisses the MPs and then leads Ace back across the tarmac to the awaiting government vehicle. "Some of the things that happened between us . . . I had to keep up appearances. You understand it was nothing personal. As for what happened in Saudi Arabia, I had nothing to do with that. I just wanted you to know."

Ace says nothing.

"Your wife and I were friends. You were away on business when Kelli found out how badly the cancer had spread. She decided to keep it from you. Probably never told you I came to see her the day she received her death sentence. I remember the vacant look in her eyes, it was the same look you have now."

He pauses, grabbing Ace's arm. "A man is not finished when he's defeated. He's finished when he quits. You know who said that? Nixon. Right after the Watergate scandal."

"You brought me here for a history lesson?"

"I'm here to get you to understand. Kelli's last eighteen months . . . she knew she had lost the battle, but she never gave up. She kept fighting. She made every day count."

Ace's eyes narrow. "You were in on it, weren't you? Her plan to derail the Neocons?"

"Who do you think gave her access to Promis?"

Ace continues walking, his blood pressure ticking higher.

Schall follows him out the gate. "I gave her what she needed . . . a cause. A second wind. The world's a mess, Ace, but at least we see the problems for what they are, and that's a step forward . . . at least it's a start. What the two of you accomplished . . . it was a good thing."

"A good thing?" Ace turns on him, pushing him back on his heels. "Tell the hundreds of thousands of cancer victims who will suffer until the day they die that this was a good thing. Tell it to the victims' loved ones. See if they buy it, because I sure don't. "

"No argument, but it could have been worse. The situation had to be defused."

"You know what the problem with you and Kelli and Cheney, and the rest of the PNAC and CFR and Trilateral Commission loonies is? No matter how bad things get, no matter how many times you screw up, you always think you're right. Well guess what? There wouldn't be any Islamic extremists if we weren't addicted to oil. There wouldn't be an Al-Qaeda if we hadn't funded an Afghanistan resistance against the Soviets. Saddam would have never been a threat if we hadn't armed him, or Iran, or the other puppet regimes the CIA set up so every administration since President Kennedy was assassinated could pull their strings. We're the United States, Schall. We're supposed to be the good guys! What if our leaders had insisted on human rights and accountability in places like Saudi Arabia in exchange for their oil? Better yet, what if Congress and the White House actually got together and decided to force our nation off fossil fuels once and for all . . . to hell with big oil, to hell with the

Haliburtons and federal banks. Let's reinvent the wheel and do it right. Imagine what a different world we'd be living in today. I guarantee you, Los Angeles would be a lot greener."

"It's a nice speech, Ace. Maybe you should practice it in Farsi."

"Up yours, Schall." Ace bypasses the limousine, heading for the airport exit and Route 1.

"Dad!"

He stops and turns, his heart leaping in his throat as Sam bursts out of the back door of the limousine and races into his arms. Tears of joy flow from his eyes as he hugs his son, the vacuum in his soul suddenly overflowing with emotion.

Leigh approaches, unsure.

Sam wraps his arms around Ace's neck in a bear hug. "Dad, we saw you on the news! Dad . . . you were on the news!"

His daughter stares at him, still feeling betrayed. "Dad? What did they do to you? Look at you—you're a train wreck."

"Felt like I was in one. Guys, I am so sorry for leaving you, and I promise I will never leave you again. Ever. Do you forgive me?"

Sammy nods.

Leigh's face breaks into sobs as she hugs him.

"It's okay, sweetheart. Daddy's home again . . .

"I'm home."

"Never before has man had such capacity to control his own environment, to end thirst and hunger, to conquer poverty and disease, to banish illiteracy and massive human misery. We have the power to make this the best generation of mankind in the history of the world—or to make it the last."

—PRESIDENT JOHN F. KENNEDY

"Then I saw a new heaven and a new earth for the old heaven and earth had disappeared."

—REVELATION 21:1

"The thing the sixties did was to show us the possibilities and the responsibility that we all had. It wasn't the answer. It just gave us a glimpse of the possibility."

—JOHN LENNON

EPILOGUE

THE MOVING TRUCK IS PACKED TO ITS ROOF, the movers wedging in the last of their belongings. Leigh and Sam are out front saying good-bye to their friends. Their grandparents are inside, speaking with the real estate agent.

Jennifer parks in the cul-de-sac. She tosses a scarf around her neck before heading up to the house. "Hey, kids. Where's your dad?"

"Where else?" Leigh says. "Saying his good-byes."

✦ ✦ ✦

A harsh March wind whips spray across the Atlantic, churning the surf into endless foam-crested waves. Ace adjusts his collar, staring at the ocean . . . ready to move on.

He and his family had spent most of November in Washington D.C., Ace testifying in Senate hearings on the Columbus Day attack. As predicted, the heavy-handed public investigation had implicated Iran and the House of Saud in the destruction of Los Angeles . . . preventing anarchy in the United States and hostilities throughout the Arab World.

Seven members of the Strategic Support Branch were eventually indicted for "failing to protect the citizens of the United States." Homeland Security Director Howard S. Lowe and Secretary of Defense Joseph Kendle stepped down for "family reasons." Details of how the two suitcase bombs actually arrived in the States were never publicly disclosed, nor was the recruitment process of Jamal al-Yusaf and Omar Kamel Radi.

Members of Congress agreed to these secret arrangements to "preserve the state of the union" in exchange for sweeping changes in the election process. Campaign contributions were banned. All monies would now be drawn from a pool of federal funds that would be divided equally among the parties and their candidates based on predetermined amounts assigned to the particular office they were campaigning for. No other monies were permitted, 527s outlawed . . . along with all lobbyists. A wartime bill was enacted, preventing private companies from reaping profits. More changes were on the horizon, pending the upcoming Presidential election.

In late December, following an "anonymous tip," a man named Armond "Dale" Proctor was arrested in the Cayman Islands by CIA agents. Proctor would later turn state's evidence against two manufacturers of voting machines that had been rigged to alter the count in key counties in Florida and Ohio during the 2000 and 2004 presidential elections. Proctor's testimony would lead to another new election rule mandating all touch-screen voting machines be equipped with paper ballot receipts.

On February 22—George Washington's birthday— Senator Edward R. Mulligan was elected forty-fifth President of the United States. His first act was to pass a sweeping new energy bill designed to reduce America's dependency on fossil fuels. His second act was to increase the speed at which troops were being withdrawn from Iraq.

A United Nations peace-keeping force took over U.S. military bases in Saudi Arabia—preparing for the former kingdom's first open democratic elections. The interim government—headed by Ramzi Karim—was supported by $600 billion in missing funds that had been sequestered into private bank accounts all over the world.

Having accepted a small "settlement," members of the Royal family abandoned their palaces and relocated to Europe.

With the more radical mullahs forced to give up power, Iranian students once more began organizing peaceful demonstrations against the ruling parties. A short time later, the President of Iran died of what was reported to be a massive stroke.

✦ ✦ ✦

"Ace!"

Jennifer joins him, her earlobes bright red from the cold. "It's freezing out here. Keep me warm." She hooks her arm with his and tucks her hand back into her jacket pocket, using his body to block the wind. "Have you heard the latest? They decided to turn downtown Los Angeles into a redwood park. They say it should significantly reduce radiation levels."

Ace says nothing, his eyes transfixed on the horizon.

"So, South Florida, huh? I guess we'll be close. What made you—"

"Southeast Wind and Power, they offered me a job. I figured we could all use a change in scenery."

"What about me? Am I part of that change?"

Ace says nothing.

"Ace . . . that night on the beach. I meant what I said . . . about having feelings for you. Do you suppose when you're in Florida—"

"You'll always be part of our family, Jen."

"But nothing more?"

"What do you think?" Ace turns to face her. "You and Kelli . . . the two of you set me up."

"It was your wife's idea, not mine."

"But you went along with it. You lied to me."

"Yes. Yes, you're right, and I'm sorry. I'm sorry for all you went through. Believe me, if we had known—"

"Stop."

They continue to stare at the ocean in silence. A slice of sun shines its way through a gray cloud, casting its heavenly beacon upon the water.

"Ace . . . I truly am sorry."

He swallows hard. "Back in college, the first time I saw Kelli, the first time I met her, it was love at first sight. I guess first loves are special that way. When we met again years later, maybe I was looking for something I had lost. Maybe we both were." He brushes a strand of dark hair from Jennifer's eyes. "I'm not looking for that anymore, Jen. That person's long gone. You know what I'm saying?"

She nods, tears in her eyes. "Have a safe trip." Adjusting her scarf, she heads back down the beach.

Ace watches her go, then returns his gaze back to the sea.

Their new home is located on the same ocean, fifteen hundred miles to the south. The water is different, the Atlantic an azure-blue. Yes, as his father-in-law has repeatedly warned, there will be the occasional hurricane threat to contend with, and yet, no sea stays calm forever, no paradise remains unblemished. He will miss Montauk, and the house that he and his wife made into a home.

Change is hard.

The company he will be working for is one of the businesses Kenneth Keene had secretly funded with the House of Saud's money. Ace is a partner in the firm, the managing director.

From oil to wind . . . sometimes change is good.

The green movement is well under way in America, spurred on, no doubt, by the nuclear devastation in Los Angeles. By late 2014, new high-tech windmills are expected to sprout up along the Atlantic, Gulf, and Pacific coastlines. By 2017 these high-tech machines should provide clean, affordable electricity to nearly 30 percent of American homes in the continental United States, helping to ease U.S. dependence on fossil fuels. Federally funded solar wind farms are scheduled to come on line as well, with a push to increase subsidies for local food farms. Scientists expect carbon dioxide levels to drop significantly, reducing the effects of global warming while improving the quality of air that has been causing severe asthma problems among children living in areas located near coal-powered plants.

Ace recalls his last moments with his wife at the John Lennon memorial.

Imagine . . .

Wiping a tear, he takes one final look to the east and then walks back to the house, anxious to begin his life anew.

"When written in Chinese, the word "crisis" is composed of two characters. One represents danger and the other represents opportunity."

—President John F. Kennedy

"I'm trying to say to you—be part of the change! No one else is going to do it. The politicians are paralyzed. Our democracy hasn't been working very well . . . that's my opinion. We've made a bunch of serious policy mistakes. But it's way too simple and too partisan to blame the Bush-Cheney Administration. We've got checks and balances, an independent judiciary, a free press, a Congress . . . have they all failed us? *Have we failed ourselves?*"

—Former Vice President Al Gore, 2007

"Be the change that you want to see in the world."

—Mahatma Gandhi

Final Excerpt:
To the Brink of Hell:
An Apology to the Survivors
by Kelli Doyle
White House National Security Staff Advisor
(2002-2008)

Where will you be when the world changes? When the gas lines are miles long and the grocery store shelves run bare. How will you cope? Do you have the land to farm your own crop? The means to protect it?

How will you react when suitcase nukes replace commercial jets as the new terror threat, and the first mushroom cloud rolls toward the heavens? Will you be caught in the maelstrom? Traveling on business? At home with your loved ones? Enjoying the night out? If you reside in a major city, will you stay at home or flee? Stuff your belongings in the car and race to the interstate, only to find it clogged in bumper-to-bumper traffic . . .

Will you ever trust your elected leaders again?

Will you ever feel safe?

What will you do when civilization and sanity go up in radioactive smoke, when anyone resembling a brown-skinned Muslim is dragged into the street and beaten to death? When nine o'clock curfews and Big Brother's eyes become the rules of the day, and our borders remain permanently closed to all but the elite.

How will you feel when the retaliation begins? When seventy million Iranians pay the ultimate price for being born under an oppressive regime . . . for the lies they were spoon-fed since birth, for the hatred it festered under the guise of religion.

Will the purple rain wash away the threat? Will the world just call it a day?

Will we ever learn?

— *Kelli Doyle-Futrell*
December 9, 2011

This novel is dedicated in memory to my Father-in-law

JAMES FRANKLIN ROOF
(July 11, 1933–June 19, 1996)

Served proudly in Korea 1950–1954
Recipient of two Purple Hearts

and

to my friend and technical editor

CHARLES "Chuck" EUGENE JONES
(May 28, 1962–December 29, 2006)
Served proudly as a ballistic missile
technician and police officer.

FACT OR FICTION

WHILE *The Shell Game* REMAINS FICTION, some of the most disturbing passages and threads of information incorporated into the story line are indeed real. While I cannot begin to cite every reference used for every detail woven into the manuscript (the studies and published articles alone number well over six hundred) I have included (below) comments on some of the more controversial references appearing in the novel. As an author, I reserve the freedom to select those references (and slants) that allow me to move the story forward; however, unlike the cherry-picking of information conducted by the Bush White House, the references cited service the truth and not a hidden agenda.

"Numerous Sources" means the references are far too numerous to list and that the subject matter can be easily found through an Internet search. "Bibliography" refers to the list of key books that follow. "Classified" is a confidential source who has requested not to be identified. For those subjects or threads I have not covered, I suggest an Internet search.

For those of you who seek more detailed answers regarding the undisclosed facts behind the September 11th attacks, I highly recommend visiting www911truth.org, as well as www.AE911Truth.org. A must-read is *"Crossing the Rubicon"* by Michael C. Ruppert. It is a disturbing, extremely well-documented accounting that makes transparent what those involved do not wish the public to see. I also recommend Ruppert's new release, *An American Energy Policy*, which explains in detail the threat of

Peak Oil, and what we need to do in order to survive. Visit his blog at http://www.mikeruppert.blogspot.com.

For those of you who still have comments or questions, my personal e-mail link is available at www.SteveAlten.com.

PROLOGUE

"I reported that Bin Laden had escaped to the Hadhramaut of Yemen, that he was being protected by Sayyid tribesmen." Reference: classified. (Note: While it is impossible at this time [June 2009] to know if this is really true, I have absolutely no doubt that the Middle Eastern Moslem source who told me this tidbit was telling me what he believed was true.)

"And the Reserves and National Guardsmen? Nice surprise, not telling them deployment doesn't officially begin until their boots hit sand, meaning the six months their unit spent at the MOB stations didn't count." Reference: U.S. soldiers.

Author's Note: Just as disturbing as reports of depression and suicide among our troops is the fact that U.S. soldiers returning from Iraq and Afghanistan are not being given proper time to "detox" before being assimilated back into society. Nor is the needed psychiatric assistance being made available. This is a dangerous reality that is impacting our veterans and their families and we owe them far better than to sweep this under the rug.

"Roosevelt knew the Japanese were readying an attack on Pearl Harbor, and guess what—he allowed it to happen!" Reference: numerous historical articles.

CHAPTER 1

"I'm not sure we're any different. After all, how many tens of billions of dollars' worth of aid to New Orleans was secretly diverted to rebuild oil rigs damaged by Hurricane Katrina?" Reference: classified.

Stats and references about oil usage can be found in numerous sources and bibliography.

CHAPTER 3

Alternative energy sources and oil info can be found in numerous sources and bibliography.

"Syn-fuel is nothing more than a giant tax dodge created by a handful of greedy companies who found a way to take advantage of a tax incentive enacted by Congress back in the 1980s." Reference: see references in the text.

CHAPTER 4

"It was a Neoconservative initiative, pushed by Dick Cheney, who believed Iran-Contra failed only because the CIA and Pentagon were involved and secrecy couldn't be maintained." Reference: OP-ED (March 31, 2007) written by Jim Mullins, Senior Fellow at the Center for International Policy in Washington, D.C., backed by numerous cross-references.

CHAPTER 5

"The opening scene, taken by a hand-held camera, is of a classroom of Arab grade schoolers, ages five to seven . . . singing a song. Neary listens carefully. Translates: "Arabs are beloved and Jews are dogs." Reference: *Obsession: Radical Islam's War Against the West.*

CHAPTER 7

Carlyle Group information: *"House of Bush, House of Saud,"* by Craig Unger, along with numerous sources.

CHAPTER 8

"Homeland Security is no longer required to have a search warrant

when dealing with acts intended to intimidate or coerce a civilian population." See Patriot Act.

KELLI DOYLE EXCERPT

"On the day of the attacks, the joint chiefs, under Vice President Cheney's personal direction, scheduled and conducted five separate war game drills that purposely pulled interceptor jets away from the northeastern airspace corridor while deliberately inserting false blips on air traffic screens to simulate, of all things, hijacked airliners. Military jets that routinely intercept aircraft within minutes were delayed an unfathomable eighty minutes, most never even entered the fray. . . ." Numerous sources and *Crossing the Rubicon: The Decline of the American Empire at the End of the Age of Oil,* by Michael C. Ruppert.

"A day before the attacks domestic and foreign investors placed an unprecedented number of 'puts' (a leveraged bet a stock will drop) on the airlines and companies that would suffer devastating losses, in some cases over ninety times higher than normal trading. These financial transactions netted upward of $15 billion in insider trading that was halfheartedly investigated before they too were dismissed by investigators and the media, the latter manipulated by the Bush Administration who were dictating which stories to run and which to kill. Meanwhile, key members of Congress who opposed the administration's plans, received packages of anthrax in the mail, the lethal spores later determined to have originated not overseas, but from labs used by the CIA. Numerous sources *Crossing the Rubicon: The Decline of the American Empire at the End of the Age of Oil,* by Michael C. Ruppert.

"In an effort to stymie the Shi'ites in both Iraq and Lebanon, the Bush Administration covertly began channeling billions of "rebuilding" dollars into Sunni resistance groups—otherwise known as Al-Qaeda." Article in March 5, 2007 *New Yorker* by Seymour Hersh.

CHAPTER 9

"Enlisted men not cutting it can be sent home. Every so often a few opt to kill themselves rather than be shamed into quitting. During Tursi's eight weeks, his squadron experienced one attempted suicide and one that succeeded when a recruit took a nose-dive out a third-story window during morning formation." Resource: Confidential (A.F. recruit).

CHAPTER 10

"Patriot Act, section 213: Any federal law enforcement agency can enter your home or business, whether you are there or not or whether they tell you about it or not and then use any confiscated evidence to convict you of a crime. Section 202 states the Feds can read your e-mail, section 216 allows them to intercept your cell phone calls." Resource: Patriot Act.

CHAPTER 11

All information cited about the assassination of Meir Kahane, the Muslim terrorist cell that planned the murder and the eventual targeting of the (first) World Trade Center attack that should have been prevented, is factual, backed by numerous sources.

CHAPTER 13

The incident described at Little Rock Air Force Base that nearly wiped out a significant portion of central Arkansas is factual. Resource: Confidential (he was one of the BMAT's who witnessed the event).

KELLI DOYLE EXCERPT

Historical information presented on Ibn Saud and the history of the House of Saud, along with their purchasing of U.S. and other weapon systems, is factual, backed by numerous sources, including *The House of Saud*, by Said K. Aburish.

CHAPTER 16

"Part of a highly classified stealth satellite program known collectively as the Future Imagery Architecture (FIA), ONYX was severely criticized by members of the Senate Select Committee on Intelligence for its extraordinary price tag ($40 billion) and its inability to penetrate underground bunkers where Iran and North Korea house their nuclear facilities. Despite these objections, the program was funded by the GOP-controlled House and Senate appropriations committees." References: numerous sources and *Space Review*.

CHAPTER 17

Haditha massacre: *TIME* Magazine and numerous other sources.

KELLI DOYLE EXCERPT

Historical information on Iran–Contra, Iran–Iraq War, Kuwait, etc: numerous sources.

"When [April Glaspie, U.S. Ambassador to Iraq] asked the dictator what else he wanted, Saddam replied that his country's aim was to reclaim the Shatt al Arab, a region of Iraq that was now part of Kuwait. Glaspie's response was that "the Kuwait issue is not associated with America." In essence, the United States had just given Saddam a green light to invade Kuwait." Reference: numerous sources.

CHAPTER 21

Historical information on PROMIS is factual. Reference: Numerous sources and *Crossing the Rubicon: The Decline of the American Empire at the End of the Age of Oil*, by Michael C. Ruppert.

CHAPTER 22

"When I was in Tehran I heard rumors that many of the Magnificent Nineteen were still alive. Mohamed Atta and Salem Al Hazni . . . that

these men were never even onboard the planes. They had been traveling on false passports, instructed the night before the attacks to get publicly intoxicated and to scream insults at the infidels so as to attract attention to themselves. We were told these men were no one's fools, that they had purposely allowed their driver's licenses to be photocopied, that they even used public library computers to send e-mail using unencrypted messages, all to leave false trails to the FBI. Author's license: Not based on any fact. Similar reports have surfaced on numerous websites and blogs, including www.WhatReallyHappened.com and www.MadCowMorningNews.com.

"See, even with oil, the planet only has a feeding and energy capacity for about 2 billion people. We manage now because 4 billion of our fellow human beings are slowly starving to death in Africa and Asia. That leaves about a billion or so of us lucky ones who get to lead the charmed life, only the rules change when the pumps run dry. Divide 6 billion into what little food and fuel resources are left after the Big Rollover and you come up with approximately 500 million people, give or take a few hundred thousand."

Reference: "Confronting the 21st Century's Hidden Crisis: Reducing Human Numbers by 80 Percent," by J. Kenneth Smail, Professor of Anthropology, and "Food, Energy, and Society," by David and Marcia Pimental, professors of Ecology and Agricultural Science, 2000.

CHAPTER 28

"Enter the Mu chip, a tiny invader the size of a grain of sand. Mu allows the government to scan you, track you, and determine what hazardous materials you've come in contact with. The next generation Mu will enable Washington to eavesdrop on our very thought process." Reference: numerous sources.

"Nineteen dead scientists in four months—all experts in the field of viruses. No arrests, everything kept out of the news and conveniently

swept under the carpet." All true. Reference: numerous sources, including *"Crossing the Rubicon: The Decline of the American Empire at the End of the Age of Oil,"* by Michael C. Ruppert.

"There were two influential Democrats poised to thwart the Patriot Act—Tom Daschle and Patrick Leahy—and they were the only ones on Capitol Hill to receive packages of anthrax. The anthrax used in those packages was traced back to the Ames strain taken from Fort Detrick, yet John Ashcroft refused to follow up on that little piece of evidence." All of the anthrax packages came from within the U.S., with origins that trace back to CIA-run covert research programs. Reference: numerous sources, including *"Crossing the Rubicon: The Decline of the American Empire at the End of the Age of Oil,"* by Michael C. Ruppert.

KELLI DOYLE EXCERPT

"A hardline group of Neoconservatives, headed by Dick Cheney, Paul Wolfowitz, Richard Pearle, Jeb Bush, and Donald Rumsfeld, all members of an organization calling itself the 'Project for a New American Century (PNAC).' Using the Defense Planning Guidance as its blueprint for America's future, the group created their own strategic military document, entitled 'Rebuilding America's Defenses.' Admonishing the Clinton Administration for its adherence to the 1972 ABM Treaty and for cutting military spending, the plan outlined a grand strategy that sought to exploit America's newfound position as the world's lone superpower." Reference: numerous sources, including the two cited documents.

"Within months Vice President Dick Cheney was organizing secret energy task force meetings involving some of the biggest players (and donors) in the fossil fuel and nuclear industry. My role in these meetings was to supply maps of Iraqi oil and natural gas fields, as well as the locations of pipelines, refineries, and terminals." Author License (but I'll tell if Dick Cheney will tell!)

"Afghanistan is the world's largest producer of the opium poppy, used

to make heroin. It is estimated $500 billion flows from poppy fields annually, the drugs ending up on the streets of the United States and other Western nations, the profits washed through banking systems across the globe. Plain and simple: Drugs finance cooked banking ledgers and the world's debt." Reference: numerous sources, including *"Crossing the Rubicon: The Decline of the American Empire at the End of the Age of Oil,"* by Michael C. Ruppert.

Author's Note: According to a 1996 IMF report, money laundered from drugs and other criminal activities accounts for 2–5 percent of the world's GDP (about $800 billion to $2 trillion).

CHAPTER 32

"And yet the Saudi slave trade remains common knowledge around Washington power circles, a tolerated "look the other way" crime that has been going on since King Fahd and his sons first ran child sex rings from their private mansions in Beverly Hills." Reference: Documented in numerous references, denied by the State Department.

CHAPTER 33

Inakesh Prison, Saudi Arabia. Resource: *"The Defilers: Sowing the Seeds of Terrorism,"* by ElSirgany.

CHAPTER 34

"At least half the monies taken originated from commissions skimmed by the House of Saud on arms contracts. Patriot Missiles, F-15s, AWACS, Canadian Halifax frigates, French Helec torpedo boats, the British Yamama sale . . . as well as off-the-book deals that can be traced as far back as the Reagan years." Resource: *"The House of Saud,"* by Said K. Aburish. Also backed by multiple cross-references.

CHAPTER 39

"The original "October surprise" dates back to the 1980 Presidential

election when the release of American hostages from Iran would have all but guaranteed a reelection win to Democratic incumbent Jimmy Carter, whose administration was preparing to implement a second rescue attempt in the event negotiations broke down. When the Reagan-Bush campaign heard about the rescue, they launched a major publicity blitz warning the public that President Carter was timing an 'October surprise' solely to win the election. Meanwhile, former CIA director George Bush and other members of the Reagan team were secretly meeting with high-level Iranian and Israeli representatives in a hotel in Paris, forging an agreement that promised to award Iran with arms and spare military parts in return for agreeing not to release the American hostages until after the election." Resources: Multiple articles and published books.

Author's Note: This one admittedly divides along party lines and is very controversial, having been the subject of several investigations, the results of which are split. If you're a Dem you probably agree it happened, if you're a Republican you'll call it a "conspiracy." My opinion: Both sides were certainly attempting to "spin" the Iranian hostage situation in an attempt to win the election. Reagan won. You decide.

CHAPTER 45

"The Executive Orders Biden just rattled off, they're emergency powers, established by Bush, that allows the President to essentially bypass the Constitution and do anything he wants." Reference: National Security Presidential Directive 51 and Homeland Security Presidential Directive 20.

SUGGESTED READING

Aburish, Said K. *The House of Saud*. New York: St. Martins Press, 1994.

Brock, David. *The Republican Noise Machine: Right-Wing Media and How It Corrupts Democracy*. New York: Crown Publishers, 2004.

Campbell, C.J. *The Coming Oil Crisis*. Essex, UK: Multi-Science Publishing Company & PetroConsultants S.A., 1988.

Diamond, Jared. *Collapse: How Societies Choose to Fail or Succeed*. New York: Penguin, 2005.

El Sirgany, Emad. *The Defilers: Sowing the Seeds of Terrorism*. Summer Publishing House, 2004.

Hall-Jamieson, Kathleen. *Deception, Distraction & Democracy*. New York: Oxford University Press, 1992.

Heinberg, Richard. *The Party's Over—Oil, War and the Fate of Industrial Societies*. Gabriola Island, BC: New Society Publishers, 2003.

Heinberg, Richard. *Powerdown: Options and Actions For a Post-Carbon World*. Gabriola Island, BC: New Society Publishers, 2004.

Johnson, Chalmers. *The Sorrows of Empire: Militarism, Secrecy, and the End of the Republic*. New York: Metropolitan Books, 2004.

Kane, Michael. "Elephants in the Barracks: The Complete Failure of the 9-11 Commission." Centre for Research on

Globalisation, March 27, 2004. http://globalresearch.ca/
articles/KAN403A.html.

Klare, Michael T. *Resources Wars—The New Landscape of Global
Conflict.*New York: Henry Holt, 2001.

Kunstler, James Howard. *The Long Emergency: Surviving the
Converging Catastrophes of the Twenty-first Century.* Boston:
Atlantic Monthly Press, 2005.

Mooney, Chris. *The Republican War on Science.* Jackson,
Tennessee: Perseus Books Group, Basic Books, 2005.

Obsession: Radical Islam's War Against the West (www.
ObsessionTheMovie.com)

Packer, George. *The Assassins' Gate: America in Iraq.* New York:
Farrar, Straus & Giroux, 2005.

Pimental, David and Marcia: "Food, Energy, & Society,"
Bioscience. May 2000.

Ruppert, Michael C. *Crossing the Rubicon: The Decline of the
American Empire at the End of the Age of Oil.* Gabriola Island,
BC: New Society Publishers, 2004.

Ruppert, Michael C.: *An American Energy Policy.* Cabot,
Arkansas: Variance Publishing, 2009.

Smail, Kenneth J. "Confronting the 21st Century's Hidden Crisis:
Reducing Human Numbers by 80%," *NPG Forum Series.*
Kenyon College, May 1995.

Unger, Craig: *House of Bush, House of Saud: The Secret relationship
Between the World's Two Most Powerful Dynasties.* New York:
Scribner, 2004.

Webb, Gary. *Dark Alliance.* New York: Seven Stories Press, 1998.

Yergin, Daniel. *The Prize: The Epic Quest for Oil, Money, & Power.*
New York: Free Press, 1991.